As a child, **Fiona Harper** was constantly teased for two things: having her nose in a book and living in a dream. Things haven't changed much since then. Fiona has found a career that puts her runa...

Fiona loves dancing, so clear the floor if you're ever at a party with her, and her current creative craze (one of a long list!) is jewellery making. She loves good books, good films and good food, especially anything cinnamon-flavoured, and she can *always* find room in her diet for chocolate or champagne!

Fiona loves to hear from readers and you can contact her through fiona@fionaharper.com or find her on her Facebook page (Fiona Harper Romance Author) or tweet her! (@FiHarperAuthor)

# The Little Shop of Hopes and Dreams

## FIONA HARPER

This edition published in Great Britain 2014
by Mills & Boon, an imprint of Harlequin (UK) Limited,
Eton House, 18-24 Paradise Road, Richmond, Surrey, TW9 1SR

© 2014 Fiona Harper

ISBN: 978-0-263-24566-0

097-1014

Printed and bound by
CPI Group (UK) Ltd, Croydon, CR0 4YY

## ACKNOWLEDGEMENTS

Thank you to Anna Baggaley and all the team at Harlequin for their hard work and enthusiasm, and also to Lizzy Kremer, my fabulous agent.

To the members of the Romantic Novelists' Association. So many of you have supported and encouraged me along the way and I have made friendships that will last a lifetime. May love always turn your pages.

# CHAPTER ONE

'What you need is another cosmopolitan.'

Nicole Harrison swayed on her high heels and frowned at her best friend and soon-to-be business partner, who was starting to look a little fuzzy around the edges. 'You sure about that?'

She squinted at the large clock behind the bar of Déjà Vu, a trendy little place not too far from Covent Garden. Quarter to twelve. One more cocktail and she might not stay vertical until midnight, and she really wanted to be conscious when the new year started. Next year was the year when everything was going to fall into place and all her plans and hard work paid off.

''Course I'm sure,' Peggy said, beckoning the bartender with an elegant wave of her blood-red nails. 'Best remedy for a broken heart.'

Nicole took a few seconds to unfocus from the clock and refocus back on her friend. She blinked slowly. For a moment she'd forgotten this was a fancy-dress party. The sight of Doris Day sitting on the next stool had momentarily confused her. The real Peggy was loud and curvy, and while she often dressed in vintage, it was always something with a little more va-va-voom than this pastel frock. As Nicole stared at her, the white polka dots started to dance around on the pale pink background.

'My heart's not broken,' she mumbled.

At least not any more. But it had been. Once. What she'd felt today had just been an echo of that.

'It was just an engagement announcement,' she said, absent-mindedly accepting the glass of ruby liquid that Peggy slid in her direction. 'And Jasper and I were over a long time ago.'

It shouldn't matter any more. It didn't.

'Well, he's an idiot,' Mia, her other best friend, muttered with her usual bluntness. 'No matter how long ago he let you slip out of his fingers.'

Mia had been sitting so quietly sipping her drink that Nicole had almost forgotten she was there, although she was hard to miss in her Lara Croft outfit, complete with chicken-fillet enhanced chest and thigh holsters. She wasn't in the best of moods this evening, seeing as her army fiancé was out of the country on active duty. Lots of women got soppy when they missed their other halves, but Mia just got feisty.

Nicole raised her glass. 'To the idiot,' she said and toasted her friend's ineffable wisdom by downing the contents in one go.

Only she knew she was lying. Jasper hadn't been an idiot. Not at all. He was the most wonderful man she'd ever known.

'Steady there, Nicole,' Mia said. 'You don't normally put this much away.'

Peggy sighed and rolled her eyes. 'She'll be fine. And

it was either this or sitting home with six gallons of ice cream in those tatty tracksuit bottoms of hers, and I know which one I'd rather watch her do.'

Mia frowned but nodded. 'Forget the jerk,' she said vehemently. 'You were too good for him back then and you're definitely too good for him now.'

Nicole saluted her with her empty glass. Too right. She'd worked really hard to become the woman she was today, the kind of woman who could bring the Jaspers of this world to their knees, reflected in her choice of costume this evening. Who embodied effortless elegance more than Audrey Hepburn in her *Breakfast at Tiffany's* little black dress?

Okay, maybe Holly Golightly herself hadn't always been cool, calm and dignified, but it was the overall image that counted. It was iconic.

'Stuff Jasper! May he marry the cow and have a brood full of boys as shallow and stuck-up as he is!' she said, trying to slide onto the stool next to Peggy's and missing.

'Exactly,' Peggy said and ordered another round of cosmos.

Lara…or Mia…tapped Peggy on the arm. She nodded at Nicole. 'I'm not sure that's such a good idea.'

Peggy turned and studied her friend, pursing her lips. 'Well, we've got to do something to cheer her up. My gran used to say the way you start a new year is the way you'll end it, and I don't want her moping around our brand-new office for the next twelve months.'

Mia sipped beer out of the bottle. 'You're all heart,' she said, giving her a very *Lara* look.

'Of course, I want Nicole to be happy too,' Peggy added, pouting a little.

Nicole listened to her friends debate the merit of a fourth—or was it fifth?—cocktail. She hadn't kept count. Probably because she really hadn't planned to drink much this evening.

She felt oddly detached, as if the room was swimming in and out of focus, sounds waning and then becoming magnified. She tried to fix her gaze on Peggy, but the spots on her dress were now involved in the complicated choreography of a Busby Berkeley number, complete with split-second timing and terrifying symmetry. Nicole could have sworn, as she tried to tear her eyes away from the swimming mass of white-on-pink polka dots, that one of them actually winked at her.

'It's just because it's been a while since you've had a man in your life,' Peggy explained, 'and that can always make you susceptible to the "if only"s.'

Mia snorted. 'So that's your excuse for not having more than a half-hour break between relationships, is it?'

Peggy glared at Mia. 'We're not talking about me. We're talking about Nicole. It's been two months since she waved bye-bye to the last boyfriend, and it's about time she got back on the horse.'

Horse? Nicole didn't think there'd been a horse that evening, but she'd drifted off for a moment there. Maybe there had been. She was starting to realise that whole swathes of New Year's Eve were a complete blank. Probably because Mia was right—she didn't usually drink much, if at all. She didn't usually like the way alcohol fuzzied up her edges, made her lose control. She ended up doing things that really weren't like her at all.

'Having a conveyor belt of men in your life isn't the answer to everything,' Mia replied. 'Sometimes a girl needs a bit of breathing space.'

Peggy waved a hand. 'Breathing space, schmeathing space. There's only one way to deal with a situation like this—she needs to find a cute guy to smooch at midnight and start the year in the way she means to go on.'

'No,' Nicole said, suppressing a hiccup. 'I don't do things like that.'

'Then it's about time you started,' Peggy said, grinning at her, then scanning the room for a likely candidate.

Thankfully, Mia rescued her. 'Who needs to pin our happiness on men, anyway? I say we refill our glasses...' she nodded at Nicole '...orange juice for you, my love, and toast ourselves and Nicole's new business venture. This time next year she'll own the first proposal-planning agency in London and we'll be rich because we had the good sense to invest in it!'

'Now, *that* I can drink to,' Nicole said, thumping the bar. 'A pint of water, if you will, bartender!'

'Classy,' Peggy said, shaking her head.

'Sensible,' Mia countered, swinging her long plait behind her head.

The bartender sloshed a glass of water in front of Nicole and she scooped it up, not even caring it was dripping on her dress. 'To Nicole!' she said. 'And her little shop of Hopes & Dreams!'

Peggy and Mia joined her, clinking their respective

cocktail glass and beer bottle with her pint glass. 'To us!' they chorused.

They were all just drinking deep when Peggy nudged Nicole in the ribs. 'Ooh, don't look now, but…two o'clock…'

*Already?* Had she missed midnight? Those cocktails must be more lethal than she'd thought!

'You're hopeless,' Peggy said, physically moving Nicole's head so she dragged her gaze from the clock behind the bar and across the seething mass of partygoers. 'I mean *two o'clock*. The guy with the black T-shirt standing over there. He's a dish. I think you should claim him for that midnight kiss.'

A *dish*? Peggy was really getting into character, wasn't she?

Nicole shook her head. 'I couldn't.'

'Why not?' Peggy said, nudging her off her stool and in the right direction. 'There's no force field stopping you, is there?'

Nicole shook her head. But there probably should be. His black T-shirt clung lovingly to his broad chest and his hair was just messy enough to be sexy but just short enough to stop him looking foppish. It was as if the air pulsed around him, the molecules excited by his presence. Or maybe that was the fifth cosmo messing with gravity… Whatever it was, there was a definite whiff of danger in the air, and if there was one thing Nicole knew, bad boys like him didn't go for good girls like her.

'Interesting choice of trousers,' Mia said, looking him up and down, 'but I suppose you can't have everything.'

And while Nicole tried to work out what Mia meant,

and if the soft fuzz of his jeans was something more than the delicious blurring effect of vodka and cranberry juice, Peggy leaned in and whispered in her ear.

'Go on, Nicole. It's almost midnight… I dare you.'

He watched the brunette over by the bar snap to attention and stare directly at him. He toasted her with his bottle of beer and smiled. Well, he hadn't seen that coming. He'd been half-watching her all night and he'd thought he'd had her pegged.

He didn't know why she'd caught his eye. She wasn't his usual type—extroverted and free-spirited—but there was something about her calmness and poise in a room full of chaos that had drawn his gaze.

But he still hadn't been able to help looking over now and then, and the more he'd looked, the more he'd noticed the good bone structure, the fine features that weren't arranged to make her conventionally pretty, but interesting.

He liked interesting.

She got up from her bar stool, straightened her black dress, adjusted the rope of large pearls circling her neck, then wobbled her way towards him.

He would have said she was heading straight for him, but halfway across the room she got distracted and veered off course until the blonde in the pink dress by the bar yelled something at her and she shook herself and started pushing her way through the heaving dance floor to where he was leaning against the wall.

He couldn't help smiling to himself. He was glad it was the Audrey Hepburn girl, not Doris or Lara, who was teetering her way towards him. He put his beer bottle down on a nearby ledge and pushed himself away from the wall.

If he'd said women hadn't approached him in bars before he'd be lying. So badly his pants would probably burst into flames. But there was something different about this girl. Instead of that hungry, almost predatory, look he'd come to expect, she was wide-eyed and uncertain. For some reason that made her approach all the more tantalising.

'Incoming,' his buddy Tom, and partner in crime, whispered out of the corner of his mouth. 'Which means I'm going to make myself scarce. In fact, now that the group at the bar is depleted a little, I might just see if Lara Croft would like to get into some one-to-one combat with me.' And with a flash of a wicked smile he set off.

'Good luck!'

Tom was going to need it. Lara had spotted him coming her way and was glaring at him, but that probably wasn't going to stop him. Tom liked a challenge, and you didn't get to be a hot up-and-coming record producer without being able to handle a few prickly customers.

He watched his friend's progress for a few seconds then turned his attention back to the brunette. She was only a few steps away now, blocked by the people on the fringes of the dance floor, but then a groping pair stumbled off to one side and suddenly she was right in front of him.

'Hi,' he said, his smile growing wider.

'Hi,' she replied, and one ankle buckled a little beneath her before she found her footing again. And then she just stared at him, as if she wasn't quite sure what she was going to do with him. He found he liked that too. There was a hum of anticipation that was missing from a more direct approach.

He saw her ribcage rise as she hauled in some air and then she stepped forward and placed her hands on his chest. Her long-boned fingers were pale and delicate, but they packed quite a punch. A jolt shot through him, as if he'd been on a hospital trolley and someone had zapped him with a defibrillator.

Suddenly, things got very, *very* interesting.

In the background the music dimmed and someone turned the television up. An overexcited presenter was bouncing up and down in a bobble hat and scarf on the Embankment, and then the shot switched to the face of Big Ben. There was a heartbeat of silence before the chimes started, but Alex hardly heard them.

'It's midnight soon,' she said and leaned in closer. He caught a whiff of her perfume, fresh and delicate with an undertone of spice. 'So I'm going to kiss you.'

He wasn't going to argue with that.

Well, not much.

Her face was inches away now, her eyes huge and dark. His heart was pumping wildly, throbbing in his ears. 'Not if I get there first,' he whispered and dipped his head to taste her lips, just briefly.

He heard her little gasp of surprise, and he decided he liked it, so he kissed her again, more deeply this time. She responded, a little hesitantly at first, which was intriguing, seeing as this had been her idea, but then her hands moved from his chest, skimming his torso through his T-shirt, until they were on his back, setting off a chain of tiny fireworks that were just as potent as the ones about to explode on barges in the Thames not half a mile away.

Big Ben's bongs went uncounted and uncelebrated, at least by him and the mystery brunette, as they took what had started as a simple kiss and kicked it up a notch.

That moment of held breath when everyone waited for the twelfth chime was long over when they came up for air. People were dancing again, although he hadn't been aware when the music had turned back on or even how long it had been playing. The brunette swayed slightly in front of him, her eyes closed, a tiny smile curving her lips, as he looked down at her.

'What's your name?' he asked hoarsely.

She didn't reply, just traced the lone dimple on his left cheek with her finger then kissed him again. Her hands slid lower to rest on his hips, and then he felt her lips purse. She pulled away, frowning. 'You're wearing furry trousers. What did you come as? Mr Tumnus? Because if you did, you should have a scarf. And an umbrella. Where's your umbrella?'

He laughed. 'No, nothing so exotic as a faun,' he said. 'I'm the back end of a pantomime horse.'

She smiled a serene little smile, as if that made perfect sense. 'Peggy said there'd be a horse…but I can't really remember how the horse was going to get here or why.' She screwed up her face, as if she was thinking hard. 'Where's your head?'

He nodded in the direction of the bar. 'Trying to chat up one of your friends,' he replied.

Lara was still scowling. It looked as if Tom had struck out for once, but he probably wouldn't mind too much. His motto in everything—especially when it came to women—was 'nothing ventured, nothing gained'.

The brunette looked over her shoulder, then turned to look him in the eye and thought hard for a moment. 'I think I need to kiss you again. Three times is supposed to be lucky, isn't it?'

He nodded, equally serious. It certainly was. And he hoped these cheap hired horse hindquarters were fire retardant, because the kiss that followed topped the previous two on the scorch-o-meter. That was the best kiss he'd had all year. And not just the one that had started. He'd included the one before that too.

'What's your name?' he asked again.

She laughed loudly, indicated her black dress and string of pearls with a hand. 'Don't you know?'

He shook his head, smiling. A few wisps of hair had escaped from her neat bun thing and she looked totally adorable.

'But I'm from *Breakfast at Tiffany's*! Everybody's seen *Breakfast at Tiffany's*!'

He shrugged. 'Not me.'

Her mouth dropped open. 'Really! Never?'

Alex shook his head. Breakfast... Now, there was an appealing idea. 'Let me guess... Are you Tiffany?'

She went from shocked to amused in a heartbeat, hitting him gently on the chest. 'No, silly!'

He caught her hand and kept it trapped under his.

'I'm Holly!' she said with a weary sigh, as if even his two-year-old niece would know that. But then again, she probably did. Women seemed to know everything about every chick flick ever made from the moment of their births.

'Well, Holly… Can I have your number? I'd like to call you.'

She closed her eyes and rested against him, mumbled sleepily, 'Sure.'

He waited for a moment. 'Care to enlighten me?'

One eyelid lifted. 'Huh?'

'Your number?'

The eyelid slid closed again. 'It's oh-nine-three…no, seven…no, three…' She lifted her head and peered at him from under half-mast false lashes. 'I can't seem to remember.'

'How about I give you mine?'

She nodded. He tore a corner off a flyer on a nearby table and scribbled his number down for her. When he handed it to her she blinked twice, very deliberately, then tucked it down in the front of her dress. All the saliva evaporated from his mouth.

He caught a flash of baby-pink moving towards him and realised her friends had come to rescue her.

She smiled dreamily at him. 'Thank you…for my midnight kiss. It was very nice.'

His smile grew wider. 'Yes, it was.'

Over her shoulder he saw Tom heading back in his direction, down but not out, according to the rueful smile on his face. His mystery woman's friends weren't far behind. They pushed their way through the dance floor, stopped a short distance away and beckoned for their friend.

The one in the pink gave him a saucy wink, while the

Lara Croft lookalike kept an eye on Tom, making sure he was heading away from her.

'Call me,' he said, as they led her away.

Pinky looked back at him over her shoulder as they headed for the door. 'If she doesn't,' she said with a little smirk, 'I will.'

Tom sighed as he leaned back against the wall beside him. 'Damn. Knew I should have gone for Doris instead.' He took a swig of beer and smiled at the polka-dotted hips wiggling their way out of the door. 'The good girls are always so much fun when they're persuaded to be just a little bit bad.'

# CHAPTER TWO

*Ten months later*

Nicole stood on top of an office building in Lambeth, arms wrapped around her for warmth. The sun had set half an hour ago, leaving just a smudge of peach peeping out between the glass towers and church spires that crowded the London horizon.

She risked a glance over the edge and instantly regretted it. Twenty storeys below, the November wind tugged papery leaves from trees then threw them carelessly in the path of the rush-hour traffic.

'Are you ready, Warren?' she asked, only just managing to stop her teeth chattering. She forced her cheeks into the soothing, yet professional smile she always used on her clients at this part of the proposal process.

Warren, a baby-faced, slightly balding forty-something, was fastening an abseiling harness over the top of his dinner suit. He looked up and nodded, nervous but determined.

Nicole caught the eye of Kirk, the ex-army guy she'd used a few times for similar stunts. He was one of those wordless, beefy types, who Nicole had been worried would intimidate men preparing to be the most vulnerable they'd ever been in their life, but somehow he inspired laddish camaraderie, and even the most timid of clients seemed more ready to do something high-risk and daring under his guidance. He finished testing Warren's harness then stepped back and nodded at Nicole.

Warren's face paled.

Nicole stepped forward and handed him an earpiece, similar to the one she was wearing. She looked him in the eyes. 'It's going to be fine,' she told him. 'A minute from now you're going to be face to face with the woman you love, and she's worth all of this, isn't she?'

He nodded and his Adam's apple bobbed in his throat.

Nicole stepped back as Warren jammed the earpiece into place. 'Now you've got your very own piece of high-tech gadgetry—just like James Bond,' she added, warming the ever-present smile up a notch.

Warren fidgeted with his harness a little. She guessed it was probably pinching in places she didn't want to know about. 'That's the idea,' he said. 'Cheryl's always had a bit of a thing for 007. I'm not under any grand illusions, but I thought if I could show her I could be the tiniest bit like him, it might improve the chance of her saying yes.'

Nicole looked across at his smooth receding forehead, his slightly chubby cheeks, the torso that suggested he'd spent more time at the kebab shop than at the gym. She wished she really could tell him he was the spitting image of Pierce or Roger or Sean. 'You look extremely dashing,' she said. 'You're going to blow Cheryl away.'

Warren smiled softly. 'Like a real Bond film... Something always gets blown away—or up—in a Bond film.'

The thought of an explosion of any kind featuring in the proposal she spent the last month meticulously planning sent a shiver of fear down Nicole's spine. However, she glued the smile in place and projected it back at Warren with even greater force. 'As long as it's an explosion of love, and love alone, everyone will be happy.'

Especially her.

She checked her watch. 'Do you remember what to do?'

Warren went back to looking very serious. He nodded. 'Abseil down slowly two floors, then wait for your signal before doing the last bit.'

'You can do it,' she said, handing him the sign he was going to clip to his harness and a single red rose. 'Just remember...Kirk is here at the top if you need help and I'll be waiting for you on the seventeenth floor.'

Warren nodded weakly and backed towards the edge. With Kirk's help he started to lower himself down. Nicole stood, calm and serene, smiling as he went. Just before he vanished she did a little thumbs-up gesture, but as soon as his eyes disappeared below the parapet, and only the thinning fluff on the top of his head was left in view, she set off running like a greyhound towards the door that led to the fire escape.

Her heels clattered on the stairs as she raced down two flights. They weren't really practical for this kind of thing, she knew, but she had a professional image to maintain.

She paused briefly outside the room where the action was due to take place and sucked in as much oxygen as she could. Five seconds was all she had, so five seconds would have to do. She tucked a strand of hair behind her ear as she waited for her pulse to stop stampeding, then slipped gracefully through the fire-exit door and into the open-plan office. No one would ever have known she'd been a heaving mess only seconds earlier.

Cheryl, Warren's fiancée-to-be, was tapping away on her keyboard right next to the floor-to-ceiling windows. Every now and then she glanced up at the large clock on the far wall and sighed. The rest of the office carried on with their business, as if it were the end of a normal Friday afternoon.

Nicole made eye contact with Felicity, Cheryl's best friend, who'd been only too happy to be the office 'mole' for this part of the operation. Then she checked her watch. 'Where are you, Warren?' she mumbled into her Bluetooth earpiece.

She could hear panting and the wind whistling. 'Just about there,' he said in a high-pitched voice. 'Passing the eighteenth floor now.'

She gave Felicity a nod, and Felicity turned and gave a signal to a large man sitting at a desk in the centre of the room. His name was Morris, and he had the most soulful voice Nicole had ever heard. He stood up, cleared his throat and started singing the opening bars to 'Ain't No Mountain High Enough'.

A few of the other workers looked up, but most kept on about their work. One by one they joined in the song until the whole seventeenth floor was singing its heart out. Nicole grinned. Those endless choir practices at Hurstdean Academy had come in useful after all.

Warren might not be James Bond, but Nicole dearly

hoped that Cheryl was going to say yes. Not only was he a really nice guy, but it said a lot about him that their work-mates had spent hours perfecting the song in secret over the last fortnight.

Nicole crept a little further into the office so she could see Cheryl more clearly round the edge of a row of cubicles. She'd stopped typing now and was staring open-mouthed at her colleagues, who sang and smiled as they gathered round her. And, just as Morris took the song to its lung-bursting climax, Warren lurched into view outside Cheryl's window, fumbling to pull the red rose out of his lapel and holding it towards her.

For a moment Cheryl didn't see him, but that sixth sense that comes when someone is looking over one's shoulder must have kicked in, because she twisted round and screamed at the same time. She would have fled halfway across the office if Felicity hadn't caught her and steered her back.

'Warren!' Cheryl shrieked, both hands pressed against her sternum, one on top of the other. 'What the heck are you doing out there?'

Warren, bless his little cotton socks, managed to stop looking quite so nervous. He flashed her a truly 007-worthy smile, then swung the sign dangling from a short rope attached to his harness up into his hands with one swift move.

On it were written four words: *Will you marry me?*

He'd wanted to go with something Bond-themed, but Nicole had convinced him to keep it simple. When it came to this part of the proposal, no fuss, no frills were needed. That was all a woman needed to hear.

The hairs on the back of her neck lifted as a hush fell

on the whole office. Cheryl covered her mouth with her hands then nodded slowly. Once. Twice. Then a flurry of bobbing as she pressed her hands against the glass and started crying.

Nicole smiled as she whispered into her headset, 'We are *go*!'

Right on cue, fireworks erupted from the park opposite and Warren and Cheryl's colleagues cheered and rushed to the windows to watch. Nicole waved at Warren to catch his attention and pointed downwards with an exaggerated action. He was just hanging there, a stupid grin plastered all over his chubby face. He'd completely forgotten the next part of the plan was to get him down and on *this* side of the glass ASAP.

She sighed and looked around at the mayhem. It was lovely. It really was. And romantic. But…

She shook her head and plucked her earpiece out of her ear. Maybe she was getting a little jaded. In the ten and a half months since she'd started Hopes & Dreams she'd helped numerous men pop the question, but maybe the daily diet of OTT was starting to wear on her.

It was lovely to see all these couples happily planning their futures, but it only seemed to emphasise that once they'd taken each other by the hand and waltzed off into the sunset, she was left standing there alone.

She'd come close—once—to being proposed to. Or so she'd thought. She shook her head to dislodge the memory of that night. She didn't need to go back there. Life was all about moving forward, about making the future count, not about moping over things that should have been but weren't.

Warren, who'd finally made it down to the balcony two floors below and unharnessed himself with Kirk's help, appeared in the doorway to an almighty cheer from his colleagues. He marched over to Cheryl looking ten feet tall, a bit of a Bond swagger in his usual lolloping gait. His fiancée watched him approach, her eyes wide and moist, and Nicole couldn't help but shake off the mood that had been troubling her a few moments earlier.

She caught Warren's eye across the top of the crowd and he winked at her as he drew Cheryl into his arms then dipped her for a kiss. Nicole smiled back and tucked her earpiece in her pocket.

Her job was done here. Everything had gone according to her meticulous plan—as everything in her life always did. And she didn't know why she was getting all maudlin about the lack of proposals in her own life. It was a moot point. She wasn't even seeing anyone at the moment. There'd been no one since...

She mentally swatted that thought.

She wasn't seeing anyone, and that was fine, because she was too busy getting a fledgling business off the ground in tough economic times. So right now she was perfectly content organising everyone else's happy-ever-afters. As long as everything kept going to plan, hers would get here eventually.

# CHAPTER THREE

Feeling a little windswept and definitely a lot tired, Nicole walked into the foyer of the Hamilton Grand Hotel and quickly disposed of her coat and bag in the cloakroom. She checked her watch. She was late. Just a little. But it didn't sit well with her. She didn't do late. Or unprofessional. Or disorganised.

Her outfit wasn't perfect, either. But that was what happened when you had to go from the top of an office block to a party in one evening. She usually preferred a cocktail dress, but her pencil skirt and classic chiffon blouse would just have to do.

Since both Peggy and Mia had both invested money in Hopes & Dreams and were hoping to join Nicole in the business full-time when things took off, Nicole had invited both her friends to come along with her. She found them in the Terrace Bar with a view over the Thames, along with a hundred or so event planners, hoteliers and media bods. The Hamilton had recently undergone an extensive refurbishment and this was their 'we're back!' party, designed to wow former clients who'd been less than impressed with gradually dilapidating facilities.

Nicole had to admit, they'd done a marvellous job. It was now chic and modern. Flat matt walls in both neutral and bold colours, textured fabrics, funky light fittings. No hint of the dated plasterwork, thank goodness. Nicole shuddered at the memory. She'd always had a hatred for that fussy eighties faux-Victorian look, ever since one of her posh boarding-school friends had come to stay, taken one look at Nicole's mother's stripy wallpaper under the glued-on dado rail and had wrinkled her nose a little.

None of the other girls at Hurstdean had homes like that. They'd had antiques instead of orange pine that had darkened to an almost radioactive tone, real oil paintings instead of Monet prints from IKEA. But that was what came from being the scholarship kid, she supposed.

But after that incident Nicole had decided it was better to go without if you couldn't have the real thing, and she'd started building her furnishings, her wardrobe—and her life—according to that code. 'Dress for the job you want…' someone had once said. Well, Nicole dressed for the life she wanted, a fabulous one.

'So, did Cheryl say yes to tubby old Warren?' Peggy asked as Nicole approached.

Nicole nodded and the other two girls breathed out a sigh of relief. While a negative to a proposal really came down to the relationship in question, too many refusals could make the Hopes & Dreams look bad. So far, though, Nicole had a really good success rate. Only one 'no', and that had been right back at the beginning, a big-headed plonker whose ill-fated proposal idea had only convinced his girlfriend that he loved himself more than he did her.

That one blot on her otherwise perfect record still smarted. Still, she'd been on a huge learning curve since then and had come up with protective measures to stop herself falling into that kind of situation ever again.

Thankfully, her proposer tonight had been nothing like Mr Arrogant.

'He got right into the part too,' Nicole said. 'Not sure what Cheryl's going to do with him now he's discovered his inner Bond.'

Peggy's red lips stretched slowly into a smile. 'I know what I'd do with a man who'd discovered his inner Bond...'

'Oh, there you are, darlings! Doesn't the Hamilton look super? I'm sure Minty and I are going to use it for one of our next parties.'

Nicole's stomach sank, but she turned round, smiling—if not genuinely—widely. 'Celeste...Araminta... How are you?'

The two women were both tall and had cascading, thick honey-coloured waves. They looked as if they'd blown in off the King's Road after an afternoon's shopping. The dresses were bang on trend, the make-up artfully suggesting a healthy glow, and the legs went on for centuries.

However, despite her irritation at their presence, Nicole couldn't help taking a mental note of how their outfits were put together, noting details like designers, fabrics, cut... As much as she didn't like them, Celeste and Minty always looked fabulous, and it was never good to be outshone by the competition.

It was a habit she'd picked up at school, when fitting in

had been as necessary as breathing. She might have not had as much money as most of her school chums, but that hadn't meant she'd wanted to stand out in cut-price high-street polyester knock-offs. As a result, she'd developed a talent for breaking down an outfit into its component parts, working out how she could copy it on a shoestring or use what she already owned to pull off the look. It had helped her blend into the privileged world of Hurstdean Academy.

'Marvellous!' Celeste said, beaming. For some reason her smile reminded Nicole of a chihuahua baring its teeth. 'And how's your cute little boutique agency doing? I don't seem to have heard much about it in ages. I Do, I Do, I Do is going great guns. Did you hear we just did the Patterson–Henley proposal? She said yes, of course. Who wouldn't when daddy-in-law is a viscount?'

Celeste broke off so she and Minty could congratulate themselves with throaty, slightly horsey laughter.

Nicole kept smiling and gently put a hand on Peggy's arm. She was sure she'd just heard a snarl from under her flatmate's breath.

Minty sighed and flicked her hair in a manner that got the attention of all the men in a ten-foot radius. 'They've asked us to do the engagement party as well, you know. Fabulous exposure.'

'I'm sure it is,' Mia said tightly. 'Congratulations.'

Celeste started scanning the crowd. Obviously, they'd ceased to be entertaining now the gloating had finished, and she was looking for her next victim. 'Ooh! There's the new owner of the Hamilton, Jayce Ryder. He did say he wanted a word with us. Come on, Minty.' She waved above the crowd. 'Yoo-hoo, Jayce…!'

Both girls flashed identical smiles at Nicole, Peggy and Mia and then headed off into the crowd without bothering to air-kiss a farewell.

The name Peggy called them when they were out of earshot wasn't nice.

Nicole shook her head. 'We shouldn't criticise the competition in public. It's not professional.'

Peggy's eyes narrowed. 'Professional, schmessional. Sometimes I just can't help myself, and I don't know how you can be so calm, cool and collected about it, either. Not after they copied your idea and set up a rival proposal-planning agency right under your nose!'

Nicole sent a laser-targeted stare after the two disappearing willowy figures. 'They only got that job because Minty's daddy plays polo with Hugo Patterson's daddy.'

Mia followed her gaze. 'Oh, yes. I forgot you used to work with them at that big event-planning firm.'

'Me and my big mouth,' Nicole muttered, turning back to her friends and sighing. 'I shouldn't have bragged to them that I was branching out on my own.'

Mia nodded understandingly. 'And have you seen a drop in business recently? I know you said you were worried about that when you started out.'

Nicole sighed again. She'd hoped for a fun, glitzy evening after a hard week with sleepless nights and ten-hour days. 'A bit. I run a full range of services. The lowest tier is personalised proposal ideas that clients buy for a small fee and then they do the rest themselves—inspiration, if you like. Next is helping to find venues and vendors who match the client's requirements, but the top tier is the no-holds-barred planning service, where I take care of everything. Not only are those the most fun to do, but they're the ones I make most money on, and it's interest in those kind of proposals that seems to have tailed off.'

She glanced over again at her rivals, who were busy fawning over the hotel tycoon who'd been responsible for the Hamilton's upswing in fortune. 'And I have a feeling I know who's hoovering up all that kind of business.'

Peggy glared over at them. 'Those two are toxic on so many levels it isn't funny.'

Nicole angled her body away from Celeste and Minty. She didn't even want to look at them. They didn't count. She wasn't going to let girls like that get the better of her ever again.

'Ever since school I've had to deal with girls like that, girls whose lives are charmed, because someone waved a magic wand over them at birth, so they get everything their hearts desire. So life comes easy to them. So success drops easily into their laps because of their names or their connections, but it doesn't mean they have to have it all, leaving nothing for us.'

Nicole was prepared to work for it. Work hard. She'd get there in the end.

'It doesn't matter how well they're doing now,' she said slowly. 'Celeste was slapdash when we worked together at Elite Gatherings and I bet she's slapdash now. She was always swanning around doing what she felt like doing and palming off the boring stuff on other people.'

'Sounds about right,' Peggy said grimly. 'Look up "entitlement" in the dictionary and you'd see her ugly mug staring right back at you.'

Nicole nodded and smiled. 'That was all fine and dandy

while Celeste was working for a big event-planning firm, with plenty of victims to take up the slack, but now it's just her and Minty, and Minty's just as bad. It doesn't matter if they've got the connections, access to the Old Boys' Club through their fathers… They'll trip themselves up eventually. What matters are drive and talent, and Hopes & Dreams has plenty of that, especially now Peggy has come on board part-time.'

All three women stared after their number one—well, their only—competitors.

'Won't matter if we go under and they continue to float around London like it's their own personal garden party,' Peggy muttered darkly.

Mia, ever the practical one, laid a hand on Nicole's arm. 'Well, if you ever want a hand with the books, just let me know. I might as well use all those fancy letters I got after my name for something I really care about.'

Nicole smiled and nodded. Mia hated her job as an accountant in a big city firm. If she could have joined her and Peggy at Hopes & Dreams, she'd have done so in a heartbeat. In fact, that was the plan if the business survived into next year.

Peggy hated any talk of boring things like numbers and spreadsheets. She let her head loll and pretended to snore softly, and when Mia poked her in the arm with a sharp fingernail she lifted her head and said, 'Time for another drink.' She handed her glass to Mia, who rolled her eyes but waved at the barman anyway.

'I'd settle for a glass of fizz and change of subject,' Nicole said. She'd been on a nice little high after Warren's triumph that evening, but Celeste's news about Hugo Pat-

terson and Sarah Henley had thrown cold water all over
it. Somehow, a draughty office building in Lambeth just
didn't have the same cachet. It was great having satisfied
clients, but what she really needed was *high-profile* satisfied clients. Ones who would shell out a ton of money on
a high-end proposal, then brag about it to all their friends
and get Hopes & Dreams mentioned in *Celebrity Life*.

'Change of subject? Oh, well in that case… Guess who
dropped by our flat while you were out being a Bond girl?'
Peggy waggled her eyebrows and waited, smiling.

'The Sultan of Brunei,' Nicole replied, not missing a
beat.

Peggy tutted. 'It's no fun if you don't play along.'

'It's no fun for *you*, you mean…'

Mia leaned over and put a hand on Nicole's arm. 'Just
humour her. You know she'll bug you until she gets it out
of her system one way or the other.'

Peggy grinned at Nicole. 'Well, if you're going to be
boring, I'll just tell you… Your dad came in to check that
damp patch on the bathroom ceiling this afternoon, with
hunky plumber Steve in tow. They were sad to have missed
you—especially Steve.'

Nicole shrugged.

'And when I say "sad", I mean *very* sad. You ought to put
him out of his misery and call him sometime, you know.
I'm sure the only reason he keeps coming back to check
the work he did on the boiler is because he wants an excuse to see you.'

'Sorry, Peg. Steve just isn't my type.'

'Then find someone who *is* your type!' Peggy said,
flicking her artfully curled platinum locks. 'It's been too

long since you've been out on a date. It's making you very crabby.'

Nicole opened her mouth to say there was a difference between 'crabby' and 'taking your life seriously', but Mia jumped in ahead of her.

'A woman can exist without a man in her life, you know, Peg. It's not the 1950s any more, even though you dearly like to pretend it is. Sometimes it's about the quality, not the quantity.'

Peggy gave Mia a well-worn look. 'There's not going to be any quality at all if the quantity is zero.'

'Well, we all know you like to prove that point with a different man every week.'

Nicole could see where this was going. Mia and Peg were firm friends really, but sometimes they really could rub each other up the wrong way. 'Calm down, children,' she said in a soothing tone. 'We're supposed to be here to check out the Hamilton and schmooze for new clients, re-member?'

Both women nodded reluctantly, but Peggy had to get the last word in, as always. 'You can't chip in anyway, Miss Mia, seeing as you've now got a ring on your finger, are sickeningly loved-up and can't even remember what it's like to be single.'

Mia suddenly stopped scowling and her whole face lit up in a beatific smile. 'I am sickeningly loved-up, aren't I? And who wouldn't be with a man like Jonathan? He's perfect, isn't he? Tell me he's perfect.'

Nicole laughed. It was true; Mia's fiancé really was lovely. He'd been so nervous about popping the question that he'd asked Nicole for help and it was then she'd realised not only was there a gap in the market, but that proposal planning was only a sidestep from event and party planning. There was so much pressure on guys these days, not only asking the question but how they did it. Suddenly booking a table at a nice restaurant and buying a ring wasn't enough. Jonathan had been very aware of all those YouTube videos out there of creative and romantic proposals. So that was where the idea to start Hopes & Dreams had been born.

'He really is perfect,' she reassured Mia. Perfect for Mia, at least. Not that Jonathan wasn't a great guy, but Nicole had yet to meet the man who lived up to her idea of Mr Right, the man who was a perfect fit for the life she was dressing to have.

The only one who'd come close was Jasper.

He'd been one of her old school friend's brothers. Their dad was head of an old and prestigious insurance company and his son had been not only rich, but gorgeous and charming. She'd fallen helplessly in love with him. Who wouldn't have done?

She hadn't been able to believe her luck. After all, his whole world was populated with girls like Minty and Celeste—confident, stylish, privileged. He'd told her he loved her. He'd said he liked spending time with her because she was spontaneous and unspoilt, such a refreshing change from all those rich girls who liked to dangle a chap from a piece of string just because they could. And she'd fallen completely under his spell, believing her own fairy tale had finally landed in her lap.

They'd been together for two years when Jasper had announced he had something important to discuss with her. It had come hot on the heels of a visit home to the rambling manor house his parents owned in the Berkshire countryside. He'd seemed nervous too, a look Nicole had seen more than once since then, in the faces of the men who knocked on the door of Hopes & Dreams.

So she'd gone out and bought a horribly expensive dress from one of the boutiques on Bond Street and had waited slightly breathlessly for him at the restaurant, with its imposing pillars and stern-faced waiters. And at the end of the meal he'd reached across the table and pulled her hand into his and had stared into her eyes.

She'd held her breath. And then her smile had melted from her face. She still hadn't been able to breathe, but not because she was delirious with joy. Because Jasper had been telling her it was over between them, that he was at that age when he needed to think about getting serious and settling down. She'd known his father had been pressuring him about joining the family firm for some time, but he'd always resisted up until that point.

After the shock wore off, as she was being ferried home in the cab that Jasper had insisted paying for, the truth had hit her. Jasper wanted to settle down, but not with her. Because in his eyes she wasn't what his family thought was the 'right sort'. The daughter of a builder from South-East London just wasn't good enough. And she'd hated him for being weak enough to give in to them.

Never in her whole life had she felt so small and worthless and insignificant.

Three months later she'd found out he was seeing a girl whose father owned half of Shropshire. Right there and then she'd realised she'd been fooling herself all along. She sighed. 'Maybe if the perfect guy fell out of the sky tomorrow, I'd make time for romance, but it's not a bad idea to concentrate on the business for the moment.'

Peggy just snorted. 'It's not a bad idea to be wrapped around a hot guy once in a while, either!' She shook her head. 'Your love life has been in drought since we started planning to open Hopes & Dreams, and the one time you did get close, you chickened out. I never understood why you didn't call that total cutie of a cowboy you pinned down under the mistletoe on New Year's Eve.'

Once again Peggy was playing fast and loose with the facts. 'There was no mistletoe, and he was the back end of a pantomime horse, not a cowboy.'

Nicole went quiet then, assailed by a rather vivid flashback of that kiss—his arms pulling her close, the scent of his aftershave as she'd let her head fall back and he'd pressed his lips to that quivery little spot just under her ear.

She shuddered, then shook herself. Damn. She hadn't had one of those for months.

'That doesn't count,' she told Peggy. 'I told you I lost his number. It was hardly surprising, seeing that under your influence, I got very...well...under the influence.'

Peggy shook her head. 'Squiffy or no, it was very careless of you. That was one dreamy cowboy...'

Nicole sipped her drink, worried that she might incriminate herself if she said any more.

Peggy wasn't the only one playing a little fast and loose with the facts this evening. Because Nicole knew exactly where that little scrap of paper he'd written his phone number on was. She'd known it all year.

She didn't know why she'd lied when Peggy had asked

about it the following day; she just had. She'd had too much of a hangover to have the energy to resist her flatmate's insistence to call him and arrange a date. This year was very important. She couldn't afford to lose focus. Besides, she didn't do that kind of thing, not since Jasper. These days she played it cool and let the guy do all the running.

Okay, she didn't usually go around kissing random strangers, either, but maybe one out-of-character action each year was allowed. One per year was certainly enough. She'd spent a long time grooming herself into the woman she was now. She wasn't about to let go of all that because of one drunken kiss.

Even if it had been one seriously *hot* drunken kiss…

Another flashback hit. Instead of being a muted aftershock, it was double the intensity. Nicole's ears grew warm and the hairs on the back of her neck stood up. She rubbed her hand over the spot to shoo the feeling away.

On a purely physical level the fizz of awareness was pleasant, but she didn't welcome it. This was how Jasper had made her feel, as if she were one buzzing, whirling mass of sensation, churning her up so she couldn't think straight, so she couldn't see the truth or even remember who she was. She definitely didn't need a man like that in her life.

So she hadn't called the cowboy. She'd tucked the scribbled number into a little pocket inside her purse and had tried to forget about it. She probably should throw it away. In fact, she would. As soon as she got home that evening. When Peg wasn't looking.

What she needed right now was a distraction, something to veer the subject away from her love life—or lack of it. She flashed her friends and business partners a smile, straightened her skirt and stood up tall.

'Come on, ladies. I spy Jayce Ryder's right-hand woman over there—and smart girls like us know that the real connection to make is the power *behind* the throne. Let's go and wow her socks off before Celeste and Minty get to her.'

# CHAPTER FOUR

The Hopes & Dreams office was east of Clerkenwell, a stone's throw from the Golden Lane housing estate. While many of the old buildings of the area had been demolished during the Blitz, there were still little pockets of Victorian and Edwardian architecture. Tucked away from the main roads was a half-forgotten little courtyard that had once been home to tradesmen's shops, like cobblers and iron-mongers.

Nicole's dad had come across the premises while repairing a leaky roof on a nearby shop. He had wandered down an alleyway in search of a decent cuppa and found a small, organic cafe in what had once been a hardware shop. There he'd spotted an old tailor's and haberdasher's shop, which he'd thought would be perfect.

Nicole hadn't been quite so sure of the location when he'd shown it to her earlier that year, but she'd realised that while she could do a lot of the proposal organising at home, constantly having meetings in coffee shops wasn't ideal. She'd really needed a base where she could meet clients discreetly and give the sense of an up-and-coming business, not a one-man-band affair.

Then her dad had taken her down the road to Clerkenwell and shown her how its regeneration meant that young and trendy businesses were flocking to the area: art galleries and bistros and independent bookshops. It would only be a matter of time before the effect rippled outwards. She should sign the lease while the rent was still within her reach.

Mr Chapman, the softly spoken, white-haired tailor who owned the shop, hadn't used the upstairs of his premises for a while, on account of his arthritis. The haberdasher's, which his wife had run and had occupied the ground floor of the premises, had been closed for years, so he'd moved his work downstairs and had put the upstairs space out for rent. Seeing as the late Mrs Chapman hadn't wanted dirty great men who needed their suits altered tramping through her shop on a regular basis, they'd chosen a place with a separate entrance to the first-floor studio.

The rent had still been a stretch, especially as the whole place would need refitting to be the kind of office Nicole had envisioned, but when she'd brought Peggy back with her for a second opinion, Peggy had come up with a solution. She was a freelance graphic designer and shared office space with three other designers, all of whom were men. She'd said she'd just about had enough of the slightly smelly testosterone-filled air and the takeaway cartons that no one seemed to clear up after an all-nighter doing a rush job for a client, so she'd suggested she and Nicole share the studio above the shop. She could do her design work without having to breathe through her mouth half the day or listen to endless discussions about 'World of Warcraft', but since her job meant work often ebbed and flowed, she could also help Nicole with Hopes & Dreams during the downtimes.

Nicole's dad had been an absolute star, doing any building work at cost, and Peggy and Nicole had got their hands dirty too, wielding paintbrushes and electric drills and sanding the original floorboards. They'd scoured salvage yards and boot fairs for pieces of furniture that went with the quirky vintage vibe of the shop and had managed to find two large desks in dark wood that had been sanded and re-stained. Nicole's remained neat and tidy, with a few pencil pots and notepads, while Peggy's was an explosion of photo frames and polka-dotted accessories.

One of the walls was filled with dark wooden shelves, probably home to thread and ribbons and buttons once upon a time, but now it housed photos of happy couples she'd helped on their way to matrimony, miniature wedding cakes, bouquets of silk flowers and just about anything heart-shaped Peggy could lay her hands on. Near the other window was a small purple velvet sofa with silver scatter cushions.

The crowning glory of their junk-shop treasures was a tailor's dummy that Peggy had found and christened Gilda. She was now adorned with a wedding dress that was mostly corset and tulle skirt and stood in front of one of the two large sash windows, her headless body staring out across the courtyard, like a fairy-tale heroine waiting for her prince to come.

Nicole hadn't been convinced about the design scheme when she and Peggy had discussed ideas, wanting something more classy and elegant, but Peggy was paying half the rent, so she'd had to compromise. They needed something fun, something different, Peggy had pointed out. Something that told Nicole's potential clients she could deliver the impossible, not just the same old, same old. While the bright fuchsia paint on the one wall that hadn't been stripped back to bare brick and the bejewelled chandelier that hung from the ceiling made Nicole wince a little every time she arrived for work in the morning, she had to agree that their little shop of Hopes & Dreams fulfilled that brief.

Behind the front studio was a small kitchenette and a toilet and they'd turned the small stockroom at the back into a cosy meeting space for Nicole to chat to her clients.

Peggy swept into the office on Monday morning and hung her coat on the old-fashioned hatstand in the corner with more force than was strictly necessary. 'I don't believe it! The Witches have gone and gazumped us again! You know the breakfast TV presenter Lottie Carlton? Well, her producer boyfriend proposed to her live on-air just before the credits rolled, and I'm sure that when a camera swung round I saw Celeste and Minty there in the background!' She collapsed into her chair and sighed dramatically. 'We'll never hear the end of it.'

Nicole had got there early to work on ideas for a client she was meeting later that day and had just come back from the kitchenette, where she'd made herself a cup of coffee. When she'd first worked here she'd nipped across to the little coffee shop opposite for caffeine, but now she was counting her pennies and had to put up with instant.

Peggy threw her vintage crocodile-skin handbag down

on her desk. 'I know she only does the local London show, but that's serious exposure for I Do, I Do, I Do.'

Nicole used a finger to smooth her hair back out of her face as she pulled her desk chair out and sat down. 'We're going to drive ourselves mad if we keep comparing Hopes & Dreams to them. I think we ought to have a Celeste-and-Minty jar in the office.'

Confusion crumpled Peggy's features. 'What?'

'Like a swear jar,' Nicole explained. 'Every time we mention them or their agency, we have to put a pound in the pot. It's about time we stopped focusing our energy on how well they're doing and concentrate on our own success. We've had another two yeses since we saw them at the Hamilton last week.'

Peggy nodded, grudgingly. 'I suppose you're right.' She tipped her collection of fluffy pens out of a polka-dotted tin that said 'You don't have to be a goddess to work here, but it helps' on the side and plonked it on Nicole's desk. 'Here…and I vote we spend the proceeds on cocktails, to drown our sorrows when Detest and Squinty schmooze all the high-profile clients in London into their clutches.'

Nicole picked the pot up and held it in her direction, raising her eyebrows.

'What?' Peggy said. 'I didn't actually use their proper names…'

Nicole waggled the pot.

Peggy flounced over and dropped a coin in the bottom. 'Fine.'

'It still counts. We need some positive energy around here. I've spent my whole life trying to compete with girls like that, and I've decided I can't be bothered with it any more.

And you know why? Because we're good. We're really good.
So the big-ticket clients will come. We've worked too hard
for them not to. We deserve them, and I believe people sow
what they reap. We don't have to stress about those two—'
She noticed the tin in her hand, broke off and smiled se-
renely. 'We don't have to stress,' she said again. 'It'll all
work out.'

Peggy stopped looking quite so affronted and a naughty
twinkle appeared in her eye. 'You really think so?'

Nicole ignored the little wobble in her tummy at that
thought of her much-loved company, the one she'd invested
all her time and energy and even more of her money in,
going down the drain. 'I certainly do,' she said, faking total
and complete calmness. She was ninety per cent there.
Fudging the final ten per cent really wasn't lying.

And she was also sure she'd conquer this childish urge to
push Celeste's and Minty's faces into the ground and stand
triumphantly over them while they tasted the mud of defeat.
She was talking the talk, doing her best to walk the walk.
If she persevered, eventually her wayward thoughts would
have to get into line with the rest of her. This was the method
she'd used in upgrading the rest of her life, and she was sure
it would work here too.

'We'll be okay in the end if we work hard,' she told
her business partner, most seriously. 'We just mustn't lose
heart.'

Peggy snorted, but as she flumped into her office chair
she looked a little less stressed. 'You sound almost reli-
gious about it.'

'Well, it is in the Bible, that sowing and reaping thing.

Why shouldn't we get rewarded for all our effort, while...
other people...get what they deserve?'

Peggy shook her head. 'Well, the last bit sounds wonderful to me. I've always been a fan of a bit of divine ret-
ribution. But are you saying that if we all just pray hard
enough, a rich, young—preferably titled—stud is going to
crash through that door on his steed and declare, "I want
you to plan a proposal for me!"?'

Nicole sent her an angelic smile. 'I'm sending up a little
prayer right now,' she replied and returned to her internet
search for a glass slipper that one of their clients wanted
to use as part of his proposal.

# CHAPTER FIVE

Later that afternoon, as the clouds hung heavy across the city, bringing a premature twilight, and the wind bounced itself off the windows at the front of the Hopes & Dreams office, the door crashed open.

Nicole looked up to find a tall, long-legged blonde wrapped stylishly in a cape, her tumbling golden waves teased slightly out of place by the wind. 'Are you the proposal planners?' she asked, bracing herself dramatically in the doorway.

Nicole and Peggy shot a look at each other across their desks, looked at their guest and nodded.

'Then I want you to plan the best proposal ever for me,' she said, a tinge of desperation in her cut-glass tone. 'The best one you've ever done!'

Peggy mouthed across at Nicole, 'You know who that is?'

Nicole nodded, ever so slightly, ever so discreetly. Either this was famous-for-being-famous socialite Saffron Wolden-Barnes or her double had just crashed her way into their office.

'Flipping heck,' Peggy muttered under her breath and shooting a look heavenwards. 'It actually worked.'

'God does indeed move in mysterious ways,' Nicole mumbled back. In the ten and a half months since Hopes & Dreams had been in business, she'd not once had a woman walk through her door.

Peggy shrugged and added, 'You prayed for her. You'd better take her.'

Nicole rose and walked towards their new client and held out a hand. 'Lovely to meet you. I'm Nicole Harrison, founder of Hopes & Dreams Proposal Planning Agency. If it's something unique you want, you've come to the right place.'

The blonde shook her hand back. 'Saffron,' she said, exhaling, and nodded towards the door, as Peggy scurried over to close it. 'Sorry about that. People expect me to make an entrance when I'm out doing public appearances and what have you. Sometimes I just forget to switch it all off.'

'Why don't we sit down and talk through some ideas,' Nicole said smoothly. She led Saffron down the narrow corridor and opened the door to the proposal-planning room.

Once inside she breathed a sigh of relief. Here, at least, she'd been allowed free hand to decorate, and it was an oasis of cream and off-white, clean lines and stripped wood. Black-and-white photos graced the walls and there was just enough room for a low glass coffee table and two oatmeal-coloured armchairs.

As they settled themselves down, Nicole took a closer look at their client. She'd seen pictures of her in *Celebrity Life*, of course, but had never laid eyes on her in person. That charisma that oozed from the glossy pages of the magazine was not exaggerated. There was something about her that made you want to look at her. Maybe it was the long, tumbling blonde waves. Maybe it was the designer jeans and boots, the way she'd slung her outfit together with a careless sophistication that Nicole had taken years to get down pat. Whatever that elusive X factor was, Saffron Wolden-Barnes had it in spades. It was as if someone had taken all the best bits of all 'those girls' Nicole had battled with all her life and rolled them into one perfect package.

A package that they sorely needed, if Nicole's diminishing bank account was anything to go by. She couldn't let that faze her, though. Pretending her heart wasn't pounding a little harder, that this was any other, non-famous, non-make-or-break client, Nicole picked up a large notebook from the coffee table, which was adorned with folders full of different proposal ideas. She removed the lid of her fountain pen, poised it ready to write, then looked up.

What she saw took her by surprise. Saffron was looking back at her, leaning forward with her hands clasped. Her knees were pressed together, allowing her to rest her elbows on them, but her feet jutted out at odd angles, giving her long legs the appearance of those of a just-born foal who wasn't quite sure what to do with them. She leaned forward, stared Nicole straight in the eye and sighed. Her eyebrows pulled upwards in the centre, creating a little arch-shaped wrinkle in the skin above her nose.

'You think I'm bonkers, don't you? Go on, say it. All my friends do. They think I should wait for him to pop the question.'

Nicole blinked. She'd expected Saffron to be the queen of 'those girls', full of confidence and easy words, but there was something about her… She reminded Nicole of the girl she'd been at school. On one hand, having everything going for her, but on the other, awkward, vulnerable, maybe a little too desperate to please. She put her pen down, stopped smiling her 'client' smile at the other woman and leaned forward. 'There's nothing bonkers—I mean, crazy—about wanting to ask the person you love to marry you.'

The rest of Saffron's eyebrows lifted and her mouth opened a little. Then she smiled at Nicole. A big, glowing smile that lit up her face and made her blue eyes sparkle. Nicole couldn't help smiling back. There was something very open and refreshing about Saffron Wolden-Barnes.

'Why don't you tell me about the man in your life,' she asked gently. 'We're going to need to find out a little about him before we start planning in earnest.'

Saffron didn't need to be asked twice. She launched instantly into a full description of the paragon she dearly wanted to marry. He was sexy. He was clever. He was cool and funny. He had the best smile in the world and made her feel safe and grounded in her crazy life.

'He's a bit publicity shy, though,' she added, thoughtfully. 'Doesn't really like the limelight. So we've been dating not exactly in secret, but quietly.'

'And you think he's ready to make this step too?' Nicole asked. Nobody—not her, not the client—wanted a 'no' after all the expense and planning, so it wasn't a bad idea to make sure the proposer had really thought about it before they put the wheels in motion.

Saffron nodded vigorously. 'I'm sure he does. At least…' She frowned again. 'No…I'm sure. I think so.' She gave

Nicole another blast of her famous smile. 'There are no guarantees when you're doing something like this, right?'

'Right,' Nicole said, heartily relieved Saffron wasn't one of those clients she had to remind about this point. She was good, but she couldn't achieve the impossible.

'I mean…part of the point of the exercise is finding out the answer to that question, isn't it? And I really want to know the answer. Now.' Her shoulders drooped a little. 'I just haven't got time to wait for the next leap year.'

'Well, what kind of proposal were you looking for?' Nicole asked. 'We can arrange just about anything you want. Intimate meetings in the midst of the city or an idyllic woodland trail with a Michelin-starred picnic at the end. Flash mobs or a romantic assignation at a castle or in a luxury penthouse. We can do big and dramatic or cosy and intimate. Obviously, we can't do magic…' she paused to smile softly, as she always did when she delivered the next bit '…but we'll do our best to make your hopes and dreams come true.'

Cheesy line, she knew. But the clients loved it.

Saffron exhaled and her shoulders relaxed. 'Thank you. You don't know what this means to me.'

Nicole smiled again. She hadn't expected to like Saffron, but she did. There was a lack of guile about her that was surprisingly disarming. Suddenly she understood why it was this girl and not the hundreds of other bright young things like her that the tabloids followed round.

'I don't even know where to start…' Saffron said mournfully, flicking through one of the folders in front of her. 'Just that I want it to be monumental, spectacular. And that I want to do it the weekend before Christmas, so it's all done and dusted by the time I get together with my father, step-mother and step-sister on Christmas Eve.'

'Well, I've got a questionnaire I can run through with you that will throw up some ideas, but we don't have to decide anything right now,' Nicole said.

'I usually do a little homework on the fiancé-to-be when someone comes to me to plan a proposal. I also try to engineer a face-to-face meeting so that we can get a feel for their personality and tastes.' After Mr Arrogant she wasn't taking any chances.

It had turned out to be a genius idea. While a lot of the men who came to her knew their partners very well, she'd discovered that there were also things many women hadn't communicated to their significant other, secret wishes that the man of their dreams should just instinctively know without being told. After her mock interview, Nicole was well placed to weave them into her proposal ideas and let the proposer take the credit.

Saffron looked a little panicked. 'You won't tip him off, will you?'

Nicole shook her head reassuringly. 'Don't worry. We're very discreet. Usually, I pose as a journalist or a market researcher doing a questionnaire and ask them a few key questions about themselves, what they feel about love and romance. It's all very quick and painless.'

She didn't add that it was usually a bit easier when the target was a woman. It wasn't hard to run into someone in a coffee shop or in a high street and start chatting about weddings and boyfriends. Saffron was spooked enough as it was. Nicole wasn't going to scare her off by mentioning this would be her first girl-asks-boy proposal.

'What we need from you is information on how we can informally "bump into" him. Preferably a public place where there's an opportunity to chat, hopefully within the next week.'

Saffron thought hard for a moment. 'I have the perfect event! Oh! It's tonight…like, in a couple of hours. That's not too soon, is it?'

Nicole shook her head. It wasn't impossible, even if it wasn't the way she liked to do things. Usually, she preferred a couple of days to do some homework before she met the 'target', as Mia jokingly called them. It would mean she'd have to meet the guy first and do her research later. She mentally leafed through her diary and rescheduled her gym session for the following morning. 'No, tonight is fine.'

Saffron immediately brightened, clapping her hands together and bouncing a little on the sofa. 'Oh, that's amazing! I am *so* excited we can kick-start this straight away. I detest waiting for things.' She pulled a scrap of paper from her handbag and scribbled down an address on it. 'It's a photography exhibition. I may well turn up at some point. That's okay, isn't it?'

Nicole nodded. 'I might not speak to you when you do. It will be better if we're not seen together at this stage, but I'll chat to your man and come up with some personalised ideas from the information you've both given me. Then we can meet again in a few days to start setting something up.'

She rose and indicated that Saffron should follow her back down the little corridor.

'Money's no object,' Saffron said loudly as they emerged into the office.

Nicole saw Peggy's ears prick up, but she kept her head

down, hiding her smile as she tinkered with a design on her computer.

'I want the whole of London talking about this proposal for months. Years, even!'

Both Nicole and Peggy smiled broadly at the socialite. So did they.

'I have one last question before you go…' Nicole said. The whole time she'd been talking with Saffron, one big thing had been puzzling her.

Saffron raised her eyebrows. 'Fire away.'

Nicole cleared her throat and asked the question she knew Peggy was also thinking. 'Why did you choose Hopes & Dreams instead of…instead of another proposal-planning agency?' She knew that Celeste and Minty ran in the same circles as Saffron and her buddies. Surely they would have been the natural choice.

For the first time since she'd entered their offices, Saffron dimmed a little. 'Well, I won't lie. I did hear of another agency first, but then I discovered who ran it and I kept searching using Google.'

Peggy shot a look at Nicole.

'I hate to speak badly of anyone,' Saffron continued, 'but I wouldn't trust Araminta Fossington as far as I could throw her.'

'Oh, yes?' Peggy piped up, before Nicole could stop her.

Saffron nodded vehemently. 'She once stole a boyfriend right from under my nose. There's no way I'd let her within fifty feet of my man.'

Nicole tried not to show it visibly, but inside she was jumping up and down. She sent a glance at Peggy that said, *See? I told you stuff would come back and bite them in the butt some day.* Peggy rolled her eyes and pretended she hadn't understood.

'Well, we're very glad you chose us,' Nicole said, shaking her hand. 'And you'll find us professional in the utmost, in every area of our service.'

Saffron gave her another of her light-up-the-city smiles. 'I have a good feeling about this,' she said as she hitched her handbag up onto her shoulder. 'See you in a few days!'

And then she swept out of the office in a twirl of fur-trimmed camel cape and a waft of perfume. It seemed her exits were every bit as impressive as her entrances.

They waited until Saffron had disappeared out of the courtyard below before they started jumping up and down and hugging each other.

'Take that, Celeste and Minty!' Nicole said, punching the air.

Peggy picked up the swear jar and thrust it her direction. Nicole smiled and dropped a pound coin into the bottom. She didn't care. That victory shout had been worth every penny.

# CHAPTER SIX

When Saffron had mentioned an exhibition, Nicole had assumed it would be an upmarket gallery in Bloomsbury or Chelsea. She hadn't expected a church, tucked away down a dusty side street in Blackfriars on the south bank of the Thames. Most of Saffron's circle wouldn't be seen dead in this postcode. She checked the slip of paper with her client's large and looping scrawl once again. Trinity Arts Centre. Yep. This was the place.

She walked up the stone steps and pushed one of the glazed wooden doors open enough to slide through. She then stepped through a second set of doors and into a large, bright space.

The original beams and pillars of the large church remained, as did the parquet floor and the organ pipes on the far wall, but the interior had been cleared and everything was painted crisp white, making the stained-glass windows sing with colour.

Off to one side as she walked in was a bar and seating area, while the other held a small shop, and deeper into the church was the exhibition space, carved into different sections by slabs of white walls about seven feet high. Some were set at right angles to each other, arranged near other walls to make a large and open maze, where the artwork was displayed.

There was a small crowd wandering around, wine glasses in hands, perusing the large black-and-white prints that adorned the display space. Before joining them, Nicole checked her phone. Still nothing from Saffron. They'd chatted not long after she'd left the office and Saffron had promised she'd send a photo through of her intended. It had yet to arrive. Until it did, Nicole would just have to mingle and enjoy the exhibition until she found the man she was here to stalk—Alex Black.

She snagged a glass of wine from a passing waiter and headed deeper into the church. She stopped by the first wall and took a sip. The print was of a windswept Highland landscape. Nicole had always loved the rich, peaty colours of a Scottish winter—the mossy greens, slate greys, the ochre of the dying bracken—but there was something about seeing it in black and white that made it look even wilder and more lonely. She could almost feel the wind sweeping off the worn-down mountain tops and into the wide, flat valley below, could almost hear the frothy sea hiss as the gale tossed the waves with no mercy.

She carried on. They were all British landscapes—rugged Cornish beaches, tranquil forest glades, ancient stone circles—but each harnessed a wild and beautiful energy. It made something inside her ache. Just a little. And she didn't know why.

She'd reached the far end of one of the maze-like avenues now, and she hesitated at which direction to go next.

It was clever. There was no predetermined route between the walls. In fact, the layout seemed deliberately designed to make visitors wander and retrace their steps, to seek out the hidden nooks they hadn't discovered yet. She glanced right, wondering if she'd been that way already, then left.

Just as she did, someone disappeared behind a wall. Nicole hadn't seen them properly. It had only been a blur at the edges of her peripheral vision, but it was accompanied by a flash of something that was very much like a memory. Something that made her think of soft fur and dancing lights. Without asking herself why, she followed.

As she turned the corner she saw a man with his back to her, talking to a couple of older men in suits. They were discussing a piece halfway down the zig-zag of wall, about fifteen feet away. He was dressed all in black, from his battered biker boots, to his jeans and T-shirt. Even his hair was so dark it almost matched them. Just a hint of chestnut brought out by the overhead spotlights spoiled the effect. His stance was easy, relaxed, as he drank from an open beer bottle and gestured towards the photo in front of him.

Nicole knew she should turn, look at the print right in front of her, but she couldn't help but linger. There was something about him. Something tickling the back of her brain. Had she met him before? She felt as if she had, but surely she hadn't, because she'd definitely remember someone like him. Not her type at all, of course, but memorable all the same.

And then he turned and smiled at a woman who joined the group, and a delectable little dimple appeared at one corner of his mouth, apparent even beneath the short black stubble.

A charge shot through Nicole like electricity. So strong it reminded her of the time her pet hamster had chewed through the wire on her bedside light and she'd foolishly picked it up, thinking it wouldn't hurt her. She'd found herself on the other side of the room a split second later, dazed and confused.

It couldn't be, could it?

It couldn't be *him*. The guy from New Year's Eve.

For some reason she clutched her handbag closer to her, as if she was protecting that slip of paper folded into the pocket of her purse, as if it might jump out and cause trouble if she didn't.

He'd been one hot cowboy, as Peggy had called him, when Nicole had been five cocktails to the wind, but the sober version was just as potent. It seemed her beer goggles had twenty-twenty vision. She knew she should feel happy about that, but she couldn't. Not while her insides were unravelling in loops.

Why, after months of coexisting in the same city, did she have to bump into him *now*? On the night she had to be on top form if she was going to bag this job of Saffron's and deliver the proposal of the century?

At least he hadn't spotted her. She should just sneak back round that wall and…

Uh-oh.

As she was backing away he turned, noticed her. His eyebrows lifted momentarily in surprise and then his smile widened and he started to stroll towards her with that easy stride she hadn't realised she'd noticed, let alone recalled. Nicole tried to move but her stilettos were glued to the floor. Her phone buzzed in her pocket but she ignored it.

'Hey, Holly...' he said, a mischievous glint lighting up his eyes. 'Long time no see.'

Her mouth moved. Up and down, up and down. She must look like a gaping frog. 'Holly?' she finally managed as he stopped in front of her.

'Holly Golightly,' he said, brandishing a smile that didn't quite reach his eyes. 'Of course, I realised that wasn't your real name pretty quickly. One quick Google search put pay to that.'

She'd told him her name was Holly Golightly?

'So why didn't you?' he asked.

Nicole blinked. 'Why didn't I what?'

He stepped forward. She started to feel more than a little claustrophobic. 'Call me,' he replied, and then he waited, a hint of a lopsided smile pulling at one corner of his mouth.

She swallowed. It was one thing fibbing to Peggy when she got too nosy, but it was another thing entirely to lie to the man himself. Her mouth felt dry, despite the fact she'd been sipping her wine and it was already half gone.

But she couldn't tell him the truth, couldn't tell him she'd been too much of a coward to call him, because something about him made her feel out of her depth, like she was a drowning woman trying to surface and gasp in some air. She didn't want to ever feel that way again with a man.

It was happening now. She tried to come up with a smooth, polished answer, but the only things inside her head were jumbled syllables, like a multitude of jigsaw pieces, none of which seemed to connect to the rest. 'Um...' she said and looked away. When she looked back he was still smiling at her, a hint of satisfaction in his gaze.

That was when it hit her like a slap. He was playing with

her. He was *enjoying* seeing her like this. That thought alone sobered her enough to thread a few of those syllables together.

'I don't know if you noticed...' she began, finding it easier with every word that slid from between her lips, suddenly finding an excuse she might be able to use to her advantage, '...but I was a little bit tiddly that evening.'

The grin she got in return told her he knew exactly how tiddly she'd been and that he hadn't minded one bit.

She closed her eyes momentarily, licked her lips.

*Focus, Nicole.*

She breathed in, turned her internal thermostat down a notch. She had to get a grip on herself. 'I lost your number...and I didn't know your name, either. There wasn't much I could have done.'

There. Smooth. Silky. Giving him back as good as she got. That was the Nicole she knew and loved, not that gibbering idiot who'd look into a man's eyes and believe every lie he told her.

He nodded. 'True. But you didn't seem too bothered about finding out before you pinned me up against that wall and had your wicked way with me.'

Although she tried not to, Nicole felt herself blush right down to her perfectly manicured toenails. She could feel heat radiating from him like a force field, and while one part of her—the sane part—was telling her to back away, excuse herself and get on with what she'd come here to do, she couldn't deny that a completely separate part was telling her to launch herself onto him again.

And he knew it. Damn him. Payback was a bitch.

'I tried to find you, you know…?' he said, keeping his voice deliberately low, so she was tempted to sway closer.

'You did?' She'd aimed for cool and unaffected. Husky and mildly perturbed would just have to do.

He nodded. 'When you didn't call I talked to friends who were there that night, the bar staff… I even called a lookalike agency. But you didn't leave me much to go on, just a naughty twinkle in your eyes and a fake name.' He reached out and touched the end of her plait, which was draped over her shoulder. 'I didn't even know if this was your real hair. You could have been wearing a wig.'

Nicole flicked her braid out of his fingers by turning to look at the picture to her left. Peggy would say this was fate intervening, that she shouldn't waste a second chance like this. Peggy was clearly a lunatic.

Yes, she was attracted to him. Yes, he knew it, the smug so-and-so… But that didn't mean she had to do anything about it. Guys like this were definitely *not* part of the plan she had for her life.

There was only one thing she could do — she was going to have to blow him off a second time.

She glanced at the photograph. It was a dark and moody shot of one of the giant monoliths at Stonehenge. 'Wonderful use of light, don't you think?' she said, trying to keep her tone breezy, searching for an 'out' so she could float off and talk to someone else. Anyone. As long as it wasn't him.

He chuckled deep in his throat. 'I think so, but I'm glad you do too.'

Nicole was too busy trying to spot a likely victim to analyse his reply. 'It's beautiful,' she added and then focused on the picture properly. The shot had been taken slightly from below, making the huge lump of rock seem even more solid and ancient. Storm clouds hung low on the horizon, but a beam of light broke through, lighting up one side of the stone, revealing its pitted and lichen-covered surface in sharp detail. She found once she started looking at it, she couldn't stop.

She'd said it was beautiful without thinking, and it really was. Almost too beautiful. But she didn't tell him that. Somehow that felt as if she'd be giving something important away.

'I waited four hours in the rain for that shot, but it was worth the week-long cold that followed.'

Forgetting she was supposed to be finding an exit ramp for this conversation, Nicole swung round sharply. 'This is *your* exhibition?'

A wry smile played on his lips for a moment. 'And there was me thinking you'd seen a flyer and come because you'd finally found me after all these months of tireless searching.' The humour in his eyes told her he was still teasing, but had turned it on himself. She'd just about pigeonholed him as a strutting peacock, but his self-mockery shot a hole in that idea. Damn. She liked a little humility in a man. And if it came with a dry and self-deprecating sense of humour it was doubly as potent.

'I…I…'

So it was back to this. Great.

His eyes sparkled with mischief as he looked down at her, inviting her to join him, to turn the joke back on herself and see the funny side. Unfortunately, Nicole couldn't stand even the hint that someone might be laughing at her and she stiffened, feeling both superior and hypocritical at the same time.

Wow. This guy really brought out the best in her, didn't he?

Which was why she was getting out before things deteriorated any further. She should have listened to her gut instinct and done it minutes ago. 'I'm sure you're far too busy and important to be standing around gassing to me,' she said, a little snippily. 'I should let you go and talk to some of your other guests.'

She moved to walk past him, pretending she was heading round the corner to a section of the exhibition she had yet to visit, but his hand shot out and his fingers lightly circled her wrist. 'Not so fast, Holly.'

She stopped dead. His touch was light and she knew she could pull away easily if she wanted to, which she did, but for some reason she didn't move a millimetre.

'This time I need a name at least.'

Nicole blew out a shaky breath. That wouldn't be a good idea. As gorgeous as he was, he wasn't her type, and he probably had 'drifter' stamped all the way through him like Brighton rock. Still, she wasn't rude enough to completely snub him. Her parents had brought her up better than that.

'Nicole,' she said, gently easing her wrist from his grasp and circling it with her own fingers. 'Nicole Harrison.'

He nodded. 'And what do you do, Nicole Harrison, when you're not driving men crazy by disappearing into the night air never to be found again?'

Her stomach bottomed out. For the last ten minutes she'd completely forgotten why she was here. She'd forgotten all about Saffron and her fiancé-to-be. She'd forgotten all about Hopes & Dreams and why this job was so darn important. She needed to stop chit-chatting and find Alex Black. The easiest way was to stop sparring with this man and just roll over and answer his questions.

'I'm a journalist,' she said quickly, then frowned at herself. She didn't know why she'd said that. It would have been okay to tell him the truth. But maybe, because she'd been all prepped to come out with a cover story this evening, that was what had left her mouth first.

'And what are you working on now? Not covering the show, are you?'

She shook her head. 'No, this is just for fun...'

Torture, more like.

'Actually, I'm doing a piece on...a piece on...'

He raised his eyebrows again. And the smile was back. The one where she thought he might be laughing at her.

'On weddings,' she blurted out. It was all she'd been able to think of. 'For *Beautiful Weddings* magazine.'

'Really?' he said and waited, clearly expecting her to elaborate.

Nicole's brain flew in three directions at once, and none of them useful. See? *This* was why she didn't like veering from her careful plans. Everything turned out messy and unpredictable.

She had to say something. Something that was easy to understand and wouldn't require further interrogation. Something to do with weddings. Something that would work for a magazine feature.

She thought of all the weddings she'd planned when she'd worked at Elite Gatherings, when she'd been part of an army of worker bees who'd found the day anything but ethereal and magical.

She refocused on him. 'I'm going to do a piece on the unsung heroes of the wedding industry, you know...all the people who work in the background to make the magic happen.' She shot him a smile. Her brain was whirring now and she went with it. 'Rather than just chatting to people on the phone and doing the superficial stuff, I want to follow each professional round for a couple of weeks, do different kinds of weddings, make it really in-depth. Then I can do an interest piece, but also with some really good tips about getting the most out of that professional when someone plans their own big day.'

He nodded. 'So who would you follow round?'

She shrugged. 'Oh, I don't know. People like caterers and waitresses, florists or bakers.'

The grin was back. 'People like photographers?'

She could have sworn her insides turned to chocolate. Melting chocolate.

'People like photographers,' she echoed, a slight dryness in her voice.

'Then you've come to the right guy,' he said then waved an arm to encompass the photos on the walls. 'This is what I really love to do, why I pick up my camera on a daily basis, but I earn my bread and butter doing weddings. At least for now.'

'Oh,' she said, forgetting to keep calm and collected, letting her eyes widen. She hadn't expected him to say that. There was nothing about this guy that made her think of weddings and rings and happy-ever-afters.

'So why don't you follow me around for a couple of

weeks?' he asked, his dimple putting in another appearance. Nicole couldn't quite tear her eyes from it.

He lowered his voice. 'I could give you the low-down on slaves and f-stops?'

F-stops? She knew it was probably a technical term, but in that voice and with that smile it sounded kind of naughty.

'So...are you interested?' he said, leaning in close enough for her to get a whiff of his aftershave.

She swallowed again. The tiniest glimmer of interest in his eyes suggested he was asking about more than a professional opportunity. He didn't want to just score a point; he wanted total defeat. Revenge for skipping out on him all those months ago.

So she would say no. To the offer to shadow him—because that wasn't her real job anyway, and it would be a total waste of time—and to the offer to spend more time with him, because...because...

Although he'd moved back, she could still smell his scent, and it prompted one of those New Year flashbacks, a particularly potent one of his lips on the soft skin of her neck, his hands round her waist. Suddenly she was very tempted to say yes. To everything.

She knew she should walk away a second time, but something was sticking her feet to the floor like Velcro. Something was telling her to go with that wild feeling his photographs had stirred inside her, to tell the voice of caution inside her head to go to hell.

He was watching her, taking in the emotions, the thoughts, flitting across her features. The knowing expression told her he knew exactly what she was thinking, knew exactly what decision she was teetering on the edge of.

Nicole was about to open her mouth, suggest they go for a coffee after the exhibition to discuss his offer, when her phone buzzed in her pocket again.

It brought her back to reality with a bump.

Oh, heck. Saffron.

She glanced up at him as she pulled her phone out of her coat pocket. 'I'm sorry… I really need to check this.'

He shrugged one shoulder carelessly as she swiped her phone screen to pull up the message.

'Maybe we can discuss this shadowing thing after—'

The rest of the sentence never left her mouth. Because the message was indeed from Saffron. An hour later than they'd planned, but that wasn't the problem. The problem was the picture message that accompanied the text.

She was staring down at a photo of a windswept photographer with a bewitching little dimple.

# CHAPTER SEVEN

She seemed to have frozen looking at her phone. She was clutching it so hard her finger joints were going white. Alex coughed softly. 'Nicole?' Still she stared at the screen, not moving, not speaking. He started to regret teasing her quite so hard. What if it was horrific news, if someone had died or her house had burnt down? 'Are you okay?'

She snapped upright then, shoving her phone back in her pocket, and bestowed a bright smile on him. 'Fine.' She blinked. 'Absolutely fine. Nothing wrong at all.'

Okay, then…

He frowned a little. In his experience women often said 'fine' when they meant 'my life is going down the toilet'. He had a feeling this might be one of those times, but he really didn't know her well enough to push. He also didn't know her well enough to read her correctly. She could be as fine as that fluorescent smile said she was.

Or she could be faking it just as hard as he was.

As much as he liked to think he'd been in control of the conversation up until now. He'd been doing what he always liked to do in a hairy situation—winging it and hoping it would turn out his way in the end—but he couldn't ignore the chemistry popping between them any more than she could. Trying to get under her skin had backfired on him spectacularly.

He should have come up with a better plan. Or maybe any kind of plan at all.

He exhaled and swigged his beer.

Their timing stank. Why couldn't he have met her nine months ago, when he'd still been free and single?

He hadn't been lying. He'd looked for her for ages. Way longer than was sensible. Maybe that was why he'd listened to that little voice in his ear telling him to mess with her a little, because his ego had taken a knock when she hadn't got back to him. He'd decided maybe he'd been wrong about New Year's Eve, that she hadn't felt the same way. However, she'd demonstrated very nicely with her stammering and blushing this evening that just wasn't the case.

So why hadn't she called? It was going to drive him crazy if he never found out. Even if he did, he couldn't ask her out again. As much as he liked women, he liked them better one at a time. Not only was he not that much of a sleazeball, but it cut down on the inevitable drama. He didn't like drama. A life that was free and easy and cool suited him much better.

She was fiddling with the stem of her wine glass. Somehow he knew what she was thinking about saying. It was as if he could see the subtitles, like watching a foreign film. And if these ones were printed out in stark white letters, hovering in the air below her face, they would say, 'Find an excuse to get away. Now.'

He made up his mind to let her.

'Well, it's been lovely bumping into you again,' she said, smiling her 'fine' smile again, 'but I've really got to...'

He nodded. So did he.

This time he didn't reach out and grab her hand, but watched her walk on to the next photograph, pretend to peruse it. He fully intended to head off in the opposite direction, but just as he was turning to go she let a little bit of that iron composure slip, closed her eyes and heaved out a weary sigh.

It was as if she'd slammed down a matching card in a game of 'Snap'. An identical tug of war was going on inside him. There were reasons he should walk away. Good reasons. Not only Saffron, but the fact that he'd promised himself he was going to stick to women who knew what they wanted, who were as easy to read as a picture book.

But...

Something was telling him he'd been a fool to let her slip away a second time.

He found himself striding back to her. 'When do you have to have this article thing done by?'

She looked mournfully at him, as if she was begging him for something. Finally she sighed and said, 'The weekend before Christmas.'

'I've got five weddings lined up between now and Christmas. Different types too—some small and quirky, a couple that have pulled out all the stops. It could be just what you need.'

This was insane. He knew it was insane. But he was still doing it.

He needed a chance to see her again, to find out if this was really something or whether he was just smarting because he wanted what he couldn't have. He also wanted to see if the warm, funny, sexy girl he'd met on New Year's Eve was hiding away somewhere inside this starchy suit. And this was a totally innocent way of being around her so he could find out. Nothing had to happen. And if he was wrong about her... Well, he'd be free and clear to walk away. No harm done.

She started shaking her head. 'I don't think... Maybe we should just...'

'Have you got any better offers?'

She sighed. 'No.'

'I could do with the extra pair of hands,' he said, sending her a begging look of his own. 'At this time of year the weather always conspires to make things more complicated.'

She opened her mouth to brush him off, he could tell, but before she could get the words out she jumped and pulled her phone out of her pocket again. It must have been on vibrate.

Her eyes widened as she read the message then dropped her hand to hang by her side. 'I'm sorry, Alex. I really have to go.'

She moved to push past him without making eye contact, but he stepped in front of her. 'At least let me take your number this time. You might regret it if you don't.' He waited until she looked at him, tried to tease a smile out of her, but there was sadness in her expression that hadn't been there before.

She shook her head. 'I can't...'

'Not even prepared to suffer my company for your art?'

Her forehead crumpled into little lines. 'Huh?'

'Well, if not your art...your article,' he said. 'If you don't find someone else to shadow—a cake maker or a florist or a dove trainer—you might regret not being my assistant for the next few weeks. Here...' He picked up her hand, phone still in it, and deftly entered his number in her address book. 'No excuses this time,' he said, watching her flush a little bit pinker. 'Use it.'

The look she gave him told him it was unlikely. 'Bye, Alex,' she almost whispered, and then she darted past him. He didn't stop her, just watched as she straightened her spine and walked out the door without looking back.

He was still standing there, only half aware of the sparse traffic darting past the glazed doors, when someone clapped him on the shoulder. He turned round to find Tom grinning at him.

'Who was that?'

Alex shook his head. 'You'll never guess.'

But that didn't stop Tom trying. He'd gone through most of the minor royals and had started on the cast of *TOWIE* by the time Alex stopped him. He would have interrupted sooner, but his head had been swirling with thoughts of his mystery woman. He knew her name now, but somehow that hadn't made her any less mysterious. It was as if he could see two versions of her superimposed on top of each other, mostly in sync, but occasionally the image jumped and he could see one more clearly than the other. He had no idea which was the real Nicole Harrison.

'It was Holly Golightly. From New Year's Eve.'

Tom let out an appreciative whistle. 'Did you flirt with her?'

Alex opened his mouth to deny it. There was a difference between playing a bit of a game and actual flirting. However, Tom, as usual, didn't stop to wait for anything as mundane as an answer.

'Of course you did.'

Alex shook his head and tipped up his beer bottle, only to discover it empty. Damn.

'You know, some people use flirting as part of the hunt, but you're the only guy I know who uses it as a defence mechanism.'

Alex smiled, looked at the photo he'd taken of Tintagel, high on a stormy coast. 'Seriously, mate, you've been spending too much time in LA. You're starting to sound like a shrink yourself. Any more startling insights to wow me with?'

He glanced to his left and found Tom smirking at him. 'Okay, I'll bite. How long have you been going out with Saffron now?'

Alex pulled his mouth down at the corners while he thought about it. 'What…? Five months? Maybe a little longer?'

Tom made a great show of looking at his watch. 'Yup. Right on time.'

Alex knew he didn't really want to ask him to elaborate, but he did it anyway. 'For what?'

'It's always around the six-month mark in any relationship that you get the jitters, start questioning everything—especially why you're with her and not some other wonderful creature you've just spotted—and ultimately end up backing out and breaking her heart.'

No. This wasn't what this was. It wasn't the same with Nicole. Besides, Tom was wrong about the six-month thing.

He'd split up with Vicky after… Well, okay, maybe that one did fit. But then there had been Meg, who'd lasted… Damn. What about Rachel…?

He shoved his empty bottle in Tom's direction. 'Shut up and get me another beer.'

Tom grinned at him and headed off to the bar, whistling.

He'd just returned and handed Alex a fresh one, before scooting off to chat to one of their other climbing buddies who'd just arrived, when Alex saw a flash of honey-coloured hair by the front door. He heard the clop of her boots as she made her way towards him, carving a wake through the throng of entranced visitors.

'Wonderful turnout,' she said, before leaning in to air-kiss his cheek, prising his latest beer from his fingers, taking a swig and not giving it back to him.

He grunted. For some reason he was feeling ticked off with her. 'Hi, Saffron. Nice of you to show up.' And then he added, under his breath, 'Finally.'

She gave him one of her saucy looks, the kind she must have given her doting daddy when she was little to make him shower her with dolls and sweeties and ponies. 'I know I'm a tad late…'

He exhaled. Normally he didn't mind that Saffron operated in her own time zone, but this evening had been important to him. He thought she could have at least made the effort for once. 'One hour and twenty-five minutes to be exact.'

She rolled her eyes and gave him a *who's counting* kind of expression as she leaned in and laced her fingers between those of his free hand. 'Well, I'm here now. That's what matters.'

He sighed. Well, at least she hadn't given him some lame story. That was why he'd been attracted to Saffron in the first place—she was who she was, no apologies, no excuses, and he'd never once caught her lying about anything. Which was just as well. Because he'd had enough of women who pretended to be one thing and turned out to be something entirely different. That was a fast track to a broken heart, and he wasn't buying tickets for a return visit any time soon.

Saffron slid her free arm in his and turned to a print of a picture he'd taken in Glen Coe. 'Now…which bog exactly did you immerse yourself in to take this one…?'

# CHAPTER EIGHT

When Nicole got back to the flat she shared with Peggy, she didn't stop walking until she crashed the door to her bedroom open. There she stepped out of her skirt, heels and blouse, pulled a soft pair of tattered tracksuit bottoms from a drawer and topped them off with a well-loved and well-stretched grey T-shirt. Leaving her clothes in a heap on the floor, she marched to the kitchen, buried her head inside the freezer, then emerged again with a carton of clotted-cream vanilla ice cream in her hand.

She grabbed a spoon and headed for the living room, where she dropped onto the neutral-coloured sofa that she'd chosen, snuggled up against the bright, psychedelic cushions that Peggy had bought and aimed the remote at the TV with more than a hint of fierceness. Sometimes the clash of hers and Peggy's very different decorating styles made their flat seem a little schizophrenic.

It was only as the opening credits to *Pretty in Pink*, her favourite 1980s high-school movie, filled the screen that she exhaled and let her shoulders sag.

Peggy wandered into the room in her polka-dotted bathrobe, rubbing her damp hair with a towel. 'Uh-oh,' she said, as she spotted Nicole on the sofa, feet stretched out on the coffee table that normally was only allowed drinks on top if a coaster was involved. 'What happened?'

Nicole kept staring at the screen as the credits rolled. A young Molly Ringwald was getting dressed in an explosion of pink lace and floral prints. 'The cowboy happened.'

'Oh?' Peggy murmured, pretending she knew what Nicole was talking about as she dropped down onto the sofa next to her.

'From New Year's Eve...?'

Peggy kept frowning and then her eyes widened. *'Oh!'*

Nicole nodded. 'Yes, *oh!*'

Peggy's forehead bunched again. 'But that's good, isn't it?'

*Good.* That was an interesting word. Not one Nicole knew if she'd apply to Alex Black, either. He looked good if you meant *want to eat him up with a spoon*, but not the wings-and-halo type of good, far from it, with that shaggy dark hair, perma-stubble and that infuriating little dimple.

An image of Saffron flashed through Nicole's memory from the meeting they'd had at Hopes & Dreams that afternoon. Saffron had hesitated, hadn't she, when she'd answered the question about whether her intended fiancé was having the same thoughts of happy-ever-after? Maybe their relationship wasn't as solid as she assumed?

*Get real, Nicole. You're grasping at straws. It's serious.* Serious enough for Saffron to propose to him, anyway. Unless there was a ring on a finger, things didn't get much more serious than that, and even if it wasn't serious, he was taken.

'*Not* good, then...' Peggy said, answering her own question as she inched closer to Nicole and laid her head on her shoulder. They both watched the movie in silence for at least five minutes. 'I don't know why you're so obsessed with this film. She should end up with Duckie, not the rich jerk.'

Nicole sighed. Part of her knew that. But another part of her knew what it was like to be the girl from the wrong side of the tracks and yearn for the perfect boy who would always be out of her league. It was nice to see the underdog triumph for once. Instead of like real life.

Peggy sat up and turned to Nicole. She prised the ice-cream carton out of her hand and stole a spoonful. 'So… it's obvious you don't want to talk about the cowboy, so tell me about the meet with Saffron's man instead.'

Nicole swiped the carton back off her friend and indulged in another spoonful of ice cream before she answered. 'One and the same.'

Peggy opened her mouth and shut it again. 'You don't mean…?'

Nicole nodded again. 'Yup.'

'Wow…' Peggy shook her head. 'Talk about complicated.' She shifted position to face Nicole fully. 'But don't give up. It'll work itself out.'

Nicole stopped watching Molly moon over Andrew McCarthy for a few seconds. 'How?'

Peggy shrugged. 'I was just thinking about *Pillow Talk* or *Move Over, Darling.* Those were really tricky romantic situations, but it all turned out right for Doris in the end.' The smile she gave Nicole was so sweet, so genuine, that Nicole didn't have the heart to tell her that Doris Day films weren't real life, something Peggy needed reminding of on a more and more regular basis.

And she thought Nicole's John Hughes addiction was weird.

She lifted one corner of her mouth in her best attempt at a smile. 'It doesn't matter anyway. It was just a physical thing. I could do without the complication.'

Peggy smiled and nodded. She took the ice-cream carton from Nicole and headed back towards the little kitchenette. 'I think ice-cream hour is over and wine time has begun.'

Nicole would have chased her all the way back to the freezer if she'd had the energy. Instead she turned back to the screen, but as much as she stared at it, the images floating through her head weren't colour, but black and white, and instead of love-struck teens, she could see wild moors and heather and billowing clouds that filled the sky. It made her feel like running out into the night to feel the icy November wind on her cheeks or climbing a tall building to see how far she could see. There weren't many mountains in the N1 postcode, so that would be the best she could do to exorcise this feeling whirling inside her.

Peggy returned and handed her a rather full glass of wine. Nicole accepted it gratefully. Usually she didn't partake on weekdays, but— Ugh. Who cared? She took a large gulp and exhaled. Hard.

'Can I take the job over?' Peggy asked. 'I am a proposal planner in training, after all.'

Nicole shook her head. 'It's fine. I can handle it. I told Saffron I'd be dealing with her proposal personally, and I don't want to do anything to spook her.' She looked Peggy meaningfully in the eye. 'We need this job to go well if

Hopes & Dreams is going to grow. In fact, if we're not doing better by the new year I might have to go back to regular event planning and do Hopes & Dream part-time, and I really don't want to do that.'

She couldn't bear the thought of having to take a backwards step.

'And then there's the money both you and Mia have put in...'

'No pressure, then,' Peggy said.

Nicole shrugged. It was what it was. 'All it boils down to is that we need a "yes". I can't let anything interfere with that.'

Peggy nodded sadly. 'Fate is cruel,' she said melodramatically, and Nicole couldn't help but burst out laughing.

'What?' Peggy asked, wrinkling her nose and looking a little offended.

'No, you're right. Fate *is* cruel. But you've gotta laugh or you'll cry, right? What doesn't kill you makes you stronger...'

Peggy nodded, instantly joining in the game they liked to play when either of them was down—coming up with inane-sounding platitudes in the hope one of them would make sense. 'You forgot "There are plenty more fish in the sea."'

'So I did.' Nicole toasted the screen with her glass and snuggled down into the sofa cushions. 'Now, shut up and let's watch this movie.'

Peggy slurped her Chardonnay. 'I mean...thank goodness it's her asking him and not the other way round. At least you won't have to spend much time with him. Just see him on the night, that's all. And we can make it so you direct things from afar, if you like, and I can do the hands-on stuff...' She trailed off as she saw the look on Nicole's face. 'Oh, no. What have you done?'

Nicole jabbed the pause button and scowled. Then she explained about the fake magazine article, about Alex's offer. When she'd finished Peggy stared at her. 'Holy crap on a cracker,' she said. 'You can't go through with it!'

'I have to,' Nicole said glumly. 'I didn't get any info from Alex this evening—I was too shocked. I know I did the questionnaire with Saffron, but she's got one of those butterfly minds that leaps all over the place. I hardly got anything useful, partly because I don't think she knows what she wants. That means I have to see him again or we can't possibly tailor her proposal to him properly. I need to find out what he thinks about love and marriage and romance...' She gave Peggy a morbid little smile while her insides churned. Maybe ice cream and wine hadn't been the best way to go. 'And what better place to do that than at a wedding?'

Peggy stared at her. 'You're insane. And that's a lot, coming from me.'

Nicole turned away and let the movie off pause. They were just about to get to the bit when Duckie slides into the record store and sings 'Try a Little Tenderness' and she needed a bit of cheering up.

'I'm only going to do the one week,' she said matter-of-factly, 'and then I'll find a reason to pull out—I'll tell him my editor doesn't like the angle or something, or that she wants it quicker and I need to investigate the other jobs instead. What else can I do?'

Peggy laid her head back on the sofa cushions and looked

at the ceiling. 'Nothing. You're just going to have to go along to some horribly romantic winter wedding, spend all day up-close-and-personal with Mr Sex-on-a-Stick. What could possibly go wrong?'

Nicole jabbed her in the ribs, making her jump and slosh her wine on her favourite velvet cushion in a particularly violent shade of lime. 'Hey!' When she'd brushed the worst of it off, she looked Nicole in the eye. 'Can you really do this? Can you resist temptation and control yourself?'

Nicole laughed softly. 'Of course I can… I'm not you, Peg.'

Peggy knew her own weaknesses too well and just rolled her eyes instead of getting upset. Besides, if there was one thing Nicole excelled at, it was keeping in control.

# CHAPTER NINE

When Nicole turned up at the chic little oyster bar tucked away behind the theatres of the West End to meet Saffron, she made sure she looked flawless. There was no way she was going to come off as second best in the fashion department, even if she was a loser in every other arena comparisons were made. Especially in the romance department.

She'd dressed carefully that morning, choosing to echo Saffron's high-end boho chic rather than her usual sophisticated office wear. She tried adding a chunky woollen scarf, carelessly wrapped around her neck, but instead of looking artsy and casual it just made her look as if she were a farmer about to go milking. Why could she never get this ultra-casual designer look right? It was driving her crazy.

When she reached the restaurant, she took a deep breath, squared her shoulders and pushed open the dark wood door and entered the cluttered space. There was a large horseshoe-shaped bar topped with smooth grey marble in the centre of the room. A brass rail ran around the edge and deep leather-covered stools were tucked underneath. The waiter showed her to a little table beyond the bar.

It was empty, of course. She ordered a sparkling water and settled down to wait. Unlike Saffron, she didn't have the luxury of turning up late. If she left a client waiting, even for a few minutes, it wouldn't look good.

The minutes sloped by. The longer she sat there, the more her mind churned with the thought that had woken her up, making her sit bolt upright, at two-thirty that morning.

She should come clean.

It was a conflict of interest or…something. She should tell Saffron she'd met Alex before, tell her they'd been romantically involved.

Except they hadn't.

It had only been a kiss, one that had lasted maybe three—possibly five—minutes. A drunken kiss that she really shouldn't remember in quite such vivid detail. But every time she rehearsed in her head how she was going to broach it with Saffron, the conversation always went badly. It was the fact that the whole thing had been so difficult to categorise that made it harder.

If she could just say, 'We went out for two months about five years ago, but we parted on good terms and I moved on and I'm madly in love with someone else now,' then maybe everything would be fine. But she couldn't say that. Even though what she'd done with Alex was *way* less intimate, somehow saying, 'I walked up to him and snogged him senseless earlier this year' just wasn't going to put a skittish girlfriend at ease.

And that was where she'd been for almost the last twelve hours. Going backwards and forward between telling and not telling, and she wasn't getting anywhere. She was always up front with her clients. Always. They trusted her to give an unbiased and sometimes not-easy-to-hear opinion when they needed one.

It was her own stupid fault. She'd known when she'd walked into the arts centre the other evening that she shouldn't have let herself get sidetracked, but she'd done it anyway. If she'd kept professional, stuck to the plan, it would never have got to the stage where Alex Black was flirting with her and she was starting to like it.

It would never have got to the stage when she'd *almost* listened to Peggy's advice about wrapping herself around a hot man, either...

Thank goodness Saffron's text had arrived when it had. Otherwise she'd have committed professional suicide as well as romantic suicide, and that really would have been too much for one evening.

Saffron appeared half an hour later, with an armful of large, glossy shopping bags with string handles that seemed to contain more air than shopping—the sure sign of some really expensive purchases.

She let the bags drop at her feet with a rustle of tissue paper and greeted Nicole, who had risen and waited patiently while the waiters flapped around their celebrity patron, taking her coat and pulling out her chair so she could sit down.

'Well,' she said, leaning forward across the table, her eyes shining. 'Did you meet him?'

Nicole nodded. 'I certainly did. That was the plan.'

The only bit of the plan that had gone smoothly, it had to be said.

'And isn't he gorgeous? Isn't he perfect?'

Nicole nodded again, but gently, giving nothing away. 'He is.' Not that Saffron would have noticed. She was in full-on gush mode and was only too happy to have someone to sing her fiancé-to-be's praises to. Which she did, for at least ten minutes. Usually, Nicole enjoyed this bit— seeing that light in a client's eyes when they talked about the person they wanted to marry—but the longer Saffron talked, the better Alex sounded, and the sicker Nicole felt.

She should tell her. Just spit it out and tell her.

But…

She remembered what Saffron had said about man-stealing Minty. And Saffron could be temperamental and rash—she knew that much from the tabloids. And from the fact she wanted to propose to her boyfriend after five months, of course. If she caught Saffron in the wrong mood, she might flush this whole job down the toilet, and Mia and Peggy were depending on her to bring it in. It wasn't only herself she'd be sabotaging, but her two best friends in the world, and the future of Hopes & Dreams, which she knew she could make a success—she just needed a little more time. And Saffron's money and profile.

*It's ancient history,* she reasoned with herself. Nothing. Less than nothing. And over before Saffron and Alex began. What good would it do to dredge it all up now?

Their drinks and appetisers arrived. Saffron had ordered a seafood platter, which was on a metal plate on a stand, lying on a bed of crushed ice. A large and rather pink prawn was facing in Nicole's direction and it fixed her with its black, currant-like eyes. *I know,* it seemed to be saying. *I know your secret…*

It was at that point that Nicole decided she had to do

something to protect her sanity. As much truth as she was *able* to tell might do it. She took the opportunity while Saffron sipped her wine to butt in. 'Unfortunately, I didn't get quite as much information from Alex as I'd like to have done the other evening. I thought I'd better let you know that I may need to meet with him again.'

Saffron threw her head back and tipped an oyster down her throat then shrugged. 'Fine. Whatever you need to do to get the job done.'

Nicole let out a breath. She'd be honest about the present, even if the past was better left in the past. 'I'm keeping up my cover story and attending a wedding posing as a journalist next Saturday,' she told her client. 'Hopefully, it'll give me some really good ideas.'

Saffron grinned at her. 'As long as those ideas are big and colourful and expensive, I'm all in. What have you come up with so far?'

Nicole smiled as she toyed with her dressed crab. At least now she was back in her comfort zone. They spent the rest of the time discussing the merits of different venues and proposal types and ended up with a shortlist of three basic outlines, which Nicole would tailor further to Saffron's requirements when she had more of an idea of what made the wonderful Alex Black tick.

When they were finished, Saffron thanked her for lunch and swept off to another urgent appointment she was already an hour late for, and Nicole settled the bill.

It had started to rain while they'd been eating. She had a raincoat with her, but it didn't have a hood, so she had to pull her collar up and jog down the alleyway that ran past a theatre and out onto St Martin's Lane. She looked sideways as she ran past the row of posters advertising the latest play. The glass was just shiny enough to send back a reflection.

She slowed to a walking pace, still glancing at her image in the dark posters as she passed them. Her eyes were large and she looked younger. She was reminded of the night Jasper hadn't proposed. She'd run away from the restaurant, down alleys like this, desperate to get to the main road and find a cab.

She'd thought she'd got rid of that woman, that only an echo of her had been left behind. It was a shock to see her staring back at her, the pale face superimposed on those of the actors in the posters.

She couldn't be that person again. Not now. And definitely not for the next six weeks as they ran up to Christmas and Saffron's big proposal. The clock couldn't turn backwards. She wouldn't let it.

She had this horrible feeling that if she didn't finish the journey she'd started after Jasper left her, she'd always be stuck in some horrible limbo between being the girl she once was and the woman she wanted to be. And that wouldn't do. She needed every bit of armour about her now.

Especially if she was going to survive a whole Saturday in the company of Alex Black.

# CHAPTER TEN

It was bright and frosty that Saturday morning when Alex pulled up outside Nicole's flat in his car. She didn't wait for him to ring the doorbell. Instead she ran down the stairs, intending to intercept him on the pavement outside before he even got out of the car. The less he knew about her the better, because if Alex found out what she really did for a living before Saffron proposed, her whole life would be toast.

She'd formulated a plan while she'd been waiting. In lieu of anything better, today's objective was to be the consummate professional—on two fronts: the real job and the fake job. She would not flirt. She would not stammer. She would forget all about how attractive he was and treat him the same as any other fiancé-to-be.

And he was, really. Despite what had happened on New Year's Eve. There was no reason to feel as if she'd known him for years, no reason to believe they were part of a secret club of two, no matter how much the air seemed to close in around them every time they were within three feet of each other. It was just physical. She had to remember that. Chemicals firing off in her brain at the sight of a nice-looking man. Nothing more.

And she didn't need to get to know him, either. At least no more than she needed to so she could do her job and provide Saffron with the proposal she'd hired her for.

He spotted her emerging from the door to the street as he stepped from his car, and one corner of his mouth lifted in greeting. Her disobedient heart went into overdrive, causing her pulse to bang in her ears. She took a deep breath and ignored it. *Talk the talk, walk the walk, and the rest will follow.*

'Will this do?' she said, opening her coat and showing him what she was wearing. He'd said she should dress smartly but practically and with a view to being as unobtrusive as possible.

It had taken a while to find something that would truly help her blend into the background. While she favoured understated elegance, she realised that she always dressed hoping others would notice the pared-down style, the subtle message that said, 'I'm not trying to impress you', even though she subconsciously was. In the end she'd plumped for a soft charcoal jumper over smart black trousers and boots with a heel that wouldn't give her nosebleeds.

Alex was dressed in a dark suit with a thin black tie and a large and slightly scruffy overcoat thrown over the top. He should have looked smart, but somehow the overall effect, including the battered boots that still graced his feet, gave him the air of a rock star who was trying very badly to be on his best behaviour.

He gave her a wink. 'It'll do,' he said.

She told herself the rush of heat to her face was down

to the icy wind pinching her cheeks. She nodded and slid
into the passenger seat of his Jeep while he rather gallantly
held the door open for her. She wished he hadn't. The only
way she was going to make it through today was if she cast
herself as lowly helper and packhorse. She didn't want him
to do the sort of thing he might have done if they were out
on a date.

'How long will it take us to get there?' she asked, as he
started up the engine and pulled away.

'An hour to an hour and a half, depending on the traffic.'

She nodded and kept her focus straight ahead as they
headed east, through the almost empty streets. She'd hoped
it would be a local wedding, something at a nice hotel in
London. Something she'd have been able to get the Tube
to, then get away again as quickly as possible. But it had
turned out they were heading across London and into deep-
est Kent, to a stately home called Elmhurst Hall. She'd
heard of it, but had never been there before. All of a sudden,
an hour and a half in a Jeep with him felt like an eternity.

'Do you mind if I put some music on?' he asked.

Nicole shook her head, and Alex prodded a couple of
buttons on the stereo. Pretty soon a rock station was blaring into the car. She welcomed the noise, hoping it would
fill the space between them, hoping it would stop her noticing each tiny movement of his arm near hers as he moved
the gear stick.

It didn't work.

It also didn't remove the subtle scent of his aftershave
from the confined space or stop her listening to the thrum
of his voice as he hummed along with a favourite song.

She decided the only way she would keep her sanity was if she *did* talk.

'Tell me about the location,' she said. Maybe, if she could keep herself in 'work' mode—even if her work wasn't just being photographer's dogsbody—then she'd survive this monster of a day.

'It's the home of Lord and Lady Radcliffe, but they open the house and gardens to the public and do a great wedding package,' he told her, only flicking a glance in her direction as he weaved through the London traffic. 'I've done a couple of weddings there before, so I didn't need to go down and scout out the place beforehand. The ceremony is going to be in the church at the edge of the grounds and the reception will be held in the grand hall. It's medieval, complete with a raised dais at one end and shields and swords on the wall. Lighting will be a bit of a nightmare, by the way, because it's a bit gloomy in there this time of year... One of the reasons I could do with an assistant today.'

Nicole's voice, when it came out, had a bit of a squeak to it. 'You want...you want *me* to help with the lighting?'

Alex laughed. 'Don't worry. I'm talking about a couple of slave flashes on tripods that'll work wirelessly with the unit on my camera. I'll just need you to set them up straight and keep an eye on them, make sure they don't get knocked. You won't have to do anything technical.'

'Thank goodness for that,' she muttered.

'I thought you wanted to get the low-down on being a wedding photographer,' he said, a hint of challenge in his voice. 'You won't manage that without getting your hands dirty.'

Nicole stared at her hands in her lap as they waited for a

red light to change. She'd been so busy thinking about Alex and how she was going to handle seeing him again, she'd forgotten she'd actually be doing things today. Things she knew nothing about. Things that could potentially mess up someone's wedding. All of a sudden she felt a little queasy.

If there was one place she disliked being, even more than crammed into this confined space with Alex Black, it was out of her comfort zone.

'I think you'd better fill me in on exactly what we're going to be doing when we get there,' she said. The squeak in her voice was back. Higher. Tighter.

As they headed out of London, Alex did exactly that, outlining all the different places and people they'd be shooting, from starting the day with the bride and groom getting ready to the reception. Her brain began to spin with all the facts and details. After ten minutes she held up a hand to stop him. 'Do you have a list?' she asked weakly. 'If you want me to help you call all these people and get them in the right place, I think I should have a list.'

He grinned as he kept his eyes on the road straight ahead. 'Of course I have a list.'

Nicole exhaled and relaxed into her seat a little more. 'Where is it?'

Alex lifted his left hand off the steering wheel and tapped his index finger to his temple. 'In here.'

All the warm and fuzzy feelings that had started to grow flushed themselves away, leaving only a pool of ice in the bottom of her stomach.

However, by the time they drove through the vast stone gateposts to Elmhurst Hall, Nicole had scribbled for twenty pages in the little notebook she always kept in her handbag.

At least the job of extracting Alex's list from his head had kept them off personal things and firmly onto the business side of the day.

Fifteen of those pages were lists of different groups of people they'd need to shoot at different times and in different locations throughout the day. The other five were notes on which lens was which and how to organise the multiple memory cards Alex would be using in his camera. And she was going to have to carry kit around and keep charge of it. She couldn't have been more nervous if she'd been guarding the Crown jewels. She'd been involved in planning numerous weddings while working at Elite Gatherings, and the last thing she wanted was to end up as some Bridezilla's breakfast because she'd accidentally deleted all her wedding photos.

How did Alex carry all of this around in his head and not go crazy? The thought of working off the top of her head, not relying on print-outs and lists synchronised to her phone, made her feel twitchy.

Alex parked his Jeep and they unloaded the boot. She took a small lens bag and a lightweight tripod, but when she moved to sling a third bag over her shoulder, Alex waved her away from the back of the car.

'I'll get these.' He threw her his keys. 'You can shut the boot after me and lock the car.'

Nicole looked at the remaining three bags. All were big. All were heavy. And there were two more tripods. 'And you usually let your assistants off this lightly, do you?'

Alex stopped and frowned. 'Well, usually they're photography students doing it for the experience. They expect to work hard.'

She straightened her back. 'And so do I. I want the whole experience. That's what I'm here for, after all.'

And it was true. It was just that it wasn't the photography experience she was after. It was the full-on Alex Black experience. But only because her job required it, of course. Only because she'd promised Saffron she'd do a stupendous job planning her proposal.

He studied her carefully, then shrugged one shoulder. 'Have it your way.' Then he handed her a bag so heavy to sling over her shoulder she thought she'd be walking like a lopsided orang-utan for weeks and piled another tripod on her waiting arms.

'This way,' he said, heading off round a wall at the corner of the car park. 'Mustn't keep the bride waiting.'

# CHAPTER ELEVEN

Alex hoisted a tripod more comfortably over his shoulder and led the way past the front of Elmhurst Hall. It was pretty impressive, with its large central square tower and two wings spreading either direction. Smaller towers finished each wing like rather large sandstone bookends. There were battlements on the roof and tall, multi-paned windows breaking up the warm yellow facade.

He turned round the side of the building, aware of Nicole trailing behind him, puffing slightly. He looked over his shoulder and opened his mouth to ask if she wanted a hand, but the look that she gave him told him he'd better not try it, so he closed it again and just kept going.

The front of Elmhurst Hall might be showy and grand, but he liked it round the back better. Here it was much more obvious how successive owners had added to it over the centuries, creating a patchwork of different styles from medieval to Jacobean.

Keeping the route as short as possible, he led Nicole through a small, studded wooden door and headed up a stone spiral staircase. By the time they reached the landing outside the room reserved for the bride's dressing quarters, Nicole was panting behind him but trying desperately not to show it. He indicated she could put her load down. She grimaced and let it gently to the ground.

She'd surprised him, refusing to let him do all the heavy lifting. Saffron would have taken him up on that offer like a shot. And she'd have engineered a way to offload the small amount she did have to carry too.

But that was what today was all about, wasn't it? Finding out who Nicole Harrison really was. He couldn't think of a better way than this. After a back-breaking twelve-hour day where they'd have to deal with the expected and unexpected, he'd have her pegged. He'd know if the spark between them was real or if it was just like Tom had said, that she was nothing more than a knee-jerk reaction because his relationship with Saffron was going beyond 'fun' and teetering on the edge of something more serious.

And he wasn't going to flirt. No matter what else Tom had said.

He was just going to be chatty and friendly, like he was with everyone else. That way maybe she'd lose the starchy librarian act she'd got going and loosen up a little.

He rapped softly on the door with his knuckles, and a bridesmaid peered nervously round the door a few seconds later. 'Alex!' she said, her face lighting up, and almost dragged him inside. 'Lynette!' she called over her shoulder. 'Alex is here!'

'Thank God!' another female voice said from inside the room. 'I'm having an earring crisis and I need someone with a good eye to help me out.'

He entered the large, low-ceilinged circular room, part

of the vast round tower that sat at one of the back corners
of the Hall. The room was covered in rich, hardwood pan-
elling, its patina darkened to almost black by the wear of
a couple of hundred years. Where the light from the mul-
lioned windows hit it, it glowed warm and rosy like a good
red wine. The antique furniture was a similar colour but
the gloom was lightened by a soft cream carpet and furniture. The bride stood by the window, being fussed around
by the bridesmaid who'd answered the door and a few others of various shapes and sizes.

Lynette turned from surveying her open jewellery box
on a large dressing table, where a make-up artist and hairdresser were both patiently waiting for her to sit so they
could make their finishing touches. 'Alex, I can't decide…'
She held up a single earring in each hand. 'Mummy gave
me Grannie's pearl earrings this morning and I don't know
whether to go with those or stick with the ones I spent three
months searching for.'

He stepped forward. If he looked hard he could see a
slight difference, but they were both pretty. However, he
knew—after learning the hard way—that brides took details like this very seriously. 'Why don't we wait until
you're in your dress and everything's finished,' he suggested. 'Then I'll take a close-up of you wearing each pair
with your necklace and you can choose between them.'
Problem solved. And he was off the hook if she later decided she'd made the wrong choice.

'Genius!' Lynette cried, clapping her hands. 'I knew
there was a good reason I hired you. And it wasn't just
because most of them—' she threw a look at the gaggle of
giggling bridesmaids over her shoulder '—begged me to.'

She leaned forward, pulled him into a hug and kissed him on the cheek. He stepped back, smiling, then gestured towards Nicole. 'I said I'd be bringing an extra pair of hands today. This is Nicole Harrison.'

'Lovely to meet you,' Lynette said to Nicole and shook her hand. 'Any friend of Alex's is a friend of ours. You'll meet Charles shortly, I should think.'

A tiny crack appeared in Nicole's composure as she glanced warily in his direction, but then she produced a blinding smile, one that felt as if it had been rehearsed a thousand times. He realised he'd been on the receiving end of that smile more than once in their short acquaintance. He also realised he didn't like it much.

'Thank you,' she said. 'I'm looking forward to it.'

That done, he clapped his hands softly and looked round the room. 'Right. Time to get some of this clutter moved away so we have a clean background for the shots. Nicole?'

'Yes,' she said, snapping to attention, any hint that she'd felt anything but totally in control completely erased.

'Can you move the clothing rail over to the far side of the room, away from the windows?'

'Done,' she said, starting off in that direction.

'And, girls…?'

The bridesmaids erupted in a flurry of giggles and eyelash batting. They were all a bit hyped up, dressed to impress, and he was the first male specimen that had seen them in their glorified state, that was all. He was used to this kind of reaction from batches of girls in identically coloured dresses. He also wasn't above using it to keep the group smiling and cooperative. Herding bridesmaids was about as easy as herding cats.

He grinned back at them. 'If you could sweep up any bits of your make-up and hair stuff and put them on that dresser over there...'

Within five minutes he had the room how he wanted it. The make-up artist was putting the finishing touches to Lynette's face. The soft winter light from the window was perfect, making her skin look like that of an old-fashioned movie goddess. He set to work instantly while the make-up artist swept yet more mascara on her lashes and applied her lipstick.

A lot of photographers would have kept quiet at this point, but he liked to chat with the bride. Not only did it relax her, but he always got a few lovely shots of genuine amusement or wistfulness, not those kind of stilted posed pictures where she looked like a shop dummy in a wedding dress staring out of a window. He asked her about her family, how Charles had proposed, where they were going on honeymoon, and then, right at the end, he took the shots of the earrings he'd promised and Lynette was feeling so mellow she chose her grandmother's without a second thought.

When he was ready to move on to the next set of shots, he looked over his shoulder. 'Nicole?'

She was standing silently, stiffly, not engaging at all in the fun going on around her. 'Yes?' she replied, standing straighter.

'I need the seventy-to-two-hundred-millimetre lens from inside that bag.'

She opened the bag and stared at the assorted lenses in there, all protected from rolling around with padded partitions, and then she looked back at him a little helplessly.

'Sorry,' he said, smiling. 'Forgot you're not my usual kind of helper. The one in the far right corner.'

He then turned his attention to the bridesmaids, getting them to help each other check their hair and arrange the wrap things they were wearing round their shoulders, all the while snapping away. It wasn't a very traditional way to do wedding photography, but this was how he liked to work. He liked action, catching a moment as if he were a news photographer, listening to his gut so he could press the shutter at just the right moment to catch a smile or a look.

The hairdresser had finished tonging or curling or whatever they called it and now she was fixing a small pearl-covered tiara onto Lynette's head. When it was done, and she stood up, the bridesmaids sighed all at once.

'Don't you start!' Lynette warned, waving a finger at her maid of honour, who was desperately flapping her hands in front of her eyes with splayed fingers. 'I want some photos of us while the make-up's still good and before I turn panda!'

Uh-oh. He knew where this was heading if he didn't do something quick—Niagara Falls. And no one needed a delay in schedule while make-up had to be hastily re-done. He had to run down to the church in half an hour and start to work on the groom and his attendants before the service.

'So...' he said, stepping into the group and starting to shoo them into a loose group around the bride, who sat back down in her chair. 'Who was the worst behaved on the hen weekend?' That instantly produced a few hoots of laughter and accusations began to flow, mainly from the direction of the bride.

He took a few last shots of them all together as they ribbed one girl about an unfortunate incident with a feather boa, and then he glanced over at Nicole. She was ticking away in that little notebook of hers. He didn't need to check with her, but he did anyway, guessing it might help her relax a little. 'All done?'

She nodded.

'Then that's our cue.' He headed for the door. 'Let us know when you're ready for us again,' he said to the head bridesmaid as Nicole dashed after him. She gave him a questioning look when they were alone on the landing together, the solid oak door closed behind them.

'Obviously, I don't stay inside while the bride gets dressed,' he said. She raised her eyebrows, looking unconvinced, so he added, 'I might be a little bit bad on occasion, but I'm not that bad.'

There was something about the hint of holier-than-thou in her expression that got under his skin and niggled him. He looked back at her, tempted to shake his head.

This woman looked like and sounded like the one he'd met on New Year's Eve, but there the similarities ended. And, yes, he knew she'd been a little drunk, but in his experience alcohol tended to loosen the inhibitions, magnify what was already there, not turn a person into a different being entirely.

While on one hand it irritated him, another side of him was curious. Where had she gone, his Midnight-Kiss Girl? He was no closer to finding out than he had been when he'd picked her up that morning. Friendly and chatty was just not doing it. At least not with her, even though it seemed to be working fine on everyone else. He gave in to the temptation to push just a little bit harder, to see if he at least could get that iron mask of hers to wobble a little. And he knew exactly how to do it, never mind what Tom would accuse him of later.

He leaned in, invading her space just enough to see her pause breathing. 'But you know all about being a little bit bad on occasion, don't you? I swear, if I hadn't experienced it for myself while Big Ben was chiming, I'd have bought the "butter wouldn't melt" thing you've got going on.'

'I'm here to work,' she croaked. 'Not…not…'

He raised his eyebrows. 'Not…?'

She swallowed. 'I know we have…history. Sort of. But I'm not here because of that. Really I'm not. I'm here on a purely professional footing today, and I'd prefer it if our relationship stayed that way. If you're not comfortable with that, then I'll leave.'

When she'd started talking there'd been the slightest tremor in her voice, but as she ended her speech her tone was calm and even. She stared back at him coolly and innocently, then flashed him another one of those smiles.

He mentally kicked himself. He'd told himself not to flirt, hadn't he? And yet somehow he'd not only done it, but talked himself into thinking it was a good idea.

There was a call from inside the door. Lynette was ready. He reached over and opened it, allowed Nicole to go first. She slipped through the doorway without looking at him.

Great. Now she'd clamped down even harder than ever, and he was the one feeling all hot and bothered. All he'd succeeded in doing was reminding himself how much he was attracted to her, of how good that kiss had been. Tom had been right: the good girls really were fun when they were being just a little bit bad.

He sighed as he followed Nicole back into the room. It was going to be a very long day.

# CHAPTER TWELVE

A flurry of confetti met a gust of wind above the bride's and groom's heads and exploded like a pastel firework. All around people cheered. Lynette looked lovingly into her new husband's eyes and he bent in to kiss her tenderly, and Alex caught it all. Nicole could hear the shutter whirring on his camera as the bride laughed, pulled away from the groom and fished a handful of coloured paper from down the front of her dress. Alex captured that too.

It was amazing to watch him. Not only did he set to work ticking every item on the list they'd created together, but he managed to catch all the unplanned moments of magic as well.

It had been a lovely service in the tiny church that sat on the edge of the Elmhurst estate. Soon the cars would arrive and ferry the wedding party and guests back the short distance to the hall, where the reception would begin.

The happy couple had elected to have a good portion of the formal group photos done outside the picturesque church, even though it was late November and frost still tinged the grass that sat in the shadow of the spire. Nicole hadn't had time to get cold, though. She was also minding Alex's coat. He'd shrugged it off when he'd really got going, darting this way and that, snapping everyone emerging from the arched doorway, getting candid shots of genuine joy and pleasure as family and friends looked on at the new Mr and Mrs Hunt.

They were getting to the end of the shot list now. Bridesmaids were shivering, pageboys misbehaving, elderly aunts needing to be escorted into the warm. Nicole was frazzled. There'd been no let-up, not since they'd climbed that staircase and knocked on the bride's dressing-room door. Her feet were sore, her eyes gritty, her shoulder muscles screaming from carrying bags and tripods. And if she had to go and find one more cousin of some sort who'd just wandered off...

But Alex...Alex was taking it all in his stride, as if he was running on the energy created by all the happiness around him. She was desperately trying to keep cool, calm and professional. On the surface she was managing it, but underneath?

Well, underneath it was all a hot mess.

Did he have to keep doing that? That thing where he smiled at her when he got a particularly good shot? It made her feel part of a team of two. A couple. She really didn't need to be thinking that way about him, not even in a professional sense. And did he have to keep needing more lenses from his bag so she had to keep getting close to him, trying desperately not to let their fingers touch? She was having to concentrate hard just to do the fake job properly. Any thoughts of doing what she'd really come here to do had flown out the window.

At that moment Alex bounded up to her again. The more photos he took, the more enthusiastic he got. And the more unbridled energy that emanated from him, the more she couldn't stop looking at him. 'Next group?' he asked.

She quelled a shiver and checked her list. 'Lynette's university friends—they're all rounded up and waiting—and then it's Charles's rugby pals. I'll make a start finding them while you're doing the next lot.'

He nodded. 'But keep close by. I might need that fish-eye lens again soon.'

'Will do,' she said in the most efficient voice she could manage, then turned to the group of eight women she'd managed to herd together only a few moments ago. The only problem was there were now only five left.

She resisted the urge to tear her list into extra confetti while screaming at the top of her lungs. What was it about large groups of people? Even well-educated, sensible people like this lot seemed to be? Get more than a handful of them together and they couldn't do what they were told for more than two minutes. If only she'd thought about bringing a sheepdog or two along with her...

Or a cattle prod.

She scanned the crowd, looking for the friends who'd gone AWOL. Ah, yes. There was the one in the red coat... She marched up to her and tapped her on the shoulder. 'Hi,' she said with a tight smile.

The woman looked blankly at her, as if she hadn't just had a conversation with Nicole five minutes ago.

'Photographer's assistant,' she reminded her. 'Would you like to come this way so we can take a picture of all of Lynette's university friends?'

Without saying anything to Nicole, the woman excused herself from the group she was chatting to and headed back over to the waiting group. But when Nicole caught up with her she realised yet another one had gone walkabout.

'Right! St Andrew's ladies,' Alex yelled out. 'Can I have you gathering round the bride? And I promise the resulting photo will have everyone declaring that you haven't aged a bit since the day you graduated.'

As one, the six women—plus the two strays, who appeared out of nowhere—formed themselves into an orderly group around their friend. Nicole almost sobbed. She'd been trying to get them to do that for ages, and all it took was one word from Alex and they obediently followed his every command.

As she rounded up Charles's rugby friends, who were all huddled together, thankfully, listening to a match on somebody's phone, she glanced over her shoulder at Alex, watching him work. She'd heard whispers as she'd followed him around for the last couple of hours that he was one of the most sought-after wedding photographers for couples who wanted something a little bit different, and now she understood why.

He threw the rule book out the window, but it worked for him. The bridal couple looked happy and relaxed as they posed for him. There wasn't a coat-hanger smile or twitchy cheek in sight. He had a gift for putting people at ease. Probably because they just liked him. Naturally. Without him having to work at it or change himself. To be honest, she felt a little jealous.

Alex finished snapping the last few shots of different groups, but decided to save the large group shot for the

Great Hall in Elmhurst, assuring the bride and groom he knew just the spot to take it from so he could fit everyone in.

Once they'd captured Lynette and Charles's Rolls-Royce leaving the front of the church, Nicole picked up as much gear as she could and loaded it into the back of Alex's car. Rather than taking the longer route round the village and then up the sweeping drive that allowed visitors to see Elmhurst Hall at its finest, they drove along a service road that ran round the edge of the gardens and managed to leap out of the Jeep and run round to the front of the building to catch the bride and groom's arrival.

'Holding up okay?' Alex asked, as they hefted the bags and tripods inside, ready to set up for the reception. 'I've built up a lot of wedding stamina over the years, but for a first-timer it's a bit of a marathon.'

The way he smiled at her made her insides go all gooey. It was pathetic. Especially as she was now starting to question if Alex had actually flirted with her today. Yes, he'd been friendly and warm—and on occasion cheeky—with her, but he'd been exactly the same way with every other woman they'd encountered that day. He teased; he joked. It was part of his charm.

Had he even flirted with her that evening at the gallery? At the time she'd thought he had, but now she wasn't so sure. Everything he'd said and done had been filtered through her reaction to him. If her heart hadn't been thudding, her skin warming, her lungs lazily forgetting to exchange oxygen for carbon dioxide, would she have come to the same conclusion? Maybe not.

Which meant whatever crazy static energy was bounc-

ing around between them might well be all on her part and
none on his. She was such a sad, sad case.

'Nicole?'

She turned to him and tried not to notice how the cold
air had given his skin a healthy glow, how the little dimple
in his cheek appeared and disappeared as his lips twitched
in amusement.

'You kind of spaced out there for a moment.'

She shook herself. 'You're right. It has been tiring…
and maybe I did zone out for a second, but I'm back now
and ready to face the next challenge.' She had to be. She
couldn't quit now—they'd hardly had more than a few
seconds of downtime for her to quiz him, the job she was
*really* here to do.

'Great. Then let's go and get these lighting tripods set
up in the Great Hall.'

# CHAPTER THIRTEEN

Elmhurst's great hall was the perfect venue for a wedding. The stone walls were adorned with stags' antlers and armour. Flagstones were underfoot and high above was a vaulted wooden ceiling, six centuries old. It would have been impressive bare of any furniture or flowers, but set up for a wedding it was a fairy tale come true.

Large circular tables filled most of the space below a raised dais, where the top table was laid out, hung with garlands of evergreen and roses. Thick linen cloths covered the tables and the low afternoon light coming through the long, arched windows bounced off the crystal glasses and silver cutlery. Tall arrangements of white roses with trailing ivy sat in the middle of every table. They'd been cleverly constructed to hold half a dozen thin white candles and the glow of the flames brought warmth and light into the formal and impressive space.

There were a couple of spaces at a table tucked into the far corner with 'photographer' written on the place holders. 'Finally!' Nicole said as she slumped into a banqueting

chair covered in white linen and tied up with a gold sash.
Her feet were killing her.

Alex sank into a chair beside her. For the first time that
day, a hint of the tiredness he must be feeling showed on
his face. 'I don't always get to eat like this at these things,'
he said. 'Sometimes it's a packed lunch in a corridor or in
the Jeep.'

'This is very nice of Lynette and Charles,' Nicole replied, helping herself to a glass of water.

He nodded. 'They're a great couple. Very generous. They
said the least they could do if I was going to be available
to capture every moment of the reception was feed me so
I didn't keel over before the cake was cut.'

Nicole relaxed a little. Then she realised what he'd just
said. 'The *whole* reception?'

'Don't worry… I reckon we've got about an hour of
downtime. Nobody wants to have their picture taken with
their mouth full of food.'

As Alex finished talking, a waiter came and placed a
delicious-looking plate of chicken in some kind of sauce
in front of both of them.

This was it, then. Downtime from the fake job, but now
she had to gear up for the real job. She took a breath to
steady herself. Every instinct she had was telling her to
move away, find something to do so she didn't have to be
near him, but she couldn't give in to that—at least not yet.

Probably better just to get him chatting to start off with,
rather than launch into an inquisition on love and romance.
Then when she did ask the questions she needed to ask,
he'd be relaxed, ready to share.

'So…' she began, looking round the grand old hall, 'can

I see some of the shots you've taken?' That was always a good 'in'—to get someone talking about their work or something they were passionate about.

He placed his camera lens down on the tablecloth and began pressing buttons. A second or so later an image of the hall, aglow with candlelight, filled the digital display on the back of the camera, obviously the last one Alex had taken. It was different, though. Not just a boring shot of a room full of people. She'd wondered why he'd tucked himself in beside a suit of armour and now she saw why. The edge of the figure just showed on the edge of the screen, making it seem as if someone from the past was not only looking on, but keeping guard, as the bride and groom sat at the top table.

'Press this button and you'll be able to go back through everything I've got on this card,' he told her, pointing to the back of the camera.

It was then she realised they'd both leaned in to look at the shot. The gloom in this corner of the room had made the screen bright and easy to see, but it also made this spot feel set apart from the rest of the hall, more intimate. She could feel the heat of him close. Neither of them said anything for a few long seconds.

Slowly, deliberately, she lifted her thumb and pressed the button where Alex's had just been, scooting back through the photographs they'd taken since coming back from the church. If she wanted to see more they'd have to swap memory cards, as he had got her to change them numerous times throughout the day.

Alex didn't move. He didn't sit back and relax in his chair as she'd hoped he would. He kept leaning forward, watching her reaction to the shots she'd helped set up. The images began to blur past Nicole's eyes and eventually she pushed the camera back in his direction, even though she hadn't finished going through them all.

'I think the shots are amazing,' she told him, making eye contact for as long as she dared, which wasn't much, 'but they're very different from your landscapes.' She picked up her knife and fork and began cutting her vegetables.

He thought about that for a moment, then nodded. 'This is all noise and colour and people. It's fun. But when I go out there…' he glanced over his shoulder towards the window and the darkening fields beyond '…it's just me and my camera and whatever the light and weather bring to the party. It's not just fun—it's exhilarating.'

Nicole felt a small smile curve her lips. 'You really love it, don't you?'

He nodded again, eyes serious.

'And what about it makes you love it so much? What keeps you going back to some of the same places again and again?'

He looked at the ceiling, studied the rough beams of the centuries-old banqueting hall, then back at her. 'I don't know how to explain it… Take Sharp Tor on Dartmoor. It's one of my favourite spots, but every time I take pictures there it's different. The seasons change. The sun is at a different place in the sky. It's cloudy or clear. Sometimes everything looks the same but it just *feels* different. You know what I mean?'

She shook her head, but she wished she did know. Alex, without the swagger, without the laid-back charm that made him seem a little superficial, was captivating.

He thought for a moment. 'It's like every time I go I get a different piece of the puzzle, that I'm unlocking the mystery of the place.'

She let her gaze wander over some of the stuffed animal heads hanging from the stone wall behind him, coming to rest on the antlers of a noble stag. 'Is that what makes it so exhilarating—the mystery of the place?'

He shook his head. 'It's about seeing something—a place or an object—in all its moods. Until you've done that you can't know if you've really captured its…essence, I suppose. Whether you've seen its truth.'

She was supposed to be asking another question, but she found she couldn't. Alex was looking at her, his usually light eyes dark, and the air in their little corner of the room grew dense. Nicole looked down and began cutting her chicken at double speed.

Time to get off this subject. Quick. It felt as if he was telling her secrets. And she didn't want to know his secrets. Didn't need to. All she needed to do was find out how Saffron could best propose to him. They'd done enough chit-chat.

She glanced up from her meal to see if he was still listening, then indicated the grand hall with a nod of her head. 'So…would this be the sort of thing you'd do when it comes time to tie the knot, or would you go for something less traditional?'

A harmless enough subject change, given their current location, and Nicole had discovered that weddings and proposals went hand in hand. Those who liked a big, flashy wedding tended to like a big, flashy proposal and those who wanted something small and intimate to celebrate their nuptials usually went for something quieter when popping the question.

Nicole waited for him to say something but he just kept slicing and chewing for the moment. For a rather long moment, actually. Strange. For a man who seemed like an open book on most things, he was oddly quiet on this subject.

She had a feeling she'd stepped over an invisible line and she didn't know why. The air grew so thick around them, and the atmosphere so awkward, that she decided to make light of it. She smiled and looked his way while she cut her food. 'I suppose you'd be happier tying the knot while abseiling down the outside of a Scottish castle or bungee jumping off a skyscraper?'

He took the lifeline she offered. Gratefully, if his eyes were anything to go by. 'That sounds more like it.'

They ate in silence for a few moments as the previous tension leached away.

'Actually,' he said, looking over at her, 'if I had to do it again, I'd go for something small. Something intimate.'

Nicole dropped her fork and it made a horrible clattering noise. 'Again?' she echoed, her voice coming out high and not very cool and professional at all. 'You're married?'

She knew that was a stupid question the moment she heard it in her own ears, but she was so shocked she hadn't been able to stop her thoughts instantly exiting her mouth. She really hadn't pegged him for the marrying kind—at least not as young as he must have been.

'Was,' he said, looking grim. 'Divorced now.' He surveyed the romantic scene around them. 'My first one was like this—but on steroids. My ex went a little OTT.'

Nicole nodded. She knew that sort of bride. Unfortunately, having discussed basic proposal ideas with Saffron, she didn't think his current squeeze was any less inclined to shy away from extravagance and glitter.

'What about location?' she asked, hardly able to look away. It was just as well the questions she needed to ask seemed to be coming out on autopilot.

His mouth folded into a dry smile as he considered her question. 'Not in a city,' he said finally, his eyes fixing on a point on the far wall. 'Somewhere different. Somewhere wild and beautiful.'

She nodded, unable to produce any other kind of answer. Yes. That suited him. Not only because of the places he liked to photograph, but because of the unexpected seriousness in his expression right now.

All day she'd believed he was a Jack the Lad sort who floated through life with only his charm and his camera to aid him on his way, but in these last few moments she'd seen a glimpse of something else. Something deeper. Something raw. And it made her ache for him in a whole new way.

Which was wrong, she reminded herself. Very wrong.

She looked away. The next question she asked wasn't anything to do with planning a proposal; it was purely for herself, to put herself back on track.

'And are you close to making those kind of plans? I mean…are you seeing someone?'

Of course, she already knew the answer to that question, but she needed that barrier between them now, and bringing it out into the open would make it harder to breach.

For a moment she thought he was going to say something cheeky, like he had about the proposal earlier, but then he looked her straight in the eye. 'I don't know and yes. In that order.'

She thought she'd feel relieved when she heard the admission out of his own lips, but all she felt was a plummeting sensation. 'What's she like?' she asked, hoping a bigger dose of reality might help her get control of herself.

He hesitated for a moment, looked a little uncomfortable. 'Great, actually.' He sighed. 'She's fun. I never know what to expect from her. And she's kind, even though you wouldn't necessarily think that of her when you first meet her. Most of all, I like her because what you see is what you get.'

Nicole nodded, trying to look as if she was just listening rather than agreeing with him. Even though she'd only met Saffron twice, her instinct told her she was all these things. She looked down at her plate. Suddenly she'd had enough of chicken.

'And that's important to you?'

He looked straight back at her, his usually expressive face still and unmoving. 'Very.'

She looked away, just for a second. The feeling that he'd unwittingly hit the nail on the head returned, making her heart race. She knew the small amount of deception was required for her to do her job well, and that under normal circumstances nobody minded when the truth came out, but somehow this felt more serious, more damaging.

'What's her name?' she asked, and her voice came out a little husky.

Alex shrugged. 'I'm sure there are more interesting things to talk about than my love life. For example...' he reached down into his camera bag and produced a second camera body and attached a lens to it '...that I'm going to let you take some shots after the meal.'

Nicole stared at the camera as if were about to bite her. 'But you didn't tell me that. I—I haven't prepared at all!'

'You won't get the true feel for this job if you don't take a few shots yourself,' he said, leaning forward and making her look back at him. 'And that's what you want, isn't it?'

She nodded, even though a voice inside her head was screaming, *No!*

'But I don't know anything about cameras like this! What if I mess up? What if I ruin the shots?'

Alex shook his head and laughed softly. 'Then you mess up and ruin the shots.'

Nicole looked at him, aghast.

'It's okay,' he said. 'I'm not going anywhere. This is my backup camera, the spare I bring with me in case my main one fails. I'll still be doing what I do, but you can take a chance to try it for yourself. If you shoot something usable, I'll add it to the proofs for the bride and groom, and if you don't... Well, it doesn't matter.'

Nicole swallowed. 'I don't even know how to turn it on,' she said, looking at the scary lump of technology rather suspiciously.

Alex laughed again. 'Lighten up, Nic! It doesn't have to be perfect. It doesn't even have to be good. But it'll be real.'

*Nic.* No one called her Nic. She even made Mia and Peggy call her Nicole, thinking it sounded less tomboyish and more sophisticated. But when Alex said it, she kind of liked it. Nic sounded like a girl who knew how to have fun, how to roll with the punches. Nic could take this un-expected challenge and run with it.

She steered herself away from that thought and let out a shaky breath. *Photographs. You're supposed to be thinking about photographs.* She did just that, pulling the words Alex had just uttered into the front of her mind.

*Not perfect. Just real.*

For some reason that seemed like an alien concept. Everything in her job was usually about creating perfection—just what the client wanted—and it was all about fantasy, not reality. Who wanted a 'real' proposal, an offhand 'Fancy getting hitched?' while you were eating a greasy kebab or watching *EastEnders*?

Alex ploughed on. 'It's not as terrifying as it looks, I promise,' he told her. 'It has plenty of automatic functions, and after a ten-minute lesson, you'll be surprised how much you can do.'

It was only after he'd finished showing her how to work the camera and she was fiddling around with it on her own that she realised he'd done a very clever dodge about talking about his relationship, something she usually tried to get her targets to do when she did one of these reconnaissance missions.

Reconnaissance missions? She was starting to sound like Mia!

But that didn't change the fact that Alex was being a bit slippery about Saffron. In her experience, once you got someone in love talking about their other half, the hard bit was getting them to shut up again.

She frowned as she twisted the focus ring on the camera, trying to squash down the little flame of hope that had just flickered into life. There were plenty of reasons Alex might want to keep his personal business to himself. Hadn't Saffron said she and Alex had been keeping their relationship quiet? Maybe that was it. And he was hardly going to spill his guts to a virtual stranger.

Because that was what she was, even if she didn't feel as if she was a stranger to him. Although being near him scrambled her head, another part of her found it easy, natural.

She looked up, raised the camera, picked a person on the other side of the room and held the button lightly so the autofocus kicked in, just the way Alex said it would. She increased the pressure of her finger on the button and the shutter clunked.

That was his gift, wasn't it?

She checked the image on the display on the back of the camera. Dark and grainy. Underexposed, she thought Alex had called it. Not perfect at all. Not even very good.

There were probably twenty other women in this room who felt exactly the same way she did about Alex. Two meetings and people felt like they knew him. It didn't mean anything. It didn't mean she was special.

And she'd heard the way he'd talked about Saffron.

Come on. Who was going to choose her over the wonderful Saffron Wolden-Barnes? It was all in her head, wasn't it? Alex hadn't been flirting with her. He was like this with everyone. Chummy with the lads, charming with the ladies... And if not for that kiss—oh, a million years ago—she probably wouldn't have paid any attention to it. She'd have seen the situation for what it was.

She pressed the small button on the back of the camera with a trash can next to it and her grainy snap disappeared.

Crikey. Maybe Peggy was right. Maybe she did need to find herself a man. It had clearly been too long since she'd had a date if she started deluding herself about guys who were on the verge of getting married. Well, engaged, anyway.

She raised the camera again, thought about what Alex had told her and chose a subject closer to her this time. The shutter went again. It was a reassuring, heavy sound. There was something final about it. The moment was captured and memorialised. Done. Time to move on to the next one.

And it was time for her to move on too.

She looked across at Alex, who was preparing his kit for the impending toasts and speeches.

It was time to do what she'd come here to do—use the rest of the few hours together so she could work out how to make all of Saffron's hopes and dreams about this man come true.

# CHAPTER FOURTEEN

The speeches started and Alex was off again. Nicole trailed in his wake, the backup camera slung round her neck, handing him lenses and memory cards, and every now and then she raised the camera and snapped at something.

She started to understand why he liked what he did. The Great Hall was beautiful. As night fell, the light from the candles in the table arrangements cast everything in a warm glow. People were relaxing, getting into the party spirit, and while the overall effect was pleasing, it was interesting to get behind the camera and pick out one image, one person or one thing, to trim and crop it with the viewfinder until you found the right shot. Then, instead of just loveliness, you got perfection. Or at least Alex probably did. Her attempts were improving, but they were definitely shaky. From the examples that he'd shown her, she was starting to see that framing things right could make them even more beautiful.

She pressed her lips together and thought for a moment. Maybe they had that in common, if nothing else. That was what she did in her job too, in a way. A proposal was always going to be special, but Hopes & Dreams provided the frame to make it truly magical.

When it came time to cut the cake, Nicole had to put away her camera, as Alex needed a succession of different lenses—a macro to get the fine details of the roses made out of royal icing that festooned each tier, a fixed-length one for the portraits, then a zoom for more candid shots.

After that, tables were cleared away, a band arrived to fill the minstrels' gallery at the opposite end of the hall to the top table and people began to relax.

'This is the bit I like best,' Alex told her as he snapped away. 'The formal shots are over and it's all about catching those magic moments that maybe the bride and groom didn't even see at the time, but will become part of their memories of the day. Go...' he gestured with an arm '...see what you can find. And don't worry about whether it's the right kind of shot or what you think I'm after—just experiment. That's where the best shots come from. There's no list for this lot.'

Nicole put the lens bag where he indicated and picked up the spare camera. Then she set off to the other side of the hall where she might be able to work without worrying that Alex was watching her make a hash of it. If even half of what she took was in focus and not too badly underexposed she'd be pleased.

She got lost in finding angles, looking where the light was coming from, just watching people. She'd organised plenty of weddings working for Elite Gatherings, but she'd always sprinted through them, bouncing from one crisis to the next. Seeing it from a photographer's-eye view really was a different experience. She hadn't slowed down much, but her focus had changed. Instead of looking at lists and charts she was concentrating on the people. It made her feel warm inside in a way she couldn't verbalise.

She took at least fifty shots. Some of them were utterly awful, but Alex had made her promise not to delete them, just in case he could do something with them. She was pleased with one or two, though. And she was pleased that for almost an hour her head had been occupied with something that wasn't Alex. Now she'd had a bit of breathing room from him, she was starting to feel like her old self again.

It was just a silly crush. It would pass. She would make sure it did.

And, in the meantime, she'd started to think about him in a different way, mulling over who he was and what he liked. She'd started her own mental list—the one she'd come here to make. He liked beauty but not spectacle. He liked the unusual, the creative. He liked reality rather than a facsimile. He was also a high-energy sort of person, so a leisurely boat ride or an amble through a forest glade wouldn't be right for him.

Would Saffron be prepared to hike up a mountain and propose at the top?

She pulled a face to herself. Back to the drawing board. While proposals were mostly about the person being proposed to, they also needed to fit with the way the proposer wanted to ask, and she wasn't sure Saffron was a hiking sort of girl.

She was just putting the lens cap back on the camera when she went still. The hairs at the back of her neck had lifted gently and her skin was warm and tingly there. She turned to find Alex standing behind her.

'Hi,' she said, glad the low lighting was hopefully hiding the heat that was travelling round from the back of her neck to colour her cheeks.

He leaned in forward to make himself heard above the general noise of the room. The band had started playing gently up in the gallery. 'Lynette and Charles are going to have their first dance soon. I'm going to take my normal set of shots, but it's always harder when people are moving.'

'What do you want me to do?'

'If you could take some wider shots, so we can see the reactions of the people watching them, I might be able to use some of them. We'll find a spot, and I'll get the camera on the right settings, so it'll just be a case of pointing and focusing.'

Nicole's mouth went dry. 'You want me to focus?'

Alex nodded. 'I reckon you can do it by now. And if you get really stuck I'll show you how to put the autofocus back on, but really looking at something, zooming in, twisting that lens until what you want to be sharp is sharp and what you want to be blurry is blurry… There's nothing like it.'

They scouted the hall for a good place for her to stand, and once he'd got her all set up, the bandleader was tapping his microphone and calling for everyone's attention. Alex gave her a reassuring smile and dashed off to the other side of the room. Many of the tables had been cleared and a dance floor laid at one end, below the gallery where the swing band was playing.

It was harder than she'd expected—keeping track of bride and groom as they did a traditional waltz. She'd been secretly hoping they were only going to shuffle from foot to foot, but obviously Charles had been practising to impress his new bride and he was eager to show off.

After the first dance, the party started in earnest. Lynette and Charles danced with their parents, each other's parents, members of the bridal party, and their family and friends filled in around them. Alex told Nicole to keep on snapping. Although many of them wouldn't be usable—people pulling faces while they were singing along to a song or caught in awkward shapes in the middle of a dance move— a few would grace the end pages of the album, and it only took a couple of shots in a hundred to get what they needed.

She let the strap round her neck take the weight of the camera and sighed, rubbing her eyes.

'You look like you need a bit of a break. Maybe a little fun?'

She turned round to find the groom staring at her. 'I won't lie,' she told him. 'This is my first wedding and I'm fit to drop.'

He gave her a rueful smile. 'Too tired to dance with me, even?'

Her eyes widened. 'You want me to dance with you?'

He nodded over his shoulder to the dance floor. 'My wife has snapped up your colleague. I didn't see why he should be the only one to have a little time off.'

Nicole was pretty sure this was breaking all the rules of wedding photography. But then again, it seemed Alex didn't mind breaking a rule or two. And she certainly didn't need to ask his permission if he'd already taken the lead.

She looked over to where he had the bride in his arms. They were laughing and talking as he guided her round the floor to a Frank Sinatra song. Nicole unhooked the camera from round her neck and placed it on the table next to her. 'Why not?' she said and smiled back at Charles.

It was just as well her mother had insisted she take those ballroom-dancing lessons before she'd gone to boarding school, just in case there was a formal dance and everyone else knew how to waltz and she didn't, because Charles was certainly very keen to include every step in his repertoire. He spun her round the floor, throwing in the odd *chassé* and dipping her occasionally. It took all her concentration to keep up.

But even though she was dog-tired, Charles was right— it did feel good to let off a little steam, have some fun. She started to smile back at him as they danced, let the music flow around her rather than counting beats.

Unfortunately, Charles's enthusiasm outstripped his skill, especially when it came to steering her backwards around the dance floor. They had a few near misses, but it was inevitable that they would eventually hit something. Or someone.

The breath left Nicole's lungs as an elbow jabbed painfully into her back. Charles was most apologetic.

'I think you'd better hand him over to me,' his new wife said from behind them. 'Before he does any more damage. At least I'm used to his defective steering and can take evasive action.'

Charles didn't need another second of encouragement; he let go of Nicole and scooped his bride up in his arms and twirled away with her. That left her and Alex staring at each other in the middle of the dance floor.

'Would be rude not to,' he said in a low voice and held up his arms.

Nicole glanced back at the table where she'd left his camera.

'It'll be fine there for another couple of minutes—and that's all we've got. Lynette just told me she and Charles are heading off after the next couple of songs, which means we'll be back on duty for the bouquet toss and their departure in a car that now looks more like an oversized toilet roll than a Jaguar.'

She couldn't really say no to that, could she? It was only a couple of minutes. Just until the current song finished, probably.

Giving him a nervous smile, she closed the gap between them and took his hand. It was warm and large against her own, and where his other palm rested on the small of her back her skin tingled a little.

It was only as they started moving that she realised her mistake.

He was close. Only inches away, his breath warm against her neck. The last time they'd been this close was New Year's Eve. The rush of memories that brought back wasn't helping her recall this little crush she had was a one-sided affair. Not when she remembered the way he'd pulled her to him, held her firmly as his lips had explored hers. She turned her face away, looking over his shoulder, but then she could feel his breath on her neck.

Alex had nowhere near the ballroom prowess that his predecessor had shown, which meant they moved more slowly, and instead of the exhilaration of spinning round the floor, it just made her more aware of how near he was.

She frowned and hoped he thought that she was concentrating on the steps, but really she was putting all her effort into not shaking.

She found, however, that she couldn't keep staring past him. As much as she tried not to, as much as she told herself it was a stupid thing to do, she lifted her head.

He was looking at her, as if he'd been waiting for her, and there was no hint of his habitual smile in his eyes. She couldn't look away. And somehow they got even closer, even though she couldn't tell which one of them had swayed towards the other. Alex's gaze dropped lower, down to her nose, then lower still…

Revelation hit her like a lightning bolt. She felt it all the way down to her toes, where the blood fizzed and danced.

This attraction, this crush, this whatever it was…? It wasn't the tiniest bit one-sided. Alex was feeling it just as powerfully as she was.

They broke apart at the same moment, just seconds before the closing bars of the song. Alex headed one way and she the other. After a couple of steps, she realised she should probably go and rescue the backup camera and veered off in another direction. At least fetching it gave her a legitimate excuse to put the width of the Grand Hall between them.

'Right, ladies and gentlemen…' the bandleader's voice boomed. 'The bride and groom will be off on their honeymoon shortly, so I'd like all the single ladies to gather at this end of the room so the bride can throw her bouquet.'

The band burst into a few jokey bars of the Beyoncé song, then segued into something in a slower tempo. Alex, still looking mutinously serious, signalled to her to hurry up. She grabbed the camera and made her way round the edge of the room as fast as she could.

'She's ready to go, and we're only going to have one chance to get this bunch of flowers sailing through the air,' he said, opening up the camera and pulling a memory card out. 'File this one away with the others and then follow me.'

Nicole reached out to take the card from him. She never knew afterwards if it was the adrenalin of the situation or the fact she was still feeling a little wobbly after that 'moment' they'd had on the dance floor, but her fingers refused to work properly. Somehow, she only got a half grip on the little blue square of plastic, and as she turned it in her fingers, trying to get a firmer grip on it, it jiggled itself free and fell towards the table.

Unfortunately, it didn't land on the tablecloth, but in a glass of abandoned champagne, where it hit the surface of the bubbling liquid with the tiniest of splashes, then sank gracefully to the bottom.

# CHAPTER FIFTEEN

They both stared at the memory card. It had been buoyed up on the tiny bubbles and now floated on the surface of the champagne. Alex told his hands to work, his fingers to grab the card out of the fizzing liquid in the flute, but it took much too long for the signal to travel down his arm from his brain.

'I'm sorry. I'm so, so sorry...' Nicole was muttering over and over.

He ignored her. He didn't want to talk to her right now. He didn't even want to look at her. That was what had caused this whole thing in the first place. He fished the card out of the champagne and gave it a good shake. It was dripping.

Thankfully, he changed his memory cards frequently. That way he didn't lose a whole day's shots if something went wrong. But he hadn't been managing the cards today; Nicole had.

'When did we last change cards?' he barked at her.

She stopped apologising and stared back at him blankly. 'Erm...'

'*When?* Think!'

'It was…' She searched the room endlessly, as if one of the sets of antlers on the walls would provide her with an answer. Then a light appeared in her eyes. 'It was just after they cut the cake…before the first dance.' And then the joy slid off her face, as she realised what that meant. 'Oh, Alex…' She looked at him, those huge eyes pleading. 'I'm so sorry.'

'We haven't got time for that now,' he snapped, glancing to where Lynette was already positioned with her bouquet. 'Just pass me a fresh one and try to dry it off the best you can.' And then he marched off, leaving her standing there, and got on with doing his job.

He didn't dare look over his shoulder for the next five minutes as he immortalised the bouquet toss and resulting rugby scrum. He was too angry.

He shouldn't have danced with her. He'd known he should have made an excuse and laughed it off, saying they were here to work, but it had seemed like a good idea at the time. Scratch that. Thinking hadn't been part of the process, had it? That decision had been made much further south.

He took one last shot of the girl who'd caught the bouquet, ran a hand through his hair and swore softly under his breath.

He'd almost kissed her.

Those big brown eyes of Nicole's had been pleading with him then too. But it hadn't been for forgiveness; it had been for something entirely more dangerous, despite all her protestations about wanting to keep this thing strictly professional.

But he didn't have time to think about that now. Aside from the bride and groom's first dance on that memory card—which he might not be able to do anything to recreate—there were countless photos of the wedding guests. At least he could try to make those up once he'd photographed Lynette and Charles's departure.

He needed a different lens for that, but he didn't ask Nicole for it. Instead he went and got it himself, ignoring her hovering there by the bag, and strode outside into the chilly November night air. The sky was clear, showing off a billion twinkling stars, and frost was already settling on the grass. He didn't care. Maybe a little sub-zero air was just what he needed as he made the short hop from the Great Hall to where Charles's sports car was parked.

He jostled his way through the well-wishers to get a few candid shots of the bride and groom as they hugged people farewell and tried to dodge the ton of confetti being lobbed their way. Bird-friendly, no doubt. He just hoped the sparrows and robins round here were hungry.

For some reason thinking of sparrows reminded him of Saffron.

Most people would think of her as something exotic, a bird of paradise or even a glittering, elusive hummingbird, but he knew the truth. She was a lot more vulnerable than she looked. Especially at the moment.

He couldn't do this to her. Not now.

She'd had a rough time recently. It had started with a particularly cutting newspaper article and then plenty of other publications had joined the Saffron-bashing. That was what they liked to do, wasn't it? Build someone up, put them on a pedestal so they could knock them down again? They called her flaky, flighty, a waste of space. Not able to commit to anything for more than three seconds, and cited her failed forays into TV presenting, DJ'ing and an overpriced sunglasses range as evidence. 'Calling her two-dimensional would be a stretch,' some bright spark had written.

And normally Saffron would have shrugged it off as she always did, saying people were jealous of her success, if not for that chat she'd had with her father recently.

She'd always been a daddy's girl, even after her parents' acrimonious split when she was small, but her father had remarried three years ago and now Saffron had a step-sister. Michelle was a clever woman who'd finished university and gone on to become a barrister. She and Saffron's father had formed quite a bond, sharing a love of books, fine wines and travel, something that had drifted by Saffron until Michelle had got married.

He'd gone to the wedding as her guest a month or two ago. He'd seen his girlfriend sit frozen, her smile carved onto her face, while her father had got up and sung the praises of her new sister, had gone on and on about her accomplishments, about what a fine woman she was.

Maybe he'd intended it to be a dig at Saffron—whom he adored, but nagged constantly about doing something productive with her life—maybe he hadn't, but the damage had been done anyway. After that Saffron had started reading all those newspaper articles more carefully, no longer laughing over them but picking through them, frowning.

Maybe that was why she'd been acting so oddly recently, sneaking around, making phone calls she wouldn't let him hear and disappearing off for appointments she was very vague about. If anyone else had started behaving that way he'd have been suspicious, but not with Saffron. She just wasn't like that. What he'd said to Nicole was true—she was a great girl.

Oh, hell. And that just brought him right back to the root of the problem.

He let his arm fall by his side, camera in hand, as the tail lights of Charles's car glowed further up the drive. Thankfully, he'd done so many weddings now, he could take shots on automatic. He hardly remembered what he'd been focusing on, but he knew his mind had been functioning properly as his fingers had adjusted buttons and settings.

He was seriously attracted to Nicole. And, if anything, the fact that he couldn't—well, shouldn't—have her was making it worse.

He rubbed his hand over his face as he headed back inside.

Aside from Saffron, this was still a really bad idea. Nicole might be attracted to him too, but she kept blowing hot and cold, saying one thing with her mouth and another with those expressive eyes. Even if she did like him, she didn't *want* to like him. And he really, really should not want to like her.

He'd ignored those kind of warning signs and mixed messages before and had regretted it. He should have paid attention to those little signals Vanessa had given out that he hadn't wanted to see. He'd have saved himself a whole lot of heartache and humiliation that way.

Oh, Vanessa had liked him. She'd been attracted to him. She might even have loved him for a short while, but it hadn't been the kind of love days like today were supposed to be based on, days where you said promises you didn't ever intend to break. And he'd been fully prepared to do that. Unfortunately, his new bride had got a bit tangled up with the 'for richer and poorer' bit.

He hadn't been her goal, just a means to an end, namely his family name and money. Like his parents, she'd thought he'd get tired of messing around with his camera and would toe the line eventually. Which just went to show she hadn't known him at all.

But he hadn't wanted to give up a job he loved to go and manage the family estate. He couldn't think of anything more boring. Besides, his younger brother Seb was chomping at the bit to fill his shoes. His father would just have to get over the fact that his firstborn didn't want to be a country gentleman, organising shoots and Christmas balls and moaning about the endless hordes of visitors that he had to let tramp through his home to pay the bills.

But Vanessa had wanted all of that, had constantly encouraged him to take that route, until he'd got tired of her not supporting his career choice. Discussions had turned into rows and then she'd finally realised she was never going to get him to put down his camera and she'd left.

He knew it was his fault. He knew he should have been less trusting. But up until that point he hadn't had a reason to think like that. He was a pretty easy-going guy, tended to accept people as they came. Tom had warned him that just because he was so straightforward, he shouldn't expect other people to be the same.

He'd known there were women like that out there, women who used men to get what they wanted, whether that was money or prestige or to further their careers. He just hadn't considered that sweet, adoring Vanessa could have been one of them. She'd had him fooled completely.

So, while some guys liked a little mystery in their women, he could definitely live without it. Even if there was something utterly enticing about the not knowing, something about the hidden things beneath the surface that could suck a man in. So, while women like that reminded him of the landscapes he liked to photograph—complex, ever-changing, one moment one thing and the next moment something totally different—he avoided them at all costs now. It wasn't worth the risk.

Better to stick to girls like Saffron, who wore their hearts on their sleeves and made life easy for a guy. He saved the adrenalin and excitement for his photography now.

Anyway, he had more important things to think about at the moment. He steeled himself as he entered the Grand Hall again. After the shock of the icy air outside it now seemed heavy and warm in there. He found Nicole near their table, the bags all packed neatly with lenses and all but one tripod folded up. She looked at him but said nothing.

He'd been a bit hard on her, hadn't he? And, really, he'd been cross with himself more than he'd been cross with her. He'd been all fingers and thumbs when he'd passed the memory card to her. It really wasn't all her fault.

He didn't quite manage one of his trademark easy smiles, but he did manage to rid his voice of that gruff quality. 'Listen… Don't freak out about the memory card. I don't know if it's salvageable, but if it isn't, you were taking shots at the same time. We might have *something*.'

Nicole nodded, but she didn't look convinced. To be

honest, neither was he, but he hated getting worked up about stuff. These days he avoided it as best he could, let stuff slide off as if it didn't matter, even if it did. That was the only way to get through life without driving yourself crazy. Vanessa had taught him that at least.

'I was going to clock off once the bride and groom had left, but we've got some catching up to do.' He checked his watch. 'We've got another hour or so. I reckon we replace what we've lost in that time.'

She just nodded and looked at him, her mouth a thin line of determination. 'Whatever you think best.'

And then they set off to work, taking pictures of the guests as the party continued, getting some of the groups of friends to pose again for certain shots. No one seemed to mind or care. But the champers had been flowing pretty well for hours now, which all served his purpose. Finally, when the bandleader called the last song and the last of the guests began to gather their belongings together, he started to pack his gear away.

He didn't talk to Nicole, didn't try to get to know her any further. He was still as much in the dark about her as he'd been at the beginning of the day, but that didn't matter any more. New Year's Eve had come and gone. They'd had their chance and missed it, and he probably should be glad about that, because he was with Saffron now. Nice, easy Saffron, who wasn't at all demanding.

Well, okay, she was a *lot* demanding, but only in the little things—like being particular about clothes and restaurants or asking him to fetch her things she couldn't be bothered to get herself. He didn't care about those things in the slightest, because she never asked him for more than he was prepared to give.

'I don't know about you,' he said to Nicole as he slung a bag over his shoulder, 'but I'm beat. I say it's time we hit the motorway.'

# CHAPTER SIXTEEN

Nicole tramped to the car behind Alex, her arms feeling longer than anyone's had a right to feel, with all the kit she was carrying. She didn't put anything down, though. Didn't reposition anything. She deserved this.

She'd promised herself this morning she'd be cool and calm, the consummate professional? Ha! She'd failed on every single count. And probably on a few more she didn't know about.

This wasn't even her real job and he was probably going to fire her. And she didn't even have the comfort that she often had in the past that people had judged her unfairly or had underestimated her. This time she deserved everything that was coming.

And so what if he was attracted to her? It didn't change anything. He was still with someone else. And when they'd had that...*thing*...there out on the dance floor, he'd backed away pretty fast. There was no doubt he was Saffron's.

That was hardly surprising, given that instead of being the sophisticated, polished woman she knew she could be, she'd reverted to her sixteen-year-old self—gawky, shy, a little clumsy. No guy had picked that Nicole above one of 'those girls'. No guy ever would.

She let out a low growl as she hefted a tripod into the back of Alex's car. Why was she thinking like this? She shouldn't want him to want her. Not if she didn't want her whole life to fall spectacularly apart at the seams. But somehow she couldn't stop herself.

The gear was all in the boot now, and Nicole slunk round to the passenger door of the Jeep and slid into the seat. Once there she waited, staring straight ahead into the almost complete darkness of the country night. The journey home was going to be even more uncomfortable than the journey out, and that was saying something.

She heard the car door slam beside her, felt the dip in the Jeep's suspension as he dropped into his seat. He put the key in the ignition and they drove away in silence. She couldn't think of anything to say, so she said nothing, and Alex seemed to be concentrating hard on the unlit country roads.

They spent the whole journey that way, the silence a spell neither of them was willing to break, but as they neared North London, she realised she couldn't just jump out of the car and run away. She was going to have to say something.

As they stopped outside her flat, she pulled in a large breath. There was no way to gloss over this. She might as well just give it to him straight. 'I know that nothing I can say will make up for the mistake I made tonight,' she said softly. 'But I want you to know that I really am very, very sorry.'

'I think I got that,' he replied gruffly, 'from the constant apologising ever since it happened.'

'But I really am s—'

'Nicole, stop!'

Oh, flip. It was worse than she'd thought.

She stared down at her hands in her lap, seeing their paleness against her dark trousers, but after a while she could feel him looking at her. She kept her focus down until she could bear it no longer. When she turned her head to see him his expression was sombre. If she hadn't known that single dimple could appear, she'd have never believed it was there. She took a deep breath.

'Stop beating yourself up about it,' he said in a low voice. 'We all make mistakes.'

Nicole frowned and stared at him. Surely she'd heard that wrong?

He let out a deep sigh and reached into the back seat. She hadn't noticed he'd stored his main camera bag there, but he must have done, because he pulled both camera bodies out of it and started flicking through the images on the spare she'd been using. 'You were taking shots all through that patch. There might be something we can use.'

She didn't answer. Mainly because she was frozen to the spot. 'B-but I ruined your wedding shoot!'

One side of his mouth hitched up. 'Are you always this dramatic? I must admit it comes as a bit of a surprise after the ice-princess routine.'

*Ice princess?*

'Or maybe it shouldn't. I can't seem to work you out. Especially as I know there's another side to you.'

She knew what he was talking about. New Year's Eve.

But he couldn't be more wrong. 'That wasn't really me,' she blurted out. 'It was an aberration… Too many cocktails…!'

The other corner of his mouth kicked up, but the smile was reluctant. 'I've never been called an aberration before.' And then he seemed to realise that maybe he shouldn't have said that, because the dimple disappeared and he went back to looking at his camera, flicking through images in rapid succession.

After a minute or so he said, 'Here…' and thrust it in her direction.

She took it from him, careful not to let their fingers touch. The image on the back display was one she'd taken of Lynette and Charles having their first dance.

'It's too dark and very grainy…not to mention lopsided,' she said quietly.

'I might be able to do something with it in my photo-editing software.' He shrugged the shoulder nearest her. 'You know, put an effect on it, clean it up a little. In black and white, grainy can look retro and romantic.'

She forgot she really ought not to look straight into those big blue eyes. 'You can do that?'

His lips pursed momentarily. 'Maybe. And I have a friend who's good with techie stuff. I haven't completely given up hope on that memory card yet.'

'Have you had a look?'

He shook his head. 'It's still a bit sticky and I don't want to mess up the contacts inside the camera by putting it in.'

She nodded. That was understandable.

He reached out and put a hand on her arm. They both looked at it, and then he drew it away. She heard him let out a weary breath. The atmosphere in the car thawed a good few degrees.

'I meant what I said. Don't beat yourself up about it. If I said I hadn't goofed at plenty of the weddings I've covered I'd be lying. Photography is like that. Sometimes you don't get the perfect shot. Sometimes you have to take something less than perfect, find its unique qualities and make the best of them. And you worked really hard today.'

She shook her head, very gently. 'Does that mean you aren't firing me?'

He just about smiled. 'You wanted the full wedding-photography experience, and you're well on your way to getting it. Besides, next week's wedding is a bit different. I really need an extra pair of hands.'

When she didn't reply he pretended to bat his lashes. 'Please?' On anyone else that would have looked ridiculous, but somehow Alex managed to make it both funny and charming.

'I don't know,' she said, but she could feel herself weakening. 'I need time to think.'

'How about I call you in a few days? Say, Tuesday?'

She shook her head. 'Maybe I won't answer.'

He shrugged, then gave her one of his full-wattage smiles. She felt it down in the pit of her stomach. 'Well, if you don't, I'll just have to call the magazine and let them know how much I need you, how great the article will be, because—of course—you're following *me* around.'

She started to laugh at his outrageous arrogance, but then she stopped. He'd call the *magazine*?

No way could she let him do that. If he found out she

didn't actually work there, he'd start wondering where she did work, and she couldn't let him start down that path.

'And you really want my inept and disastrous help?'

'I really do.'

They stared at each other a moment more and then Nicole smiled back at him. A big, goofy smile that showed all of her teeth. Something she never usually did these days.

'Okay,' he said, and she could see a soft warmth appear in his eyes, even in the dark of the car. She should go. Before she did something else monumentally stupid.

'Okay,' she whispered back, and then she climbed out of the car and made her way to her front door. She could feel him watching her from the car, hear the dull thrum of its engine as he waited for her to disappear inside. She forbade herself to look back.

When she'd shut the door behind her and leaned against it, she heard the engine rumble into life, then get quieter as he drove down the street and merged with the rest of the late-night traffic.

It was then, and only then, that she realised what an idiot she'd been.

# CHAPTER SEVENTEEN

Peggy stumbled into the living room at around ten on Sunday morning and found Nicole curled up on the sofa. She took one look at the tracksuit bottoms and the pile of biscuit wrappers and said, 'That bad, huh?'

Nicole kept staring at the screen. 'Worse' was all she said.

She'd avoided *Pretty in Pink* this morning. Mainly because she'd had a convoluted dream all night that had cast her as unlucky-in-love Duckie, Saffron as the rich girl who got the boy and Alex as Molly Ringwald. It had been a little bizarre and a lot disturbing. Instead she'd plumped for *Some Kind of Wonderful*, but the story of one boy caught between two girls wasn't helping any.

Peggy snatched the remote from her hand and froze the image on the screen. Nicole looked sideways at her.

'Oh, God. You kissed him again, didn't you?'

Nicole gave her a scornful look.

Peggy started striding round the living room, doing a circuit round the sofa. 'I know he was cute and all, but *really*, Nicole? You've been on and on that this is your shot to take

Hopes & Dreams to the next level and you got off with the groom-to-be?'

'No, I didn't kiss him.'

Peggy's ire deflated with a large sigh and she flopped down beside Nicole. 'Then what's the problem?'

'I wanted to.'

'But you didn't…'

Nicole shook her head.

'Again, what's the problem?'

Nicole buried her face in her hands and spoke through her fingers. Just thinking about it was giving her a hot flush. 'I think he wanted to kiss me too.'

Peggy didn't say anything for a while. 'Oh,' she finally managed.

Nicole nodded. When Peggy was reduced to monosyllables things were pretty serious.

'But nothing happened?'

She slowly let her hands drop and looked at Peggy. The look of sympathy on her friend's face was almost worse than the anger had been. 'No,' she replied heavily.

'And did you find out enough about him to start planning Saffron's proposal?'

She nodded again. More than enough. That had been the problem. The more she found out about Alex, the more she liked him. And it had nothing to do with the charm and swagger that had had the bridesmaids swooning and everything to do with the silent, serious man who hid beneath that.

Peggy, who'd been leaning forward more and more as she'd been interrogating Nicole, sank back into the squashy sofa cushions. 'Mission accomplished, then. Good. Problem solved. Now we can get going with the proposal and you won't have to see him again.'

When Nicole didn't answer, Peggy bounced back onto her bunny-slippered feet again. 'What did you do?' she asked, more than a little desperately.

Nicole stared at the screen, where a suitably pained Eric Stoltz was leaning against a locker, dreaming about a bright and perky Lea Thompson. 'Remember how he offered to let me shadow him for a few weddings and I said I was going to back out after this one?'

Peggy nodded.

Nicole scrunched her face up so she didn't have to look at her friend properly. 'Well, I kind of forgot to.'

Peg threw her hands in the air. 'How did you manage to do that?'

Nicole motioned for her to sit again. She couldn't explain with Peggy towering over her like that. Her own conscience was doing pretty much the same thing, and that was bad enough.

When Peggy had sat down again, Nicole launched into the whole story, from the moment in the corridor outside the bride's dressing room right through to when Alex had dropped her home again. 'And I was just so stupidly pleased he didn't think I was a waste of space, that he actually appreciated all the hard work I'd put in, that I waltzed out of the car and completely forgot the plan.'

'That's what I'm worried about,' Peggy said as she fished one of the biscuit packets off the floor and searched it for contents. She found a Hobnob and took a bite. 'You never lose focus like that. It's not like you at all.'

'I know!' Nicole wailed. 'I don't feel like myself at all

when I'm with him and it's…it's…' She'd been going to say 'horrible', but she realised it hadn't felt horrible at all at the time. In fact, it had been rather nice. '…unsettling.' That was the best she could manage.

Peggy sighed. 'Maybe so, but he's right about one thing.'

Nicole turned sharply to look at her. 'What?'

'You are too hard on yourself.'

Nicole stared at her. Never in a million years had she expected Peggy to say something like that.

'I mean, when I look at you I see this amazing business-woman who's brave enough to put everything on the line and go after her dreams, and all you can see are things that you still need to work on.'

Peggy offered her the biscuit packet. There was one last Hobnob hiding in the bottom. The packet rustled loudly as Nicole dug her way down to it.

'So…' Peggy said softly, 'you'll just have to phone him and put him off.'

The biscuit stopped halfway to Nicole's mouth. 'I don't think I can. That's the point!' She told Peggy what Alex had said about phoning *Beautiful Weddings*. 'I can't blow my stupid cover. The one thing our clients rely on us for above all else is not to give the game away before they've popped the question. We can't risk that…' She sighed. 'So I'm going to have to go.'

Peggy sighed too. 'Sheesh! And I thought my life was complicated.'

'I know.' It seemed as if everything had turned upside down since that day when Saffron had swept into the shop. Nicole realised she really ought to be careful what she wished—or prayed—for.

'So what are you going to do?'

Nicole shrugged. She was just going to have to try extra hard to be the person she knew she could be. Nothing got to that woman. Nothing made her lose her cool. Not even a sexy photographer with a killer dimple. She could do it. She knew she could. She'd made harder and more lasting changes to herself before.

'It'll be easier this time,' she muttered, more to herself rather than to her flatmate. 'It's not a big fairy-tale do— no castles, no moonlit battlements, no candles and roses. From what Alex has told me, the next one is going to be a little…different.'

# CHAPTER EIGHTEEN

Alex met Saffron at Arch, one of her favourite restaurants to see and be seen in. To be honest, it really wasn't his kind of place. He liked a place with a good buzz, didn't mind a crowd occasionally, but Arch seemed to attract a certain type, the sort who liked to wallow in their own fabulousness. He really didn't have time for it, but this was Saffron's crowd, and a lot of her so-called friends came here. She saw it more as popping down to the local pub to catch up with her mates than going to a thriving hot spot.

But instead of flitting between different groups of friends before sitting down at her favourite table, Saffron went straight to it. She sat, her arms folded across her middle, bottom lip slightly protruding.

'Hey,' he said softly, when he found her gazing out across the restaurant, unusually quiet. He reached over and placed his hand over hers and she jumped. 'What's up?'

She sighed heavily. 'I don't suppose you saw the article in this week's *Buzz*?'

He shook his head. That trash was only good for lining budgie cages, but Saffron had a bit of a love-hate relationship with the publication, in that she loved it when they loved her and published the tidbits she fed them and hated it when they dished the dirt instead.

'It was horrible. They did this split-page thingy—"A Tale of Two Sisters", they called it. And there was Michelle on one side and me on the other.' She trailed off. 'They listed all her marvellous accomplishments, along with photos of her looking elegant and gracious, and then all my little indiscretions. Let me tell you, the photos weren't as nice.'

Alex swallowed. He could imagine. Saffron was calming down now she'd reached her mid-twenties, but she'd been more than a little wild as a teenager, and there'd been plenty of paparazzi only too willing to catch her every fall from grace.

She looked across at him, her eyes large and full of hurt. 'I've been trying really hard to create a new image for myself. I haven't been photographed drunk outside a club in more than a year, but nobody seems to notice! They just want to keep rehashing the past...'

He gave a sympathetic look. 'It takes time for people's perceptions to change, but you'll do it if you don't give up, if you just stay below the radar for a while.'

Saffron looked at him as if 'staying below the radar' was a foreign concept. 'I'm not giving up,' she said rather determinedly. 'In fact, I've got a plan that should... Never mind.' She looked away. 'I'll tell you about it another time.'

Alex frowned. That was most unlike her. She usually spilled every bit of news about herself the moment it happened, every thought from her head. Maybe she was starting to mature a little, just as her father had hoped?

Her expression turned from distant to sad. 'She's pregnant, you know… That breaking news is what prompted them to run the story.'

He raised his eyebrows. 'Who's pregnant?'

'Wonder-sister Michelle. My father's fit to pop with pride.'

Oh, hell. That was bad. Not for Michelle, obviously, who seemed like a perfectly nice and together woman, but for Saffron, who was already suffering under the weight of all the comparisons between them, especially since Michelle's wedding to a man due to be the next Viscount Hadley had catapulted her into the same spheres as Saffron.

Saffron shook her head and she stared at somewhere just over his shoulder. 'I heard it, you know, at the wedding… That little catch in his voice as he finished his toast to the bride. I saw the way he used his napkin to dab his eye when he sat down, and I just thought, *Will he ever stand up at my wedding one day and almost burst with pride?*'

Alex reached across and took her hand. 'Of course he will. When that day comes…'

He hoped he was telling the truth. Godfrey Wolden-Barnes adored his little girl. It was just that recently he'd realised what a monster he'd created by spoiling her, and he was—too late—trying to take a tougher approach. Unfortunately, his timing was terrible. But Alex had no doubt her father would give her away just as proudly as he'd done his step-daughter. He just needed to calm down a bit first, and it wasn't as if Saffron was about to tie the knot any time soon, was it?

He looked at her as she worried her napkin and fiddled with the cutlery. Ever since he'd known Saffron, her world had fallen apart on an almost weekly basis—or at least she'd thought it had. But those dramas usually had to do with not being the first one to own a particular designer handbag or her favourite table in a restaurant not being available. This was different.

Which made the whole situation right now that much more difficult.

Their relationship had started in a blaze of passion and excitement, but now it had settled down to a more pedestrian pace. Despite the crazy nature of Saffron's life, what they had together was easy, comfortable. He'd been quite happy drifting along, not really thinking about where it all was going. He'd thought that was a good thing, but now he was starting to wonder.

Tom was right about one thing—he had avoided serious relationships in the four years since he'd split from Vanessa, but who wouldn't have? However, he didn't like this feeling that he was just drifting aimlessly, being pushed where the current of his life took him. Usually he was a pretty 'take charge' kind of guy. He supposed he *should* be thinking of wanting something more serious.

And Saffron was the obvious candidate. She didn't make him feel as if he were living on shifting sand, but…

An image of Nicole, her eyes large, her face unreadable, drifted into his mind. He felt a surge of adrenalin hit, but he squashed it down again. This was not the time. Saffron needed him at the moment. Even if he'd decided that this…thing…that simmered between them was not a commitment-phobic mirage, he wasn't that much of a cad that he'd dump Saffron when she was at her lowest ebb.

And, thinking of Saffron being a bit low, he decided to talk about something that would cheer her up, which would have the added bonus of distracting him from his own thoughts as well.

'How's that party you've been planning with Sara?' he asked her. She'd been mulling over restaurant and hotel websites for weeks now, looking up all sorts of bizarre things on the Web. When he'd asked her about it she'd just mumbled something about planning an 'event', which was usually Saffron-speak for a party. He'd thought it was a great idea at the time, something to take her mind off her current troubles, but that didn't seem to be working, especially as she looked blankly at him for a second.

'Oh, *yes*!' she finally said, brightening considerably. 'It's all going along splendidly. We're having great fun planning it all.'

He frowned for a second. 'And when is it again?'

She put her glass down and laughed, a little nervously. 'I've told you before, Alex—honestly, I'm sure you don't listen to a word I say—it's a Christmas party.'

He nodded but his forehead creased again. 'Yes, but what's the *date*…?'

Saffron flicked her hair back from her shoulder. 'The twenty-first— No. I mean the twentieth. Sometime around then. We haven't quite nailed it down yet.'

He sipped his beer, still staring at her. Saffron might be a bit ditzy in most areas of her life, but one thing she took very seriously was her social calendar. She never kept a diary, not even on her phone, but she always knew the exact date and time of every party she attended, every function she'd agreed to go to. So why couldn't she remember the date of her own Christmas bash? It was most odd.

He decided to change the subject. If Saffron needed to

keep busy to stop her from moping, he had an idea. 'What are you doing this afternoon?'

'Why?'

'There's this great new space in Shoreditch, a converted fire station that the owner is intending to use for events and all sorts of artsy things. They've got gallery space. I've arranged to go and meet the owner to chat about doing an exhibition. Why don't you come and keep me company?'

She grimaced. 'Sorry, darling. Can't make it.'

'Oh?'

She didn't elaborate, just summoned a waiter to take their food orders.

Once he'd scurried away, Alex pushed a little bit harder. 'What are you up to?'

Saffron blinked at him, eyes wide and innocent. 'When?'

'This afternoon. Or are you still thinking you need a passport to travel into the East End?'

Instead of smacking him playfully, like she usually did when he made a crack like that, she looked back at him seriously. 'I'm meeting someone.'

'More party planning with Sara?' he asked.

Saffron looked both surprised and happy all at once. 'Yes. Of course. That makes complete sense, doesn't it? Sara and I are getting together to check out a venue for the Christmas thing.' For some reason she avoided making eye contact. Then she spotted someone she knew in a crowd coming through the front door and leaped out of her seat to run over so they could squeal and air-kiss noisily. It was as if the pensive Saffron he'd walked in with had disappeared.

Alex stared straight ahead and tore his bread roll open. For the last week or so he'd thought all of Saffron's strange behaviour—her faraway moods, her being incommunicado for chunks of time when she normally was glued to her phone, her vague explanations for where she'd been—was because she was stewing over this latest round of press attention.

Now he wasn't so sure. There was only one conclusion he could draw from the exchange they'd just had.

If Saffron was meeting Sara this afternoon, then he was just about to don Darcey Bussell's tutu and dance *Swan Lake* at the Opera House.

No, it was absolutely clear that Saffron—the girl he'd picked precisely because of her openness and lack of guile—was hiding something from him.

# CHAPTER NINETEEN

Saffron flicked her long golden waves over her shoulder and stared at the folder Nicole had presented to her. Nicole sat on the edge of one of the armchairs in the meeting room at the back of Hopes & Dreams, her hands clasped together as she searched her client's face for a reaction. She kept telling herself not to hold her breath, but she kept finding herself doing it anyway.

'What do you think?' she finally said, when Saffron had been staring at a particular page for at least a minute.

Saffron looked up, seeming slightly dazed. 'Oh... It all looks, well, splendid.'

Nicole swallowed. Saffron did not seem her usual self today. She was trying not to overthink that and come up with a million reasons why that might be her fault, but she wasn't doing very well. Mainly because she felt like an utter heel sitting here with Saffron like nothing had happened.

Okay, nothing actually *had* happened.

But it felt as if it had. And that was what counted.

'We tend to try to come up with key themes and words

for our proposals—to capture the essence of the person being proposed to—and use those to keep us on track when we get down to setting details in stone,' she explained. 'The three words we came up with for Alex, and his proposal, were: *dynamic*, *wild* and *intimate*.'

Saffron just blinked at her.

'*Dynamic*, because Alex seems to be a full-on kind of guy,' she carried on, hoping the reason Saffron had left the way open for her was because she wanted a fuller explanation. 'We thought something different, something exciting would be up his street. We also came up with *wild*—not in the party-till-your-brain-falls-out-your-skull kind of sense,' she added, attempting a smile, 'but *wild* in the sense of rugged and untamed. Doing something outdoorsy might well be up his street.'

Nicole had come to understand that if you really wanted to show the person you wanted to marry that you meant business, then giving them what they yearned for in their heart was the key. Like Warren had done with Cheryl—she'd secretly yearned for a bit of Bond excitement and he'd worked that out and had given it to her.

All anyone had to do was take a look at Alex's photographs, his landscapes, to see where his heart was. It was all about letting the person you loved know that you really got them, really saw what was inside. Nicole knew that if she could get her clients to not only dazzle their prospective fiancées with glitz and show, but to find a way to let the proposal touch that secret place in their heart, then a 'yes' was just about guaranteed.

'What was number three again?' Saffron asked.

'*Intimate*.' Nicole's voice came out a little husky. She

closed her eyes and looked away, trying to hide the blush that was creeping up her cheeks. 'It's hot in here, isn't it? I'll open a window.'

She got up and walked away from Saffron, cracked the large sash window on the back wall open a little, glad of the chilly air that quickly rushed in and cooled her skin. She'd settled on *intimate* because that was how Alex always made her feel—as if the world had closed in and it was only the two of them. Everything else was just peripheral. She couldn't seem to imagine him without feeling that sense of intimacy.

He must make Saffron feel like that too. No wonder she wanted to marry him.

Nicole felt sick, even though she knew Saffron held all the rights and it was she who was the interloper.

She cleared her throat and turned back to Saffron. 'I think something simple, just the two of you, but unusual and exciting would be the ticket. Now we just have to narrow down the different ideas and pick one.' She walked back over to her chair and sat down. 'Did you see the one where we'd hire a boat to take him to a restored Victorian lighthouse on the white cliffs of Dover? Think crashing waves and wild and dramatic coastline. It's not in use any more, but has been turned into a luxury getaway. We'd leave a trail of candles and clues to lead him up to the top, where you'd be waiting for him...'

Saffron snapped the folder closed and looked at Nicole with sudden and unusual intensity. 'Do you believe in love? The kind that lasts forever?'

Nicole took a moment to reorient herself. She gave Saffron one of her best smiles. 'I'm kind of in the wrong business if I don't.'

Saffron nodded, as if she'd said something meaningful and important.

Nicole leaned forward and looked at her sympathetically. 'It's perfectly normal to get a case of the jitters, you know, especially at this point in the proceedings, when everything starts to get a little…well, real.'

'It's just…' Saffron broke off and looked at the closed folder on the coffee table. 'I wonder if I have it in me to be a good wife. My father… Well, he doesn't think I can stick with anything. And the whole of the UK press seem to back him up.'

To be honest, she didn't know Saffron well enough to answer that question truthfully. 'It's not for me to judge you, Saffron. What do you think? Do you think you'll be a good wife?' She was going to add 'to Alex', but she couldn't seem to make the words leave her mouth.

The look of fear and concern disappeared from Saffron's face. 'I'm so glad I came to you for this, Nicole.' She let out a little laugh. 'It's funny—you remind me of Alex in a way.'

Nicole's heart jolted at the mere thought that anything, even a tenuous observation of Saffron's, could link her with him. 'I do?'

Saffron nodded. 'He's just about the only person I know who takes me as I am, who doesn't try to change me, to make me "better". Do you know how tiring it is to try and live up to something you're not?'

Nicole bobbed her head in agreement. She had a funny feeling she did.

'But Alex doesn't look down on me, doesn't make me

feel as if everything I do is wrong. And I need someone like that in my life at the moment…especially with what they've been saying about me in the papers. He helps balance that all out. When I start to doubt myself, he makes me feel I'm okay.'

Nicole held back a sigh. Yes, Alex did that for her too. Even when she messed up and veered completely from the plan. She knew just how warm and tingly it could make a girl feel inside.

'And when you find that sort of person, you really should hang on to them, right? Not let them go…'

She nodded again. If only she could, she thought to herself. If only she'd realised that back at New Year, before Saffron had even met him. But she'd been too blind, too stupid, too focused on her own idea of perfection and what she needed to do to achieve it, to see what the universe had dangled under her nose. 'No, you shouldn't let that kind of person go…' She looked intently at Saffron as she said her next words. 'If you love them.'

Saffron made a large, slightly dismissive gesture with her hand. 'I adore him! But you've met Alex… Everyone loves him, don't they?'

Nicole nodded quietly, not sure she'd really got the answer she'd been fishing for.

Saffron stopped smiling and became a little more serious, catching her mood maybe. 'I know Alex and I had a rough patch a little while ago… I think he thought I was encased in my own little "Saffron bubble", as he likes to call it, and I wasn't really there for him unless I needed something, but I've matured. I'm ready to prove him wrong. I'm ready to prove everyone wrong!' She grinned at Nicole, a sparkly little smile inviting her to be a co-conspirator. 'And I can't wait to see the look on my father's face when I tell him I'm getting married!' She threw the folder down on the coffee table with a triumphant slap. 'Let's go for it!'

'Which option?'

She shrugged and made a dismissive gesture with her hands. 'They're all lovely, but I think we need to work on some more scenarios—I'm thinking a big flash mob in Trafalgar Square with a party at the Savoy afterwards, everyone invited, or going to a West End show and dragging him down from the balcony to propose to him live onstage before the last curtain call. Can you come up with something along those lines?'

She looked so hopefully at Nicole that Nicole couldn't do anything but nod silently. She thought of the hours of work she'd put into that folder, each idea that was perfectly tailored to what she'd found out about Alex, to what she thought he'd really like. 'Of course I can,' she said, stretching her cheeks into a smile.

What the client wanted the client got. It was Saffron's proposal, after all, not hers.

# CHAPTER TWENTY

'Oh, my goodness! Sit down, will you?' Peggy exclaimed loudly and suddenly.

Nicole had been staring out of the front windows at Hopes & Dreams. She turned and stared at her friend. 'What's got into you?'

Mia was sitting at Nicole's desk. She'd left work a little early to drop in and give Nicole some help with her accounting software. So far she'd been squinting at the screen and frowning a lot. Now she looked up.

Peggy shook her head. 'You've been pacing backwards and forwards for the last half an hour. It's doing my head in. And every time I think you've finally stopped and you sit down, you're up again two minutes later. I'm a very visual person,' she said with a dramatic flounce. 'And I'm supposed to be designing a website banner, and I can't concentrate with you prowling around in my peripheral vision.'

'Sorry,' Nicole said, maybe a little tightly, and since her chair was occupied, she walked stiffly over to the purple sofa and sat down. 'Pacing helps me think. You know that.'

Peggy shook her head. 'I didn't think I'd ever say this,

but I think I'd prefer to watch an endless loop of *Pretty in Pink* to all this extraneous movement.'

Nicole found herself tensing her leg muscles, ready to stand again, and forced herself to stay seated. Okay. She hadn't realised she'd been doing it, but maybe Peggy had a point.

Mia took her hand off the mouse and turned to look at Nicole. 'What's got your brain tied up in knots? Is it Saffron's proposal?'

Nicole shook her head. 'No. That's not it. I'm actually thinking about here…the shop.'

Peggy picked herself up from where she'd sprawled her top half across the desk. 'What about the shop?'

Nicole stood up again, took one look at Peggy's face and perched herself on the edge of the desk. She took a moment to scan the room, took in the cutesy hearts, the funky photos, the blaring fuchsia wall. 'I think we need to redecorate,' she said simply.

Both Peggy's and Mia's mouths dropped open.

'But you've only been in here since April,' Mia said. 'And you worked really hard getting it the way it is. Why on earth would you want to change it all again?'

'Because we may need to if we want to keep attracting new clients like Saffron,' she explained, folding her arms.

Peggy narrowed her eyes and looked at her. 'You've been acting weird all week. First of all it was Sunday's Brat Pack marathon, and then come Monday morning you were all spruced up, superefficient, supercool, more than a little scary…and you've been gathering momentum all week! Thank goodness it's Friday tomorrow, or I'd start to get really terrified.'

'I'm fine,' Nicole said lightly. 'Really I am.'

Or she would be. Once she remembered who she was aiming to be, all the things she wanted from life, instead of yearning for other people's boyfriends.

She shouldn't want him. Not just because he belonged to her most important client, but because he was a clear and present danger to her goals. How could he be anything else? Every time she was around him, everything unravelled.

She glanced across at Peggy to find her friend still studying her intently.

Peggy stood up and rested her curvaceous derrière against her desk. 'Has this got something to do with the cowboy?'

Nicole blinked in surprise. 'No,' she said, rather quickly. 'It's got nothing to do with him. After this weekend, our working relationship—our fake working relationship, I might hasten to add—will be over and it'll be back to business as usual.'

Peggy pouted. 'I like our office the way it is, and I don't see why we have to change it.'

Well, that was understandable, thought Nicole, seeing as Peggy had steamrollered her into some of the design decisions—especially the colours. She took a moment to collect herself. She had to say this the right way or she'd offend Peggy further, and that was the last thing she wanted to do.

'I just think that if we're going to be attracting more upmarket clients, maybe we need to start thinking about having premises to match.'

Peggy stiffened.

'It took all of our three combined savings accounts to get this place up to scratch,' Mia said. She was starting to look a little bit agitated too. Her jaw tensed and she gave

Nicole a hard look through her glasses. 'It makes no business sense to spend yet more money on something you don't need. Aren't you getting a little ahead of yourself?'

Nicole shook her head. She really didn't think she was.

'You're forgetting that Saffron came to us anyway,' Peggy said, turning round and flumping back down into her desk chair. 'She liked us just the way we are. Why do we need to change anything?'

Also forgetting she was supposed to stay anchored, Nicole stood up and walked over to the window, looked out across the courtyard to the cafe. A group of young mums had congregated near the shop door and there was a bit of a traffic jam with the pushchairs. She looked back at Peggy and Mia. 'Saffron was the exception, though, not the rule. She would have hooked up with Minty and Celeste if she hadn't had a very good reason not to. If we don't want them to wipe the floor with us and steal all the best clients, we're going to have to make it an even playing field.'

Or open war, she added mentally, but she kept that to herself.

'And that might require a little bit of an image overhaul, whether we like it or not. Like I say, sometimes you've got to—'

'Dress for the life you want,' both Peggy and Mia chimed in.

'Right,' Nicole said, noticing the way both of them folded their arms and looked at her as she did so. 'And the same applies to Hopes & Dreams. We need to dress for the clients we want… They're not going to come otherwise.'

Peggy picked up one of her pens and fiddled with the fluffy, baby-pink feather tip. 'Okay,' she finally said grudgingly. 'You might have a point. I don't like it, but you might have a point.' She sighed. 'If you can't beat 'em, join 'em.'

Nicole was grateful for Peggy's nod at their platitude tradition. She even joined in with one of her own. 'One door closes and another one opens, right?'

The only problem was that Peggy and Mia didn't look very convinced. She decided to stop being silly and start being honest. 'Anyway, thank you. Thinking about it is all I'm asking for right now—I'm not off to get a paintbrush any time soon.' Even if she dearly wished she could. Some days that flipping pink wall gave her a headache.

'Now…who's up for a latte? My treat.' She had just enough change in her purse to cover that, and since she still had the urge to stride around, she might as well put her legs to good use before something polka-dotted of Peggy's came flying towards her across the office. Both Mia's and Peggy's hands shot up in the air.

'I'll be back in ten,' she said and grabbed her coat and headed for the door.

# CHAPTER TWENTY-ONE

When Alex had said this wedding was going to be a little different, he hadn't been kidding.

'Where's the church?' Nicole had asked as they'd sped through the East Sussex countryside. 'Which village?'

'We're not going to a church,' Alex had answered, smiling to himself, and had refused to be drawn on the matter any further. 'Just you wait and see.'

And now they'd reached their destination, Nicole certainly did see.

No quaint village church with a pointed spire and flint-decorated walls, stained glass and flagstones. Instead, they'd pulled up outside Luttingford Steam Railway and when Nicole spotted the assembled guests she thought she'd wandered into a time warp.

As they unloaded the bags and tripods from the Jeep, she couldn't help but stare. Every single person, from babes in arms to octogenarians, was dressed in full Victorian finery—but with a twist.

'Ever been to a steampunk wedding before?' Alex asked

as they set off towards the vast Victorian railway shed that now formed the main part of the museum.

Nicole shook her head.

There were ruffled skirts and crinolines, corsets and button-up boots. The men wore tails and cravats, waistcoats and top hats, but here and there on everyone there were a few details that weren't strictly historical. Like the old-fashioned driving goggles the groom and best man wore on their hats, the gun belts some had slung round their middles. The buttonholes, instead of being the bog-standard rose or carnation with a pin, were beautiful contraptions made out of cogs and curling metal filigree, with a small sprig of heather sticking out the top.

'What exactly *is* steampunk?' Nicole whispered as they made their way inside.

'I'm not an expert, but I believe it's inspired by science fiction set in worlds where steam machinery is dominant. Think H. G. Wells or Jules Verne.'

'Oh,' Nicole said. That made sense, even if she still didn't quite get why people wanted to dress up in that style, especially for a wedding.

Inside the museum there were rows of chairs set up in front of a massive steam locomotive. Even the celebrant was dressed in full-on steampunk costume, from the feather in her jaunty little hat to the satin corset enhancing her already ample chest.

'I love things like this,' Alex said, grinning at her. 'Sometimes it's nice not to have the same old pastel bridesmaids and boring white flowers. There's certainly room for some creativity at a gig like this.'

A gig.

Only Alex could get away with calling a wedding, possibly the most serious and meaningful day of a person's life, a gig. She was about to smile, tell him off good-naturedly about it, but then she stopped herself. This wasn't what she'd promised herself when she'd been waiting at the end of the street for him to pick her up this morning, was it? But it was so hard when it just felt natural to talk to him as if she'd known him all her life.

The only way she—and Hopes & Dreams—was going to survive this day was if she doubled the efforts she'd made last week. Nothing personal. She would keep a little—okay, maybe a lot—of professional distance between her and Alex. Chatting kept to the absolute minimum and definitely not even the wrong kind of smile sent in his direction. Nice, professional, *safe* smiles only.

She nodded and gave him her most serene effort. 'It's certainly going to be an interesting day.'

Alex gave her a bit of a funny look, but they didn't have time to analyse anything. The service was going to start in twenty minutes, just enough time to do a few preliminary snaps. The bride and groom had chosen to have the shots of the bridal party done after the ceremony, rather than lots of 'getting ready' shots, preferring to be seen in all their finery, rather than without.

Nicole trudged after him as he set up a tripod off to one side of where the bride and groom were going to stand. At least she knew what to expect this week. The fact they'd be rushed off their feet would help her plans. It was the lulls she would have to watch for. Thankfully, she knew she was going to fill one of them by telling Alex she couldn't do the other weddings he had planned for them. She had a good excuse all worked out and had even rehearsed it with Peggy last night.

Before she knew it, the doors of the museum were closing and they were scuttling outside to take a few pictures of the bride before she and her attendants made their way down the aisle.

If she'd thought the guests had gone to town, the bride truly was something to behold. She wore a snow-white Victorian dress with a bustle and a narrow skirt that flared at the bottom. The front was mostly plain, but the back was a waterfall of ruffles. On top of the tight-laced corset she wore a fitted jacket, and a miniature top hat with a veil graced her elaborately coiled dark hair. Her bouquet, while containing traditional white roses, also had heather and ivy, but amongst all that were all manner of cogs and clockwork parts, metal curls and even a few tiny old-fashioned keys. Alex must have used twenty shots on that alone.

Once that was done, he and Nicole dashed back inside to await the bride's entrance. She walked slowly down the red-carpeted aisle towards the steam train and her groom, a small nervous smile on her face. The poor groom had looked so terrified that all he'd been able to do up until that point was stare fixedly ahead, his jaw clenched and his hands clasped so tight in front of him his knuckles were going white. His best man gave him a nudge and he finally turned round.

From where Nicole was standing, on the opposite side of the banks of chairs, she could see his face quite clearly. His look of terror melted away as he watched his bride walking towards him and he broke out into a grin that rivalled one of Alex's. He looked as if he was smiling right down to his toes.

She let out a little sigh. Sometimes she got so caught up in organising the romance that she forgot about the magic. This wedding was totally different from any other she'd ever been to before, but that look that passed between bride and groom as she took her final steps towards him was one Nicole had seen a hundred times over.

And then the work really began. Everyone left the cover of the Steam Museum to stand on the platform of a lovingly restored Victorian station. Nicole helped herd the different groupings of family and friends in front of the big green steam train that looked as if it had just pulled in from some far-off destination, complete with white ribbon tied to the front. The driver was even persuaded to let off a jet of steam so the bride and groom could pose in a romantic clinch as it swirled mistily around them.

Nicole did pretty well, even if she did say so herself. She managed to hand Alex lenses, take care of memory cards and flash units, without engaging in anything remotely resembling flirting or chatting. Cool, calm, businesslike. And silent. Perfect.

As they started to do the larger group shots, which ended this part of the job, Nicole looked around. The big locomotive shed, while fine for a short ceremony, was a bit too large and draughty for a reception, and there was no evidence of caterers waiting in the wings, ready to spring out with tables or canapés.

It all became clear a few minutes later: everyone bundled onto the train. And, after the driver had tooted the horn and fired up the engine, it pulled out of Luttingford Station and headed down the track through the frosty countryside.

The insides of the carriages were fabulous—every bit as glamorous as the Orient Express—even if there were no sleeper cabins, only dining cars and seating cars. The whole wedding party sat down at immaculately laid tables, covered in white cloths with well-polished and well-loved silverware, where they were served a three-course meal, carried with amazing precision and efficiency by a fleet of sure-footed waiters.

Nicole made a mental note to check this place out when she got back to the office. If a wedding was wonderful on board the Belle of the Weald, then it could be an amazing proposal venue too.

As the bride and groom and their guests tucked into moist pink salmon in a champagne sauce, Alex flitted from carriage to carriage, snapping away, getting shots of whole carriages, different seating groups and any quirky little details that caught his eye—like the little lamps with shades that sat in front of every window or the way the steam drifted past the carriages, making the pale tones of the winter countryside seem even more ethereal.

Even though Nicole's arms were tired and she lost her balance and bumped against the tall wooden partitions between the seats more times than she could count, watching him work was still fascinating. He was just so...creative. And energetic and talented.

Alex saw the world differently to her. Where her challenges were items to be ticked off a list, his were adventures. Where she saw an ordinary bit of cutlery, he saw a photo opportunity. And not only that, he'd find the right angle, the right lighting, to make that very functional thing look unique, exquisite, interesting.

He spotted an antique pistol, owned by one of the guests, and asked to borrow it. Nicole would never have thought that guns and weddings went together, but when Alex had whispered a suggestion to the bride and she'd been delighted at the idea of a cheeky picture, where she pretended she was coercing her besotted husband into marriage with the aid of a loaded pistol, Nicole had to admit it captured the atmosphere of this fun-filled wedding perfectly.

As the train neared the end of its journey and the passengers started getting ready to disembark, she and Alex took a moment to catch their breath. He leaned in close and showed her some of the shots he'd taken on the LCD display on the back of his camera. He grinned at her as she glanced up at him.

'They all look amazing, don't they?' he said, nodding towards the carriage full of Victorian weddings guests. 'I've hardly known which way to point my camera, there have been so many great shots.'

Nicole nodded, remembering her vow to keep chit-chat to a minimum. The guests did look great, even if, now they'd finished their meal, some of them were videoing each other or the scene out of the window on their mobile phones, which kind of spoiled the effect.

'I could even be tempted to dress up like this, given half the chance.' The dimple put in a well-timed appearance. 'It has to be better than my last fancy-dress outfit—the bit of the horse that produces the manure.'

Nicole nodded again, quickly, abruptly, and looked away. She didn't want to remember that horse costume, how soft the fur had felt under her fingers, or how his chest felt through his T-shirt as she'd started to explore, but she also didn't want to think about him dressed like an adventurer in a top hat and flying goggles, a crisp white shirt and a waistcoat. It suited him too well.

'What about you? Would you dress up in those long skirts and hats? And what are those hoopy things that go under the skirts?'

'Crinolines,' she replied quietly and studied one of the guests near to her. She wore a dark green dress with black velvet stripes. The skirt was layers of ruffles, stopping short above her daintily heeled lace-up ankle boots. A black corset pulled her in at the waist and gave her some serious cleavage, and it was all topped off with a parasol and an ostrich-feather fascinator.

'It's not really my style,' she added, thinking of her wardrobe of clean lines, neutral colours, understated...everything. 'I'm not sure I could pull it off anyway. All those frills and layers.'

'Pity,' Alex said as he hauled his camera back over his shoulder. 'I think you'd look great.'

The train was slowing now, and any further conversation was cut off by the need to collect up equipment and disembark before the bride and groom so Alex could take a few shots of them on the steps of the train.

They'd arrived at Chillingham, a quaint little railway station that looked like something off a film set. The old-fashioned signs were lovingly painted wooden boards in deep greens with gold lettering. There wasn't a rotating advertising sign or an electronic departures board in sight. Neither were there any cold and uncomfortable metal seats, but slatted wooden benches with wrought-iron ends, the wood varnished so it gleamed in the afternoon sun. Flower baskets hung from the network of old studded girders that held up the corrugated roof, and vintage leather suitcases were artfully stacked on a handcart near the exit.

There was a picturesque church right next to the station, with hall attached, where the rest of the reception was being held.

'Why didn't they just get married there?' Nicole asked Alex quietly as they hauled the equipment through the graveyard and round to the hall's entrance. She'd gathered while unintentionally eavesdropping on the train that the bride's family came from this village.

Alex looked shocked. 'What? And miss that wonderful train ride?'

Nicole rolled her eyes. 'Seems boys never do grow up, do they? Anything with wheels or a propeller and you're happy.'

'Too right.' And he jogged off with a big smile on his face.

Nicole shook her head and followed. If she couldn't convince Saffron to choose a proposal venue outside of London, she might just have to persuade her to opt for a speedboat racing down the Thames.

# CHAPTER TWENTY-TWO

A lot of thought and attention to detail had gone into decorating Chillingham village hall. There was bunting and balloons, but all in white, purple and black to match the bridesmaids' dresses. Tables and chairs were laid out round the edges with a space in the middle for dancing, but pride of place was a five-tier cake that blew Nicole's mind away. She *needed* to find the name of that baker for future reference.

It was the palest cream fondant icing and the detail was minimal, but what was there was a work of art. The baker had piped intricate swirls and flowers, cogs and keys in both thick and thin black icing, delicate and lacy, but the swirling patterns also suggested ornate Victorian wrought iron. It was topped off with flowers similar to those in the bride's bouquet. It was as if the baker had condensed the whole spectacle and essence of this unusual wedding and had fashioned it into a cake.

Since everyone had already eaten the wedding break-fast, champagne was served and speeches were done before the cutting of the cake, giving hardly any let-up. It was only when the lights had dimmed and the party was well under way that Nicole managed to collapse onto a stackable wooden chair that looked as if it had been sitting in the church hall since World War II.

Alex plonked a bright purple plastic tumbler down in front of her. 'There you go.'

'What is it?' she asked. It was bubbling, but it didn't look like champagne, which was probably for the best, given the events of the previous week.

'Lemonade. I asked for sparkling water, but they didn't have any.'

'Thanks,' she said, meaning it. The first sip was sweet and sharp and the bubbles tickled her nose. 'I haven't had lemonade in years... When I was little, I always used to ask for it as a treat on my birthday, and my dad insisted on serving it up every year.' She laughed. 'Even after I'd gone to uni.'

Alex pulled out a chair and sat down beside her. 'Are you close with your family?'

She opened her mouth to say yes, but she realised she felt slightly adrift from them now. She was always working so hard, and when she did see her family she felt as if she'd been slowly morphing into someone who didn't quite fit in with them any more. She frowned. 'Not as close as I should be.'

Alex let out a gruff laugh. 'Nobody is as close to their family as they should be, but for some of us it's by choice.'

She knew she should just drink her lemonade and shut up, but she couldn't help turning to him and checking the expression on his face. He looked resigned, weary. That strange little tug in her chest happened again. 'You don't get on?'

He gave her a rueful look. 'We'd get on a lot better if they'd just accept that being a photographer is what I want to do and let me get on with my life.'

She nodded. 'That must be tough.' At least her mum and dad supported her whatever she did. She was the one who was always pushing herself to change, driving herself forward.

He shrugged it off. 'We've kind of reached a stalemate now. It's not important.' And he sipped his plastic glass of cola and stared out across the dance floor.

Nicole joined him. There were a group of men by the hatch into the little kitchen, which was being used as a bar, drinking beer and swapping stories. Uncles. For some reason she thought of them as uncles. Probably because her dad and his four brothers all did the same at family gatherings, and when her dad was one of five and her mum one of four, there was always a wedding or an engagement or a surprise birthday party to go to. In fact, take away the fancy coats and top hats, the corsets and parasols, and this family was very much like hers. She really ought to make time to see them more often.

She turned and continued looking at the guests. Two little girls, aged about eight, were strutting their stuff with one of the bridesmaids on the dance floor. It was a little odd to see them in their petticoats and pinafores, wiggling away to Lady Gaga, but whatever...

She leaned in closer to Alex so he could hear her and pointed them out, and he picked up his camera and snapped a couple of shots.

Nicole sighed. 'I remember dancing like that at my cousin Helen's wedding when I was nine.' Dad had bought her a new lilac dress with a sash and Mum had given her an Alice band with matching sparkly bits. She'd thought she was the bee's knees and hadn't thought twice about getting up and dancing in front of everyone. 'At the time I thought I was as good as Janet Jackson, but now...' She looked at the two girls, jerky and out of time on the dance floor. 'I was probably just like them.'

Part of her wished she could return to those days, when she'd expressed herself however she wanted and no one had judged her. She sighed and looked further round the room.

The DJ was playing crowd pleasers now, and lots more of the guests, full of beer and cider and slightly warm white wine, rushed up to the dance floor to join in the 'Macarena'. Even a couple of the uncles. One stuck his pot belly out and wiggled his hips suggestively. Alex, never one to miss a good shot, stood up to get a better view. When he sat down again, Nicole was still smiling.

'What?' he asked.

She shook her head. 'For a moment there, that big guy reminded me of my dad. He was always the first one to do something to embarrass me at parties.'

Alex grinned and looked back across the dance floor. 'This is my kind of party. These people...they're *real*.'

Nicole snorted. 'What are you saying? That everyone dancing at Elmhurst Hall last week were robots?'

He gave her a dry look. 'No... And you know I think Charles and Lynette are great.'

'That's what weddings are about. For most happy cou-

ples it's about living a fantasy for the day. What's wrong
with that?'

He shrugged. 'Nothing, I suppose.'

Nicole raised her eyebrows as she surveyed the crowd of
grinding wedding guests in their waistcoats and top hats
and frills. 'And you don't think this lot are dressing up and
pretending to be something they're not?'

Alex stared at the crowd for a moment, deep in thought.
'There's a difference...' he said slowly. 'Yes, this lot get
into the fantasy when they've got an event to go to, but
this is them expressing themselves, showing on the outside
something about who they think they are on the inside, and
other than that there's no pretence here.'

Nicole didn't say anything. In a weird kind of way, Alex
had a point. But this conversation was getting uncomfortable. She didn't want to think about insides and outsides
and whether they matched or not, so she decided to steer
the conversation onto something else. She was supposed to
be posing as a journalist, wasn't she? So she really should
act like it and ask him some questions about his job.

'So...how did you get into wedding photography?'

He shrugged. 'Kind of fell into it by accident. An old
school friend knew photography was a passion of mine and
was getting married on a tight budget, so he asked me to
help out. He and his new wife loved the results and it oc-
curred to me that instead of doing a boring office job to
fund my photographic expeditions, I could do this instead.
It took a few years before I could do it full-time, but I got
there in the end.'

She smiled and took a sip of her lemonade. 'So all your

Saturdays are booked up for the next couple of years, are they?'

He gave her a rueful look. 'Pretty much. I'm a victim of my own success.'

She thought about the photos at the exhibition, how beautiful they'd been. 'And has it helped? Do you get more time to travel and take the kind of photos you love?'

Alex frowned and stared into his empty plastic cup. 'No, actually. I don't. The weddings fill up my calendar, especially during the summer months. I'd love to go to the Shetlands then—to catch the light on those long, almost endless days when the sun hardly sets.'

'You said at the gallery that this was bread and butter, that you did it so you could go and do the stuff you really loved.'

He raised his eyebrows. 'Have you got a photographic memory or something?'

She shook her head. For some reason she seemed incapable of forgetting even the smallest details of every meeting between them. 'I don't get it,' she said.

'Get what?'

'Well, if this—' she waved a hand at the packed reception '—is the bread and butter, then I think your sandwich is a little short on filling.'

Now he looked really confused. Obviously, humour was not her forte. 'What I mean is…if doing the landscapes is what you love, why don't you cut back on the weddings and make the time for it? Is it the money?'

He shook his head and thought for a moment. 'No, it's not the money. I do very nicely these days. I really should do just that…'

Nicole smiled in bemusement. Why hadn't he ever thought of that? 'If it's your dream, why aren't you chasing it with everything you've got?'

'And that's what you do, is it?'

She didn't hesitate. 'Yes.'

'With everything?'

She nodded, then swallowed as he looked at her more intensely. 'With everything,' she echoed.

He leaned forward. 'And what do you dream about, Nicole?'

He was close enough for her to smell his aftershave again. Her face started to feel warm and her stomach started to flutter. *You,* she wanted to say, but she couldn't do that. For a hundred different reasons she couldn't do that. Neither could she tell him about Hopes & Dreams, so she was kind of stuck. But she wasn't supposed to be doing chit-chat, was she?

She looked away. 'Can I have a go on your spare camera?' she asked, scanning the crowd. 'I'd like to see if I can improve on last week's offerings.'

Alex looked at her for a long moment. She thought he was going to say something, something he shouldn't say, something she probably wouldn't want to hear, but then he nodded and handed her the camera body and then a lens to go with it. She snapped it into place and hung the strap around her neck.

'Oh, I thought I ought to let you know... My friend rescued some of the shots off that card, and I managed to tidy up some of yours that will do as great candid shots.'

She exhaled. 'Thank goodness for that! Did you save any of the first dance?'

'A few. Mostly the long shots. The close-ups were destroyed.'

She looked down at the floor. 'I'm so sorry.'

'Hey…'

She kept her eyes on the floor. Not because she didn't want to look up at Alex, look into those pale blue eyes, but because she really did. A little bit too much.

'Nic?' he said softly.

She licked her lips, took a deep breath and cast him a sideways glance. 'Yep?'

'It worked out fine in the end. You took a couple of great shots of Charles and Lynette later in the evening. They were dancing, looking into each other's eyes and smiling. I cropped them down and I'll put those with the first-dance shots when I make up the album.'

She forgot all about the safety of sideways and turned to face him full on. 'You're using *my* shots in the album?'

One side of his mouth hitched. 'If the bride and groom choose them for the final layout. Yes.'

She shook her head and blinked. 'Wow.'

'They're actually better than the close-ups I took. In those, their faces were tense, because they knew everyone was watching them. By the time you came along they'd relaxed and it was obvious that all they were thinking about was each other.'

'Aww…' she said, without even thinking she shouldn't.

Alex gave her one of his knowing smiles. 'See? I knew you were a big softie underneath all that starch.'

She blinked and looked at him. 'Starch?'

He wiped the smile off his face, looked contrite. 'Sorry. Didn't mean that.'

The twinkle in his eyes called him a liar.

Nicole couldn't fold her arms, because the camera was in the way, so she put her hands on her hips and angled away from him a little. She might as well pretend to be offended at his remark. Which she was—a really tiny bit. She didn't like it when he said personal things about her. Partly because it made her think of that ill-considered New Year's Eve kiss, but partly because it made her feel funny. Exposed. As if he could look past all the layers of varnish she'd purposely built up over the years and still see the Nicole Jasper had rejected hiding underneath, the Beta version she was doing her best to upgrade.

She didn't want to feel like that. She needed to remember about Saffron, why she was really here. And maybe she needed to remind him too. Not that he'd done anything inappropriate. But it felt like he might. Or, even worse, that she would.

It was odd, thinking that he'd been married once, but she supposed that gave Saffron an even greater chance. He wasn't the drifter she'd thought he was. Or hadn't been.

She knew he probably didn't want to talk about it, but she needed to smash this warm little bubble they'd created around themselves. How had a simple conversation about the memory card turned so personal?

'So...if you did it a second time, would you go for one of these steampunk bashes? You seem rather taken with the whole thing.'

He gave a nonchalant shrug of his shoulders. 'No idea. Haven't really thought about it.'

She swallowed. While she hadn't expected him to wax lyrical about dress designers and party favours, surely a man who *might* be on the verge of getting engaged, even if he didn't know it yet, should be a little less...apathetic... about the whole idea of marriage?

She stared straight ahead, the mass of bodies on the dance floor a blur. 'Do you think it's on the cards...eventually... with this wonderful girlfriend of yours?'

There. She'd said it. That should drive a couple of miles of much-needed professional distance between them.

Alex didn't answer.

Nicole resisted as long as she could, but she had to check his face to see the reason behind his silence. Was he deep in thought about Saffron, or was he shocked at her question, or was he truly chewing the idea over? She turned her head, keeping her gaze low at first, then lifted her eyes to look at him at the last moment.

There wasn't a hint of a smile on his face, but he didn't look conflicted or love-struck, either. He just looked... open. As if she could read everything about him that she wanted to know in those blue eyes. That air-thickening, bubble-type sensation came back, faster, harder, enclosing her and Alex from the noise of the party. Something inside Nicole's chest started to ache and she felt curiously short of breath.

He shook his head.

Nicole had to take a moment to remember what her question had been.

Oh, right. Marriage. To Saffron.

'Why?' she whispered, still unable to look away.

A weary but honest expression passed across his features. 'I think you know why.'

# CHAPTER TWENTY-THREE

'Did you hear me, Nicole?'

She seemed to have frozen, a look of shock on her face. Alex was starting to wonder whether he should go and find a first-aider.

He was in deep now. He might as well keep digging. 'I like you. More than I should.'

Her eyes, which were already large and round, widened further. Her mouth moved, and he thought she was going to say something. She bit her lip but she didn't look away.

He'd spoken the truth. Nothing else. But he hadn't re-alised just *how* true it had been until the words were out of his mouth, the thoughts and feelings he'd had for the last couple of weeks made concrete in sound.

There was no hiding from it now. No pretending he was just bantering with her as he did with other women, that it was harmless. That just made the situation all the more dangerous.

As much as he'd tried not to, he hadn't been able to stop thinking about her. And it wasn't just about wanting what he couldn't have. She'd finally started to let down those barbed-wire fences of hers, let him see her more clearly, and he liked what he saw. Tom had been dead wrong. This wasn't the six-month thing. It was something more. But it was also something dangerous.

As prickly as she could be, he found himself talking to her, telling her things he didn't normally share with anyone else, the things no one else thought to ask about. Not even Saffron.

He closed his eyes momentarily. He'd thought he was happy with Saffron, that what they had worked, but now... he just didn't know any more.

He ran his hand through his hair and broke eye contact. 'I know...' he said, replying to the look he'd just seen in her eyes. 'I know I'm involved with someone else. I know this is complicated.'

He glanced back at her.

'But I also know that if what I have with her is real, then I shouldn't be feeling the way I do when I'm with you. But I don't want to be the kind of guy who juggles two women, who tells lies...'

He saw relief in her eyes. It made him feel as if he'd passed some kind of test.

She took a deep breath. 'I like you too,' she said shakily. 'But you're right. It is complicated.' She shook her head and let out a little bark of dark laughter. '*So* complicated.'

A look of anger, a faint hint of disgust, tinged her expression. But it didn't seem as if she was angry with him, thank goodness, more that she was annoyed with herself. He could understand that. He was feeling much the same way.

She looked him straight in the eye. 'There's so much I want to tell you, but I just can't.'

He nodded. He understood all of it. The frustration, the regret, the feeling of loss that was creeping up on him, even though she was only standing a foot away. Even though what she made him feel both excited and terrified him, he couldn't do anything about it. Not now. Not yet. Man, their timing stank.

But he needed something. Something more than this endless circling round each other pretending nothing was going on. It was the same feeling he got week after week, wedding after wedding. Part of him liked the routine, the easiness of it all, but another part of him yearned for the wild open spaces, for that indescribable feeling he just couldn't seem to do without.

Suddenly that feeling came bubbling up from inside of him and pushed words from his mouth. 'I want to dance with you,' he suddenly said, surprising them both.

# CHAPTER TWENTY-FOUR

Nicole started to shake her head slowly, gave him a plead-ing look. As much as she wanted to, it would be like tor-ture.

'Just a dance,' he said. 'No funny business, I promise.' He waved an arm, indicating the dance floor, where uncle was dancing with niece, cousin with cousin, all quite ap-propriately and platonically. 'At least let's have this.'

She knew she should say no, but she really didn't have the strength. Alex must have seen her capitulation in her expression, because he unlooped the camera from around her neck, put it on an empty chair, then stood and offered her his hand. She took it and he led her to the edge of the dance floor. In the sea of Victorian fussiness, their plain clothes marked them out as a unit of two.

The chart tracks had given way to something slower, smoother. She walked into his arms and laid her head on his shoulder, turning her face away from him, unable to look him in the eyes.

They must have moved, but she wasn't aware of it. She just closed her eyelids and concentrated on the feel of him.

It was different from New Year's Eve, when it had all been hands and lips and pheromones. She placed her hands on his chest. His circled her waist. The two of them just stayed like that. Breathing. He was solid and warm in a way that made her want to cry.

Even this was too much, it turned out. Even this wasn't safe.

As they shuffled round the edge of the dance floor, she could swear she heard the sound of a thousand tiny cracks appearing in those layers of varnish she'd been applying to herself for years. She felt as if she were coming apart, that she wanted to spill everything she was—unedited and unfiltered—at his feet, and that would never do. People didn't like that Nicole, not as much as they liked the new, improved version, anyway. Especially men. Especially gorgeous, wonderful men.

She drew in a breath and her whole torso shuddered.

He dipped his head, so close his lips were a mere millimetre from hers. She held her breath. It would be so easy to kiss him, so easy to give in to everything she'd been feeling but had been trying to hold at bay. Her pulse thudded in her ears.

But this was more than just a kiss. This… It would change everything. Risk everything. Her whole life could be wiped away in one heady moment.

The thing that scared her most was that she was ready to do it, that she was ready to see her company crumble and fold, ready to disappoint her friends and leave them poorer, all for this one moment.

She breathed in through her mouth. She felt like a high diver on a platform, rising onto her toes, stretching her arms out wide. In a moment gravity would work its irre-vocable force and pull her down.

But there was one thing she was not prepared to risk, and for that reason, although the song hadn't quite ended, she stepped back and put some much-needed air between them. She could not let herself be hurt the way Jasper had hurt her. She could not go back to square one and build herself up from scratch again.

He didn't argue. In fact, the nod of recognition he gave her told her he hadn't taken it as a slight.

She walked back to where he'd left the spare camera, but instead of slinging the strap round her neck again, she handed it back to him. Then she began the speech she'd rehearsed with Peggy in their living room the night before. It had seemed so simple then, so easy and reasonable to say, but now it felt as if the words were being ripped from her body.

'I don't think I need to come to the next three weddings,' she told him plainly, looking him in the eye. 'I don't want to let you down, but I've got enough material for my article, and my editor is hurrying me along. It seems they want to start the series a month earlier than planned, so I need to get on and research the next profession.'

He nodded. She knew he understood. All of it. And that he agreed.

'What next?' he said lightly, taking the out she'd given them.

'Waitress,' she said, picking a job out of the air.

'I have some contacts,' he added. 'Wedding profession-als get to know each other after a few years on the circuit. I'll talk to some of them, give you a call.'

'Text me,' she replied hoarsely. That way she wouldn't have to hear his voice.

Alex looked at her for a long moment. Then he looked towards the exit. 'It's late, and it looks like this party is going to keep going for a while longer before bride and groom are ready to leave. I think it's time for you to call it a night.'

It felt like a dismissal, even though she knew it was an escape. She nodded, not knowing what else to say.

He pulled a battered leather wallet from his back pocket. 'I'll pay for a cab to take you back home.'

She shook her head. 'Are you insane? That'll cost a fortune!'

He shrugged. 'To answer those questions: probably, and seeing as you've pulled two twelve-hour days with hardly any breaks, all without pay, it's the least I can do.'

It made sense. And he was right. They were finished here. But the irony wasn't lost on her that the last time a man had paid for a cab like this, she'd been feeling pretty much the same way.

He handed her a wad of notes and she accepted them then went to fetch her coat. He followed her to the door. 'It was nice working with you, Nicole.'

Her head bobbed up and down in lieu of a verbal response. She concentrated on breathing properly so she didn't make a noise that would give her away. Then she opened the door and let it swing closed behind her, cutting her off from him. She felt sick.

She tried to distract herself from the sensation by copying the number of a local minicab firm pinned onto a cork noticeboard into her phone.

Sick for having unwittingly poached her best-ever client's boyfriend. Sick for having to walk away from him. But most of all, sick because she knew that even if she could have him, Alex was a man who looked for the truth, who valued what was real. And she'd been lying to him in one way or another from the first moment they'd met.

# CHAPTER TWENTY-FIVE

Sunday morning always had its own brand of quiet, Nicole thought, as she crept to the front door with her shoes off. There was a completeness about it that made every noise she made a hundred times louder. She tried putting her toes down first and walking like a ballerina.

Peggy always described this tiptoeing through a flat at the dead of morning, careful not to disturb the other occupant, as 'the walk of shame'. It really shouldn't count in Nicole's case, since she had woken up in her own bed. Alone. That didn't stop her feeling the weight of the previous night's events as she reached the front door and pulled her boots on.

It was nine-thirty and she really needed to get moving before Peggy woke up. There was no way she could face another inquisition like last week, so she'd decided to go and grab breakfast at a local cafe, and then she'd text Mum and see if it was okay to crash Sunday lunch. A day hidden behind Mum's sparkling white net curtains in the suburbs was exactly what she needed.

Once she'd reached the cafe and bought a cappuccino

and yogurt, she fished her phone out of her handbag and sent a quick text off to her mother. It dinged only moments later with a rather enthusiastic reply. That only served to heap more shame onto Nicole's shoulders. She knew it had been a long time since her last visit, and they only lived an hour or so away by public transport. She'd been meaning to go, she really had, but she'd been so busy…

And going home wasn't the same as it used to be. She'd grown up on the fringes of London in Orpington, in a nice middle-class area with tree-lined streets and well-kept front gardens in front of the 1930s semi-detached houses. Mum was a teacher, and her father—Nicole's grandfather—had been a police inspector, but Dad was from decidedly more working-class roots.

He'd always used to joke that his wife was too posh for him, and Nicole had smiled at that growing up, liking the fact that he thought her mum was special. And she'd felt special too. Some of her friends had even teased her for being posh when Dad had bought his Mercedes, even though it had been a few years old and previously loved. She'd felt lucky, privileged.

Securing a scholarship to Hurstdean had been the icing on the cake. But when she'd got there, she'd realised that there was posh and then there was *posh*. Having one Merc didn't qualify. Two or three, maybe, along with a Ferrari or an Aston Martin, not forgetting the obligatory Land Rover. It had been a whole different world. One she'd had to do her best to fit into. Or at least not stand out too badly in.

It was only a quick hop on the Tube and a train out from Charing Cross before she arrived at a virtually deserted Orpington Station. Her dad was waiting for her in the car park with the motor running—the same Mercedes—and he leaned over and gave her a peck on the cheek as she slid into the passenger seat.

'Hello, love. How's tricks?'

She gave him her best smile, the one she usually reserved for nervous clients. 'Oh, you know... The business is growing. Life is busy...'

He nodded, put the car into gear and pulled away. Nicole exhaled. She'd got very good at that, being vague with her parents about the actual details of her life.

When they pulled up on the drive outside her parents' house, her mother opened the door wearing a Laura Ashley apron. Nicole walked up the path smiling and went happily into her embrace. She closed her eyes. There was something about Mum's hugs that always made her feel better. When she'd been little, Dad had always joked they were magic, but Nicole wasn't sure he was far wrong.

'It's lovely to see you,' Mum said as she pulled back and took a good look at her daughter. 'You look a bit tired. Late night?'

Nicole tried not to give anything away in her expression. 'Something like that.' And then, because she really didn't want to delve any further into that subject, she added, 'Sorry about the short notice.'

Mum shook her head. 'You know there's always plenty for Sunday lunch. You should do it more often, even bring Peggy with you, if you wanted to. Or a man...'

Oh, they were back to that again, were they? Mum's not-so-subtle hints.

'There's no one special at the moment,' she said. Only that wasn't quite true, was it? Another lie. They seemed to come so easily at the moment, as if they were a habit she hadn't realised she'd developed. 'I mean, I'm not seeing anyone.' She smiled brightly back at her mother. 'I'll bring Peggy next time, I promise.'

Peggy loved coming here. She went gaga over the original features that Mum had stopped Dad ripping out of the house, like the fireplaces with their ceramic tiles and the picture rails on the walls. Peggy called her mum 'Mrs H' and flirted with her dad shamelessly. Not that Dad complained.

'Anyway, come inside. It's perishing out there.'

Mum turned and walked down the hall, leaving Nicole and her dad to follow. The scent of roast lamb and home-made mint sauce hit her squarely in the nostrils. It was such a warm, comforting smell, reminding her of long, rainy Sunday afternoons and board games round the dining table after lunch. She'd always wished she'd had a sister or a brother to make up a foursome, but one had never arrived. For some reason she'd never asked her mother whether it had been out of choice.

'So…how's the agency going? Any exciting proposals recently?' her mum asked as they started tucking into their roast dinner.

Nicole smiled and told them all about Warren popping the question in true 007 style, and then she went on to tell them about the steampunk wedding, casually fudging over the details of why she'd been there and whom she'd been with.

Her mother looked over at her father across the mint sauce. 'We didn't make such a fuss over that sort of thing in our day,' she said, and a smile blossomed behind her

eyes. 'Your father proposed to me on a park bench after
we'd been out for a Sunday afternoon walk. No fuss, no
flowers. Didn't make it any less romantic.'

Dad snorted. 'Just as well. There's no way I'd get dressed
up like ruddy James Bond and work my way down the outside of a windy building. I do enough of that in the day job.'

Mum leaned over and patted his hand. Her father main-
tained his scowl, but Nicole saw the answering warmth in
his eyes as he stared back at his wife.

Mum shrugged. 'Sometimes you just know,' she said, re-
turning to her dinner and chopping up a piece of broccoli.
'It's that simple. Just didn't need a lot of fanfare to prove
it to ourselves and everyone else. Didn't make it less real.'

'Just as well not everyone thinks like you do, or I'd be
out of a job,' Nicole said, laughing.

Mum smiled across the table at her. 'I think so too. It's
not our cup of tea, but we're very proud of you for setting
up your own business and making a success of it. And you
make lots of people happy. I'm really glad you've found
something you love to do.'

Nicole nodded. Her smile stayed in place, but her insides
sank. While she hadn't been planning on going into profit
and loss statements, she'd wondered if Dad would be a good
source of advice when it came to running a small business.
Now they were looking at her with that 'glow' again, the
kind of glow they'd developed when she'd got her scholarship, the kind of glow she'd seen every half-term and
every holiday when she'd returned home. It made it very
hard to tell them things weren't as rosy as they thought,
as they needed them to be. She turned her attention to her
carrots instead and stacked the orange discs onto her fork.

They'd been so proud of her when she'd got her scholarship. She hadn't been able to tell them in those first few years how much of an outsider she'd felt. Even when she'd established a group of good friends and felt as if she was fitting in, something would happen to bring everything sharply back into focus again—usually a trip that she couldn't afford to go on—and the differences, the boundaries, between her and her friends would be drawn again. But she'd refused to ask Mum and Dad for more. They'd given her more than enough already. Besides, making her way in the world was her job, not theirs.

After the roast lamb came her mum's famous apple pie. Nicole wolfed it down with relish. She might have eaten in a top London restaurant or two in her time, but she hadn't yet met a dessert that could beat it. She was just scooping up the last crumbs, along with a healthy serving of cream, when her mum spoke. 'Are you okay, Nicole darling? You seem very quiet today.'

Nicole stopped chewing and looked up at her mother. For a few seconds she didn't do anything, but then she swallowed and put her spoon down.

*No,* she wanted to say. *I've got myself into a terrible mess and I don't know how to get out of it.*

But she didn't say it. As much as she wanted to curl up on the sofa with a cup of tea and tell her mum some of what was going on, she realised she couldn't. It was such a disaster that even telling a small part of it would mean the rest of the story would unravel around it. Part of the reason for all her hard work, all the changes she'd made to her life to make herself better, was to show her parents she was worth all the sacrifices they'd made for her over the years. They didn't need to know their only daughter was on the verge of dismantling everything she'd worked for bit by bit.

'I'm fine,' she said eventually. 'Well, mostly fine. But it's a long story. Perhaps I'll fill you in another time. I realise I have to get back and do some prep for tomorrow.'

Her mother nodded, even though she didn't look entirely convinced.

And maybe Nicole would tell her, when it was all over, and she'd managed to salvage as much as she could, knew how to spin the bad bits so it didn't sound so awful.

She did stay for the obligatory board game. Dad insisted, saying he'd drive her back to the station and make sure she caught the four o'clock train, so she'd be back home by teatime. At least working out if Professor Plum or Miss Scarlet had committed a heinous crime left her out of the firing line.

It was almost dark by the time her mother waved her goodbye on the doorstep and she climbed into her dad's car. When she said goodbye to him outside the station, she gave him an extra squeeze.

*Thank you,* it said, *for everything. And sorry for a lot more.*

Her dad just squeezed her back and kissed the top of her head. 'Hurry up,' he said, sounding a little gruff. 'Or you'll miss it, and it's a half-hour wait for the next one.'

Nicole nodded and hurried away, but as she disappeared from view inside the station, she slowed. She had plenty of time. And she wasn't even sure if she cared if she did miss the train at six minutes past. She had some thinking to do, and sitting on a windy platform watching the sky darken to a murky grey-blue seemed to be a fitting location.

Her plan for today had failed. Like most of her plans were failing at the moment.

She'd wanted to visit her parents to escape the things plaguing her in London, but all she'd done was bring it all with her. And being back home had brought some new truths she didn't want to know about sharply into focus.

Most of her life she'd been trying to fit in, to feel part of something, to feel like an insider rather than the perpetual outsider, but she had to face facts that, despite all her attempts, sometimes she felt lonelier than ever.

The only person she didn't feel that way with was Alex, and soon he'd be forever out of her reach.

# CHAPTER TWENTY-SIX

Early on Monday morning, Alex met Tom for a run round Weavers Fields, not far from his flat, which lay between Shoreditch and Bethnal Green. It was cold and grey, but a part of him welcomed the feeling of chilly damp air on his skin. They did a quick warm-up at the edge of the park before setting off.

'So...' Tom said, while grasping his foot and pulling it up behind him into a quad stretch. 'How was it seeing Cinderella again?'

Alex looked straight ahead and pushed his heel down to lengthen his calf. For some reason everything was feeling very tight today. 'Who?'

Tom chuckled. 'Cinderella. Your mystery girl who disappeared at midnight. That's two Saturdays in a row now. In your younger days that would have been considered a serious relationship.'

Nope, this calf just wasn't wanting to give. Alex exhaled and tried to relax his leg muscles. 'It was work,' he said, not giving Tom the satisfaction of reacting to his dig. 'And I'm with Saffron.'

Tom snorted.

'You're wrong about the six-month thing, by the way. Saffron and I are in a very comfortable groove. I could keep going out with her quite easily.'

Tom dropped his foot and picked up the other one. 'But are you happy with her?'

Right. He was giving up on this leg and trying the other one. 'Yeah.' He glanced across at Tom. 'We have fun.'

Tom shook his head. 'That's not what I'm talking about.'

Alex was tempted to give him a shove and watch him fall into the mud. Instead he ignored him. Tom was always a little bit feisty on a Monday morning. His low mood just needed to catch up with his high energy levels. Until then, he was often a bit argumentative.

'Anyway,' Alex said, 'it's coming up to that time when we need to plan the annual hiking trip. Jack and Phil say they're up for it.'

'What about Matt?'

Alex shook his head. 'His missus is about to have a baby, so he's grounded. I know we always stick to the UK, but I wondered about somewhere further afield, somewhere with some more interesting terrain.'

Tom stopped stretching his legs and started swinging his arms. 'And by "more interesting", you mean "more dangerous".'

Alex grinned at him. 'Of course.'

They both set off walking at a brisk pace. Tom laughed. 'Well, we all know you're a bit of an adrenalin junkie, and I suppose you've got to get your kicks somehow these days.'

Great. Tom was turning psychologist on him again. It wouldn't be as bad if he came out and said what he wanted to say without just dropping big hint bombs and then watching for the resulting fallout. Alex knew he shouldn't take the bait.

'What does that mean?'

Eh. He'd never been one for listening to good advice. Or any advice, it had to be said. He liked to do things his own way and in his own sweet time, thank you very much.

'It means you never used to be one for playing it safe, mate.'

Alex just gave him a quizzical look. It was that or punch him.

Tom shrugged. 'Think about it.' And then he picked up speed and jogged away down the path.

Alex shook his head and kept striding. With his calves the way they were today, he needed to take a bit longer to get up to speed, even if his so-called best mate was going to rib him about 'losing' when they got to the end of their run. To be honest, he'd had enough of Tom's pearls of wisdom today. He could do with the solitude.

He took his earphones, which were hanging round his neck, and jammed them in his ears, then pressed play on his iPod.

Playing it safe? What utter rubbish.

He walked for a few more minutes, the pounding of a Muse track in his ears fuelling his pace, then began to pick up speed. As he ran, hardly noticing the trees and bushes, or the dog walkers clustered in clumps and having a gossip, he pushed Tom's words out of his mind.

Unfortunately, that just left space for other thoughts to creep in, ones that were equally unwelcome, despite their allure. What had Nicole said about his work on Saturday?

About him not taking the chance to follow his dreams? That wasn't what Tom was talking about, was it? It was just a crazy schedule that prevented him from taking more time to do his landscapes. When he had a moment to plan his next trip, he would.

*Then why haven't you?* a little voice in the back of his head whispered. *It's been almost a year since the last one. It's almost as if you're avoiding it.*

He huffed out a laugh as he ran. Also ridiculous. Why on earth would he put off doing what he really wanted to do? Why would anyone?

His feet hit the ground rhythmically and he concentrated on his breathing, keeping his shoulders loose and his form good. Okay, maybe it had been easier when he'd been further back in his career, when the hopes of becoming a well-respected landscape photographer were just a dim and distant dream. Back then, his dreams had always been dangling in front of him, calling to him, but still bright and shiny and totally out of reach.

But they weren't that far away any more, were they? If he wanted to he could stretch and see what he could do, if he could make it.

*Thud, thud, thud,* his feet went.

*So, why aren't you?* said his head.

He swallowed in an effort to quell the chilly feeling in his gut. Maybe because he knew what it was like to trust a dream, to trust the future, to believe it was all about to come true before having it ripped out from underneath him. Divorce tended to do that to a person. Anybody would think twice after something like that.

*Nicole goes after her dreams.*

*Oh, shut up,* he told himself. So what if she did? So what if, despite the mystery surrounding her, that at least was crystal clear. Bully for her.

He picked up speed, legs and arms working harder. Okay, so maybe he was a little bit nervous. Everyone was when the thing they were passionate about hung in the balance. Maybe he was just a little bit worried of finding out that he only had the talent to be a small-time amateur landscape photographer and that another twenty or thirty years of weddings stretched into the future like a life sentence. If that was the case, all that confetti and cake nonsense wouldn't be so much fun. It was easier to pretend he was doing it because he chose to, rather than because he had to.

Okay.

So maybe Nicole had a point. Maybe he should just do it. No matter what. That was the kind of guy he'd always thought he was anyway.

As he ran he started to play his conversation with Tom back over in his mind. But Tom hadn't mentioned work, had he? He'd been talking about Saffron.

But no way was he playing it safe by being with Saffron. She was one seriously crazy chick, always coming up with some new hare-brained scheme she hadn't thought through properly. Saffron was the complete opposite of safe.

He shook his head and laughed softly as he eased off his pace a little. So much for Tom's little lecture. The man obviously had no idea what he was talking about.

# CHAPTER TWENTY-SEVEN

'Nicole! What have you done?' Peggy stood, mouth open, and stared at the wall opposite the shelves at Hopes & Dreams. Where there once had been an expanse of eye-watering fuchsia was now an oasis of fresh Caramel Latte paint.

Nicole, dressed in a pair of her dad's old overalls, with her hair in a messy ponytail and a paintbrush in her hand, turned to survey her handiwork. 'It looks great, doesn't it? Much more classy.'

Peggy turned to look at the shelves. 'And where have those funky little heart-shaped frames I got from IKEA gone?' she demanded. 'I only put them there last week!'

Nicole stopped smiling. Peggy was making an awful lot of fuss over a bit of paint and a knick-knack or two. 'I know I said we wouldn't do anything drastic, but I decided the office could do with a little bit of an "edit", just to get us started in the right direction. I just removed a few bits of clutter... More turns up every week, Peg, and it was getting a bit crowded. Now we can see the individual pieces more clearly again.'

'That wasn't what we agreed,' Peggy said and let her cardigan slip off her shoulders. She caught it and hugged it to her, arms across her middle. 'I specifically remember you saying something about there being no paintbrushes, not yet.'

Nicole frowned. Yes, she supposed she had said that. Somehow she'd forgotten.

'And do you know how long it took me to find exactly the right shade of hot pink? Why didn't you talk to me about it first?'

Nicole laid the brush down very carefully on the lid of the paint tin and stepped off the dust sheet she'd covered half of the office with. She frowned. 'I don't know. I just woke up this morning with an idea in my head and decided to run with it. I didn't think it'd be such a big deal.' She'd had a can of the same colour she'd used in the meeting room left over. Mia had said she shouldn't spend more money, and she hadn't.

'You did it on an impulse?' Peggy said slowly, looking at Nicole as if she'd just announced she was going to dance the lambada down Oxford Street, naked. 'It's not part of some big refurbishment plan you've forgotten to tell me about?'

'That's right.'

Peggy turned and made her way swiftly to the kitchenette behind the office space. When she returned with two cups of coffee, she led Nicole to sit on the purple sofa, which had been pulled away from the wall and was now sitting slap bang in the middle of the room. Nicole sat as she was instructed, mainly because she realised she'd upset Peggy somehow, and compliance was probably the safest option at this point. 'I know we said we'd wait until we had new offices,' she explained in a calming voice, 'but I really don't think we can hang around.'

Nicole took the mug gratefully. She'd got here at 5 a.m. and she was starting to realise just how thirsty—and hungry—she was after all that painting.

She looked at Peggy. 'You're right. I should have waited and talked to you. I don't know why I didn't. But it's done now, and we agreed we needed to have a makeover eventually.'

Peggy didn't look convinced. 'I know that if our whole business goes that route we might need to change our image a little, but Saffron is only one customer, and the rest of our clients like us the way we are. We're turning ourselves into blooming Squinty and Detest!' She lobbed a coin from her purse in the general direction of the swear tin. 'And I really do not want to model myself on those two—'

'But we need to do this!'

Peggy laid a hand on Nicole's arm. 'No, Nicole. I think *you* need to do this. And it's more than just business planning gone mad, isn't it? What on earth happened this weekend? I hardly saw you all Sunday, and when you came back from your parents' you just sloped off saying you wanted a bath and an early night with a good book.'

Nicole stared at her coffee mug. She hadn't taken a sip yet. 'I did want an early night with a good book.' Anything to take her mind off what had been whirling round her head.

'And I took you at your word, because other than that you seemed fine—no tracksuit bottoms, no high-school flicks...' She leaned in and looked at Nicole. 'What happened at that wedding? That's what this is all about, isn't it? Alex?'

Nicole nodded. She had a horrible feeling it was, even though that had been the furthest thing from her mind when she'd picked up the paintbrush that morning.

'I think you need to tell me,' Peggy said softly.

Nicole sighed. She looked at the wall. Suddenly it didn't look so classy and wonderful any more. In fact, it looked a little bit...beige. Like the rest of her life had been until Alex Black had sauntered into it again and turned it upside down.

Yes, she really did need to talk about it. To finally stop pretending this was all part of the master plan and admit what a screw-up she was. Before she did that, though, there was something else she needed to say.

She turned to look at Peggy. 'I'm really, really sorry about the wall. I honestly don't know what came over me.'

Peggy gave her a soft little smile. 'Love makes idiots of us all.'

Nicole's first instinct was to bat that comment away, pretend it hadn't hit the mark at all, to say it was nonsense to suggest she might be in love with Alex after only a few weeks. But when she looked deep into herself she found that wasn't entirely true.

She might not be head over heels in love with the guy— yet—but she'd been down that slippery slope once before and recognised the start of the uncontrollable slither down it. She'd promised herself she wouldn't do this again, wouldn't fall helplessly and hopelessly for a guy who was so out of her league he might as well be on a different planet.

'We'll put the frames back…' she mumbled.

'Don't worry. I'll just take them home and find a place for them. I think you might have had a point about over-doing it.' She stood up. 'If we're going to have a good old gossip session, we need breakfast.' She glanced through the window to the little coffee shop over the way. 'And don't worry. It's my treat. Give me three minutes…'

With that she disappeared out the shop door and across the courtyard. When she returned the pair of them sat on the floor with their coffees and pastries and Nicole filled her in on everything that had happened over the weekend, including Alex's startling confession.

'What are you going to do?' Peggy asked, when Nicole had finished.

Nicole gave her a glum little smile that only just about lifted her mouth at the corners. 'What can I do? I can't do anything, can I? I certainly can't tell Alex that his girlfriend has hired me to help her propose to him! And I can't tell Saffron I'm smitten with the man she wants to marry. It'd kill the agency dead.'

Peggy said nothing. It was such an unusual occurrence that Nicole was tempted to laugh. Instead she unfolded her legs and got up off the floor. 'I'm just going to have to keep going.'

'That's the plan?' Peggy said a little nervously, as she also rose and brushed her skirt down. Nicole could tell from her eyes that she wanted her to say yes. Strange. The amount Peggy moaned about Nicole's plans, you'd think she didn't like them.

Nicole shook her head. 'The plan's shot to pieces. Having a plan suggests you have a choice in what's about to happen and we just don't.'

'Actually, I shouldn't have asked what you were going to do,' Peggy said. 'I should have said, "What are *we* going to do?" We're in this together, you know.'

Nicole smiled weakly at her friend. When she spoke she sounded a lot calmer than she actually was. 'We're just going to have to ride the roller coaster and look for an exit when the opportunity presents itself.'

For the first time in almost five years she was outside the lines of the life she'd drawn for herself, and she didn't like it one bit.

# CHAPTER TWENTY-EIGHT

Alex had always liked covering registry-office weddings, especially when they weren't the kind with the full-on fairy-tale bridal treatment. There was something so refreshing about a couple with a few select friends and family members who rushed down to the local town hall and tied the knot—no fuss, no rigmarole.

Carol and Mark were an older couple compared to some of the other brides and grooms he'd photographed. They were both in their forties, both had been married before with all the trimmings and, despite the fact they both had highly paid jobs in the City and could have afforded anything they wanted, they'd decided that all they wanted was a fun and informal day to mark the beginning of their new life together. His son was the best man and her daughter the bridesmaid, but there were no floor-length gowns or morning coats, and only the bride carried a bouquet.

Carol wore a stylish red shift dress with matching jacket and a large wide-brimmed black hat, and Mark a well-cut suit. The witnesses had worn what they liked, although it was obvious they'd coordinated enough not to clash with each other too badly.

'Ready?' Alex yelled, looking at the display on the back of his camera as it perched on a tripod at the bottom of the steps at Chelsea Old Town Hall.

The dozen or so guests surrounding the bride and groom all either nodded or yelled their answers, confetti clutched in their fists.

'One, two, three—'

Alex's 'go' was cut off by a loud cheer from the confetti-throwers and a few passers-by who joined in for the heck of it. Little bits of coloured paper spiralled into the air and floated down again. He kept his finger on the button and just kept snapping, catching each moment like the frames of a motion picture. Some would be terrible. A few would be good. One might even be perfect.

As the last of the multicoloured cloud rained down past the bride and groom, Mark picked Carol up and spun her round.

Alex knew he'd just got his shot.

He turned to grin at his assistant, share the moment with her…

And realised she wasn't there.

He shook his head and got on with his job. Weird. He'd been doing weddings for eight years now, and Nicole had only done two with him. How was it possible for him to miss her, to feel that there was a hole next to him that ought not be there?

He sighed as he rummaged in his bag to change the lens.

And how was there a hole in the rest of his life too? In his workshop-cum-office, in his flat, when she'd never even set foot in those places? He felt as if he'd undergone a seismic shift, and the life that had seemed exciting and fulfilling last week now seemed drab and pointless.

He must be coming down with something.

That was it. It had to be it. Because he didn't want to let it be anything else. He didn't want to feel this gnawing sense of loss, of the warm tingle in his chest when he thought about her. And not just because he couldn't have her. He should be grateful things had ended, that he was going out with a no-nonsense woman like Saffron.

The shots outside the Town Hall were done now, and Alex gathered up his pared-down kit and followed the wedding party to the kerb, where they all hailed taxis and bundled into them so they could travel to the reception venue. He rode with Mark and Carol, sitting on one of the flap-down seats facing backwards and snapping away at them as they held each other's hands and stared into each other's eyes on the back seat, oblivious to his presence.

Those were going to be great shots, with the happy couple sharply in focus and the blur of the London scenery out the back window of the taxi behind them. Shots full of life and movement and colour. Shots where the love they clearly felt for each other was almost a tangible thing.

He leaped out of the taxi ahead of them when they got to Kensington High Street. The reception was to be in the Roof Gardens, an exclusive little venue perched on top of an old department store. Above the honking, noisy traffic and busy pre-Christmas shoppers was an oasis of calm. The wedding party had hired out one of the function rooms and the Spanish Garden for their guests to stroll in in the winter sunshine—an amazing space. It was hard to believe it sat hidden amongst the London skyline, with its palm trees and fountains and terracotta-tiled covered walkway.

He was just catching Mark helping Carol out of the taxi, when something in his peripheral vision caused him to lift his head. A flash of honey-coloured hair and a pair of big sunglasses.

At first he thought it was Saffron, but that couldn't be, because she'd told him she was meeting her father for lunch on the other side of London. Besides, this part of the city was almost entirely populated with girls like her, with their giant handbags and five-inch heels.

He started to turn away, but then the girl spun around and waved at the taxi driver who'd just put his 'for hire' sign on again as Carol and Mark had exited his cab. Alex took his camera down from his face and stared.

It *was* her.

In a different part of the city from where she was supposed to be, not with the person she was supposed to be with. All the little things that hadn't been adding up, all the holes in Saffron's timetable, the faraway stares out the window, the vague answers to innocent questions, all rolled themselves into one unavoidable truth.

Up until now it had just been suspicion. His paranoia, he'd told himself. After Vanessa had pulled the wool over his eyes so completely he'd always been a little bit that way with women. People thought he was an easy-going sort, who didn't care about anything, and he let them. Mainly because it was a good disguise and much better than being thought a pathetic sap.

He shook his head as the taxi did a U-turn in the middle of Kensington High Street, prompting not a few horns to blare and hand gestures from other motorists, and picked his lying girlfriend up from the other side of the street. As usual, she was so lost in her own little world that she didn't even spot him, even though he was only thirty feet away.

He watched the cab disappear into the traffic, until it met and blended with four or five other taxis and he couldn't tell which was which. Then he turned and went into the building in front of him.

It wasn't possible, was it? But what else could he think?

There was only one explanation that came to mind. And that was that his transparent, what-you-see-is-what-you-get girlfriend was cheating on him.

# CHAPTER TWENTY-NINE

Nicole walked briskly along Piccadilly. She was due to meet Saffron at The Ritz in ten minutes to view their function rooms. She hadn't even caught sight of the hotel, when someone grabbed her from behind and hustled her through a wrought-iron gateway and into the little courtyard outside St James's church. She was about to scream until she turned and saw Saffron standing there, looking more than a little spooked. She looked furtively around before dragging Nicole away from the gate and into the little craft and souvenir market that occupied the courtyard most days of the week.

'What's going on?' Nicole asked, rubbing her arm where Saffron had grabbed her.

Saffron pretended to be perusing a stall of handmade felt…somethings. 'I just saw my best friend Sara walking out of Fortnum's, so I had to duck out of the way. This was the safest place I could think of.'

Nicole looked around. Saffron was right. She couldn't imagine any of her client's friends wanting to browse the odd mixture of second-hand jewellery, odd craft objects and 'I heart London' T-shirts. 'What's wrong with being seen down Piccadilly on a Thursday lunchtime?' she asked Saffron.

'Nothing. But I told Alex—and Sara—that I was meeting my father for lunch in St John's Wood. I don't want to make her suspicious.'

Nicole's eyebrows rose. 'You haven't told her about the proposal?'

Saffron shook her head. 'Love the girl to bits, but she's not very discreet.'

Nicole stifled a laugh. No wonder they got on so well.

Saffron frowned. 'I don't want Alex to get wind of it, not when it's only weeks away. He's already asking lots of questions.'

'Is he?' Nicole asked breezily, ignoring the jolt in her pulse at the mention of his name.

Saffron nodded and picked up a strange-looking wood carving, which might have been a turtle, from one of the stalls. 'How much is this?' she asked the vendor.

He mentioned an exorbitant price. Nicole was just about to tell him to stop having a laugh, when Saffron handed over some cash and tucked the wooden creature in her pocket. 'For my friend's little girl,' she explained. 'She likes tortoises.'

Nicole couldn't fault her generosity, if not her bargaining skills. 'He charged you far too much,' she whispered. 'Next time, let me do it.'

Saffron smiled at her and tucked her arm through Nicole's. 'Okay,' she said. 'This is nice, isn't it? Shopping. Just us girls.'

Nicole smiled and nodded back. It was nice.

Or it would have been, if not for the sliding sensation she was feeling inside. If Saffron knew the truth about her, about what she was feeling for the man she was about to propose to, Nicole doubted she'd be smiling at her like that. She felt like the lowest kind of worm, even though she'd done the right thing and had walked away from Alex.

Saffron eyed a pink T-shirt with a rather dodgy Union Jack printed onto it. 'Do you think I could get away with this if I was being ironic?'

Nicole cleared her throat and looked at Saffron. As nice as shopping was, they had appointments to get to. 'We should really head towards The Ritz.'

Saffron wrinkled her nose. 'I had a think about The Ritz while I've been hiding in here. I've been to plenty of events there and I'm not sure their biggest suite will be large enough. I've definitely decided I want the party to be massive. Why don't we go straight to the Savoy?'

'Okay,' Nicole said slowly. She'd been hoping Saffron would make it more of an exclusive and intimate party, but it seemed that was not to be.

'Only...' Saffron crept towards the gates and peered round '...do you think you can nip out and hail down a cab? I'd rather not bump into anyone else I know.'

Nicole nodded and set about doing just that. Once one had slowed outside the entrance to the church courtyard, she ushered Saffron inside and soon they were zooming through the London traffic.

Saffron was looking out of the window, frowning, as they turned from Haymarket to pass Trafalgar Square.

'And you're definite about the big party idea?' Nicole

asked. Secretly, she was hoping none of the big party venues Saffron wanted would be free this close to Christmas and that Saffron would be forced to go another way. 'It's not too late to go with one of the other London-based options if you think it'd be more Alex's cup of tea. How about the speedboat down the Thames? Or the helicopter ride that takes you over the city and out to Hadsborough Castle for an intimate evening together in their turret suite?'

Saffron shook her head. 'No, I want a party. Something that'll get in the papers and the celebrity magazines. Something to let them all know...' She shook her head. 'Never mind.'

Well, Saffron was her father's daughter all right. The media mogul had a reputation for not just setting his mind, but setting it in concrete. It hadn't mattered how many great suggestions she'd fired in Saffron's way; they'd all been batted away without a moment's consideration. Which was irritating on a professional front—after all, Saffron had hired her to do a job and now wasn't letting her do it. If Nicole had wanted to be a glorified dogsbody, who did all the legwork for someone else's ideas, she'd have stayed at Elite Gatherings.

But it also niggled on another front, the way crumbs did when you'd had breakfast in bed. Every time she tried to make peace with what was happening, she just couldn't settle down comfortably and rest.

Even if she totally ignored her own feelings about Alex, Saffron wasn't planning the proposal Alex would want. Which meant either she didn't know Alex well enough to choose well, or she was just ignoring his needs and doing what she wanted. Neither option was a good omen for a long and happy marriage.

If it was any other client she'd say something, give a gentle hint, but she hadn't quite been able to let the words out of her mouth. Probably because she couldn't guarantee they would be free from her own ulterior motives, that the personal side of why she didn't want Saffron to marry Alex might hijack her mouth and take over.

The taxi turned into Savoy Court and drew to a stop under the black-and-gold Art Deco canopy that shielded the entrance to the hotel. She paid the cabby and followed Saffron into the lobby, where they were met by a member of the hotel's events team and were escorted to the Lancaster Ballroom. The man gave them a quick and informative rundown of the services they could offer, then left Saffron and Nicole to discuss matters in private.

It was odd, being in the centre of this grand old room, no tables, no chairs, no people. As if its soul were missing. Nicole turned to ask Saffron something, but she was tapping away on her phone.

'It's Alex...' she said, 'asking where I am.' She shook her head. 'He's never been the clingy type. That's one of the reasons that I like him. So easy-going, so relaxed... If I didn't know any better I'd think he was being a little...'

'A little what?'

Saffron shrugged one shoulder. 'Well...jealous.' Then she broke into one of her wide, dazzling grins. 'Cute, huh? But it's making it very difficult to meet up with you or even research anything on my phone. He keeps asking who I'm texting when I'm browsing the websites you recommended.'

Nicole's stomach dived. Alex was jealous?

'Are you sure that's what it is?'

Saffron shrugged again. 'What else could it be?'

Nicole swallowed. Suddenly her mouth was very dry and her words felt like they were dragging on the edges of her throat before they made it out.

'He's been very protective recently,' Saffron added, nodding to herself. 'Especially with all the mess that's going on in the papers.' She glanced at Nicole. 'I expect you've seen it… Everybody has.'

Nicole wanted to say she hadn't, but she couldn't. She couldn't have avoided it if she'd wanted to. And she seemed to have developed a special kind of radar for spotting her client's image on the front of a magazine. The things that journalist had said hadn't been kind. Or true. Okay, Saffron was a little impulsive and immature, but she wasn't evil. As blasé as Saffron seemed about the whole thing, it had to have hurt, right?

She felt a sudden pang of sympathy for her client. And she suddenly understood why Alex had called his situation "complicated".

Saffron needed him. That was what he'd been trying to say, wasn't it? And, sap that she was, she liked him even more for doing that, for standing by Saffron. But it still wasn't going to wave a magic wand over Saffron's off-base proposal idea and guarantee a 'yes', would it?

What if he said no? It wouldn't just be bad news for her, for Hopes & Dreams. The tabloids would have a field day when it came out. It would just cause Saffron to be even more of a laughing stock than she already was, and that was something she didn't deserve. Just because she'd jumped into this proposal with both feet, it didn't mean that she wasn't being incredibly brave.

Nicole heaved in a breath. She needed to act on her client's best interests, and suddenly it was really clear what she needed to do. If she'd got the same vibes from another prospective fiancé, she'd have said something, and it wasn't as if she was going to tell Saffron to pull the plug, either, which made her feel less guilty, but there was something she could suggest that might help everyone involved.

She walked in a circle, taking in the powder-blue paintwork, the elaborate plaster moulding that covered the walls and ceiling, reminding her of a grand French palace. 'What with everything going on in the media at the moment, are you sure it's the right time to plan your proposal? We could always wait until the new year, you know... Maybe do something stupendous for Valentine's Day?'

Alex and Saffron clearly were on very different pages about their relationship. A little extra time might help things become clear to both of them.

Saffron shook her head. 'I've got Christmas lights in my mind when I think of this proposal and I can't seem to shake them. Valentine's would be all...well, wrong.'

Nicole nodded glumly. 'Really? Because we—'

'Really.' Saffron was wearing a most determined expression. Then she looked round the room. 'You know what? Even though this is fabulous, I think we should keep looking. I want somewhere with stairs... You can't make a great entrance without a good flight of stairs, can you?' She smiled her sparkly smile at Nicole.

'Okay, then,' Nicole said, looking down at the list she'd written in her book as they'd been talking. Her handwriting was appalling and she hadn't even managed to stay on the ruled lines. 'Stairs it is. In that case, what do you think about the Hamilton?'

# CHAPTER THIRTY

A s Nicole walked through Victoria Embankment Gardens towards the Tube station, her phone buzzed in her pocket. She pulled it out, but when she saw the message alert on the screen, she almost put it straight back.

Alex.

Was he trying to torture her?

Here she was, trying to remember all the very good reasons she should forget he even existed, and everywhere she went, everyone she spoke to, it was Alex, Alex, Alex...

Got a job 4 u if u want it?

Oh, flip.

Amidst all the other Alex-related problems going on, she'd completely forgotten about the fake job—and the cover story that wouldn't die.

She'd just exited the park and reached the entrance to Embankment Tube station. She stopped in the midst of the chequered ticket hall, about ten feet short of the barriers. Not sure, she texted back. Perhaps, if she was vague enough, he'd get tired of tapping in questions with his thumbs and give up. But when another message arrived, she had to admit it didn't look as if that approach was working.

Next Sat. Big wedding. Great for your article.

Someone bumped into her in their rush to get down the stairs and catch their Tube, but Nicole hardly felt it.

She typed another wishy-washy message. Not sure I can make it.

??? he texted back.

*Why?* she screamed inside her head. *You know why!* Or at least he knew one of the very good reasons why. She scowled at her phone and replied:

I've got a… She paused while she searched for the right word. …thing to go to.

Well, the right word hadn't come and that was the best she'd been able to do.

She waited for her phone to ding again, but it stayed silent. Had it worked? Had she finally put him off? She was starting to assume she had, when it started to ring. Peggy said she was going to call after the Savoy for an update on the Saffron situation. Nicole was so flustered she picked it up without thinking.

'Hi,' a voice on the other end of the line said. Deep and rich with a hint of gravel. Definitely not Peggy. She didn't know how, but she could hear him smiling.

'Hi' was all she could manage back. And why did her voice have to sound so soft and breathy? Couldn't she even maintain some much-needed professional distance from this man when he was miles away?

'I've been speaking to a contact of mine who caters big weddings,' he finally said. 'He's got a job for you, if you want it. Just the sort of thing that would be perfect for your article.'

'Alex... You don't have to do that.'

'Yes,' he said very firmly. 'I do. It's my fault you didn't get your in-depth look at wedding photography.'

Ah. He hadn't bought her pathetic excuse for pulling out of the rest of the weddings she was going to do with him. She didn't really blame him.

'The least I can do is make sure the rest of the articles go well,' he added.

She closed her eyes and told herself not to fight him. Arguing would only prolong the conversation.

When she didn't answer, he added, 'How's it coming along, by the way? I hope you haven't trashed my character too thoroughly.'

Now she couldn't just hear the smile; she could hear the dimple too. Which was just plain ridiculous. 'Erm... fine,' she replied, finding it hard to squeeze the air out of her lungs.

'Good,' he said. 'Well, it's a big society affair—around three hundred guests, silver service. If you want to really find out how waitressing is done at these things it's a perfect opportunity.'

It would be. If she was even writing a flipping article. But she couldn't tell Alex that. He'd want to know why she'd been lying, and that was something else she couldn't tell him. She rubbed the palm of her hand over her forehead as the commuters flowed round her. She didn't want to talk to him any more. Not that she didn't want to hear his voice, because she stupidly did, but because she was just so tired of the empty words she'd been spouting, all the lies.

'I'll see if I can rejig my schedule,' she replied wearily. And then she couldn't help feeling just a little bit warm inside. He'd gone to the trouble of setting this up for her. It was very sweet of him. 'Thank you,' she said, her voice softening.

'No problem.'

Such 'Alex' kind of words. On the surface so laid-back, so simple, but she heard the answering warmth in his tone. A warmth that said way more than the syllables ever could.

Their business was done. She should hang up now. Or he should. They both knew it, but neither of them did. Just hearing silence from him was better than hearing a thousand words from someone else.

She stared at her phone for a good thirty seconds and guessed Alex was doing the same. Then she took a deep breath. There was something she needed to know, even if she was going to phone his catering guy up and wriggle her way out of whatever he'd set up for her.

'Will you be there?' she asked. 'At this wedding?'

The silence continued, and then he said, 'Yes.'

Her heart flipped, despite the fact she wasn't going. Despite the fact that even if she was telling the truth about writing the article, she probably shouldn't. Nothing had changed. Alex and Saffron were still together. She should not be getting excited at the thought of him *possibly* wanting to see her.

She closed her eyes and shook her head as he answered. Once again, Alex had eaten through her defences like acid, and all she had left was as much truth as she could tell him. 'Is that why you're keen for me to do it?'

More silence.

She sighed. 'I thought we both said this…us…wasn't a good idea. Not now.'

His voice was low when he answered. 'I know.' There was another pause, but when he continued he sounded much more like his normal, nothing-gets-to-me self. 'But you know first-hand how busy I get at these things. Between me snapping away and you serving a zillion guests, we probably won't even catch a glimpse of each other, let alone have time to interact.'

She nodded, even though he couldn't see her.

'If that's the case, why are you so intent that I do this?'

She could almost imagine him running his hand through his shaggy dark hair as he thought about his answer. 'Because it sounded like this article was a big thing and, like I said, I don't want your career to suffer because of me. Especially when neither of us has done anything wrong.'

Nicole didn't know about that. Okay, she hadn't slept with him, hadn't even kissed him, but that dance at the steampunk wedding… The way they'd communicated just because their bodies had been close, even though they hadn't spoken a word, even though they'd hardly looked at each other. It felt as if a betrayal of *some* kind had taken place.

'Okay,' she told him. 'I won't let it ruin my career.' At least that was the truth. By not going, she was doing her career, and him, a huge great favour.

'You'll think about it?'

She let out a soft breath. 'Yes.' Another truth. She wouldn't stop thinking about it, but that didn't mean she was going to go.

It was time to rip the plaster off, end this painfully long

conversation that shouldn't have been, that should have been left to her voicemail. She waved her hand in the air. 'I should probably...'

'Yes,' he said. 'So should I.'

But as she was drawing the phone away from her face, ready to end the call, she heard him speak again and held it back to her ear. 'I ran into an old friend and his wife the other day. She works at *Beautiful Weddings* too. What was her name? Sharon? No... Shona, that's it. But when I mentioned your name, she said she'd never heard of you. That is where you said you worked, right?'

Nicole gulped. Never, ever was she going to say she was a journalist ever again when scoping out a potential target. 'I don't know if those were exactly my words,' she said, brain whirring away in search of an excuse. 'I'm...I'm a freelancer.' And then the rest of the explanation rolled easily off her tongue, tasting bitter as it went. 'There's an editor over at *Beautiful Weddings* who really liked my idea and we're trying to make it work.'

He didn't say anything, which was what she'd wanted a moment ago, but now it was making her nervous.

'Maybe I didn't make it clear when we met at your exhibition. I was a little...thrown...by seeing you again. It must have just come out wrong.'

'Me too,' he said. And he was smiling again. 'Thrown, that is...'

She let go of a breath she hadn't been aware she'd been holding.

'Nic...? I know this thing between us is complicated, but—'

'Alex?' she said loudly, saving them both the only way

she knew how. She couldn't let him finish that sentence. 'You're breaking up. What did you say?'

'I was saying that—'

She started walking, eyes fixed on the stairs down to the platforms. 'No. Still can't hear you. Listen, text me the details of this thing and I'll…'

She trailed off as she jogged down the steps, phone still clamped to her ear. When she got to the bottom she looked at the display. Only one bar of signal, and as she walked towards the barrier even that disappeared.

Thank goodness. She couldn't have had that conversation with him. But she also couldn't bear to tell him one more lie.

# CHAPTER THIRTY-ONE

Alex stared at the huge collection of bones. For some reason Saffron had decided that instead of a Sunday afternoon installed in a favourite cafe with a steady stream of lattes and pastries on tap, she wanted to come to the Natural History Museum. They stood in the grand entrance hall, studying the diplodocus skeleton that had silently guarded it for more than a century. Alex didn't know if you could tell much when the muscles and skin were gone, but if he had to guess, he reckoned that the dinosaur looked a little hacked off.

He turned to Saffron, who was studying the tail bones quite intently. He could tell she wanted to reach out and touch them, but wasn't sure if she should. Which was odd in itself, because Saffron usually just did whatever she felt like.

'My dad always promised he'd bring me here,' she said softly, 'but he travelled a lot. He was always so busy.' She turned to smile up at him. 'Can you believe I've lived within a mile of this place my whole life and I've never once been? Not even on a school trip.'

Alex just grunted. He wasn't really in the mood for chit-chat. He hadn't seen Saffron since Thursday lunchtime in Kensington High Street. She'd been doing some media thing on Friday, and he'd had another wedding yesterday. He knew he could have made the time to see her if he'd wanted to, but he'd been too angry. He was still angry, but there were things he needed to say to her, the kind of things a person needed to say face to face.

And he found he couldn't keep it all bottled up a moment longer. Not now she was standing beside him, acting as if she hadn't a care in the world, that everything was the same way it had always been between them.

'Where did you go for lunch on Thursday?' he blurted out, surprised by how deep and booming his voice sounded in the high, vaulted space.

Saffron froze for a second, but then continued her inspection of the diplodocus's tail. 'I told you. I went to see my father.'

She moved a little further down the chain of bones, so Alex followed. 'In St John's Wood?'

She sent him a cross glance. 'Yes.'

'At noon?'

She put her hands on her hips and turned to face him, scowling. 'Yes.' Then she gazed upstairs and set off at a trot. 'Come on. I've had enough of dusty old bones. It's the gems I want to see. That's why I wanted to come in the first place.'

Alex stared after her for a second, his jaw gradually growing more and more tense. Then he stuffed his fists in his pockets and followed her with long strides. Saffron, despite the ridiculous height of her shoes, managed to keep just in front of him until they reached the room with the precious-stones display.

'Look at the size of that emerald!' she exclaimed, pointing to a green rock the size of a baby's fist. 'I've never seen one so big. But I can never quite decide if I like emeralds or not. They're rather green, aren't they?'

Alex didn't have an answer for that.

Saffron moved on to the next case, which was full of sparkling clear stones. 'I think, despite the pretty colours, I'll always prefer diamonds,' she said, sighing. 'There's something so classic about them, don't you think?'

He didn't even have time to grunt his response before she turned and gave him a look that reminded him of his mother. 'Are you even listening to me?' she asked. 'You might need this information one day. You know, the kind of gems I like…'

Actually, Alex didn't give a hoot whether she thought emeralds should be pink with blue stripes and sapphires were only fit to use as kitty litter. He had more important things on his mind, things he wasn't going to let her flit away from again quite so easily.

'If you were meeting your father for lunch at twelve in St John's Wood, why did I see you forty-five minutes after that in Kensington High Street?'

Although Saffron still had her nose pressed against the glass of the display cabinet, and her back was to him, he saw her eyes widen and her mouth drop open in her reflection in the glass. She must have not realised he could see her, because he also watched her close her mouth again and set her jaw in a most determined way.

Her voice when she spoke, however, was neither hard

nor determined, but bright and breezy. 'You know me…
I'm always running late.'

She was getting better at it. Lying. The thought made
his stomach churn. On the rare occasions she did fib, she
usually just lost her temper if she got caught out.

He waited until she glanced up at him, even though she
was pretending to inspect the gems in the case and it was
a good minute before her curiosity got the better of her. He
needed to be in control of at least some part of this situation. 'I don't believe you,' he said flatly.

That was what he'd said to Vanessa when she'd had second thoughts a couple of months after she'd ditched him,
tried to convince him she wanted to give things another
go. He'd just come out with it. He found the blunt truth was
a great antidote to all the lies and fantasies she'd woven
around him.

He still saw her around town sometimes and wondered
how he could have been so wrong. When she'd been with
him, she'd said she liked the great outdoors, had developed
an interest in photography, had been sweet and warm and
open. Now, if he ran into her, it was like meeting a completely different person with her face. Hiking? Don't make
him laugh. The closest Vanessa probably ever got to hiking these days was running across the pavement from a
designer boutique to a cab when it rained.

She'd found herself the rich husband with the name in
the Domesday Book she'd always wanted, lived between a
London town house and a Georgian stately home in Wilt-
shire. The man was obviously more malleable than he had
been or more ready for a trophy wife who loved the things
he'd inherited more than she did him.

He had to give her credit for one thing, though. She'd obviously been completely committed, even going to the gym so she could keep up with him on the long treks across Dartmoor to photograph some of the rocky tors. Her deception had been total and complete. And if there was one thing he'd promised himself once he'd brushed himself down and picked himself off the floor, it was that he was never going to let another woman lie to him again.

Saffron was looking at him now, with those big blue eyes open and pleading. He didn't care. He'd been prepared to stand by her and support her through her family crisis, but not any more. If she had someone else on the side, let him do it. He felt no loyalty to her at all now.

'Who were you with?' he asked, his voice low and controlled, even though inside he felt anything but.

She shook her head. Her phone must have gone off, because she reached into her pocket and pulled it out, checked the message then looked back up at him. 'It's none of your business.'

Without thinking, he snatched the phone from her hand. Not very gallant, he knew.

He checked the message alert that was still visible on her lock screen. '"Meet up on Monday. N",' he read out. 'Who's "N"?'

Saffron grabbed her phone back. 'I told you,' she said, her brows pinching together. 'None of your business.'

He recognised that look. She hadn't been able to keep cool, calm and collected up for very long. She might be getting better at lying, but she was still a novice. This was the face she pulled when her father asked her to do something she didn't want to do, a sulky, childish pout. That didn't mean it wasn't effective. He knew she'd dig her heels in until she got what she wanted—and despite her daddy's reputation for being a ball breaker when it came to his multinational media empire, she always did.

He turned away and walked a few steps, running his hand through his hair. Suddenly, he just couldn't be bothered any more.

'Fine. If that's the way you want to play it, then you've got your wish,' he told her. 'We've had fun, Saffron, but I can't do this any more, not if you're going to lie to me—'

'No!' A distressed squeak escaped her lips. She hadn't expected him to take that tack. Not many people stood their ground with her.

'Then be a grown-up and take responsibility for your actions,' he continued, discovering he had quite a lot to say now he'd got going. He shook his head. 'Whatever you say, you're not ready for a long-term relationship. You don't care about anyone but yourself, not really. You float around in your Saffron bubble, thinking you can do whatever you want, use people however you want, and I've got news for you—I'm the man with the big sharp pin, and I'm getting out.'

Now she really did look like a child. Her bottom lip quivered and her eyes filled with tears. She stepped forward, whispered 'no' again…

On another day he might have taken pity and pulled her into his arms, but not today. He folded his arms and stepped back when she moved towards him.

'Don't say that!' Her voice was thick with tears. 'I am ready. I am. I've got it in me to go the distance, and I'm going to prove it to you! To everyone!'

She looked so passionate, so fierce, he almost believed her.

'Relationships are based on trust,' he said. 'What can I trust you to do, Saffron? Turn up late? Forget the important events in my life? Sure, I can trust you to deliver those things on a regular basis...'

Her eyes widened, as if she'd never even considered her actions could be seen as insensitive. Alex almost laughed. She'd just proved his point very nicely. He found it fuelled his anger enough to keep going.

He shook his head. 'But I can't trust you in the things that count. And you know what that means—'

'No!' Saffron rushed towards him and flung herself at him, latching her arms around him like a baby octopus. 'Don't say it!'

He didn't want to be rough with her, so he peeled one arm off at a time. It didn't do him much good. As soon as he went to work on the second arm, she grabbed hold of him again with the first one. After a couple of frustrated attempts he stopped. People were looking, and this was getting them nowhere.

He looked down at Saffron. Her eyes were red and puffy, her nose was starting to drip and she looked totally and utterly miserable. Something inside his chest squeezed. He couldn't make his mind up whether she truly was devastated by the prospect of what he hadn't actually managed to say yet or whether this was just another part of the charade. His gut told him the former, but his gut had been wrong before.

Whichever it was, he found he wasn't as steaming angry as he'd been minutes earlier. What was it about women's tears? They were as effective as acid when it came to eroding a guy's resolve.

She swallowed and looked him in the eye. 'I know what you're thinking, Alex, but it isn't true. I'm not seeing anyone else.'

She might have her arms round him, squeezing herself to him, but he felt as stiff as a wooden pole. 'Then who is this "N" person?'

She shook her head. 'I can't tell you.'

He began to pull away.

'But I have a good reason for not telling you, I promise,' she said, begging him to look her in the eye, to see the truth of her words in her face. Maybe he was a big sucker, but he saw it there in her eyes. 'Just give me another chance, a week or two, and I'll be able to tell you everything!'

He started to shake his head, but then the tears started to flow thick and fast. She released her grip and started to sob into her hands. 'P-please,' she said, hiccuping slightly. 'I need you...'

Alex had been witness to more than a few tearful outbursts from Saffron, but usually these were a mixture of sulk and show, designed—albeit subconsciously sometimes—to get what she wanted. The hanky she often dabbed to the corners of her eyes rarely suffered more than a molecule or two of moisture. He'd never seen her like this before. Had never seen her cry so hard the snot came out her nose and her face went all pink and crumpled.

Something inside him snapped and he stepped forward and put his arms around her. He might be going crazy, but he was starting to believe her.

Eventually, she stopped sobbing and looked up at him,

her eyes hopeful. He didn't know what to tell her, so he didn't say anything. She stood on her tiptoes, pressed a soft kiss to his lips and linked her arm through his.

He let her pull him along as they both stared silently at the sparkling stones inside the cases, using the time to gather themselves back together after the emotional outburst. Alex saw colours and light, but he didn't make sense of much else.

There was one thing that was really clear to him, though, especially now he'd got some distance from losing his temper and could analyse the scene for what it had really been. It was like taking a snapshot of something in the moment, never really sure how it would turn out, then being able to study it later, to see which bits were light and dark, see what was in focus and what was fuzzy.

He'd been angry with Saffron, yes, when he'd been on the verge of finishing with her, but he realised now that it hadn't been the overriding emotion. When he'd thought Saffron was cheating on him, that he'd had the escape route he needed, all he'd felt was a wonderful sense of relief.

# CHAPTER THIRTY-TWO

Mia took her glasses off and relaxed back into the office chair. Nicole, who'd been sitting at Peggy's desk while Mia went over the accounts on her computer, leaned forward. 'How does it look? Have I missed anything?'

Mia shook her head. 'No. For someone who's never had any bookkeeping training, you're doing a solid job.'

Nicole slumped back into Peggy's chair and stared at the fluffy pink pens in Peggy's pen pot. 'I was hoping I was wrong, that the future of Hopes & Dreams didn't hang quite so squarely on Saffron's proposal.'

Mia gave a weary shrug. 'Sorry. Saffron's job gives you a much-needed cash injection, but that's only going to last a few months. You're right that you need this proposal to go well so you can attract more of the same kind of business. What you really need is a big advertising push.'

Nicole's shoulders sagged. 'I just haven't got the money for that.'

'Well, here's your solution,' Mia said. 'If the recession means that the ordinary Joes are mostly paying for ideas packages and not for the full-on service, then you're going to have to go after clients who do have that kind of disposable income. Saffron's proposal going well is the best kind of promotion you could have. I don't doubt the story would hit all the gossip mags.'

Nicole nodded. She'd seen herself how Saffron, if she wanted to work with a magazine, could find ways to make a story run for weeks. 'Wait there,' she told Mia and nipped to the kitchenette. She returned with a bottle of wine she'd pulled from the tiny fridge and two clean mugs. 'Emergency supplies,' she said as she put the bottle down on the desk. She poured each of them a generous helping and glugged a few mouthfuls down immediately.

'Well, that's it. My life is officially going down the toilet.'

'No,' Mia countered, ever the voice of reason. 'Your business has hit a rocky patch, that's all. The rest of your life is fine.'

Nicole raised her eyebrows. 'You don't know the half of it.'

Mia just gave her a steady, unflinching look that said, *Then why don't you tell me?*

Nicole exhaled and shook her head. Where did she start?

'I just got off the phone before you came in, but I thought I'd let you check the figures before I dropped the bombshell.'

'Uh-oh,' Mia said, but she was still calm and unemotional. Suddenly Nicole was glad that Peggy was off doing some last-minute freelance design job for a big cosmetics company. Her old office mates had roped her in, needing an extra body, and they were planning on pulling an all-nighter to get a series of photos retouched. While Peggy was a fabulous cheerleader and all-round supporter, she did tend to get a bit dramatic, and what Nicole needed now was someone who could help her keep on an even keel, not wind her up then let her loose like a crazed mechanical toy. She'd made enough gaffes during this job already.

She kept her voice steady and even as she regaled Mia with her tale. 'You know Alex got me that catering job?'

'Mm-hmm...'

'Well, I'd been calling Brian, the caterer, fairly regularly to cancel, but all I'd been getting was his voicemail. Since there's no real magazine article, there's no reason for me to do the job, but I still wanted to call and back out nicely. I didn't want Alex to look bad because of me.'

Mia picked up her mug and took a sip of wine. 'That makes sense.'

Nicole got up and paced to the other side of the room, then turned to look back at her friend. 'Well, today I finally managed to talk to him.'

Mia brightened. 'That's good, isn't it?'

'You'd think. But when I finished saying my piece the guy went ballistic. It seems Alex pulled some pretty big strings to get me this gig.'

Gig.

Listen to her. She was even starting to sound like him.

'It turns out that "Brian the catering guy" is actually Brian Roscoff.'

Mia's eyes popped. 'The Michelin-starred chef? The one who's just taken over running the restaurant at the Wardesley Hotel?'

Nicole nodded. 'Boy, that man has an extensive vocabulary. I'm surprised my phone handset didn't turn blue!

And once he'd finished ranting in general, he moved on to screaming about Alex, saying he'll blacken Alex's name on the London wedding circuit if this "favour" meant he was even one waitress short tomorrow.'

'I have a horrible feeling I know where this is going,' Mia said.

Nicole walked over to the purple sofa and dropped down onto it almost as dramatically as Peggy would have done. 'Alex was just trying to help me out...'

Mia came over, mug in hand, and sat next to her. 'It's not really your responsibility.'

Nicole sighed. 'I know. But Alex only lined it up because I lied to him. I feel really bad about letting him deal with the fallout of my bad judgement.'

'I know. While I said it wasn't your responsibility, I also knew there was no way in hell you would do that to him— to anyone. You're just not that selfish.' Mia paused for a moment. 'So what are you going to do?'

Nicole let out a weary little laugh. 'I don't suppose you're doing anything tomorrow afternoon, are you?'

Mia shook her head. 'I'd do it, you know that, but Jonathan and I are supposed to be going down to Elmhurst Hall to check it out as a wedding venue. After all you told us about the place, I just had to see it for myself, but if we don't book it this weekend we'll lose the date we want, and it's been hard enough finding one when Jon's parents are in the country as it is.'

'It's okay. I wasn't really serious.' She went over and fetched her mug of wine, finished it off. 'But that's not the worst of it. Once Chef Roscoff mentioned the date and the location, all the pieces fell into place. You know whose wedding it is, don't you?'

Mia stretched her legs out. 'Society wedding? It's not Selena Marchant and the earl of something, is it? The glossy celebrity magazines have been abuzz with that for months.'

If only.

'Nope. Worse than that. It's as if the universe has decided to play one humungous joke on me at the moment.' She turned to look mournfully at Mia. 'It's—'

At the same moment, a flash of revelation hit Mia's eyes. 'You don't mean…?'

Nicole nodded. 'Yup. It's Jasper's wedding. Of all the lousy five-star hotels in the world…'

'It never rains but it pours,' Mia whispered quietly.

Nicole was all out of platitudes. She decided to put it a little more pithily. 'In other words, I'm screwed.'

Mia sat up. 'Forget Elmhurst Hall,' she said, looking quite fierce. 'I'll do it for you. There are plenty other lovely places to get married.'

Nicole shook her head. 'No. Thanks, but no. This is my mess and I'm just going to have to deal with it.' She couldn't let Mia do that. One of the reasons she'd waxed so lyrical about Elmhurst was because she'd thought it was perfect for Mia and Jonathan. She already had one doomed proposal on her conscience; she didn't need to add a wedding to that list as well.

Mia looked seriously into her mug. 'Maybe this is a good thing.'

Nicole was too tired to laugh, otherwise she might have

howled until the tears rolled down her face. 'How do you reckon that?'

Mia put her mug on the floor and turned to face Nicole. 'It's been more than five years since you split with Jasper. You really should have found someone else by now, but there's been no one. No one really serious, anyway.'

'I've been busy,' Nicole said. 'Hatching the idea for my own business while working full-time for Elite Gatherings wasn't easy. I took all the extra hours I could to pad my start-up fund. And since launching Hopes & Dreams, I just haven't had the time or the energy.'

'I know,' Mia said patiently. 'But sometimes I get the feeling that your hectic schedule, the pace at which you live your life, isn't a reason but an excuse.'

Nicole frowned. 'What do you mean?'

'I mean I think you keep yourself deliberately busy so you don't have time for romance. I mean that the ghost of Jasper is haunting you still. And that's why I think this wedding might have a silver lining. You can go, see him again, put that ghost to rest, as well as paying Alex back for his kindness.'

Nicole's stomach churned at the thought. 'Get some closure, you mean?'

'Yes.'

'Can't I just sleep with a rugby team and get a tattoo?' she asked a little desperately.

Mia shook her head then took another measured sip of her wine. 'If that would have worked for you, I think you would have done it already.'

Nicole huffed. Now she wished Peggy was here instead. Why did Mia have to make so much sense? 'So, basically, you're saying I've got to endure a whole day in the company of the two men who have ballsed up my life the most, and I've got to get sore feet and aching legs doing it.'

'That's pretty much it.'

Nicole stood up and marched over to the desk, where the wine bottle was dripping condensation on her block of Post-it notes. 'In that case, I think we're going to need another one of these.'

# CHAPTER THIRTY-THREE

Nicole pulled down the white blouse of her waitress uniform. It just wouldn't sit right, confirming that her life was slowly becoming a nightmare that would never end. She gave it one last tug and headed off to where the other waitressing staff was waiting for a briefing.

Unfortunately, Mia had been right about her. What else could she have done but turn up at the wedding? She couldn't get Alex into hot water just because he'd been trying to help her out. She sighed. Unfortunately, all Alex's efforts to 'help' in the last few weeks had done was make her life even more complicated.

And then there was the fact that this was her ex's wedding and that the bride, Penelope, was clearly worth walking down the aisle with, whereas Nicole hadn't come up to scratch. Lovely.

It was going to be a bit awkward if she and Jasper came face to face. However, she was counting on the fact that just wouldn't happen. She was the lowest of the lowly servers and wouldn't get within fifty feet of the top table. That much had been made clear to her already. Thankfully, the scale of this wedding meant that she'd be able to lose herself amidst the hundreds of bodies.

One thing she'd also realised when she'd woken at five that morning, eyes wide open, heart pounding, was that she might know some of the guests. Jasper's sister, Helena, had been a good enough friend for her to keep in touch with after school, although communication had dwindled to the occasional comment on each other's Facebook posts after Nicole had split with her brother. Thankfully, Helena was four years younger than Jasper and since Hurstdean had only taken girls he'd gone to an equally exclusive boys' school. Brother and sister shouldn't have too many old friends in common.

And if they did? Well, Nicole was counting on the fact that after so many years, she'd just be a vaguely familiar face out of context, that she'd remain as anonymous as the rest of the army of servers who'd be working there that day. All she had to do was keep her head down, do her job quietly and efficiently and everything would be fine.

She stifled a yawn as she listened to the head waiter's instructions. She'd had to be here at seven for a lengthy training session, which she hadn't dared fail. Thank goodness she'd done plenty of waitressing in her university days to help pay the bills. It wasn't quite the same as the silver service they used at the Wardesley, but at least she knew the basics already and the rest had come fairly quickly.

After the talk they were assigned to their jobs. Nicole was fairly relieved to discover she wasn't going to be required to carry plates. First, she was going to stand with trays of champagne to offer to arriving guests, and then she'd be responsible for filling up water jugs and making sure the tables had enough butter and things like that.

When she was given her tray, she went to stand on duty in the reception area where the guests would be gathering before luncheon was called. She checked the clock on the wall. One-thirty. The service had ended more than half an hour ago, according to the timetable the staff had been given. Some of the wedding guests—the thirstier ones who didn't want to stand around in the cold throwing confetti, she guessed—started to trail in.

She managed to bag herself a spot away from the entrance, so she wouldn't be the first person people saw when they walked into the room, but made sure she had a good view of the doors. Not only because her heart was thudding slightly at the thought of seeing Jasper with the woman who'd outclassed her, but also to see if there were any other guests she needed to avoid.

The doors swooshed open and a group of women entered. Nicole closed her eyes and sent a thought heavenwards. *You're having a joke, aren't you?* she mentally whispered. *Minty and Celeste? Really?*

What she wouldn't have given for a long fringe. She angled her face away from them while still keeping them in her sights. She should have known this wasn't going to be that easy. Okay, she'd spotted them tucked away somewhere in Helena's long list of Facebook friends, but she hadn't realised they'd been close. Either that or the divine Penelope knew them.

Uh. It didn't really matter, did it? They were here and she was going to have to deal with it.

Thankfully, with a couple of hundred guests to lose herself in, it turned out to be not as hard as she'd anticipated. When Celeste and Minty, who always seemed to travel as a pair, looked as if they were heading her way, Nicole just turned and altered her trajectory, smiled at a group of guests on the other side of the room and offered them a champagne cocktail.

She'd just performed a particularly effective manoeuvre, when she became aware of a commotion outside, lots of cheering and whistling. The bride and groom must have arrived. The noise got louder. Nicole's heart went into overdrive. This was it. The moment she'd been dreading. The moment Mia had said she needed to endure in order to find some closure. That didn't mean she'd been looking forward to it. She pressed herself back against the wall, tray in hand, and slapped on her best professional smile. No one needed to know she was shaking inside.

But then she heard a noise that made the hairs on the back of her neck stand up on end.

The whirr of a camera shutter.

How she detected it above the hum of conversation, she'd never know, but her hungry eyes found him instantly, shooting the guests at the entrance to the reception room. Her heart felt as if it had heaved to a stop, just for a few seconds, before starting up again at double the speed.

Moments later, Jasper and his new bride appeared in the doorway and swept past the guests and into the ballroom in a cloud of joy and trailing confetti. Nicole hardly noticed them. She was too busy looking at Alex, drinking him in. It was at that moment she realised the nerves that had been skittering up her spine all day had nothing to do with seeing her ex get married and everything to do with a consummate charmer who hid his artist's soul deep away inside.

He didn't see her at first, too busy chatting with a group of women in hats, before taking their photograph, but then he turned his head. Their eyes met for just a split second, but she felt as if a crossbow bolt had shot through her, impaling her to the pillar she was pressing herself against.

Oh, she was a sick little puppy. While most of her had been frustrated at not being able to wangle her way out of a twelve-hour day on her feet handing other people drinks, a tiny part of her had been pleased. A tiny, masochistic part she hadn't realised existed. She'd felt as if there'd been an inevitability about ending up here today. Something she just hadn't wanted to fight, if she were honest with herself, even before that conversation with Mia. How could she have denied herself one last chance to see him before Saffron proposed?

It was only a week away now. Everything was booked, even a top-notch venue. Saffron's credit card had opened doors that would have been firmly closed to normal mortals. Guests had been invited. It was real now. And the closer she got to the twentieth, the sicker Nicole felt. That was all wrong. She should want it to happen. It was her job to *make* it happen, after all.

And he was all wrong for her. It was as if he had some destructive force field around him, so every time she got near she turned into someone else, someone she thought she'd forgotten who to be.

A psychologist would have a field day with her, probably suggesting she only wanted him because he was Saffron's, because Saffron represented "those girls", and this was her chance to finally come out on top.

She blamed the whole thing on Molly Ringwald. Without that Cinderella scene in the car park with Andrew McCarthy, she'd never have been holding out for her own *Pretty in Pink* moment all these years.

*But you liked him before he ever met Saffron. What about that?*

She ignored that thought and turned and smiled brightly at another group of mingling guests, thrusting the tray of champagne glasses into their midst. Instead of taking any, they all looked at her, puzzled. It was only when Nicole took a good look at her tray she realised why. Somewhere along the way, all the full glasses had been taken, and she'd offered them four empty glasses and a half-drunk one with a napkin stuffed into it.

See? Even thinking about Alex had her messing up and doing stupid things, a pattern that had emerged from the very first moment she'd laid eyes on him.

But the empty tray wasn't all bad. At least it gave her an excuse to leave the room, to get away from him for a few moments and gather herself together.

She needed to do this. To prove to herself and the rest of the world that she could cope with being around him without falling apart. Otherwise, come the night of the party, when Saffron was all dressed up and on bended knee in front of him, she was going to fall to pieces.

With a fortifying breath, Nicole straightened her spine and headed for the kitchen.

# CHAPTER THIRTY-FOUR

Nicole was stationed at the back of the large rectangular ballroom, as far away from the top table as she could possibly get, a tray of champagne flutes balanced on her hand. The main course had been both eaten and cleared and other waiters and waitresses were similarly poised around the room, waiting for the signal to start placing a glass in front of each of the two hundred and ninety-six guests.

She looked across the ballroom to the bride and groom, deep in conversation with each other. It was weird, seeing Jasper after all this time. Like a dream. As if he was a person who resembled someone she'd known well once but wasn't actually him.

They looked happy, he and his new bride. Penelope was petite and blonde, pretty and elegant. They were perfect together. If she hadn't had a personal connection to him, she'd have applauded him for his choice. Maybe she did anyway, because standing here looking at him, she could finally remember the good times, the way he'd boosted her confidence and made her feel special, but she didn't ache for him the way she once had. No, he'd passed that privilege on to someone else.

She slipped her aching foot from her court shoe and carefully rubbed it against her other leg just as the signal came to start serving the champagne. She quickly slid her toes back into her shoe and made her way to the first of her allotted tables.

She'd thought the team had been huge when she'd first arrived, but now they were all separated and dotted around the vast ballroom, she realised how badly they were outnumbered and just how much energy was required if she was going to do her bit. And it didn't help that the sheer hard graft wasn't the only thing sapping her energy this evening. Just the effort of *not* sneaking constant glances at Alex, filtering out his voice through the clink of cutlery and glasses, was draining her last reserves.

As she reached the final table in her section she got a shock. Celeste was right there. That wasn't where she'd been for the first part of the reception!

It didn't take long to work out she had eyes for the floppy-haired blond on that table and had ousted the rightful occupant of her current chair just before dessert. Nicole spotted the other woman sitting next to Minty over on table fifteen with her arms folded, sending Celeste daggers and refusing to eat her white-chocolate-and-lavender profiteroles in protest.

Still, no one had even glanced Nicole's way all day while she'd been serving. It was almost as if she'd been invisible. And if she just did her job well, Celeste would probably never even realise she'd been there.

Four glasses to go… Three… Two…

She leaned in and placed a flute in front of her rival, dipping in silently to the right, the way she'd been taught. Celeste glanced up slightly at the sight of the champagne coming her way, but her gaze only made it as far as Nicole's hand. Like the rest, she didn't bother looking at her face.

Nicole controlled the urge to exhale long and hard and saved it for the moment when she'd strode quickly from the ballroom and leaned back against the wall. Unfortunately, she hadn't noticed the tray of empty glasses on a nearby table and she toppled one or two as she put out her hand to steady herself.

They dived towards the carpet in a graceful arc, but the thickness of the pile saved them from shattering. Nicole quickly bent to scoop them up and felt a rush of warm air as the double doors that led to the ballroom opened.

'Nicole?'

Oh, no. She recognised that voice.

Of course she did. True to form, this day just kept getting better and better. Slowly, she rose and turned to face Celeste Delacourt, who was smiling sweetly back at her.

'It *is* you!' she said. That smile was about as genuine as an alligator's. She looked Nicole up and down, taking in her plain black skirt and her badly fitting blouse, and her mouth widened just a fraction. 'I didn't realise things were so sticky at Hopes & Wishes that you were having to do a bit of moonlighting to make ends meet. That's too bad.'

Nicole corrected her through clenched teeth. 'It's Hopes & Dreams.'

Oh, and look now. Where Tweedle Dum was, Tweedle Dee was sure to follow. Minty slid through the heavy doors that led to the ballroom and stopped in her tracks.

'I didn't know you knew Penelope,' she said to Nicole. 'Or that you'd been invited. Great wedding, isn't it?'

Nicole wasn't fooled for a second. Minty knew she wasn't a guest. Nicole stared back at her, daring her to say something else.

Minty took in her stony expression and let out a musical little giggle, pretending she'd just realised her mistake. 'Sorry, darling,' she drawled. 'Too much champers... Should have realised.'

Nicole just picked up the tray of empties and prepared to take them back to the kitchen.

'No,' Celeste said in a cloying tone, 'it's not Penelope she knows...it's Jasper. Helena told us all about it.' She narrowed her eyes. 'Didn't you have a fling with him once?'

'Actually, we went out for two years.'

Celeste shrugged the information off as unimportant.

However, it seemed that Minty wasn't finished with her yet. Nicole was quickly realising that she was the more vicious of the two. 'Well, it's quality that counts, not quantity,' she said. She glanced at the doors to the ballroom. 'Didn't he start going out with Penelope not long after he dumped you? They're so good together...a perfect fit.'

She must have seen a flicker of emotion in Nicole's eyes, because she stepped in closer, went in for the kill. 'Helena said you got quite hysterical about it, went all stalker on him.'

Nicole said nothing. Yes, she had been heartbroken when Jasper had finished it. She'd loved him, for goodness' sake! Jasper hadn't been very forthcoming with explanations at first, probably too ashamed of his own snobbishness. A couple of phone calls to try to work out what the heck had gone wrong between them hardly constituted psychotic behaviour!

But it wouldn't do her any good to tell these two any of that. They'd made up their minds about her from the first day they'd met her, hadn't they? She'd been labelled *inferior* and *worthless* because she Wasn't Like Them.

Celeste came to stand next to Minty. 'Didn't you go to Hurstdean with Helena?'

She took in Nicole's uniform again. The blouse had continued to misbehave and was now riding up on one side.

'Ten years on and you're reduced to waitressing? God, what a waste of a good education.'

'Well,' Minty drawled, joining in the fun. 'It goes to show that you can take the girl out of the council estate, but you can't take the council estate out of the girl.'

Nicole knew that the words were designed to hurt, that she should just laugh them off, but that didn't stop the stinging sensation deep down in her stomach. It didn't stop humiliation flooding her face, warm and red. What had she ever done to these two?

She looked at the carpet, cross with herself that tears were prickling in the corners of her eyes, that her nose was burning. She'd come too far to let them reduce her to this state. The new Nicole she'd become was supposed to shield her from feeling like this, but after all these years, all the changes she'd made, it hadn't worked.

That was when her anger changed course, when it stopped eating inwards and started radiating out through her pores. It grew and grew, until the urge to whack the pair of them upside the head with the reassuringly heavy metal tray became almost irresistible.

But Nicole wasn't as stupid as they were callous. She placed the tray back down on the table—just in case the daft side of her that kept hijacking her life decided to put in another appearance—and pulled herself up to her full height.

'I have nothing to be ashamed of,' she told them. 'Even if I was a waitress full-time, there's nothing wrong in that. Maybe some of us don't have the luxury of starting life at the top of the heap, but that doesn't mean we can't work our way up there.'

They were looking back at her, too stunned to say anything, so she just kept going. 'I'm proud of where I come from, proud of my family, who've worked so hard to give me opportunities they never had. So my dad hasn't showered me in diamonds from birth, but he's taught me about love and respect, the value of an honest day's work. Those things are far more precious. But if you haven't got that by now, you probably never will, and because of that I refuse to be intimidated by you. In fact, I feel sorry for you.'

Celeste's mouth flapped and Minty looked as if she were about to have a stroke.

Nicole picked up the tray. 'Nice to see you again, girls,' she said, looking at them each in turn. And it had been. She felt as if a chapter of her life had slammed shut. 'You'll have to excuse me now. I need to get back to work.'

With that she turned and strode away, leaving them staring after her.

'This isn't over!' Celeste called after her, finally finding her voice.

'It is for me,' she yelled back. Not a single glass on her tray wobbled as she made her exit.

# CHAPTER THIRTY-FIVE

She was standing on the terrace overlooking the Thames, the only soul daring enough to brave the sharp December winds, especially now the slash of pale blue low on the horizon was the only hint the sun had graced this day with its presence. Alex slipped through the door and let it close behind him. Nicole flinched, indicating she'd heard it, but didn't turn round.

'What now?' she asked, staring out over the river. 'You've come back to make fun of my voice? Where my parents live? The fact I take the Tube rather than being carted around in a litter by serfs?'

Alex stepped forward. 'I don't want to make fun of you.'

She spun around. 'Oh, it's you.'

While she'd been facing the other way, her voice had sounded strong, defiant, but now he could see silvery streaks down her face. It made him feel as if he'd been kicked in the chest by a horse. 'Don't cry.' He walked over to her, brushed away the wet trail on one of her cheeks with his thumb. 'Who did you think I was?'

She shook her head and backed away. He couldn't tell if

it was because she didn't want to talk or because she didn't want to be near him.

'Just stupid girls I used to work with. They're guests here at the wedding. For some reason they've always had it in for me and I've never understood why.'

Alex glanced back towards the hotel. He knew there had been hundreds of people there that day, but it didn't stop him trying to picture whom Nicole had had her run-in with. 'They're probably jealous.'

She turned away again and leaned on the stone balustrade that circled the small terrace, let out a dry little bark of a laugh. 'I don't think so.'

Alex just looked at her. 'I do. You've got drive. You've got intelligence. You've got heart. Why wouldn't they be?'

She shook her head, rejecting his explanation. 'It doesn't matter why. Either way I'm stupid to let them get to me, even a little bit. Especially as I gave as good as I got. I suppose it's just that after the adrenalin high, you get the crash...'

A shiver rippled from the top of her spine downwards and, still leaning her elbows on the stone railing, she hugged herself. Alex knew what he did next was cheesy and old-fashioned, but he just couldn't stop himself. He slid his jacket off and draped it loosely around her shoulders before stepping back out of her personal space.

He needed to talk to her. Properly. And he got the feeling she was a bit skittish this evening. He didn't want to scare her off before he got a chance to say what he needed to say.

'I've been looking for you,' he said, joining her at the balustrade, staring out over the Thames with her.

She shook her head again, still refusing to look at him. 'You shouldn't have.'

Maybe. They were both supposed to be working. But the speeches had been done; the cake had been cut. He had a bit of time before he needed to get going again. But before he launched into what he'd come here to say, he needed to know if she was all right. 'People like that... You can't pay attention to them.'

She sighed. 'I didn't think I had, but the more I look back, the more I realise that's all I've ever done. And that's why I hate doing this—' she took another angry swipe at her eyes '—not because they got in a few well-timed digs, but because I've wasted so much time and energy on something that didn't matter.'

He wanted to touch her, but he put his hands in his trouser pockets to stop himself. He had the feeling that it wasn't the right moment.

She shook her head again and began to laugh. 'I'm so stupid. My whole life has been an exercise in proving them wrong, proving that I *am* good enough, no matter what they say.'

His control snapped a little. He moved closer, into her personal space now, so close he was almost touching. He could feel the warmth of her body, the heat carried the couple of millimetres between them. 'Of course you are,' he said softly.

Fresh tears began to roll down her cheeks and she stood up and hugged herself harder. She sniffed. 'I always thought I knew that, but now I'm not so sure I ever really believed it.'

To hell with waiting. He closed the tiny gap left between

them by folding his arms around her and pulling her close. She clutched on to his shirt and buried her face against his shoulder. He closed his eyes and just breathed her in. It felt as if he'd been waiting for this moment for years, when really it had only been a couple of weeks.

'Why wouldn't you believe it?' he asked, his voice incredulous. Didn't she know how amazing she was? Didn't she know how clever and determined and funny? He couldn't look at anyone else when she was in the room, couldn't even think of anyone else.

She tipped her head up to look at him. 'I don't know. I just know that I didn't.'

He stared down at her. For so long she'd puzzled him, one moment being one thing, the next something entirely different, but now he felt as if he was seeing her fully for the first time. There were no secrets in her eyes, no barriers. He'd been wondering who the real Nicole was. Well, here she was, clear and unobscured. He knew that with the same inner certainty as he did when he got a perfect shot of a landscape, found just the right angle and light to bring its essence alive.

And what he saw in Nicole was just as wonderful as getting that perfect shot. It made him feel alive in a way he just couldn't describe. He dipped his head, touched his lips against hers. They were cold at first, but promised such warmth. For a second she let him, strained towards him just the barest amount, but then she shook her head and looked away. 'We can't, Alex. What about Saffron?'

He moved his hands from her back to twist her head gently back to face him, so she was looking him in the eye. 'There is no Saffron. Not when I'm with you.'

'Pretty words, but I'm not going to—'

'Nic,' he whispered, and she stopped talking, closed her eyes and absorbed the soft sound of his voice as if it had been a blow.

'What?' she said back, her lids still closed.

He waited for her to open them again, and when she did he couldn't help smiling. It started somewhere deep down inside and spread up through him and then onto the outside, stretching his mouth wide and making him feel as if he were fizzing.

'They're not just pretty words. There is no Saffron, not for me…'

She frowned and opened her mouth, but he cut her off before she could say anything.

'Because I broke up with her a few days ago.'

# CHAPTER THIRTY-SIX

'B-but…but…' That was all Nicole could manage. Nothing more intelligible came out of her mouth.

Alex was smiling at her. She wanted to close her eyes, sink into whatever fantasy this was and never come out again. Unfortunately, she didn't have that luxury. Had he *really* just said what she thought he'd said? It certainly would explain why Saffron hadn't returned any of her calls in the last few days.

'You did what?' she finally managed to croak.

And then she went cold all over.

Had she been the one to mention Saffron's name? She wasn't sure. She hoped Alex didn't notice if she had. As far as she could recall, he'd always been discreet, had never actually revealed his girlfriend's identity to her.

Alex released her head and moved his hands to her shoulders, then slid them down to her elbows, before pulling her closer.

Alex had dumped Saffron?

She shook her head, unable to really process the full

implications of that information. What did that mean? For her, but also for Hopes & Dreams?

'We had a long chat on Sunday, and she almost convinced me to give her a second chance, but I just couldn't do it. In the end I had to come clean. I told her I was breaking it off.' He looked for her reaction and frowned. 'I thought you'd be more pleased.'

'I am,' she said.

She was. Or at least she thought she was. This was a good thing, right? She'd been trying to hint to Saffron that maybe Alex wasn't ready for the big declaration of love. She'd be spared that humiliation now. That had to be good news.

*And you get to steal Alex away all for yourself.*

No. She wasn't stealing. You couldn't steal something that didn't belong to someone else.

Then why was the joy she should be feeling marred with great, dirty smudges of guilt? She closed her eyes and rubbed her forehead with one hand, before opening them again and looking at Alex. That darned dimple was working overtime as he watched one emotion then the next flow undisguised over her features. For some reason he seemed to be enjoying every one of them.

She cleared her throat. 'I thought you said it was complicated.'

'It was. But I found a way to make it simple.'

'How...? Why?'

His smile slid a little. 'It wasn't easy, but I came to the decision I'd be hurting us both to live a lie. I couldn't have gone on seeing her feeling the way I feel about you. Until I met you I thought I was happy. I thought what Saffron and I had was okay… She was my safety net.' He frowned, looked very serious. 'I don't want a safety net any more. That's not what life is about.'

Nicole swallowed the lump that had appeared in her throat. She wasn't so sure everything was as simple as Alex made it sound.

'Nic?'

'Yes?' she replied on a whisper.

'You're overthinking everything again.'

'Am I?'

Was she? Did she do that?

He leaned forward. 'Yes.' His voice was low and rumbly in her ear, sending tiny shock waves out from that point, raising the hairs on the back of her neck.

Maybe he was right. She let out a great, heaving breath. She'd tied herself up in knots all these years with her warped thinking about Minty and Celeste and all those kind of girls. Maybe life wasn't supposed to be as hard as she made it for herself. Maybe it could all work out if she didn't plan everything to death, if she just went with the flow the way Alex did.

Maybe good things happened anyway sometimes. She certainly hadn't planned for Alex, yet the way he was pressing his lips to her neck at that moment was really rather nice.

But lips and neck weren't enough, as delicious as those feather-light little kisses were. She wanted the real thing. The thing she'd been waiting for for eleven and a half months, even if she'd pretended to herself—and everyone else—that she hadn't. She wanted Alex to kiss her. Really kiss her.

She released her hands, which had been bunched in fists, crumpling his shirt, and slid them up and around his neck, pulling him to her and angling her head so lips met lips. Alex guessed what she was doing, and he kissed her lightly, slowly, smiling against her mouth as he did so.

Alex's jacket slid off her shoulders, but Nicole didn't notice the slicing wind coming off the Thames under a cloudless and starry sky. All she could think or feel or remember was Alex. It was such a relief after keeping it all at bay for so long.

And she knew he was enjoying it, enjoying the way he was sweeping away every last bit of her control. What was worse was that she didn't care. Kissing Alex squiffy all those months ago had been good. However, kissing him stone-cold sober, with no touch, no sensation, dulled by half a dozen cocktails, was much better than she'd ever dreamed it would be.

# CHAPTER THIRTY-SEVEN

The National Portrait Gallery was quiet on a Sunday morning. Nicole found Alex staring at a series of black-and-white photographs just beyond the entrance hall. He'd mentioned that there was an exhibition he wanted to see, a famous photographer who'd snapped everyone from supermodels to rock stars, politicians and old lovers throughout his forty-year career. Alex turned as he heard her approach and her heart did a little skip.

This morning, she felt as if she'd woken up in a parallel universe where everything looked the same on the surface but somehow it all *felt* different.

He smiled at her broadly, as if he hadn't been quite sure she was going to turn up and was pleased that she had. Nicole smiled back. She had spent hours this morning chewing it over in her mind, wondering if this was the right thing to do. She still didn't have an answer for that question.

'You came,' he said.

She nodded. 'I did.' And then she glanced at the entrance to the exhibition area. 'Why don't we go and look at photos?'

'Nic?'

She'd started walking ahead of him and now turned to face him. 'Yes?'

'Are you okay after yesterday? You seemed pretty upset when I found you on the terrace.'

A wash of heat went through her at the mention of the terrace. Alex's pupils dilated a fraction and she guessed he was having a similar flashback. She coughed and glanced away, not sure she wanted to broach that subject yet. Better to stick to the one he'd led with.

'I'm okay,' she said honestly. It felt very good to just be herself with him, to not have to lie to him. At least, not about this. 'Yesterday made me think very hard about my life, about where it's going and what I want out of it.'

He gave her a sympathetic look. 'Don't let those bitches get to you.'

She shook her head and smiled back at him. She didn't even have to fake it. 'They haven't. In fact, I decided I'm glad it happened.'

Today, when she'd got up she hadn't gone straight to her wardrobe and chosen her outfit with 'those girls' in mind. Instead, she'd dressed for herself. Jeans, comfy boots and the grey jumper she'd worn at the first wedding with Alex, because it was warm and she liked it, and because it felt like an anchor to a pleasant memory. She'd even slung a colourful knitted scarf round her neck, even if it did make her look like a farmer.

They wandered from picture to picture in silence for a while. Nicole was glad. She wasn't sure what she was going to say to him today, where this thing between them could go. They stopped in front of a picture of Kat de Souza, the acoustic singer-songwriter whose every album topped the chart for weeks. Instead of her posing in jeans and T-shirt, her guitar slung round her body, as she was usually photo-graphed, this one was taken outside on a sunny day. She was wearing a simple floral dress, sitting in long grass, her knees pulled up and her chin resting on them. The sun was behind her, creating a kind of mistiness, and the soft smile in her eyes was bewitching.

'I can see why you idolise this guy,' she told Alex. 'I've never seen her look so soft, so…approachable.'

He nodded. 'That's why I like Gatson's work. He strips stuff away, gets to the truth of a person with his camera. In these days of constant retouching and airbrushing, it's a rare thing.'

Nicole studied the picture again, wondering if this soft vulnerable creature was the real woman behind the chart-topping success, not the angry young woman who graced her album covers.

'Why don't you take more portraits?' she asked.

'With all the weddings I do, I take hundreds of portraits every Saturday. When I get to choose my own subjects, I suppose I want a rest from faces, to do something dif-ferent.' He sighed. 'I would like to do this kind of thing, though. Be able to take my time, create an atmosphere, not just snap away like a mad thing, trying to make sure I don't miss an essential moment.'

Nicole turned her head to look at him. 'You should.'

'Do you remember what you said to me at the wedding the other week, about dreams?'

She nodded.

'Well, it's time for me to start chasing mine, to do the

kind of photography I really want to do. I'm cutting down my wedding commitments and making time to travel. Maybe I'll do up my studio, think about doing portraits as well.' He looked at her. His voice was light but his expression was serious. 'One life, one shot, right? It's time to get rid of all of my safety nets.'

Nicole smiled at him. 'I'm so pleased. I think you'll be amazing.'

He smiled back, just enough for his dimple to hint at an appearance, and he raised his hand to gently trace his fingers over her cheekbone. 'I'd like to photograph you.'

As much as Nicole wanted to lean into his touch, she stepped away. She wasn't sure if she was ready for Alex to take her picture—for a whole lot of reasons. What would he see if he looked at her down the lens? She wasn't sure either of them was ready for what he might discover.

His smile faded as she backed up. He dropped his hand. 'Are you having second thoughts?'

She shook her head. 'No.'

He didn't look convinced. She closed a little of the distance between them. 'No, really, Alex.'

'Then what is it?'

She sighed, stared back at the photograph. If only she could look so free, so peaceful. 'We both said this was complicated...'

Hope flared in his eyes, causing the corners of his mouth to lift. 'But I told you...I dealt with that.'

'You dealt with *your* complications. I still have a few.'

His mouth thinned into a line. 'Are you telling me you're involved with someone else? That you need to end it?'

She shook her head. 'No... It's nothing like that.'

'Then what is it?'

She sighed and moved along to the next photo, an old rocker who wore the excesses of his life on his face. Gatson had caught every line and wrinkle, but he'd also caught the rebellious spirit that was still raging strong. She turned and found Alex standing very close, his expression serious.

She swallowed and sent him a pleading look. She so badly wanted to tell him. Not just about her job, but everything. She felt as if she'd been wearing a corset that was too tight for years and was desperate to unlace it, just so she could breathe properly again. And it was because of Alex that she'd realised just how tightly it had been knotted, just how much it had restricted her. If it wasn't for him she'd never have realised how stale and…beige…her life had become.

But not every secret that needed to come out was hers to tell. And even if they were, she would still have to move cautiously. She remembered what Saffron had said about Minty stealing her boyfriend. Would she see Nicole in the same light? While, technically, Alex hadn't cheated on Saffron, it might be too soon for her to find out there was someone new in his life, especially someone she had sent across his path.

And then there was the proposal.

Would Saffron tell him what she'd been planning? Most girls would save themselves the humiliation, but Saffron wasn't most girls. She was used to putting everything out there. Nicole had to give her the chance to tell him, or at least have some closure on the relationship, before she discovered the man she'd wanted to marry had moved on.

She needed to tread carefully. Not just for herself and Alex, but for Saffron's sake too. Nicole really didn't want to see her hurt. And then there was Peggy and Mia, depending on her not to mess things up for Hopes & Dreams and lose them all their savings. If Saffron got angry about this, there was no telling what she would do, no telling how the bad publicity would affect their business at such a crucial time.

'What do you need?' Alex asked, his voice soft.

She fell a little bit more for him because he was willing to wait, willing to give her the space she needed.

'Time,' she said hoarsely. 'To sort things out.'

He nodded. His hand returned to her face and he stepped in and rested his forehead against hers. 'I want to see you still.'

She let out a shuddering breath. 'I want to see you too. But I don't want to sneak around.'

He leaned forward and brushed his lips against hers, just briefly, before pulling away again. 'Then we'll see each other.'

She shook her head. 'I don't think dating is a good idea.'

One side of his mouth hitched up. 'Who said anything about dating? If you need space before we make it anything official, I can handle that.' He glanced at the photographs on the walls around him. 'But if I go to an exhibition, or a certain coffee bar, and you happen to turn up...' His smile kicked up a gear. 'Or if you wander into Déjà Vu again this December thirty-first, for a New Year's Eve party...'

She smiled back at him, grateful for his ingenuity. They

couldn't be together, not yet, but at least she might be able to see him sometimes. That would have to be enough for now.

She hoped it wouldn't be too long, though, because she'd finally grown weary of planning everyone else's happy-ever-afters. It was high time she started nailing down her own.

# CHAPTER THIRTY-EIGHT

Nicole stood in the courtyard outside Hopes & Dreams. It was late on Sunday afternoon, the kind of time normal people were tucked up in their living rooms, drinking hot mugs of tea and arguing about who really should have gone through on *Strictly* the night before. Her dad's Merc pulled into the yard.

Normally the landlords were pretty hot on parking outside the shops, but nobody minded at this time of day on a Sunday. When her dad got out of the car, she went over and hugged him. 'Thanks so much for this.'

'What else have I got to do with my Sunday afternoon but search round all the hardware shops in South-East England for a couple of cans of Pouty Pink?' he grumbled, but he kissed her on the cheek all the same.

'You found it?' Nicole said as he went round to the boot.

He just shook his head and lifted two cans of paint out. Nicole squealed and ran over to hug him again. 'Dad, I don't know what I'd do without you!'

A glimmer of a grudging smile crossed his lips. 'I know.

Now…how about we get this stuff on the walls so I can get home before midnight?'

Nicole grinned and took a can from him then led the way upstairs. She'd had a flash of inspiration riding home on the bus after meeting Alex at the National Portrait Gallery. She just hoped Peggy didn't go nuts at her for changing it back without asking, but somehow she guessed her friend wouldn't moan if there was one less beige wall in the world.

As she put the can of paint down on the sheet she'd laid out to protect the floorboards, her phone buzzed in her pocket. She smiled and pulled it out. It was a message from Alex. The third one today. Like the previous ones there were no words; it was just a photograph.

The first had been a shot of Trafalgar Square, one he must have taken on his route home from the National Portrait Gallery. Nelson's Column had risen proud and silent against the silver grey of a winter's afternoon. Then there had been a picture of a funny advert on his Tube carriage. This one was a close-up of a leaf in a wonderful shade of gold floating on a near-black puddle.

They were little things that had made up Alex's day. Ordinary things. The landscapes of his life. Somehow it made her feel as if she were with him, spending time with him, even when she couldn't physically be near him. She smiled, but left her phone on her desk and went over to help her dad start prepping the wall.

'I know what your brush skills are like,' her dad said as he opened a can of Pouty Pink with a screwdriver. 'So you can do the roller and I'll do the cutting in. Otherwise we'll be here all night cleaning the mess off the skirting.'

Nicole saluted him and he called her a cheeky brat, but

they chatted amiably while they worked on their respective patches of wall. By seven-thirty they were cleaning their tools and folding up the drop cloth.

'What do you think?' she asked him, as they both stood there, hands on hips.

'Looks like a tart's boudoir, if you ask me,' he said. 'But if you chose it, it must be perfect.'

Nicole hugged her dad again. For some reason she had a real urge to do that today. 'You're the best,' she whispered into his ear. He patted her on the back in an indulgent way, but when he pulled away there was a twinkle in his eye and he was looking a little redder.

She felt sad to see him go when he pulled out of the courtyard in his beloved car and headed back to Orpington. He'd hated the colour, no matter what he'd said, but he'd helped her anyway, no criticism, no trying to persuade her to change it to something else, and she realised what a gift that was.

Saffron had only talked about her father a little bit, but Nicole had got the feeling she'd had to fight for every scrap of attention she'd got from him, and even when he was paying attention to her, he forced her to measure up to his own high standards. Her parents had never done that. They'd always loved her so completely, so unconditionally. Maybe that was why she'd subconsciously tried to pay them back all these years, by being the best daughter she could be.

They always accepted her, no matter what, and it made her heart heavy to think she'd been taking them for granted. Giving that speech to Minty and Celeste yesterday had made that crystal clear in her mind. She shouldn't have to apologise for who she was or where she came from.

Her phone beeped again. She went over to her desk and swiped the home screen. This time it was a picture of a clear and frosty moon that had turned the edges of the clouds silver. She walked over to the window and looked up in the sky. The same moon was there. The wind had moved the clouds a little, but it was almost identical. She closed her eyes and tried to imagine him wherever he was right now.

As yet she hadn't been brave enough to send him a message back, but now she impulsively grabbed her phone and snapped the fuchsia wall. He didn't know where it was, so it couldn't give her away, but it felt nice to share a secret with him rather than hide it.

She sighed. This had to work out. It just had to.

But she wasn't looking forward to tomorrow. Not only because Peggy was going to find out she'd changed the office single-handedly again, but because she had a two o'clock meeting scheduled with Saffron to go over some last-minute details of the proposal. It was possible that Saffron might not even show, and even if she did it wasn't going to be easy.

She felt so bad about this. But what could she do? You couldn't help whom you fell in love with.

Hang on… *Whom you fell in love with?*

Shaking her head, she gathered up her paintbrushes and headed for the little kitchen. It was too soon for that. Far too soon. Wasn't it? It went a lot deeper than just 'like', but that was as far as she was prepared to label it right now. It would be different in the new year, when they might be able to see each other properly.

A fluttering started up in her stomach. She supposed

tomorrow's meeting would be an indicator of whether that could ever happen. If Saffron was sad but determined to bounce back, it might be okay. But if she was a snivelling mess… It might be a long time before Nicole and Alex could be together, if at all.

# CHAPTER THIRTY-NINE

When Nicole and Peggy arrived at Hopes & Dreams the following morning, Peggy didn't say anything. She just walked over to Nicole and hugged her tight. After about thirty seconds, Nicole tapped her gently on the arm. 'Peg…? I think you're cutting off my air supply.'

Peggy laughed and released her. 'Sorry. It's just…' she pressed her lips together and smiled '…you've been behaving a bit oddly for ages now, but I suddenly feel as if I've got my friend back.'

Nicole closed her eyes and shook her head. 'I know, I know… The last few weeks… This whole thing with Alex and Saffron. It just got to me.'

'It's more than that,' Peggy said. 'You've been more and more uptight ever since you started planning Hopes & Dreams.'

Nicole frowned. 'Have I?'

Peggy nodded. 'When I think back to the fun-loving girl who answered my flat-share ad about a million years ago, she seems like a different person.'

Nicole searched Peggy's face for the truth in her words,

found it in the little nod her friend gave her. Really? She knew she'd changed, but surely that wasn't a bad thing. Surely that was all about growing up?

The door opened and Mia walked in. Nicole had sent her a message the night before asking if she could make time for an emergency investors' meeting. She needed Mia's practical and no-nonsense advice if they were going to save Hopes & Dreams now Saffron's proposal was going to be cancelled. Obviously, having done all the planning already, they'd get paid, but they weren't going to benefit from that all-important publicity boost.

'Wow,' Mia said, looking at the wall. 'It's back.'

Nicole gave her a sheepish look. 'I shouldn't have changed it in the first place. I don't know what got into me.'

Mia dumped her coat and bag on her desk then came back to join Peggy and Nicole, who were still staring at the wall. 'So…what brought all of this on?'

Nicole sighed. 'I think it was the wedding on Saturday.' And she launched into the whole tale of Celeste and Minty. Peggy had heard it already, of course, but she didn't seem to mind getting second helpings of all the gossip.

Mia frowned when she'd finished. 'Well, good for you for telling those girls what for, but I don't quite see what this has got to do with repainting the wall pink.'

Nicole went over and sat on the purple sofa. Mia joined her and Peggy leaned against the old-fashioned shop counter. 'Since school, I've always felt I had to compete with those kind of girls, be better than them to be happy.'

Peggy folded her arms. 'That's ridiculous!'

Nicole nodded wearily. 'I know. But what's even worse was that I realised I wasn't just trying to outdo them. I was trying to be like them. I don't like to admit it, but I think I've just been plain jealous that girls like that seem to have everything.'

Mia shook her head, laughing.

'What?' Nicole asked. 'What's so funny?'

Mia sighed. 'Those girls don't have everything.'

Nicole folded her arms. It sure seemed like that to her.

'Their lives are just as complicated as ours, just in different ways.'

Peggy nodded. 'Yeah, just look at poor old Saffron!'

'It's that stupid school you went to,' Mia said, 'and that stupid man who let you slip through his fingers. They've got you believing this is all about class and privilege and it isn't.'

'It isn't?' Nicole echoed, slightly dazed by the way Mia had nailed her down so effectively when she was only just coming to realise some of these things herself.

'No,' Mia replied firmly. 'There's only one thing those girls have got that you haven't got… Self-confidence.'

Peggy gave her a rueful smile. 'Bingo.'

Nicole looked at both of them in turn. That couldn't be right, but Mia's words had lodged inside her like a stone, something solid and real that wasn't going to be moved, probably because it was the truth.

She'd always known she hadn't had Mia's quiet self-assurance or Peggy's belief in her own inherent wonderfulness, but she realised that not only did her parents love her the way she was, but she had two amazing friends who accepted her with all her foibles and neuroses. And then there was Alex… He liked her. And he'd seen all of her, even the bits she didn't normally let people see.

Nicole breathed and looked round the room, craned her neck to see the expanse of pink behind her. 'You're right, Peggy.' She turned back round to face them. 'We don't need a new office. We're fine the way we are. Maybe we don't have to always be trailing in Detest and Squinty's wake, trying to do business the way they do.'

She walked over to her desk and picked up the polka-dotted pot, prepared to drop a pound coin in, but Peggy followed her and took it from her before paying the fine herself. 'Just for using those nicknames, this one's on me,' she said, grinning, and then she put the pot down on the desk and gave Nicole another hug.

Mia, not wanting to miss out on the bonding session, skipped over from the sofa and joined them. When they all pulled apart, smiling, Nicole said, 'And what's wrong with planning proposals for the Warrens and Cheryls of this world? They deserve love and romance just as much as the beautiful young things. We'll just have to find another way to encourage them to go all out and book the full proposal service with us, maybe tweak the business model a little bit. Let Celeste and Minty have the society clients… They're welcome to all the drama that goes along with them!'

Peggy and Mia looked at each other and grinned.

'I'm right with you on that,' Peggy said. 'I was just trying to work out a way to tell you, but I was going to wait until after Saffron's job—it seemed to be turning you a little loopy.'

Nicole laughed softly. She'd definitely been a bit weird recently. 'Well, money can't buy you love,' she said, teasing.

Peggy picked up on it instantly. 'Every cloud has a silver lining.'

Mia even chimed in. 'All's well that ends well!'

'And who wants to plan proposals where everything has to be beige and white and dripping in diamonds?' Peggy added, looking slightly affronted at the thought. 'I like a do with a little more pop and pizzazz. I mean, you gave Saffron all those wonderful ideas, and in the end all she plumped for was an outrageously expensive party for all her friends at a posh hotel. I'd rather be known for our creativity and originality, not for just how much money we can throw at something. If we can survive this rough patch, that's what's going to attract the clients—all sorts of clients. We'll just have to make sure we're so fabulous they can't bear not to ask us to do the whole thing for them!'

Nicole had to give Peggy another hug for that. She really hoped that things did go well, that both her friends could join her in her business full-time in the future. She needed them; she'd just tied herself up in knots trying to do it on her own.

Peggy pulled away and grinned at Nicole. 'Anyway, don't forget that apart from the earful you gave those two posh cows the other day, you've got what you wanted anyway and proved you're every bit as good as "those girls" you go on about.'

Nicole raised her eyebrows. 'I have?'

Peggy looked puzzled. 'Of course you have. You always said that kind stuck together, but you've bagged one of "those boys" from under their noses, haven't you?'

Mia looked at both her friends' frowns of confusion. 'I don't think she knows, Peg.'

Nicole stepped back and examined their faces. 'Knows what?'

Peggy looked at Mia then started to explain. 'Alex… He's the son of Lord Westerham. The eldest son. Marry him and you'll end up a proper toff one day.'

Nicole had a sensation similar to when she'd ridden a glass-bottomed elevator up to the top of the CN Tower when Mum and Dad had taken her to visit Auntie Mags in Toronto. The speed of the lift and the fact she couldn't see a firm floor below her as the ground sped away had made her feel disoriented and queasy. However, this was ten times worse. She felt as if there were no floor at all, that she was suspended on fresh air, ready to plummet back down to reality.

'He's *what*?' she whispered.

Peggy and Mia looked at each other.

'I thought you already knew,' Mia said.

'Or at least that you'd be pleased now you've found out,' Peggy added.

Nicole didn't know what she felt. Only that, once again, the world had shifted and she hadn't quite managed to keep up.

'But he can't be… His name doesn't match.'

'I thought you'd have looked all this up on Google weeks ago,' Mia said. 'He's got his own Wikipedia entry…'

Nicole shook her head. She'd been doing her level best *not* to think about Alex while she was planning Saffron's proposal. Why would she torture herself searching the internet for information about him?

Peggy looked crestfallen she'd said anything. 'He changed his name—or uses a professional name. I don't know which.

I read he didn't want to trade on his family's status, that he wanted to make it on his own.'

Nicole nodded, feeling a little numb. That made sense. It fitted in perfectly with what she knew about Alex. Suddenly his comments about his family not accepting his choice of career all made horrible sense.

'This doesn't matter,' Mia said, rubbing her arm. 'It doesn't change anything.'

'I know…'

At least it shouldn't matter. Her head knew that, but another part of her was running around screaming and freaking out.

'Jasper might have been weak enough to get brainwashed into preserving the family bloodlines or what have you,' Peggy said, 'but Alex isn't like that, is he? He likes *you*. He broke up with Saffron Wolden-Barnes for *you*. That has to say something, doesn't it?'

Nicole nodded again. 'Of course it does…'

Then she shook herself, blasted her friends with her usual 'everything's fine' smile. They looked back at her a little strangely, and she didn't blame them. Her features felt weird contorting themselves into that shape, but she didn't drop it. It was all she had left.

She walked over to her desk. She needed to think about something else for a bit. 'Anyway…Saffron's due in this afternoon. Before that we've got to put our heads together and try and work out a low-cost but effective way to publicise Hopes & Dreams without the advantage of a string of articles in *Buzz Magazine*.'

# CHAPTER FORTY

Nicole had just about regained her equilibrium when Saffron arrived for their two o'clock meeting. She rose from her desk and went to greet her, taking a deep breath as she crossed the office. She put on what she hoped was a welcoming but sympathetic smile; however, when Saffron walked through the door she beamed back at her.

Nicole's heart went out to her. She was doing a very brave job of covering it all up.

'Shall we go straight through?'

Saffron nodded and Nicole followed her through to the meeting room. Once there, they sat down. Nicole folded her hands in her lap and waited. This was not going to be easy to hear. 'How are things?'

Saffron was silent for a moment. Her face, as always, was eminently readable, and Nicole watched a whole spectrum of emotions flit across her features before she settled on determination. 'Fine. Or they will be.'

What did that mean? And how could things be fine? Her boyfriend, the man she was about to propose to, had just told her he didn't think things were working out between them. If Alex had said that to her, Nicole would have been a snivelling wreck. Heck, she was a snivelling wreck just thinking they might never even *start* anything. That made her feel a little bit relieved. Maybe Saffron hadn't been in love with Alex as much as she'd thought.

'Oh, by the way,' Saffron added dreamily, 'I gave your name to Jimmy Hunter and Marcus Babbington. They both happened to mention they were getting serious with their other halves and I said I'd heard of a good proposal planner—without giving myself away, of course.'

Nicole nodded. 'Thank you.'

A silver lining to the situation, thank goodness. Maybe, even with Saffron's proposal going south, they'd benefit a little from the connection.

She didn't really know how to react to Saffron's stiff-upper-lip approach. Saffron was always so open that Nicole had just expected her to break down and tell her everything as soon as the meeting-room door shut behind them. She decided to carry on—sort of—as usual and hope that her client would eventually come clean. After all, they couldn't possibly keep planning a proposal that wasn't going to happen.

'So…' she said tentatively, 'are you still happy with the plans we've talked about? Do we need to change anything?'

Saffron shook her head. 'No. I know I take a long time making my mind up, but once it's made, that's it. I can be very pig-headed like that.'

'Ok-ay,' Nicole said, pretending to write something on the pad in front of her. 'And you're sure…? That there's nothing you want to change or…erm…' she swallowed '…cancel?'

Saffron leaned forward, clasping her hands together. Her eyes were large and full of emotion.

*This is it,* thought Nicole. *The deluge is about to start.*

'Are you okay, Nicole?' she asked, her voice warm. 'I know we're really client and proposal planner, but I've come to think of you a little bit as a friend too.'

Nicole was struck dumb, partly because she was touched, but mostly because of the crushing weight of guilt that had just started pressing down on her chest. She just nodded her response.

'Oh, good!' Saffron said brightly and sat back against the sofa. 'What is it, then? Had a wild weekend?'

Nicole nodded again. 'Something like that.' While not the party-filled few days Saffron was probably imagining, her weekend certainly had been unexpected and exciting, and now it had given way to a Monday that was getting more bizarre by the second.

'And what about you?' Nicole managed to finally ask, realising that turning the spotlight back on her client was probably the safest thing to do, given the circumstances. 'How have you been?'

At last Saffron showed something other than her dazzling smile. She frowned, but even that looked cute on her. 'Well, Alex has been a bit funny recently...'

Nicole leaned forward. 'Oh, yes?'

Saffron laughed and shook her head. 'You'll never guess what the daft man thinks I did!'

Nicole's insides grew as dense as lead, making her feel as if she'd sink through the armchair cushion if she weren't careful. 'No...what?'

'Well, he found that text from you about our meeting on my phone and he thought I was seeing someone else!'

Nicole swallowed. Suddenly her throat felt very dry. 'A text from me?'

Could Alex have found out? And if he had, how come he'd still kissed her at the wedding, invited her out on Sunday afternoon...?

'Yes,' Saffron said, laughing harder now. 'He kept on and on about "Who's this 'N'?" and "Where are you meeting him?" It was so funny.'

'It was?' Nicole said, feeling increasingly bemused. This didn't sound like what Alex had told her of the conversation at all.

'Yes, but I didn't mind,' Saffron said, looking happy. 'I was right. He's jealous! And that proves I'm doing the right thing after all, doesn't it? I know I said I was sure about doing this proposal when I first came to you, but I had a few doubts—I mean, who doesn't in a situation like this—but now I know for certain that Alex has strong feelings for me too, don't you see?'

Nicole nodded, even though inside she was shaking her head.

Saffron folded her hands in her lap. 'I know he's still cross with me, but it's all a silly misunderstanding. He'll see that, won't he, when I pop the question and the truth comes out? He'll see he needn't have worried.'

Nicole rubbed a palm over her forehead. Suddenly she was developing an awful headache. 'So...what you're saying,' she asked slowly, more for her own benefit than for Saffron's, 'is that, despite the current...problems...between you and Alex, that we're going ahead with everything as planned?'

Saffron beamed at her. 'Yes,' she said, nodding emphatically. 'I'm going to propose to Alex at my Christmas party—and you're going to help me.'

# CHAPTER FORTY-ONE

Alex had snapped a pigeon pecking around on the windowsill of his office-slash-darkroom on his phone and sent it off to Nicole. One of the more random shots he'd sent her, to be honest, but she seemed to like the little snippets of his life, had even started sending back ones of her own.

Like the picture of her furry slipper boots that had made him laugh. Nicole Harrison *so* did not seem like a slipper-boot kind of girl, although, for some reason he was secretly pleased she was. She'd also sent him a photo of the frothy cappuccino she'd obviously had for breakfast. The strangest one was a frame that had contained nothing but hot fuchsia pink. He was tempted to guess it was a wall, but he couldn't be sure.

He'd carried on sending pics to her, but her messages had stopped coming back. The last one he'd had was a shot of worn cobblestones, sent sometime on Monday morning. After that, nothing. Not for two whole days.

But then a text—all words, no pictures—had arrived a couple of hours ago, saying simply, I need to talk to you. Face to face. N

He'd got stupidly excited when he'd read the message. He knew she'd said she had 'complications' in her life, that she needed time. He'd been thinking on a timescale of weeks, maybe even months, but maybe he'd been over-estimating. Maybe she'd had all the time she needed. The picture messaging was cute and all, but it would be nothing to *really* being with her.

Shall I come to yours? he'd texted back.

No was the reply that had pinged back almost instantly. Meet me at Trinity Arts Centre. Eleven o'clock.

So here he was. Eleven o'clock on the dot. He walked through the double doors and nodded at Tia, who manned the little shop. The exhibition space was filled with the local watercolour society's annual show and a handful of people milled around. He checked quickly to see if Nicole was amongst them, but a movement out of the corner of his eye made him turn and look in the little coffee-bar area instead.

It was her. He had that heart-stopping, defibrillating sensation again, and this time he hadn't even touched her. She was waving at him, her smile nervous. He wanted to wipe it away with his lips, change it to that sweet little just-kissed smile he liked so much. He started walking towards her, but instead of rushing to greet him, she sat back down and clutched her handbag in front of her on the table.

He slid into the chair opposite her. 'Hi,' he said, smiling.

'Hi,' she replied, not smiling back. She hadn't even taken off her coat, he realised. A tan trench coat was tied tightly round her waist and he could see a business suit underneath, caught just a glimpse of matching high heels below the table. Her hair was scraped back into a low plait. All in all, it reminded him of the very first time he'd seen her in this place, but for some reason these clothes made him feel as if there were a wall between them.

She looked around furtively as he sat down. He didn't know why. She'd chosen the table in the furthest corner, half-hidden behind one of the old church's ornate pillars. It wasn't as if anyone could see them properly, even if they had been feeling nosy.

'What's up?' he asked.

She pulled in a breath, hard, through both nostrils and released it again. 'I'm sorry, Alex, but I think this all has to stop, even the messaging.'

'What?'

She shook her head, but her face remained just as expressionless, just as unreadable. 'I can't contact you any more. I'm sorry. I thought at least I owed it to you to say it to your face.'

He blinked. This was not what he'd been expecting at all. 'Why?' he asked, realising he'd been reduced to one-syllable questions.

She sighed and for the first time he saw just a flicker of emotion in her eyes before it quickly disappeared again. 'This has all happened so fast. What if what we feel is just the pressure-cooker effect?'

'The *what*?'

'You know… When two people work together in a high-pressured, tense environment and it magnifies the emotions, making them think they feel things they don't really feel.'

He shook his head. That wasn't what it was like for him. No way.

'Maybe we both need a complete break for a bit, some time to think.'

He stared at her, felt his jaw clench a little. Just when he thought he'd finally got her worked out. 'I don't need time to think,' he told her. 'I know what I want.'

Her. Simple as that. As scary as it was, he wanted to start taking risks again, particularly in the areas of his life that mattered the most.

She shook her head, as if she'd heard his silent answer and was rejecting it as erroneous. 'You've only just split up with someone... Are you sure she's not right for you? Maybe you should...' her voice caught, going hoarse, but then she continued '...give her another chance?'

He shook his head. 'Why are you saying this?'

Finally her mask of composure sagged a little. He saw the sorrow in her eyes. 'Because those complications I told you about? Well, they just got a whole lot more complicated.'

He felt his blood pressure rise a notch. 'Are you saying there's someone else?'

She'd told him otherwise, but he didn't know what to think any more. He hadn't thought Saffron capable of that kind of deception, either, and while she'd spun a good story, he still wasn't sure he bought it.

'Yes,' she replied, and the chill of the big open space, the centuries of hallowed air swimming in the vaulted ceiling above them, got to him. 'But not in the way that you think.'

What did that mean? All this woman gave him was riddles.

She leaned forward a little, covered his hand with hers and waited for him to meet her gaze. 'I promise,' she said, her lashes clogging with moisture, 'that you will know everything there is to know soon. But I can't see you again or talk to you or even text you until it's all out in the open, because only then will you really be able to decide what—or who—it is you really want.'

She still made no sense, but he couldn't fault the sincerity in her eyes. Whatever else she might be hiding from him, she meant that.

'Nic...?'

She shook her head and stood up. 'I can't...I can't stay any longer.' Her ankle wobbled, the same way it had done back in that club almost a year ago, when she'd walked across the dance floor towards him. And then she rushed from the coffee bar and out into the street. He rose to follow her, but as she turned the last corner he thought he saw her wipe something from the corner of her eye with a long, slim finger, and he sat down again.

Why did this whole damn thing have to be so hard? From the first moment he'd laid eyes on her he'd known she was special. But fate seemed to keep messing with them, teasing them by throwing them together then tearing them apart again.

As he sat there, trying to decide whether he might as well order a coffee now he was here, his phone rang. He checked the caller display. Oh, God. Not again. He really was going to have to do something about this. As much as he wanted to send it to voicemail, as he had the previous five calls, he decided it was better to face it head-on.

'Hi, Saffron,' he said wearily.

'Hi,' she said back. 'Glad I finally caught you.'

He traced a coffee ring on the table with his finger. 'You

can't keep calling me,' he said, the softness of his tone taking the edge off the blunt statement, he hoped.

'Alex, if you'd only let me explain… You're just being silly!'

'No. I'm not.'

He could almost hear her pouting down the other end of the line. 'There's no reason we can't still be friends, is there? Why don't we meet up and have coffee one afternoon?'

If it had been anyone else he might have said yes, but he could see through this as easily as he could see through the rest of Saffron's schemes—well, most of them. She was hoping she'd be able to nudge friendship along into something more, that maybe they could pick up where they'd left off, and that just wasn't possible. Stringing her along, giving her hope where there was none. If he got back with her just because she needed a shoulder to cry on, he'd be lying, and that wasn't fair to either of them.

'I don't think that's a good idea,' he said firmly. 'I'm sorry, Saffron.'

The irony that he was giving her the same kind of speech Nicole had just given him didn't escape him.

He heard her sigh. 'Really? Not even one tiny espresso?'

'Sorry.'

There were a few seconds of silence. He wondered if she was going to start getting cross with him, as she usually did when she didn't get her way, but she surprised him with what she said next.

'Okay, if that's how you really feel. But will you do me one favour?'

He knew he sounded suspicious when he answered, but he just couldn't help it. 'What's that?'

'Come to my Christmas party? I'll send you an invite.'

'I'm not coming as your date, Saffron.'

She sighed again. 'I know. You don't have to worry—there's going to be a huge crowd. Just come, will you, Alex? One last night of fun, like we used to have. And I promise after that you can disappear from my life forever, if that's what you want.'

He rubbed his hand across his forehead. It didn't sound too unreasonable. And he did feel the teensiest bit guilty for having ended things when she was in such a low place. Perhaps he should do this one thing for her so he could walk away with a clear conscience.

'Okay,' he said and braced himself against the ear-splitting squeal that came out of his handset. 'I'll come.'

# CHAPTER FORTY-TWO

Nicole closed her eyes and rested her body against one of the fluted Ionic columns of the Hamilton Hotel's newly renovated Palm Court. It had been a long, long day, and the most gut-wrenching part was yet to come. She just needed a moment to compose herself, a brief second to shut her lids against the winter wonderland Hopes & Dreams had created for Saffron. All that glitter and bridal white was making her stomach churn.

The venue was beautiful, originally used for tea dances, and had been returned to its former glory during the recent refurbishment. One entered through mirrored doors onto a white marble terrace that ran round three sides of the room. A black-iron-and-polished-brass balustrade guarded the edge, sweeping downwards where three short flights of steps—one at either end of the terrace and one in the middle—dipped to meet the main floor.

Once, this had been the home of potted palms and other exotic plants, string quartets and clinking teacups, but to-night it looked like an ice palace, a magical kingdom.

'Oh, my God! It's gorgeous!' someone squealed beside

her, and she opened her eyes and found Saffron standing at the top of the steps, on the verge of jumping up and down.

Nicole stood up and looked again at the scene with fresh eyes. Silver birches wound with tiny white fairy lights stood in pale earthenware pots both on the terrace and on the lower level. The tables that circled the dance floor were flowing with white flowers and silver baubles, and a million silver and white streamers hung from the ceiling like delicate stalactites.

The pale blue and lavender lights placed on the floor around the room created shadows, picking out the decorative trellis plasterwork and reflecting off any one of the mirrored panes that filled the walls. Not only were the entrance doors and those opposite that led to another room filled with mirrors, but arched panels all around the walls were decorated the same way. The original intention must have been to use the reflections of the greenery inside to make it seem as if the Palm Court was a regal glasshouse, like those at Kew, looking out over impressive gardens. Tonight, however, it seemed as if this were just one magical cavern in a network of underground ice caves.

'It's stunning!' Saffron said, giving in to the urge to bob up and down.

'I know,' Nicole murmured and sank back against the pillar. It looked as if a snowy wilderness had been imported into the heart of London—with a few little sparkly extras here and there.

What a pity she suspected Alex would have much preferred the real thing. Real snow. Real frost and hard rocks. An icy wind that was both chilling and invigorating. If she had been proposing to him, she wouldn't have done it this way.

She sighed and pushed herself upright again. But she wasn't proposing to Alex. She wasn't even *with* Alex, and she needed to remember that, or she'd be carted off to the loony bin once this evening was over.

It was all so surreal. She believed what Alex had said about breaking up with Saffron. The truth had been there in his eyes, and he could have taken advantage of the situations they'd found themselves in at the weddings if he'd wanted to run around with two women. But he hadn't.

Reading between the lines of Saffron's story, she guessed Saffron, in her usual I-always-get-what-I-want-eventually way, had just refused to believe him, and the fact that she knew her reasons for being less than open with him were legitimate just cemented her determination further.

'Everything you hoped for?' she asked Saffron.

The other woman nodded. 'More.' And then she turned to Nicole and smiled. 'It's perfect! And you're looking pretty snazzy yourself.'

Nicole mumbled her thanks. She was wearing one of three little black dresses she owned. Not the one she'd worn last New Year's Eve—that would have been too close to the bone. This one had a higher neck and didn't cling quite so lovingly. Very businesslike while still being smart enough for a party. And the black would help her blend into the shadows.

She needed this front tonight. Needed to be as smart and sophisticated and polished as she knew how to be. This dress was her armour against all that was going to happen.

'The flash mob are all here and ready and waiting for

a final rehearsal,' she told Saffron. 'Do you want to run through in what you're wearing or do you want to change into your dress?'

'Ooh, the dress! I want to see if the sequins catch the light the way I thought they would.'

'Come this way, then.' Nicole led her client through the double doors back into the lobby and indicated a lift with a single button. 'This takes you all the way up to the penthouse, to the suite we reserved for you...' She trailed off, finding she was completely unable to add the words 'and Alex'. 'For after the main event, so you can have a little privacy. The hair and make-up artists are waiting for you up there already.'

Saffron lurched impulsively forward and gave her a hug. 'Thank you, Nicole! I don't know what I'd have done without you, and I'm so glad you're going to be with me every second of the way, to back me up and make sure I don't blow it.'

Nicole patted Saffron's back awkwardly. 'Just doing my job,' she said quietly, but her insides felt like a muddy whirlpool, swirling faster and faster, sucking all the usual joy at a job well done out of her.

She stood back and looked at Saffron. 'And you're sure you want to go through with this? That this is what you want? It's not too late to pull the plug and just have a great party if you change your mind, you know.'

Saffron laughed. 'Nicole! If I didn't know better I'd think you were trying to talk me out of it!'

She'd tried to warn Saffron in countless ways over the last week or so, but it had all fallen on deaf ears. Saffron Wolden-Barnes didn't do subtle, and the other approach just wasn't an option. Not if she wanted to stay in business past the end of December.

She pushed the button for Saffron and the lift doors purred open. 'I'll see you in about half an hour,' she said, as they closed again and whisked her away up to the love nest Peggy had spent all afternoon decorating with heart-shaped balloons and rose petals. Nicole hadn't been able to face going up there, and it hadn't been because of a fear of heights.

She re-entered the Palm Court and searched out her friends for a powwow. Not only was Peggy here, but Mia too. She'd insisted on coming to lend a helping hand, although Nicole suspected she was here for moral support more than anything else.

She found Peggy chatting up the good-looking bartender and signalled for Mia, who was talking with the choir leader, to join her under one of the twinkling silver birches.

'Okay,' she said briskly as they came within earshot. 'Shall we go over the timings again?'

Mia laid a sympathetic hand on her shoulder. 'How are you holding up?'

Nicole kept her mouth closed and pulled oxygen in through her nostrils. 'Okay.' It was a lie, they all knew it, but what else could she say? Admitting she was shrivelling inside would just open the floodgates.

'I think you should let me and Peggy take over in here,' Mia added.

Nicole's eyes grew wide. 'But I can't bail now.'

'No one's saying you should bail,' Peggy said in her husky voice. 'But there's no reason why you can't take over liaising with the hotel, with the caterers and whatnot. It'll keep you away from the Palm Court for great chunks of time. I can swap with you and do all the "front of house" stuff, give the signals to the flash mob and everything, and Mia can keep an eye on Alex, make sure we know where he is when the crucial moment arrives. There's no need for you to be in here at all once the singing and dancing starts if you don't want to be.'

Nicole forgot all about prim and professional and pulled both of her best friends towards her, one with each arm, and hugged them hard until they started to complain about squashed ribs and smeared make-up. 'Thank you,' she whispered.

That, at least, was a tiny silver lining in the evening. She'd been dreading the ringside seat for watching the man she thought she might be falling in love with being proposed to by another woman.

She didn't want to see the look in his eyes when Saffron asked the question. If he was going to say no, she'd see it, and then she'd feel like the most horrible person in the universe. She didn't want to see Saffron hurt, even though her own feelings—and sometimes actions—had unwittingly contributed to that.

But part of her was scared. Scared he'd do exactly what Jasper had done and choose the safe option. He'd talked about Saffron being his safety net. What if he needed one of those now? Nicole had pushed him away so many times, hurt him. He couldn't keep bouncing back to her, could he? So what she was scared of most was *not* seeing regret in his eyes when Saffron popped the question, that instead she'd see them light up in amusement, that he'd give Saffron a flash of that dimple, the one she was starting to feel quite territorial about.

What if he said yes?

She'd seen it before, a dithering or undecided other half swept along by the sheer romance of what had been created for them. It happened. And it could happen here tonight.

'Okay,' she said, releasing her grip on her friends and picking up her clipboard from where she'd left it on a nearby table. 'Let's run through this baby just one more time...'

# CHAPTER FORTY-THREE

Nicole checked her watch and fired off a text to Saffron. It had been more than an hour since she'd seen her last, and the flash mob—thirty singers and almost as many dancers— were starting to get fidgety.

Saffron had plumped for a full-on musical number for the proposal, with herself as the star. While the music followed a romantic Christmas theme, Nicole had persuaded her to go for tango dancers rather than the ubiquitous street-dance flash mob. It was classy and elegant, sexy… And the Hamilton's Palm Court had been famous for its tango sessions back when the dance had still been shocking and risqué.

Nicole checked her watch again. It was also only an hour until the party started. If Saffron didn't get down here and rehearse soon, she'd miss her opportunity.

Thankfully, she arrived ten minutes later, looking resplendent in a short dress covered with large silver sequins. The neckline was sexy without being too revealing, but when she turned round, the back dipped away. The look was finished off with a pair of silver shoes so gorgeous Nicole was tempted to weep. With Saffron's willowy limbs and long blonde waves, the effect was stunning. No one was going to be looking at anyone else this evening, that was for sure.

'Ready to go through the routine?' Nicole asked, eager to get the rehearsal done before the troops got any more restless.

Saffron nodded, but she was frowning. 'Sure. But I keep forgetting when I need to do my bit. You will be there to give me my cue, won't you?'

Nicole nodded. She'd been to all the rehearsals in the previous week, knew exactly what Saffron had to do and when. It wasn't anything too demanding. The choir and dancers would be strategically planted all around the Palm Court, both on the floor and on the terrace. The choir would start with a soloist who'd sing the beginning of 'All I Want for Christmas Is You' a cappella. At the same time a lone pair of tango dancers would start the action on the dance floor during the slow and dramatic opening bars of the song, and then, when the tempo picked up, more of the singers would join in, shaking sleigh bells, and the band would fill in. More dancers would start in their positions around the room, then gradually make their way down to join the opening couple in the centre of the floor.

By the time the song reached its climax, four of the male dancers would split from their partners and come and collect Saffron from where she'd be waiting at the top of the steps to make the grand entrance she'd been so insistent about. They'd pick her up and carry her down the stairs on their shoulders, while she held her arms aloft, and bring her to Alex, wherever he might be standing in the room.

If they did a full circuit, so much the better, Saffron had said, liking the elevated position that garnered maximum attention. The dancers would let her down gracefully and, once delivered, she was going to go down on one knee and pop the question.

All she really needed to remember was to step out from where she'd be hidden behind one of the pillars at the right time.

'I just can't remember if I come out on the second "Ooh, baby" or the third,' Saffron said, sighing.

'The second,' Nicole said with conviction. 'We're just about to run through it so we can double-check. I'll be right over here…and Peggy knows the cues too. Everything is going to be fine.'

She hurried Saffron into her hiding place as the dancers and singers took their positions and one by one fed into the song at their appointed times. Right on cue, the four male dancers spun away from their partners and surged up the steps.

'Second!' Nicole hissed to Saffron as they approached and Saffron popped out, looking somewhat nervous, and lifted her arms in the air. From then on she just had to stay still and remember to keep her legs rigid so the dancers could carry her easily. Peggy was standing in for Alex, and they deposited her at Peggy's feet.

'Well, *I'm* tempted to say yes,' she quipped and Saffron beamed at her.

Nicole hurried forward. 'You know what you're going to say?' she asked. 'Do you want to practise it now?'

Saffron looked around nervously. 'Not in front of all these people…'

Nicole got that. After tonight she'd be able to tell Alex the truth about all her so-called complications. She was nervous enough about that, so it was no wonder Saffron didn't want to freak herself out by getting all tongue-tied before the big moment. Some things were better not re-hearsed anyway. Proposals were one of those things that should come straight from the heart.

'You're happy with the dance?' she asked Saffron.

'Can we go through it one more time?'

Nicole nodded to Peggy, and she signalled for the flash mob to take up their places again. 'I just need to go and chat to the catering team,' she told Saffron before she went back up the stairs to her opening position. 'If you need anything, or want any details about what time everything's happening, just ask Peggy or Mia.'

Saffron looked forlorn. 'You're not going to be here?'

Nicole blinked. 'Of course I will, but I've got some last-minute details to see to.'

She didn't mention the fact that while she might be in the hotel, she might not be in this very room, but that really shouldn't be a problem. Both Peggy and Mia were well briefed and ready to step in. As much as she liked Saffron, and as much as she wanted this job to outdo anything else they'd ever done, there was no way she actually wanted to be inside the Palm Court when the proposal went down.

Alex strode through the lobby of the Hamilton and headed for the Palm Court at the back of the building. He'd done a couple of weddings here before it had been refurbished, so he knew exactly where it was. He checked the time on his mobile. Nine-fifteen.

How long did he have to stick this out before he disappeared again? An hour? An hour and a half? He really wasn't in the mood for a party tonight. The only reason he was here was because of that rash promise he'd made Saffron, a promise born of guilt and confusion. Not the best kind at all.

He hadn't dressed for this do. He didn't have any designer labels on, just his usual jeans, a good T-shirt and his boots.

Muffled music thumped from the double doors at the end of a wide corridor and he made his way towards them. When he'd barged through them he ground to a halt. What the flipping heck had happened in here? It looked like Santa's grotto on speed.

A waiter drifted past him, offering spiced cranberry champagne cocktails. He shook his head and headed for the bar. If he was going to survive this evening, he needed beer. And lots of it.

He was just making his way down the short flight of marble stairs to where the bar had been set up, when out of the corner of his eye he saw movement. Familiar movement. His heart stopped and he felt as if a freight train had slammed into him. He twisted round, trying to catch a glimpse of the phantom that was responsible for the spike in his heart rate, but she was gone.

Dammit. He strode to the bar even quicker.

He'd been doing that all week and it was driving him nuts. Everywhere he went, whether working or socialising, he kept thinking he saw Nicole hovering on the fringes of his vision. Of course, every time he took a proper look he'd realise it wasn't her, that it was just someone with a coat the same colour or dark, glossy hair pulled into a neat style at the back of her head in a similar way.

This time it had been a black cocktail dress, one that reminded him of the Holly Golightly version of her. He leaned in and ordered a drink then scanned the crowd. Nope. She was gone. It was probably just his imagination screwing with him again.

He sighed as the bartender handed him a cold bottle, beaded with condensation, and took a long swig. He didn't think he could take much more of this. It was the not knowing that was driving him crazy. What *were* these 'complications' she talked about, and when would she be free of them? If only he could talk to her tonight, see her face again, hear her tell him that he just needed to wait a little longer…

He scrubbed a hand over his face and let out a low chuckle. He had it bad, didn't he? He hadn't been this obsessed about a woman since Vanessa. He should probably be worried about that, but he wasn't. Despite Nicole's initial wariness, he felt that he knew her. She'd tried to hide from him at the start, but she just couldn't seem to do it any more.

He liked that.

Other people might only see the glossy exterior, the slightly prickly career woman, but he saw what was underneath.

'Hey, you…' a soft voice behind him said.

He turned to find Saffron smiling at him.

'Like it?' she asked and gave him a twirl of her very sparkly and very short dress.

'Lovely.' He knocked back a bit more of his beer. He preferred something less showy, something black that came with ropes of pearls and long black gloves. Something with a certain brunette inside.

'I'm so glad you came! I wasn't sure you would after our last little…misunderstanding.'

He shrugged. He'd said he'd come, so he'd come. He still wasn't sure he could trust Saffron, but he'd promised to give her the benefit of the doubt. He looked her up and down as she stood in front of him, smiling. As always, she looked sensational, and her eyes were shining, her cheeks flushed.

She didn't look very heartbroken about him at all.

He hadn't realised he'd been holding so much tension in his body, but his ribs suddenly allowed him to take an extra pint or two of air in and his shoulders dropped an inch. Thank goodness for that. Now he could just do his time here, say his goodbyes and walk out of her life forever. He felt as happy as a greyhound who'd just been let off the lead.

'I hope you have a really great party, Saffron.' And he meant it.

She gave him a knowing smile. 'Oh, I think I will. Stick around and have another drink. The fun is really going to start in about half an hour.'

He gave her a non-committal nod and watched her glide away.

The party was really thumping now. The dance floor was filled, a DJ playing the latest hits, and people were talking and drinking, laughing and having fun. He felt like a lone slab of unexciting granite in the middle of it.

This scene had been fun when he'd first met Saffron,

but now he was getting really tired of it. He looked up at the ceiling, at the fake silvery things that were supposed to resemble snow or ice or something like that.

No, what he wanted was something real.

What he wanted was Nicole.

# CHAPTER FORTY-FOUR

Nicole checked her watch for what seemed like the millionth time. She was torturing herself, she knew, but she just couldn't seem to stop herself. Peggy had texted through a while ago that Alex had arrived and they were due to start Saffron's number at nine-thirty.

Only ten minutes to go now. And Alex was somewhere here in the building. Her stomach did an odd little quiver at the thought and she forced herself to tune into what the hotel's on-duty events manager was saying. Some minor problem with people trying to crash the party, but security was on top of it. Nicole didn't really need to be there dealing with this, but everything else was running so smoothly. She'd done her job too well, but the only other option was to go back into the party, and she wasn't going to do that, not until Peggy texted again to say the coast was clear.

She didn't know how she was going to handle the aftermath of the proposal, whichever way it went. If Alex said no, the need for secrecy would be done away with and she'd be free to tell him everything. Should she do it tonight? Or should she keep out of the way, contact him tomorrow when things were less crazy? She'd been so busy gearing up to the actual proposal, she realised she hadn't thought this bit through at all.

Her phone buzzed and her heart jumped, feeling like a rocket shot from the middle of a firework display. She pressed her hand against her breastbone and told herself to calm down. It was too soon for it all to be over, probably a random message—her mother or something like that.

But when she'd excused herself from talking to the events manager and pulled her phone out of her bag, she realised it was indeed Peggy who was contacting her.

Code pink! was all it said.

Nicole started running. That had been Peggy's little in-joke. Ages ago, she'd said that Nicole would need a signal in case everything went belly up during a proposal and had come up with that cute and seemingly non-threatening phrase. They'd chuckled about it at the time, but somehow it didn't seem so funny any more. What on earth could have gone wrong? She knew Peggy wouldn't have called her back to the Palm Court unless it was an emergency.

She slid in the entrance and kept to the edges of the terrace, using the heavily decorated birches for cover. Alex could absolutely, positively not see her yet. Peggy was in the corner with a rather frantic-looking Saffron. When she spotted Nicole she lurched for her, grabbed her by the hands and looked pleadingly at her.

'Oh, Nicole! Thank God you're here!' she gabbled. 'I can't remember when! I thought it was the second, but then I remembered it was the one that I didn't usually think it was, which made me think it was the third, but then I just got all confused and couldn't remember which at all!'

Nicole squeezed Saffron's hands and made her look at her. 'What exactly are you talking about?'

'*Ooh, babies,*' Saffron said, looking as if Nicole was being extremely dense. 'Do I go on number two or number three?'

'The second,' she replied firmly. They'd checked it out earlier with Julio, the lead dancer-slash-choreographer. Twice.

'I told her that,' Peggy said from the side of her mouth, 'but she wouldn't have it unless she heard it from you.'

Saffron ran a hand through her shaggy waves. 'I know, I know...' Most people would have destroyed their hairstyle by doing such a thing, but it just gave her a sexy, just-fallen-out-of-bed look. 'But I just wasn't sure and Nicole has been my rock throughout this whole thing.'

'It's going to be fine,' Nicole said, pulling her usual speech out of the bag. It was all she could come up with at the moment. 'And you're going to be standing in front of the man you love in a few minutes,' she reminded her. 'He's worth all of this, isn't he?'

Saffron swallowed. 'Let's just say I hope I never have to do this ever, ever again. Seriously, I don't know how guys do it. It's a wonder anyone ever gets married at all!'

Even though her hands were still clasped in Saffron's and she couldn't see her watch, Nicole could feel the seconds ebbing away. She had to get out of here and she had to do it fast. She was just about to tug her fingers loose of her client's, when the DJ faded out the end of the song and everything went silent.

Guests looked around, wondering what was going on. Then when everyone was suitably puzzled and quiet, the soloist opened up her mouth and belted out the opening line of 'All I Want for Christmas Is You' for all she was worth.

Nicole glanced mournfully towards the door. Everyone was still. Everyone was silent. Most people were focused on the singer and the pair of tango dancers in a spotlight in the middle of the dance floor, but a few were looking around, trying to work out what was going on.

She flattened herself against the wall.

Oh, heck.

There was Celeste, standing right there, only a few feet away. She hadn't known she'd been on the guest list, but Saffron had been tinkering with it constantly since the invites had gone out, and she had mentioned there were a handful more people she'd just told to come along. Which meant they probably had an extra fifty beyond what she'd been expecting in the room.

Well, there was no way she was going to make it out of here without being spotted now. If she tried to leave, the movement would draw attention. People would look round. Her only option was to keep back against the wall and slowly shuffle behind the pillar in the far corner.

She really, really didn't want to witness this.

She scanned the room, trying to see if there was a side exit she'd forgotten about, then frantically ran through the dance routine at triple speed inside her head, trying to work out if there was a certain bit of the choreography when everyone else would be looking in the other direction and she'd be able to slither along the wall and out the door.

She held her breath.

There he was. Alex. Standing near the short flight of

steps at the far end of the C-shaped terrace, holding a bottle of beer loosely in his fingers, watching the show with
a bemused expression on his face.

She twisted her head and looked at Saffron, who was
hiding behind the next pillar along. She was nodding along
to the music, her mouth working, and Nicole could almost
hear her mentally reciting the lyrics while her silver shoe
tapped out the beats.

Nicole wanted to cry.

Not just for herself, but for Saffron. This was really happening, wasn't it? It was actually going down. Suddenly
the life-altering seriousness of what was about to happen
shot through her.

This would change everything.

Everything.

For Alex, for Saffron, even for her. There was no coming back from this.

The song had speeded up now and more dancers and
singers had joined in. Nicole watched, frozen, as the routine progressed, her stomach sinking further with each leg
flick and vocal trill.

She couldn't move, couldn't think. Couldn't do anything
but feel the moment of the proposal coming, hanging like
a guillotine blade above her head.

She glanced at Saffron, who was looking pale and nervous. She'd stopped counting now and was just staring
straight ahead. Nicole swallowed. Even though she thought
Saffron was doing the wrong thing, had jumped into this
with both feet a little too hastily, hadn't really found out if
she and Alex were on the same page, Nicole couldn't help
admiring her.

It took guts, this. Guts to step into a spotlight alone and strip every bit of protection away and lay yourself out there emotionally naked, with every chance of being rejected. With shame, she realised it was something she wouldn't have had the courage to do, no matter how much she'd changed herself.

The song was reaching its climax now. The four male dancers peeled away and headed for the steps. Nicole wanted to shout out, but she didn't dare. *No!* she wanted to yell, because it had just become heart-stoppingly clear that this was all her fault. She wasn't about to make Saffron's hopes and dreams come true; she was sending her into an ambush.

Time seemed to slow as the dancers reached the terrace, as Julio held out his arm—Saffron's cue to spin out from behind the pillar and join them.

But she didn't do it. Didn't spin anywhere. Because Nicole suddenly lurched forward and grabbed on to Saffron's other arm, even though she didn't remember deciding to do it. Saffron's head whipped round and she scowled at Nicole.

'Wh-what are you doing?'

'I can't let you do this!' Nicole shouted, quietly enough that anyone more than a few feet away couldn't have heard it.

Julio looked at her, a question in his eyes, and she shook her head. A couple of the other dancers hesitated, but Julio just improvised a bit of a tango-inspired strut back down to join his partner on the dance floor and, one by one, they followed. She could see some of the choir frowning, but they carried on regardless.

While she was still trying to get her head around what

she'd just done, a firm hand gripped her shoulder and pulled both her and Saffron across the short terrace and out the door into the lobby.

# CHAPTER FORTY-FIVE

'Why did you do that!' Saffron spun round to face her, furious.

Nicole gulped for air. Peggy let go of her shoulder and she stumbled a little. It took her a second or so to orient herself, but the cooler air of the lobby compared to the heat and warmth of the party helped snap her out of her fuzzy state. 'I...I...'

The door moved again and a smooth voice said, 'I know exactly why she did it.'

Peggy, Saffron and Nicole turned round to see Celeste standing there. A second later, Mia barrelled through the door behind her.

Celeste smirked at Nicole before fixing Saffron with a knowing look. 'I can spot a proposal coming a mile off. That's what was about to happen, wasn't it?'

Saffron nodded dumbly.

Celeste gave her a rueful smile and shook her head. 'You should have come to us, Saffron. Minty and I would never have let this shambles happen.' She gave a dismissive, one-shouldered shrug. 'But then we're used to this level of sophistication and exclusivity. You really needed proposal planners with a bit more class...'

Saffron frowned. 'What do you mean? Up until now Nicole's done a fabulous job. She's very classy.'

Celeste just smiled. It made her look like a Siamese cat. 'Really?' Her eyebrows rose. 'That's not what I'd heard at all.'

Peggy stepped forward, 'Now, listen. You and Squinty can—'

Celeste spoke over the top of her. 'I suppose, if you think it's classy for your proposal planner to be seen snogging the face off the man of your dreams a fortnight before the happy event, then that's up to you.'

Saffron laughed. 'Don't be ridiculous! Nicole would never...' She trailed off as she realised no one else was finding it funny. In fact, the silence in the large empty lobby was rather telling. Slowly, she turned to look at Nicole. 'Is this true?'

Nicole heaved in a breath to help her give her answer, but it got stuck in her chest. Her mouth moved as she tried to get the words to come out.

Saffron's eyes widened and her jaw went slack.

Celeste just smiled. 'That's what Helena Parkhurst told me, anyway. Saw it with her own eyes at Jasper and Penelope's wedding.'

'You went after my boyfriend?' Saffron said, shaking her head. She was too shocked to be angry at present, but Nicole knew that wasn't going to last long. 'The man I asked you to help me propose marriage to?'

Nicole shook her head too. 'It wasn't like that! If you'd just give me a chance to—'

'Yes, Nicole,' Celeste said, folding her arms. 'What good explanation is there for stealing your client's prospective groom?'

'Right! I've just about had enough of you!' Peggy grabbed hold of Celeste and propelled her back through the double doors. Celeste tried to stop her, but her spindly skinny legs were no match for Peggy's healthier curves. Unfortunately, removing Celeste from the situation did nothing to solve the problem.

Saffron drew herself up to her full height. 'I want an explanation and I want one now!'

Uh-oh. She was about to go into full-on meltdown mode. Nicole opened her mouth to answer, but someone tried to push their way through the doors again. Peggy attempted to block them, assuming it was Celeste, possibly with Minty as backup, but whoever it was was strong enough to send Peggy stumbling forward and knocking into Nicole.

She just about managed to stop herself from faceplanting on the lobby's luxury carpet and was in the process of straightening again, when a low voice rumbled out behind her.

'Nicole? I thought I saw you...'

She turned. And came face to face with Alex.

# CHAPTER FORTY-SIX

Alex blinked. He couldn't quite believe what he was seeing. There he'd been, wishing he'd known where Nicole
was, and she'd just appeared out of thin air. He moved towards her, smiling, but Saffron stepped in front of him,
facing Nicole, and holstered her hands on her hips.

'He knows your name? What Celeste said was true,
wasn't it?' She let out a dry laugh. 'So much for being
an anonymous market researcher or something like that!'

Alex frowned. What was Saffron talking about? Nicole
wasn't a market researcher. He was just about to say as
much, when the door bumped open again. A small group
of people ambled into the lobby. He guessed the show—or
whatever that had been—was over and the crowds were
starting to move again.

As more people came through the entrance, Nicole's
friend—the slender one who always seemed to have a very
determined expression—hit the button to a nearby lift, then
shoved him inside when the door dinged instantly open.
Her other friend grabbed Saffron and Nicole, and soon
they were all shooting upwards to the top floor of the hotel.

When they spilled out of the lift into a large suite filled with balloons and silvery confetti, he started frowning. The pleasant feeling of surprise at seeing Nicole here was wearing off and now he was starting to think something was going on. It was as if everyone else in this little scenario knew the script and he was the one left to improvise.

He turned to Saffron. 'Do you know Nicole? And what's all this about market researchers? This isn't some new scheme to keep your name in the papers, is it?'

'Yes, I know Nicole, but what I want to know is: how well do *you* know Nicole?'

He had the grace to feel a little shimmer of heat travel up his neck. While he hadn't been unfaithful to Saffron, he had moved on pretty quick.

'She's a journalist,' he replied. 'She was doing a piece on weddings and the people who work at them. I helped her out.'

Saffron gave him a disbelieving look, and then she lifted her chin. 'Wrong again, smart guy. Nicole isn't a journalist.'

He turned to look at Nicole. She looked very much the way she had moments after she'd dropped that memory card into a glass of champagne. He didn't have to ask her if it was the truth.

'You lied to me?'

An icy wave washed over him. He didn't like this, didn't like it one bit. One moment his evening had been going on fairly normally, and now he felt like Alice falling down the rabbit hole, knowing he had to make impact at some point, but everything was getting stranger and stranger the longer it took to hit ground zero.

'Yes, she lied to you,' Saffron said, a look of dark triumph on her face. 'And she lied to me too. She's not a journalist, Alex. Never has been. She's my proposal planner.'

He closed his eyes. Proposal planner. On the face of it the words made sense, but he just couldn't seem to work out what that meant.

'Who's proposing?' he asked, realising it was probably a really stupid question.

The fire in Saffron's eyes wavered and that lost-little-girl expression flickered over her face, just for a second. 'I was. To you.'

Okay. He'd obviously already hit the ground and got concussion in the process, because now things were getting seriously screwy. 'But we broke up...'

Saffron's eyes narrowed. 'Yes,' she said, shooting a venomous look at Nicole, 'and now I understand why.'

He shook his head. 'No.' That wasn't the reason, or at least it had only been part of it.

Saffron's voice broke. 'Don't you lie to me too, Alex! I don't think I can stand that.' She marched over to Nicole and delivered a blistering slap to her face. 'You'll pay for this,' she snarled. 'I'll make sure Hopes & Dreams never gets another customer. And I can do it! You know that I can!'

And then she turned to him. 'And you...! Mr I'm-so-honest-it-hurts! You're nothing but a big fat hypocrite! I'm suddenly very glad I didn't make a fool of myself for asking you to marry me in front of all those people—and even gladder I won't ever have to go through with it.'

He knew what was coming next and he didn't move. When Saffron got in a slapping mood she kind of built up a momentum. And when she'd finished with him and his cheek was stinging hard, she turned and stalked away back to the lift and disappeared.

That left him, Nicole and her two friends all staring at each other.

# CHAPTER FORTY-SEVEN

'Erm…I think we should go and check on Saffron. Don't you, Peggy?' the slender one of Nicole's friends who'd been Lara Croft on New Year's Eve said.

'Huh?' The other one's head twisted in the direction of her friend, but her eyes stayed fixed on him and Nicole.

'Oh, for goodness' sake!' Lara hit the lift button and grabbed Doris by the arm. When the doors slid open, she bundled her inside. Nicole sent them a pleading look, but it was too late. All Doris could do was shake her head and shrug as the doors whispered closed again.

Nicole licked her lips. 'Listen…I know this looks bad, but I can explain!'

He crossed his arms over his chest. 'I'm sure you can, but I'm not sure I want to hear it.'

Nicole stepped forward, but he backed away. Right at this moment he didn't want her anywhere near him.

'You've been lying to me all along,' he said in a low, deceptively controlled voice.

Her shoulders sagged and she let out a heaving breath. 'I told you it was complicated.'

Alex closed his eyes. He was tempted to laugh. Great, bellowing, dry cackles. There was normal people 'complicated' and then there was Nicole Harrison 'complicated'. A bit like comparing a puddle to the mid-Atlantic trench.

'It's part of my job,' she said softly.

He turned before he opened his eyes so he didn't have to see her. Then he walked to the windows and stared across to the awkward and leafless trees in the square opposite. He could just about see her reflection behind his in the dark glass and he moved to eclipse her.

'When someone asks us—Hopes & Dreams, that's my company—to plan a proposal, we arrange to "bump into" the girlfriend. It's usually a girlfriend... You were our first... Never mind.' She sighed. 'It's normally a harmless ten-minute chat, and when the proposal is over we all have a good laugh about it, even the party who's been kept in the dark.'

Alex didn't move. He wasn't finding his current situation even remotely amusing.

He heard her take a step towards him on the thick carpet. 'I didn't know it was you... Not until after I'd arrived at the gallery and had already been chatting. Saffron was supposed to send a message through with your picture, you see, and she was a little bit late.'

There was the tiniest upswing in her tone at the end of that sentence. As if she was asking him a question, as if she was asking him if he understood. He thought back to that evening. He remembered her looking at her phone, the way she'd been spooked and had rushed off straight after.

He turned to face her. 'You didn't have to keep on with it after that. What was all that business about following me round at weddings—surely that wasn't necessary? What on earth were you trying to do?'

She shook her head and sat down on the end of the bed. A couple of the rose petals that had been strewn there slid off the silk comforter and onto the floor. 'I was just so flustered when I saw you again that I forgot to do my job. I hadn't found out anything about you. I had to keep going with the cover story in case you got suspicious, and it seemed like the perfect opportunity.'

He nodded. Details were coming back to him now, about things she'd said, the way she'd reacted. Problem was, he didn't much like knowing any more than he had not knowing. The mystery of Nicole Harrison wasn't as enticing as he'd imagined it would be. 'So that's why you asked me about my relationship…? About what kind of wedding I'd like?'

She nodded, then looked at the floor.

'And there was me, thinking you'd wanted to talk to me because you actually liked me.' He strode back across the suite towards the door. For some reason he needed to move. When he'd gone as far as he could go, he turned again. 'But why the next wedding after that? Why waitress the other week? I just don't get it!'

Scratch that previous thought. Nicole wasn't becoming more transparent the more he knew her. Every answer just threw up more questions.

'Why?' he asked again. He needed to know. For his own sanity, he needed to know.

She rested her elbows on her knees and covered her face with her hands, spoke through her fingers. 'It seems really lame to say so now, but at the time it didn't seem as if there was any other option.'

He nodded. Those were just excuses. 'I want the truth,' he said. 'You didn't need to go to those lengths. Why did you? Is this another service that your wonderful company offers? Is that why you batted those big brown eyes at me?'

Nicole looked up and frowned. 'I don't know what you're talking about.'

Alex marched towards her, stopped a few feet away from the bottom of the bed. 'What's it called? Ah, yes! A honey trap! Is that what you did, Nicole? Tested my fidelity so Saffron could be sure of me?'

He wanted her to jump up and shout *no*, to slap him in the face or say something nasty right back, so he'd have a legitimate reason to unleash all the rage that was racing round his bloodstream. Instead she just sat there looking wounded. He forced himself not to soften, not to give her an inch. He'd fallen for that look before.

'You really want to know why? Because I've been asking myself the same thing.'

He nodded. 'I really want to know.'

She swallowed, even as she kept looking him in the eye. 'Well, the only explanation I could come up with, and it's not a very good one, was that I suppose I just wanted to see you again.'

'Even though you knew what Saffron was planning?'

She didn't have to answer: her guilt was swimming in her eyes.

'I tried not to feel that way,' she added in a hoarse whisper. 'And I tried to warn Saffron, but you know what she's like…'

He realised he was too close to her. Too close to those pleading brown eyes, to that crazy, nonsensical pull he felt every time he was around her, and he walked away, back to the window where he'd first started. He didn't want to feel that tug, not now.

'Yes, I do know Saffron.' He looked over at her, sitting all vulnerable and Audrey Hepburn–like on the bed. He'd watched that stupid movie last January, when he'd been searching for Nicole, and she reminded him of the tragic heroine now, all sophisticated in a little black dress, but also looking like a lost child.

Who was this woman? Was she this vulnerable waif? Or was she the warm and funny sex kitten who'd kissed him on New Year's Eve? Or the down-to-earth, capable girl who'd been his wedding assistant? He really didn't know. The real Nicole could be someone different, someone he hadn't even met yet. And that was something that scared the crap out of him.

'You used me,' he said, and his anger, which had been slowly turning to embers, leaped into life again.

She shook her head, stood up. 'That's not true!'

He stared at her as she walked towards him. There'd been something bothering him, and he knew what it was now. The dress. It wasn't the same one from New Year's Eve. The neck was different, the skirt longer... Once again, she'd skewed his perception, making him see a mirage instead of the real thing.

'Alex?' she said, her eyes soft and her tone pleading.

He shook his head, moved away from the entrance to the lift to give her plenty of space. 'I don't know who you are,' he told her, 'and I don't want to.' He rubbed his face

FIONA HARPER

with his hand. 'I liked you, Nicole. Really liked you.' He hated the way his voice had caught when he'd said her name, hated himself for being so weak, so stupid, so easily fooled again. So easily snared by a woman just using him to further her ambition, because booking Saffron must have been a plum job. 'But I can't be with someone like you.'

She opened her mouth to speak, but he held up a hand and punched the lift button before moving out of the way, giving her plenty of clearance.

'But I think I'm—'

'Goodbye, Nicole. And I don't care what you think. I'd have rather said yes to Saffron than be with you...because at least I know what I'm getting with her.'

She went completely still, looked at the floor for a few seconds. Just as the lift doors dinged open he thought he saw her shoulders trembling, but he turned away. He didn't want to care if she was upset.

He heard her shoes on the marble tiles of the lift floor, heard the muffled sniff, but still he didn't turn. It seemed like an age before the lift doors sighed closed again. He held his breath until they did. And once the machinery had begun to whirr, he strode over to the well-stocked bar and cracked open a bottle of whisky.

# CHAPTER FORTY-EIGHT

Nicole stood shivering outside a boxy-looking brick building in a back street in Shoreditch. She checked the business card in her hand. Yup. This was where Alex's studio was. To be honest, she didn't know why she was here. It was ten o'clock on a Sunday evening. Only the completely insane would be standing out here in the light drizzle, hoping against hope he might be there.

He was probably somewhere else. With friends. Alex had lots of friends. He probably wasn't moping about, wondering where she was or what she was doing.

A large breath deflated her ribcage. Just how had she come to this? Two months ago her life had been perfect, right on track.

She hadn't even been able to face Mum and Dad today for Sunday lunch, even though she'd said she would go. Yesterday's events were too fresh, too raw. In the end she'd called up first thing and told them she thought she had a touch of flu. Another lie. But that was what she seemed to do best these days, wasn't it?

She was just about to turn round and walk the half-hour

back to her flat, when a dark Jeep drove past her into the little car park round the back of the building. She thought her heart would never start beating again.

And then there he was, striding towards her. Or striding towards the door, to be more exact. As he passed under a street light, he was looking pretty grim, even though he didn't seem to have noticed her standing there.

She called out to him, but it was barely more than a rasp. That was what crying half the day did for you. She tried again. 'Alex?'

He pivoted on the ball of his foot and stared right at her. For a moment he looked menacing, but then surprise broke through his grim expression. 'Nicole?'

She walked closer. 'I—I really need to talk to you.'

The shutters went down in his eyes. 'I think we said all we needed to say yesterday.'

Her insides felt as if they were melting into cold, dark goo. She closed her eyes, breathed in and took another step closer. The rain looked liked golden fuzz in the aura of the street lamp. 'There was a lot I didn't say. I wanted to explain—'

He opened his mouth, but she carried on.

'—and apologise.'

He closed it again.

'Please,' she said, hating the pathetic tone of her voice.

Alex huffed out a breath, but then stomped up some black fire-escape stairs and pulled his keys out of his pockct. 'I must be insane,' he mumbled, 'but since you're standing outside my studio in the rain late on a Sunday evening, clearly, so are you.'

She quickly hurried after him, the high heels of her

boots clonking on the stairs and echoing off the building opposite. When they got inside he hit a switch and blinding white light filled the whole room, supplied by racks of lights hanging in between the air-conditioning vents. She blinked. After the soft yellow of the street lights it seemed unbearably harsh. There were no shadows, nowhere to hide.

Alex threw his keys on a trestle table covered with black-and-white prints then turned to face her. 'Fire away,' he said, folding his arms.

This was what she'd come here for, but now the moment had arrived her mind had gone blank and her mouth had gone dry. She moistened her lips and took a deep breath.

'I'm sorry, Alex. Really I am. I never wanted to lie to you.'

He rested back against the wall. 'Then why did you?'

Suddenly she felt very weary. Maybe it was the walk here. Maybe it was the weight of all the lies she'd told pressing down on her. She'd thought she'd be free of them once the proposal was over, yet they seemed heavier than ever.

'Confidentiality is essential in my line of work,' she said, starting slowly. His expression didn't soften one bit. If anything, she could tell he was inwardly shaking his head and rolling his eyes. 'The clients who come to me are about to plan the biggest surprise of their possible future husband or wife's lives. I cannot let the secret slip, no matter what. How can I let the client spend hundreds, sometimes thousands, of pounds only to gazump them by letting the cat out of the bag?'

Alex shifted his weight. 'I suppose that makes sense.'

Okay, Nicole thought to herself, feeling her shoulders soften a little. She'd got him listening. For now.

'I agreed to do the first wedding because I couldn't think how to get out of it without giving the game away—and I needed to find out more about you, so I could plan a proposal that suited you.'

He let out a dry, barking laugh. 'Ha! You thought some fake trees and three hundred people I hardly knew was my dream come true? You're worse at this than you thought!'

Nicole flinched, but brushed the comment aside. 'Those weren't my original plans. Saffron was very…set…on a particular idea.'

He laughed again, but this time there was a tell-me-about-it warmth to it. He still had his arms folded and he wasn't smiling at her, though. She'd better carry on before her luck ran out.

'And then you practically ambushed me into doing the second wedding—I really thought you might contact *Beautiful Weddings* if I didn't show, and I couldn't let you find out where I really worked. The game would have been up.'

'So you said.'

She sighed again. 'And I tried to get out of the Wardesley job, but Brian was threatening to blackball you round town if he was a waitress down, and I…well, I'd caused you enough trouble. I didn't want to make things worse.'

He looked down at his boots and then up again. 'So you're telling me you pulled a twelve-hour day just to save my butt?'

She nodded. 'Sort of. I didn't really want to, but I couldn't see a way out of it.' She rubbed her forehead with the heel of her palm. She used to be so good at seeing way, way into the future, planning ahead, but ever since she'd met Alex again she seemed to have lost the knack of navigating even the simplest situations with grace.

'And I tried to get Saffron to slow down and think about what she was jumping into. I really did.'

He grunted his acknowledgement, and then he looked up at her. 'Why are you here, Nicole?'

Nicole. Not 'Nic' any more.

She gulped in some air. 'Because I like you too, Alex. More than I should have done. More than I wanted to. But I do.'

He scuffed the concrete floor with the toe of his boot. 'And you want me to say that now it's all over and I'm free of crazy old Saffron we can just walk off into our happy-ever-after? It doesn't work like that.'

'I know.' Her throat felt very tight. She paused for a moment. 'But we have *something*, don't we? Something that's worth not letting it slip away a second time.'

Alex just stared back at her, jaw clenched.

'So there it is,' she said, clasping her hands in front of her, mainly to stop her fidgeting with the buttons on her coat. 'I'm sorry I lied to you, and I'm sorry I hurt you. I don't exactly know what I could have done differently, but I know I messed up. I'm not perfect.' She looked hopefully at him. 'You seemed to think that wasn't such a bad thing once upon a time, that maybe even something wonderful could come from mistakes…'

He shook his head and pushed himself away from the wall, walked around the empty space. 'I don't care about you being perfect,' he said slowly as he paced. 'I care about you being real. And there lies the problem—I have no idea who you are. Are you the smart, slick woman standing before me?'

She looked herself up and down. Okay, she hadn't quite been able to bear coming to see him in her tatty tracksuit bottoms with all her mascara smudged down her cheeks, but she hadn't especially dressed up. It was just that most of her wardrobe looked a certain way.

'Or are you the girl who drops memory cards in champagne glasses? Who goes gooey at other people's weddings? Or were you just being who you needed to be to keep that all-important confidentiality going?'

'You want the truth?'

He nodded. Instead of looking just plain angry now, there was sadness in his expression.

She wanted to tell him that she was the latter, the girl he liked, the girl who knew how to be a little bit impulsive, to go with the flow like he did, but she wasn't sure if that was really her or if he just rubbed off on her when she was with him. She sighed and then gave him his answer. 'The truth is that I don't really know, either.'

He pressed his lips together, looking resigned. She knew he was going to pull the plug. She saw it in his eyes before the words even formed in his brain.

'All I know is that I'm being real now,' she said quickly. 'There's no job to lie for, no reason to pretend to be anything that I'm not.'

He nodded, walked closer. Far too close for her sense of composure not to flitter up to the ceiling like the dust he'd disturbed with his striding. 'The problem is that you talk a good talk... But if you don't know who you are from one moment to the next, how am I supposed to?'

'I don't know,' she said again. She seemed to be saying that a lot tonight.

He shook his head. 'It's no basis for a relationship.'

She nodded. She knew that much.

He finally touched her, lifted his hand to stroke her hair as he looked into her eyes. 'Maybe it was only ever supposed to be what happened on New Year's Eve, that one perfect moment. I don't think you're ready for it to be anything more, Nicole.'

She wanted to argue. She wanted to tell him he was wrong, that she wanted everything from him. But she couldn't. Because he was right. The girl she'd turned herself into didn't know how to be real, and maybe she never would.

She had one last thing to tell him before she left, though.

'If it had been my proposal,' she began, 'I would have done it differently.'

He stepped back, stared back at her, unblinking.

She took a steadying breath. 'I would have taken you hiking, along the shores of a remote loch in Western Scotland, a place where the water is as clear as glass, even in the weak winter sun. I'd have told you we were staying at a youth hostel, but as the sun set I would have led you to a little castle perched on an outcrop that looked over the loch. The air would have smelled of heather and the clouds would have huddled round a large and pale full moon, so clear you could have photographed the individual craters if you'd wanted to.'

She paused for a moment, swallowed to moisten her dry throat. 'Inside there would have been no one, but we'd have walked in to find a roaring fire and a picnic in a large wicker hamper. There, on a small table beside a small and cosy leather sofa built for two, would have been a bottle of exceptional single malt and two glasses.

'We'd have shrugged off our coats and warmed ourselves on the outside with the fire and the inside with a dash of what was in the bottle. I'd have kissed you slowly, softly, the taste of whisky on my tongue, a promise in my touch, and then I would have whispered in your ear. No fuss, no rigmarole. No fireworks, no choirs. Just simple words. Just the truth.' She inhaled, aware the burning in her nose would soon make any further speech impossible. 'That is how I would have asked you to marry me.'

Alex stood there like a statue. He looked as if he'd just been slapped. Nicole waited for him to come out of his trance, but he didn't move, didn't speak. Eventually, she just dropped her head, turned and walked out the door.

# CHAPTER FORTY-NINE

Peggy and Nicole's doorbell went at 8 a.m. Peggy was still in her fluffy pink dressing gown, so she shooed Nicole, who was mostly dressed, down the stairs to open the door. She found Mia standing there, a cardboard tray containing three takeaway coffee cups in her hand.

'Hello,' Nicole said, rubbing the corner of one eye with her index finger. 'What are you doing here?'

Mia often looked a bit serious, Nicole thought, and she did so this morning. 'I brought cappuccinos,' she replied, giving nothing away. Nicole let her inside and followed her back upstairs to the flat.

Mia put the coffees on the kitchen table and yelled for Peggy to join them. Peggy appeared with only one false eyelash attached, but Mia refused to let her go and sort the other one out. 'We need to have an emergency meeting,' she explained.

Peggy yawned and slid into one of the mismatched wooden chairs that surrounded her vintage Formica table, which she'd rescued from an old cafe that had gone out of business. 'I wouldn't exactly call cappuccinos and pastries an emergency, but I'm prepared to go with the flow…' She eyed the paper bag that Mia had placed on the table beside the coffees. 'Got an almond croissant in there?'

'Of course,' Mia said and nudged the bag in her direction. Once Peggy had snaffled her pastry, she handed the bag to Nicole.

'I thought you might need fortification when you saw this…' Mia slapped a tabloid newspaper down on the table. It took a couple of seconds for Nicole to compute there were faces she recognised on there, and that Saffron's almost filled the front cover. She snatched it up and stared at it, mouth open.

'How…? What…? How…?'

Peggy leaned in over her shoulder and read the headline beside the picture of Saffron. '"Proposal Planner Stole My Fiancé". Hey, that's you, Nicole!'

Nicole's gaze drifted to the two smaller pictures flanking the one of a forlorn-looking Saffron. One was of Alex and Saffron together, smiling at each other. The grainy texture suggested it was a personal photo, probably taken on someone's mobile phone. And the other was a fuzzy one of Nicole, looking tense and, well…the only word Nicole could think of to describe the look on her face was 'bitchy'.

Peggy swore. 'They must have taken that sometime since Saturday!' she added, tapping a hot-pink fingernail against Nicole's unflattering image.

Nicole couldn't do anything but stare. Peggy was right. There was a certain puffiness around her eyes that had marked it out as a recent photo, a certain deadness in her expression.

She shook her head slowly. 'Someone has been following me? Taking my picture without my knowledge?'

Peggy shrugged. 'Look on the bright side! You did say you wanted Hopes & Dreams to be a little more high profile...' She looked at the headline again. 'This certainly accomplishes that.'

Nicole turned to look at her. 'Are you insane? I said we needed more high-profile clients! Not to become notorious...infamous...' She closed her eyes to block out the words and images swimming in front of them. 'This is not what I meant and you know it!'

'I was just trying to find the silver lining,' Peggy mumbled, sounding a little hurt.

Nicole opened her eyes and pulled Peggy into a loose hug. 'I know. I'm sorry. I shouldn't have shouted at you. It's just... It's just...' Her eyes were drawn to the picture of her again. She was turning into the bitch the photo suggested she was, obviously.

Peggy squeezed her back. 'It's okay. I know this has to be hard for you.' She pulled away and shrugged. 'If it was me, I'd probably just laugh it off, but I know this kind of stuff matters to you.'

'What kind of stuff?'

'What people think of you.'

Mia pulled out a chair and sat down. The other two followed. 'I thought you should see this straight away, before you opened the office,' she said.

Nicole knew that was true, but her brain had snagged on Peggy's comment. 'You think I care too much about what people think about me?'

Peggy and Mia looked at each other, then back at her.

'A little bit,' Mia said tactfully.

Nicole shook her head and looked at the picture. How stupid of her. How stupid to care so much about something so artificial. She had a feeling she didn't even know who she was any more, so how could she get upset if people drew their own conclusions—ones based on her actions, no less. The horrible thing was they might be right.

'What does it say?' she asked quietly. 'Inside?' There had to be a spread to go along with that headline.

Mia sighed and pulled the paper over to flip it open. Nicole deliberately kept her focus on her cappuccino. She took the lid off and downed a large, scalding mouthful.

'Pretty much what you'd guess, given the circumstances...' Mia said as she skim-read the article she'd obviously digested earlier. 'She hired us... You met with Alex... On the night of the proposal it came to light that you'd been seeing each other behind her back.'

'But we weren't!'

Peggy shoved the cinnamon roll in her direction. 'We know that and you know that, but clearly Saffron doesn't. I can see how she joined up the dots and got the wrong picture.'

For a moment Nicole couldn't move, but then she slumped down until her forehead rested on the table. She didn't even care she could tell the ends of her hair were sticking to one side of her cinnamon roll.

Well, that was it. Even if she hadn't been tempted to pull the plug on her hopes and dreams, they were blown to smithereens now anyway. It didn't help that she knew she was the one who'd pressed the detonator. She'd wanted to build a name for herself, a reputation, but it certainly hadn't been this one. 'Shoot me now...' she mumbled with her lips against the table. It was the only humane thing left to do.

She raised her head. 'I'm so sorry, girls. I really am so sorry.'

Mia reached across and rubbed her arm. Peggy reached across and did the same, but then stole half her pastry too. 'It's okay...'

Nicole sat up then stood up. 'You don't get it, do you? No, it isn't!'

Peggy waved at her to sit down again. 'We'll weather this storm. It'll all blow over in a couple of weeks.'

Nicole shook her head. 'No, I don't think we will. This business is built on trust.'

'They trust us to give them a show-stopping proposal and we certainly did that for Saffron,' Peggy said. 'It even said so in the article!'

Nicole sighed. 'But our clients also trust us to keep their secret and not give away what they're up to, but most importantly, they trust us with their future, their happiness.' Her voice got quieter. 'They trust us with their hopes and dreams... Who is going to book us now? Nobody wants to hire a proposal planner more likely to make all their nightmares come true by stealing the groom than give them a happy-ever-after!'

Both Mia and Peggy opened their mouths. Nicole knew they both wanted to say something to contradict her, to cheer her up. She could even see their brains whirring away behind their eyes. There were plenty of platitudes Peggy could have come out with: *If at first you don't succeed*...or *Live to fight another day*...but even she was silent.

Eventually, they all just started drinking their cappuccinos and eating their pastries in silence. Just like that, their emergency meeting felt as if it had turned into a wake.

# CHAPTER FIFTY

Alex stood in front of a large display of bouquets in the supermarket and wondered which one Saffron would like best.

See? This was why things had got so screwy. They didn't even know each other well enough for him to remember her favourite flower. How on earth had she thought they were ready to walk down the aisle together? Especially when he'd broken up with her!

That was why he needed to go and see her. They needed to clear the air so they could both move on. He'd hurt her, by accident of course, but he'd still hurt her, and he didn't like that. Saffron was a delicate creature, like a butterfly— showy and beautiful, but so, so fragile.

He grabbed a bunch of yellow roses and headed for the tills, hoping she wouldn't read too much into his gift of appeasement. He stopped before he got to the 'baskets only' line, headed back to the floral display and chose something more architectural, all sorts of weird things he couldn't name mixed with a few he could, including giant blue thistles. Surely she couldn't read the wrong message into that?

He was waiting in line behind an old lady who couldn't find her purse at the bottom of her rather roomy handbag, when he glanced around, just for something to do to pass the time until it was his turn. That was when he saw it—the monstrosity in the magazine rack.

He leaped out of the line and grabbed the offending newspaper off the shelf, so hard he ripped a couple of pages as he did so. He knew he probably shouldn't say the string of words he wanted to say out loud, so he yelled them inside his head, all the while his gaze fixed on the headline in front of him.

"'Scuse me, dear...'

He turned to find the old lady looking at him.

She nodded at the flowers in his hand. 'I don't think your lady friend will appreciate it if you've deadheaded them before they're ready for it.'

He looked down at the bouquet. Somehow, in his dash to the magazine rack, one of the big woody-looking flowers had got a bit crushed and he'd lost the top of a thistle all together. 'Thanks,' he mumbled and shoved both flowers and newspaper in the direction of the cashier.

What, oh, what had Saffron done now?

Ten minutes later, he was standing outside her swanky apartment building in Chelsea. Someone on the way out buzzed him in and he took the stairs two at a time until he reached her landing. Then he pounded on her glossy black door.

She opened it a few moments later, barefooted and sleepy, even though it was well after midday. 'Alex!'

'Yes, Alex,' he said, barging past her into the flat. He marched into the living room and then turned and waited for her to catch up to him. When she padded through the door he let out the string of words he'd been trying to hold back. He wasn't proud he did it, but he'd just reached that pressure-cooker stage when there was nothing else he could do with them.

'Hello to you too,' she said drily and then threw herself onto the corner sofa, arms folded, lips pouting.

Alex resisted the urge to throw the bouquet against the windows. Instead he dropped it on the coffee table, where the damp ends began curling the cover of one of her fashion magazines. 'What did you expect?' he asked and threw the newspaper so it landed on the sofa cushion next to her. 'You've made me look like a philandering jackass!'

Saffron's eyes grew wide and she covered her mouth with her hand. 'Oh!'

Give him strength! 'Yes, oh.'

She shook her head and stared at the paper. 'There was a journalist at the party and I was so furious…' She looked up at him. 'I just wanted to get back at *her*. I totally forgot that—'

He turned away and strode to the opposite side of the room, effectively cutting her off. Typical Saffron. She never thought things through, always went on impulse. The reasoning behind the ill-considered proposal suddenly became much clearer. As in, there hadn't been any.

When he turned back again, Saffron had folded her arms and was looking less penitent. 'But you did cheat on me…'

He shook his head. 'You need to get your facts straight before you start spouting off to the press. Yes, there was something going on between me and Nicole—'

'I knew it!'

'—but I kissed her. Twice. That was all.'

'Twice more than you should have done,' Saffron mumbled.

Alex took a deep breath. He was on the verge of losing it, and he really didn't want to do that right now. He had a pretty long fuse, but once it was lit… Well, people just needed to get out of the way.

'I kissed her for the first time on New Year's Eve last year.'

Saffron's eyebrows shot up.

'Yes. That's right.' Satisfaction flowed through him, warm and comforting. 'I met her at a party before I even knew you. And I didn't see her again until she came to spy on me—at your request.'

'Oh,' Saffron said softly. 'She was *that* girl.'

Alex frowned. 'What girl? How did you know about that?'

Saffron did a little shrug. 'Tom kept teasing you about her when I first met you. I knew at the time she must be my competition if he was still going on about it months after it had happened. But then he stopped mentioning her and I forgot all about it.'

Alex blinked. He didn't remember that at all. Okay, the ribbing he did remember, but not that Saffron had been witness to any of it.

'And the second time?' she asked.

'After I broke up with you,' he replied. 'Because I did break up with you, Saffron, even if you chose to pretend otherwise.'

She pulled a cushion to her chest and hugged it to her, looked down at her lap. 'I know.'

Those two words were as effective as a pin in the bubble of his anger. He exhaled and dropped onto a small two-seater sofa opposite her, sitting forward, his feet apart and his arms resting on his knees. 'I didn't cheat on you,' he said firmly. 'Not that the rest of the world is going to believe that now.'

She had the grace to blush, just a little. 'I could ring the guy up? Offer him another exclusive?'

He shook his head. 'Spare me.' There was no knowing what other damage she could do if he consented to that. It would be better to ride the current frenzy out as fast as possible. There'd be someone new for the tabloids to tear to shreds in a few minutes anyway.

He glanced at the paper, to the blurry photo of a tight-lipped Nicole on the cover. 'You weren't fair to her,' he said. 'If I didn't cheat, neither did she.'

Saffron rolled her eyes. 'She must have done something—bat her eyes at you while she was supposed to be doing that "research" she talked about.'

He shook his head. 'No. She didn't. In fact, she told me quite clearly that our relationship would be purely professional.'

Saffron punched the cushion she was hugging and let out a snort. 'That didn't last, though, did it?'

'It lasted long enough,' he said quietly. 'Long enough that I did right by you, anyway.'

They fell quiet after that. He stared at the slightly bedraggled bouquet, picking out the different colours and shapes, wondering what they'd look like in black and white with a good strong light to one side...

When he looked up again she was studying him. She

looked very young, clutching that cushion to her, like a twelve-year-old with her favourite teddy bear. He sighed. There were things he needed to say, questions he needed to ask, and he wasn't going to take any joy in it.

'I realised you and I were just coasting. Surely you sensed that too?'

She twisted her mouth, biting her lip while she considered his question. 'A little bit.'

'So the solution was to propose?'

She sighed, stroking the cushion. 'It seemed like a good idea at the time.'

Alex put his head in his hands. He was tempted to either scream or laugh. That was the thing about Saffron: you couldn't stay angry with her for very long. 'Seriously, though,' he said, raising his head.

'You know what it was like for me a couple of months ago… Michelle had just got married, and Dad gave that speech at her wedding. And when I talked to him afterwards he said he loved me, but he wished I was more like her, more…grown-up.'

Alex sucked in some air through his nostrils. Saffron worshipped her dad. He knew that had to have hit her hard, especially after all the nonsense in the press about her just before that.

'I was so cross with him,' she said, shaking her head and frowning. 'It felt like he wasn't on my side any more, and he'd always been on my side. And there you were… the only person not looking down on me and judging me. I just… I suppose I just thought I didn't want to lose that. And it felt as if you were drifting away from me…'

He pressed his lips together. In that case, she'd cottoned

on to it even before he had. 'Are you sure just a little bit of it wasn't because you were thinking you'd show him how wrong he was about you?'

A smile, a slightly naughty smile, played on Saffron's lips for a minute. 'Maybe. But then once the impulse had struck I got caught up in it. I began to think how nice it would be to have you around always.'

He smiled back, a soft sympathetic kind of one. 'We can't be each other's security blanket, Saff. Marriage is supposed to be more than that. *Love* is supposed to be more than that.'

She nodded. 'I know that now.' Then she looked up at him, her eyes clear and soft. 'Is that how you feel about her? Nicole? That it's the *something more*?'

He stiffened, sitting up straight. 'I don't know where you got that idea from.'

She tilted her head. 'You seemed quite intent on defending her earlier on.'

He took in a breath and held it. Had he? It hadn't seemed like that at the time. He'd just been being clear about what was real—what was true—and what was not.

Anyway, it was time to change the subject. He shook himself and stood up, walked over to Saffron and pulled her up too. Then he gave her what he hoped came off as a brotherly hug. 'I will always be on your side. You know that,' he said softly.

She pulled back and nodded, her eyes shimmering.

'I just can't be by your side as your boyfriend any more. But I will always be your friend, if you want me.'

She let out a chuckle and punched him on the arm. Surprisingly hard, actually. 'Of course I want you, you big wally.' Then she heaved in a breath and let it out again, before looking at him through her lashes. 'Are you going to see her now?'

He looked at his shoes, stopped smiling. 'No, I'm not going to see her. We're not together. Not after what happened the other night.'

Saffron might be maturing a little, but a glimmer of satisfaction passed across her features. 'Why?' she asked, sounding very nonchalant while she fixed him with her eyes.

'Because she lied to me,' Alex said. 'Because I can't trust anything she said to me.'

Saffron looked at him for a long while, and then she nodded. 'Wow. That Vanessa really did a number on you, didn't she?'

He stepped back, crossed his arms. 'Don't know what you mean.'

He picked up the slightly decimated flowers and offered them to her. 'Here. You'd better put those in a vase.'

She shrugged and took them from him. 'I don't know how.'

His face crumpled into an amused frown. 'I thought girls like you learned that kind of stuff at finishing school.'

She smiled softly back at him. 'You should know me well enough to guess that girls like me were secretly on their mobiles all the way through lessons like that.'

She let the bouquet drop on the sofa behind her and followed him as he headed to the door. He turned to say goodbye in the hallway and found her leaning on the jamb, looking at him. 'I really am sorry about the newspaper article.'

He shrugged. 'I'm a big boy. I can take care of myself. I'm sorry about the proposal thing, that you and I didn't work out. Part of me kind of wished it had.'

That was the truth. He wished he had found it in himself to love her. Life would be simple then. Far less painful. Far less complicated. He was beginning to hate that word.

'No, you don't,' she said as she began to close the door. 'But I don't think you want it to work out with anyone.'

'Don't be daft,' he said, wishing he'd just walked away and hadn't waited for her to see him out. 'Why on earth would you think that?'

Saffron gave him a penetrating look. She didn't make sense very often, but when she did it was often hard to ignore.

'You always say you want "real", Alex, but that goes out the window once emotions are involved. You never want to see real emotions. You just push them all away and pretend they don't exist. You didn't let me get close to you, and I'm not sure you're going to let her, either.' She looked sad for a moment, then shook herself, smiled softly. 'I should probably be happy about that. Bye, Alex.'

And then she closed the door and left him standing there, while she went back to her fabulous life.

# CHAPTER FIFTY-ONE

Nicole slumped on her desk and looked at the old tailor's shop's clock with one eye. It seemed to take an age for the second hand to move from one little mark to the next. In her head the soundtrack to *The Breakfast Club* played, as she imagined the scene where the five main characters got more and more bored as their detention stretched on, doing more and more outlandish things in the deserted school library. But just as long as Peggy didn't do a Judd Nelson and set fire to her own shoe, they'd probably be all right.

Nicole had a bad feeling about this. It had been like this since Saffron's article had hit the newsstands. Not that the phone hadn't been ringing in the five hours since the office had been open. It had. But it was all journalists wanting a comment and now they'd switched it to answerphone. The one ray of light had been a call from Saffron's friend Marcus, who Peggy had met for an initial meeting, but it turned out he was letting them know he was putting his proposal plans on hold.

Nicole had a bad feeling about that too.

It shouldn't be like this. It was too quiet. The period be-tween the beginning of November and Valentine's should be their busiest patch, according to the blogs of similar long-established agencies in the States. They hadn't even had any email enquiries about the basic ideas packages.

Nicole wanted to believe that it was just because it was Christmas Eve and most people were busy panicking about last-minute shopping or prepping for their Christmas din-ners tomorrow. She tried to tell herself things would perk up again in the new year.

She sighed and changed position. 'Want another cup of coffee?' she asked without picking up her head.

Peggy made a gagging noise. 'If I drink any more I think I'll slosh when I walk. Maybe we should—'

She was cut off by the phone ringing. Both of them sat up straight and listened attentively, waiting to see if it was yet another journalist.

'Hello?' a slightly nervous male voice said. 'This is James Hunter.'

They stared first at the phone and then at each other. Jimmy Hunter? Saffron's friend?

Peggy lunged for the phone and snatched the receiver up. 'Hello?'

Nicole sat up straight, ears straining, but with only Peggy's half of the conversation to go on, it was very hard to make out if it was good news or bad news.

'Yes…I see…Of course, we understand entirely…Good-bye, and thank you.' Peggy put the phone down. She looked over at Nicole. 'A firm, but polite, "I'm going another way" when it comes to planning his proposal. In other words, he's scurrying off to Detest and Squinty. Out of loyalty to Saffron.'

Nicole propped her elbows on the desk and rested her chin in her upturned palms. 'Well, that's it, then, isn't it? Both of Saffron's contacts—the only new bookings we had—have now cancelled, and after that article it doesn't look as if anyone else is beating down our door. This could be the end of Hopes & Dreams.'

The end of her hopes and dreams too. She'd busted a gut to get herself this far, and look where she'd ended up— worse than being back at square one. At least she'd had her reputation back then.

'What we need is a miracle,' Peggy muttered, and then she looked over at Nicole. 'Why don't you give it another whirl? It worked last time.'

Nicole shook her head. 'Nah-uh. No way. That's what got us into this mess in the first place.' This time she was keeping her mouth shut.

But even as she pressed her lips together and forced herself to check her empty inbox one more time, her heart couldn't help whispering a tiny plea. Not for herself, but for Peggy and Mia. They didn't deserve to lose all their savings because she'd been too proud to tell the truth. And she loved this place, loved the work she did helping people start their lives together. She glanced at the other end of the shop. She'd even come to love that stupid pink wall.

She didn't know if it would make a difference, if her prayer would do anything more than bump into the ceiling and disappear. She'd also run out of faith and was too tired to take the 'fake it until it happens' approach anyway. All she could do now was try to navigate the chaos of her life as honestly and humbly as she could and hope that she'd learned her lesson enough for life to give her a second chance.

# CHAPTER FIFTY-TWO

Nicole pushed a chipolata wrapped in bacon round her plate. Usually, Christmas lunch was her favourite meal of the year. Her mum's turkey dinners were legendary, with home-made bread sauce, pork-and-chestnut stuffing, crispy roast potatoes. And then there was the gravy. Occasionally, Nicole fantasised about bathing in that gravy...

The table around her was full of noise. Mum liked a houseful at Christmas. Auntie Pat was here, along with her two sons and their wives and assorted little ones. Nicole put her fork down, deciding to stop worrying the life out of the sausage and leave it alone. At least there was so much commotion with all the other guests that no one seemed to notice she was a bit quiet. She felt as if she were in her own little bubble, insulated from the noise of crackers and the petulant refusals to eat anything green.

However, after lunch, as everyone else was flopped out in the living room watching a film and she was helping her mother with the last of the washing-up, Mum put down her tea towel. Nicole could feel her watching her as she attacked the roasting tin with a washing-up brush.

'What's up, darling? You don't seem your usual self today.'

Maybe that was a good thing. She wasn't sure if she liked the 'usual self' she'd fashioned herself into over the last few years. That girl was a fake and a snob.

She wasn't going to tell her mother that, though, and prepared to churn out one of her standard non-committal responses as she really got into the corner of the roasting tin with the brush, but then she also abandoned her task and turned to face her mum.

She had the best parents in the world, and yet sometimes she felt so lonely in their company. It was hard—being this perfect daughter, this perfect person—and she didn't want to feel this sense of distance between her and them any more. If she was really honest with herself, she was tired of dressing for that ever-elusive perfect life she wanted. What had been so wrong with the one she'd already had?

'I've messed up,' she said simply. 'That's all there is to it.'

And the whole story came out—Alex and everything—over a cup of tea while the roasting tin sat in washing-up water that was rapidly turning cold and greasy. She shook her head as she finished her tale. 'He's never going to forgive me.'

Her mother sighed and looked at her. 'Do you remember the Ashers who used to live next door?'

Nicole blinked. Of course she did. But what did that have to do with her life going down the toilet? 'Yes. I loved their tree house, remember?'

Her mother nodded. 'I also remember that you were always round there playing with Jeremy and Isla and

Kate. Sometimes I had to drag you back here kicking and screaming.'

Nicole chuckled softly. Yes, she remembered that. Even aged eight she'd been able to dig her heels in and cause herself and everybody else trouble.

'You used to pretend you were one of them,' her mother added. 'You'd borrow the girls' clothes and talk the way they talked. Once I even caught you calling yourself Nicole Asher, you wanted to be part of their gang so badly.'

Nicole pulled a sad face, shaking her head. 'I'm sorry, Mum. I probably didn't realise how hurtful that must have been at the time, thinking I didn't want to be part of this family.'

Her mother shrugged her words off. 'I understood. I think it was more about wanting to have brothers and sisters and have that sense of fitting in. I knew you found it hard being an only child.'

'It was…sometimes. But you know I think the world of you and Dad.'

Her mother nodded, looked a little wistful. 'I wanted brothers and sisters for you too, but it wasn't to be. There were complications when I had you… I always knew it might be difficult after that.'

Nicole couldn't stand that look in her mother's eyes. She leaned over the table and hugged her. 'I'm sorry I let you down,' she whispered. With only one child to bet on, she'd felt the pressure to fulfil all their dreams, not that they'd pushed for that. It was just that she'd loved them so much she'd wanted to make them proud, to prove she was enough all on her own. And look at her life now.

She sat back down again. She probably shouldn't have

spilled the beans about Hopes & Dreams, Saffron and Alex, but she found she couldn't regret it. She felt cleaner, calmer. And she and Mum were having a proper talk for the first time in ages.

'There's nothing to be sorry for,' her mother said, looking quite determined. 'We're proud of you no matter what, because of who you are, not because of what you do.'

Nicole couldn't respond to that. There was a lump the size of an undigested Brussels sprout in her throat.

'You've blossomed into such a lovely woman, Nicole. Only, I don't think you see it, and it breaks my heart. You're always so hard on yourself.'

A tear slid down Nicole's cheek. 'Peggy said that to me too.'

Ever practical, her mother reached for the box of tissues and handed one to her. 'That girl might have some strange ideas about what to wear, but she's got a good head on her shoulders.'

'And he said it,' Nicole added, her voice breaking a little. 'Alex…'

Her mother nodded, smiling softly. 'He sounds like a keeper.'

Another tear escaped. Just when she thought she'd got all the ones clogging her lashes marshalled and behaving properly. 'I think he is. I'm just not sure *I* am.'

Her mother's expression changed instantly. 'Nicole Amelia Harrison, don't you dare talk like that!'

She looked down at the top of the kitchen table, scarred by years of use, but nonetheless beautiful for it. 'Sorry,' she mumbled.

'If he likes you as much as you say he does, then there's

hope,' her mother said, and then she laughed gently. 'You've got to give the poor lad a chance to regroup. All of that coming out in one night must have been a heck of a shock.'

Nicole nodded. She supposed that was true. 'But he says he doesn't know who I am.'

Her mother patted her hand, stood up and retrieved her tea towel. 'There's only one answer to that—show him.'

# CHAPTER FIFTY-THREE

Nicole still didn't know how to do what her mother had said to her. She did, however, know something else she needed to do, and that was to face Saffron. Peggy had offered to meet with her in Nicole's place, but Nicole had refused. It was her mess and she needed to deal with it, not try to buff it away and hope it didn't show, the way she had done with all the other things she didn't like about herself for so many years.

Knowing that didn't make it any easier as she approached the little Italian cafe just off the King's Road where she'd arranged to meet her former client. To be honest, she'd been surprised that Saffron had agreed. Or maybe there'd be some paparazzi waiting to snap the inevitable catfight and the whole thing would go a second round in the papers. Who knew?

She was five minutes late, having got caught up by a delay on the Circle Line, but she assumed she'd probably have at least fifteen minutes to choose a table, sip a fortifying espresso, before Saffron turned up. It was a surprise, then, to walk into the cafe and find her sitting at a table near the window.

She looked up as Nicole walked through the door. The expression she wore wasn't hostile, but it wasn't that welcoming, either. Nicole drew in a shaky breath through her nostrils and walked over to her. Saffron motioned for her to sit down and she took the chair opposite.

'Thank you for seeing me,' Nicole said, as she tucked her handbag under the table. Not a designer one this time. Just a little patchwork floral thing she'd picked up in Clerkenwell market. And she hadn't dressed in her usual uniform of expensive neutral shades, either. What was the point in trying to out-Saffron Saffron? She was never going to win.

Saffron didn't say anything, just summoned the barista to come over and take their order. Nicole guessed this wasn't the sort of place that usually did table service, but no one was going to argue with Saffron, were they?

'I want to put the record straight,' Nicole began.

Saffron gave her a superior look. 'I don't want to hear a string of excuses.'

Nicole nodded. She so wanted to give them, to make herself look better, to explain why none of it was her fault, but she was trying to nix that habit. 'Firstly, I want you to know that whatever Celeste Delacourt may have told you, nothing happened between Alex and I while you were a couple.'

Saffron blinked. 'Alex said as much. I'm tempted to believe him.'

'Alex?' Her stomach dropped at the mere mention of his name. 'You've seen him?'

'Yes.'

The barista brought their coffees, cutting any further

conversation on the subject off. It was only then Nicole realised just how hungry she was for details about him. Was
he okay? Had he seemed upset? Angry? A thousand questions flew through her mind, but she knew she couldn't
ask Saffron any of them.

'I should have told you the truth after that first meeting with Alex,' she said, stirring a lumpy sugar cube into
her espresso. She'd worked out that that had been where
things had taken a wrong turn. She might not have been
able to control the fact that fate had thrown Alex back into
her life again unexpectedly, but she'd had the chance to be
totally open and honest up front, and she'd chickened out.

'Then why didn't you?'

Nicole looked at the grey marble tabletop, followed one
of the feathery veins as it flowed across the table, connect-
ing her and Saffron. She looked up again. 'Because I was
proud. I didn't want you to think badly of me, not when
Hopes & Dreams really needed your business.'

Saffron raised her eyebrows, a look that said she didn't
necessarily like what she'd heard, but she couldn't fault
Nicole's honesty.

'And I really didn't think it was going to be an issue at
first—or maybe I just kidded myself into thinking that.'
She'd made a lot of bad judgement calls throughout this
whole mess of a situation, hadn't she? 'After all, I believed
that you and Alex were a very serious item and I was just
a blip—a moment—in his past. Not even a relationship. It
shouldn't have made a difference.'

Saffron sipped her coffee. 'But it did.'

'I know.' She exhaled. 'Even though I tried very, very
hard not to let it. I really want you to believe that.'

Saffron gave her another one of those looks. Nicole hung her head. Yes, she knew. Lame. Stupid. She seemed to be excelling in these things at the moment. And she'd worked out why—she hadn't only been lying to everyone else about who she was; she'd been lying to herself too. No wonder she'd got so badly off track.

'I just wanted to apologise, on behalf of Hopes & Dreams, but more importantly on my own behalf. I like you, Saffron, and I really didn't set out to hurt you.'

There was a faint softening in Saffron's expression. 'Okay.' She flicked her hair back over her shoulder. 'I thought we were becoming friends, Nicole. That's what hurt. I wish you'd said something...'

Nicole sighed. 'I did try to warn you that Alex maybe wasn't ready...'

Saffron gave a reluctant nod. 'I know.'

There was silence for a few moments while they both sipped their coffees. Then Saffron put her cup down and looked Nicole in the eye.

'Listen, Nicole, I do appreciate you coming here and being so honest. I wasn't sure how I'd react, but the fact you've taken responsibility for your part helps, and I suppose I ought to take responsibility for mine.'

'Really, you don't have to—'

'Actually, I do. It's time I started acting like a grown-up, you see. That's what my father has been telling me for years, and it's finally sunk in. I thought I was doing that when I decided to propose to Alex, but it turned out I was just embarking on another stupid scheme that I hadn't properly thought through. I can't say I've enjoyed the past week or two, but I've learned something from it. At least, I hope I have.'

Nicole couldn't help but smile, just gently.

Saffron gave her a wry look. 'I'm not sure if I'm ready to like you again, but I think I have an apology of my own to make—the newspaper article? You deserved taking down a peg or two, but you didn't deserve that.'

She nodded. 'Thank you.' It meant a lot to hear Saffron say that. That blasted article had been the worst of it, almost. Even though she'd promised her mother, and Peggy and Mia, she'd stop worrying so much about her image, what other people thought of her, it still hurt to see her reputation so thoroughly cut to shreds.

At that moment, a burly, dark-haired man walked through the door. He scanned the room then headed towards them.

'Hang on a minute… Isn't that…?'

Saffron waved a hand. 'Yes. It's Julio…the tango dancer. He was very sweet to me when he saw me crying and running through the lobby of the Hamilton the other evening.'

Julio arrived at their table. He hardly even noticed Nicole. His gaze was fixed intently on Saffron, as if she were some rare and precious jewel that he couldn't quite believe existed. It was almost funny to see the epitome of macho swagger turned into a big cuddly teddy bear that way.

'Julio, be a darling and get me a *pain au chocolat*, will you? And another cappuccino—to go.'

Julio immediately jumped to attention and headed for the counter while both women watched him go.

'He's been such a comfort…' Saffron said. There wasn't the same dreamy, besotted look in her eyes as there had been in his, but there was definitely a hint of warmth. And

then she rose and swept from the cafe, leaving a dutiful
Julio to follow in her wake.

Nicole sat shaking her head for a moment. Once again,
Saffron had staged an exit that was both fabulous and surprising.

# CHAPTER FIFTY-FOUR

Hopes & Dreams stayed open during the soggy patch between Christmas and New Year. Nicole wasn't quite ready to give up hope completely yet, but Monday the twenty-ninth was just as quiet as Christmas Eve.

At least it was until about three o'clock in the afternoon when a guy in jeans and a hoody knocked on the door. He marched across the office and looked Nicole up and down. 'Are you her?'

Nicole was starting to wish she'd done as Peggy had suggested and started keeping a baseball bat beneath her desk. 'Listen, I don't know what paper you're working for, but we've told them all the same thing—no comment!'

The guy stepped back and put his hands up. 'Whoa! I'm not a journo. What made you think that?'

'You're not?' Nicole replied, her eyes widening. 'Then why are you here?'

He looked a little confused. 'You're that proposal-planning girl, aren't you?'

She nodded.

He waited, as if what he'd said was self-evident, then

rolled his eyes and carried on. 'Well, I want you to do one for me.'

'Me?'

'Yes.'

'To plan your proposal?'

She glanced back at Peggy, still at her desk, open-mouthed, then back at the man.

'That's what you do, isn't it?'

She nodded. Then she remembered that she really better stop acting like an idiot or she'd scare the only customer they'd had in the last week away. She smiled at him, not her fake, 'everything will be okay' client smile, just a real one. 'Yes. That's what I do. In fact, it's what I love to do, but...' She frowned a little, looked down at her shoes and then back up again. 'Can I ask you something before we start discussing it?'

He shrugged and nodded.

'Why...why did you decide to come to Hopes & Dreams?'

He grinned. 'I saw that story in the paper... My Shelley gets that one every day.'

Nicole's stomach sank, but he carried on regardless.

'And I'd been thinking about popping the question, but I want to do it with style, no expense spared. Something classy. She's had the hump with me, you see, since I took her to see Arsenal play away to Bayern Munich for her birthday trip...'

There was a muffled snort from the direction of Peggy's desk.

'Exactly,' he said. 'I thought I was killing two birds with one stone, but apparently I wasn't being very romantic, so I thought I'd need a bit of advice—and I reckoned if you could steal a bloke from that Saffron Wolden-Barnes, then you might have a trick or two up your sleeve to help me.'

Nicole blinked slowly and her mouth hung slightly open. She had *not* been expecting that at all. 'Oh… Okay…' she finally managed. 'That's good to know.' Seemed her new reputation was starting to work for her rather than against her. And, maybe, since most of their clients were men, they weren't so worried about her stealing their fiancées-to-be, especially not now she'd been outed as a notorious man-eater.

She led him through to the meeting room. 'And when do you think you'd like to propose?'

He did another little shrug. 'I thought Valentine's Day. That's not too cheesy, is it?'

Nicole smiled again and shook her head. 'No, that's not cheesy at all. What could show a girl more that her man loves her than him telling her he wants to spend the rest of his life with her? I think it's perfect.'

She kept smiling as she sat on the sofa opposite him and they began to chat about ideas and budgets. She wasn't sure she was entirely comfortable with gaining clients through her new-found notoriety, but she'd do it. For Mia and Peggy's sake. Whatever it took, from now on, even if it meant she crushed that glossy, polished Nicole even further into the dust.

# CHAPTER FIFTY-FIVE

Nicole was standing in her underwear at the foot of her bed, staring at the three outfits laid out there. She'd tried each of them on at least four times and she was still no closer to making a decision. She'd thought a lot about what her mum had said only a week ago, about showing Alex who she really was. She'd also thought a lot about what that meant.

He was going to be at the fancy-dress party at Déjà Vu tonight, and she'd decided she was going to turn up too. One last chance to see him. One last chance to prove to him she wasn't the manipulating chameleon he feared she might be. But she wasn't going to be able to do any of that if she couldn't decide what to wear.

Aware that she might be dithering as a subconscious attempt at self-sabotage, she made herself go through the options once again. The first outfit was a flouncy and frilly steampunk dress in sapphire satin, complete with corset, eyelet boots and a pair of fake brass goggles. It looked great on, especially the corset bit, which pinched in her waist and pushed her boobs up in a gravity-defying fashion, and she knew Alex liked the style.

He'd been right about the people at the wedding they'd gone to. The costume they chose wasn't about taking on another persona, but about expressing something that came from the inside, something that connected with the outside image. Unlike her, whose classy, neutral wardrobe had all been about hiding behind the facade of who she thought she should be to impress everybody else.

She looked at the three lumps of clothes lying on the bed and sighed. It seemed she was rather out of practice choosing what she wanted to wear for herself and no one else.

She picked up the middle selection and held it up against her body so she could look in the mirror again. It was the Audrey Hepburn dress from last year, the day they'd first met. He'd liked her then. Enough to try everything he could to find her afterwards. It would be a way to remind him he'd seen the real Nicole, loosened from her shell temporarily by a few too many cocktails.

Maybe.

She laid it down again and picked up the third dress. It was a little floral number with large peacock-blue flowers on a white background. She'd pulled it out from the back of the wardrobe after not having worn it for years. It had once been her favourite dress, but it had been eclipsed as her designer wardrobe had grown, consigned to the back of the cupboard for its loud colours and supermarket-clothing-range heritage. Thankfully, it still fitted. And, despite the fact the fabric wasn't the highest quality, it was as flattering as ever.

She sighed and hung it back up in the cupboard. Even if it did look great, this was a fancy-dress party she was going to, and she wouldn't know what to label herself as. Girl In Floral Dress didn't quite cut it.

So it was Audrey or the steampunk effort. She tried both on again, then threw them back on the bed.

The clock said it was almost nine. She'd told Peggy and Mia she'd meet them at the club in half an hour and it was going to take her at least that long to do her make-up and hair—once she'd decided which outfit would dictate the style. And then it was another half an hour to get to the party.

Peggy had wanted to stay behind and help her choose, but she'd told her to go ahead and meet Mia. She'd join them later. For some reason she felt this was a decision she had to make on her own.

Maybe a break would help.

She went into the kitchen, poured herself a half glass of wine and flopped down on the sofa in her bra and knickers. The silence was too complete, so she reached for the remote and turned the TV on. After thirty seconds flicking through the channels, she came across one that did vintage movies. The picture that flashed up on the screen made her heart leap—Molly Ringwald, in her hideous pink dress that was supposed to be really beautiful, standing at the top of a flight of steps and looking at Andrew McCarthy, all uncertain and gorgeous in his tux.

*Pretty in Pink.* That had to be fate, right?

And, as she settled down to drink her wine, intending to take her mind off her wardrobe dilemma for just ten minutes, she had a flash of inspiration. She plonked the glass down on the coffee table, sloshing some of its contents over the edge, and stood up.

Suddenly she knew exactly what she should wear to the party.

# CHAPTER FIFTY-SIX

Alex stood against the bar of Déjà Vu, a bottle of beer in his hand. He'd forgone being a horse's backside for full steampunk dress this year. He thought it'd be fun, had even emailed the groom from the wedding the other week to get some tips and addresses of costume suppliers.

Rather than opting for the look of a steampunk dandy, with embroidered waistcoats, cravats and silky top hats, he'd gone more the intrepid-explorer direction. He wore a white shirt rolled up to his elbows with a battered brown leather waistcoat over the top and a gun belt slung round his waist. A pocket-watch chain looped from one of the waistcoat buttons.

The appreciative looks he was getting from a few of the women in the club told him he hadn't done a bad job. Pity he wasn't in the mood for doing anything about it. All he could think about was if it were possible to invent a steam-powered device to turn back time one whole year.

As much as he was angry with Nicole, he still couldn't help wishing that they could do it all over, that this time he'd chase her out of the bar and make sure he got her number. Then all this stuff he was feeling would go away and he'd be his normal self again. Instead, he felt as if he'd been run over by a truck.

He shook his head and took another swig of his beer.

He shouldn't want her. Not after all that had happened. He should be content to be the easy-going guy who drifted through life with a smile for everyone, but never settled anywhere too long. Life was easier that way. Women were certainly easier that way.

Which was why he should do something about one of the girls batting their lashes at him from across the room. What about that one in the sexy kitten outfit, all soft black fur and fishnets? He glanced her direction and she smiled coyly at him.

Alex turned away and rested his elbows on the bar.

He was such a loser.

He knew he shouldn't have let Nicole get to him like this. Every sense in his body had been screaming at him to keep away, and not just because of Saffron, but because...

He didn't even want to face that thought.

*Because you're more wound up in her than you ever were in Vanessa.*

Damn. It had sneaked out anyway. *Way to cheer yourself up in the middle of a party, mate. Well done.*

He glanced at the clock. It was close to eleven. One more hour. He couldn't quite bring himself to be a total wimp and duck out of the party before then. That would be too sad. But once the new year was in and everyone was jumping around acting like idiots, he'd slip away back to his flat or maybe his studio if he couldn't sleep.

'Alex?'

The voice that came from behind him was soft and hesitant. Benign even. But it still chilled the blood in his veins.

He steeled himself, took a few moments to prepare before he turned round. She was probably dressed as something amazing, that Holly Golightly outfit or something even more dangerous to his blood pressure. He had to be ready to resist it, whatever it was. He took a deep breath and put his beer bottle down on the bar.

Nothing could have prepared him for what met his eye when he turned round to look at her.

'Wh-what…? What on earth are you wearing? What have you come as?'

So *not* the cool, don't-care greeting he'd planned. But that was hardly surprising, seeing as Nicole was standing in front of him, dressed in an outfit he'd never have even imagined her in, let alone seen her wearing.

'Me,' she said simply, calmly, but he could see the hint of nervousness in her eyes.

He looked her up and down again. Couldn't help it.

No heels. Instead the soft cream furry slipper boots she'd sent him in that picture message. On top was a stretched and oversized grey T-shirt, with the *Flashdance* logo printed across it. It was old enough that the colour was cracked and worn, peeling off in a few places. Its only saving grace was that it had dipped off Nicole's shoulder the way the girl's in the film did, revealing a rather tantalising glimpse of smooth skin. And under it she wore the tattiest, ugliest pair of tracksuit bottoms he'd ever seen.

She swallowed and held his gaze when it finally travelled back up to meet hers. He realised her face was totally free of make-up too and her hair was pulled back into a messy ponytail.

'This is me,' she repeated quietly. 'The me that no one ever sees outside the four walls of my flat. The me that I turn into after a hard day at work or when I've got a broken heart...' She looked away as her voice turned husky, but was brave enough to look him in the eye again when she'd recovered herself. 'I've been this me a lot lately.'

'B-but...? Why...?'

*Smooth, Alex. Really cool and in control of yourself.*

He didn't get it. It was the ugliest thing he'd ever seen Nicole wear and yet he could hardly control the raging heat that had started to pulse through his veins. He must be sick. Very sick. It was all he could do to keep his arms welded to his sides so he didn't reach out and touch her.

'You said you wanted to see the real me,' she said, lifting her chin, not looking apologetic, but looking a little proud, a little defiant. 'Well, here I am. It's taken me a long time to work out who she is. I didn't even know she existed until I met you, but no matter how hard I tried to lock her up, she just kept leaking out. And that's because you made me feel it was okay to be this girl...' She trailed off, her voice hoarse again.

He felt a lump form in his throat.

She sniffed and straightened her spine. 'For the first time in as long as I can remember I am *not* dressing up. That's why I came here tonight... To tell you that you did see the real me, that the Nicole you laughed and danced and snapped photographs with was the real deal. And that she's all yours...if you want her.'

Nicole felt as if her heart were going to jump out of her ribcage and tap-dance along the bar. Alex was just staring at her. She'd seen him do this before, hadn't she? Just shut down when anything involved deep emotion. Had she left it too late? Was the whole proposal deception too much to come back from?

But then he stepped forward and smoothed her messy hair away from her temples, held her face in his hands and looked into her eyes. Without heels she was a good few inches shorter than usual and she had to crick her neck to look back up at him.

'I think you're beautiful,' he said, his voice hoarse, his eyes intense. 'Just like this. Always like this.' And then he kissed her, softly at first, but then deeply, as if he couldn't get enough of her. Nicole finally stopped holding her breath and joined him. Inside, she felt as if she were flying. She felt as if she were running up the side of a mountain, then standing at the top, shouting her joy into the wind.

She was reminded of the prayer she'd sent up, just before Saffron had crashed into her life and set this whole mess in motion. She'd asked for someone, hadn't she? Someone to fulfil her hopes for the future. She just hadn't expected the answer to come in a package with shaggy black hair and a killer dimple.

Because that was what he'd done, and not just because she was a pathetic sap who needed a man in her life to make her complete, but because he'd pushed her into taking a good hard look at herself; he'd challenged her to be more than she'd even planned to be. Because he'd seen the best in her before she'd even seen it herself.

They broke apart for a moment. She heaved in some oxygen and tried to get her breathing under control. Alex wound his arms around her back and pulled her close.

'That was almost as good as last year,' she whispered into his ear.

He pulled back and looked at her, expression stern. 'What do you mean *almost*?'

She smiled sweetly at him. 'It's just an incentive to do better when midnight rolls around.'

Alex clearly wasn't patient enough to wait for midnight. He set about delivering a kiss twice as scorching. When he'd finished Nicole felt dizzy. For a few moments there, she'd forgotten they were in a crowded bar full of people. The bubble around them had pulled so tight it had shut the rest of the world out completely.

'You know,' she whispered, smiling at him, watching the little dimple appear as he responded, seeing the warmth in his eyes as he looked at her, warmth she could just curl up and float away on, 'Peggy's gran says the way you start a new year is the way you end it. I didn't think it was going to be quite so literal.'

Alex glanced over his shoulder to the clock behind the bar. 'It's not quite midnight yet. But, hey, I don't mind finding a way to fill the next hour if you don't.'

'That,' she said, reaching up and pulling him down towards her again, 'sounds like a plan.'

Somewhere behind her she heard Peggy's trademark wolf whistle and Mia's triumphant cheer.

Alex ignored them, just smiled against her lips and held her tighter. 'And if Peggy's gran is right,' he said, kissing the corner of her jaw in a way that made her toes tingle, 'I think I'm going to make sure I'm going to be doing exactly this every New Year's Eve for a very long time to come.'

Nicole kissed him back. There was no way she was going to argue with that.

*One year later*

Alex Black, landscape photographer, and Nicole Harrison, proposal planner, arc pleased to announce their engagement. The groom-to-be surprised his new fiancéc by proposing at the stroke of midnight on New Year's Eve while they enjoyed a romantic break at a secret location.

Ms Harrison described the moment as a total surprise and 'utterly perfect', but has remained tight-lipped, only consenting to say that she was thrilled it was one proposal she didn't have to plan herself and that she intends to keep the details to herself so it will always remain one of a kind.

The couple plan to have a winter wedding at Elmhurst Hall in Kent.

Below is a photo, taken in black and white, of Alex in a sharp sixties suit and Nicole in a little black dress and pearls, smiling into each other's eyes, clearly besotted but caught sharing a moment of private laughter.

The caption reads: *Photographer—Michael Gatson.*

\* \* \* \* \*

# *Feeling Christmassy?*

**Don't miss more festive treats from
FIONA HARPER**

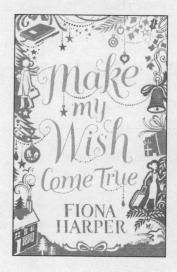

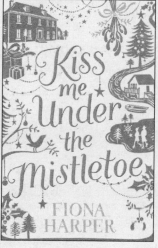

Available now at
millsandboon.co.uk

# Fall in love with the O'Neil brothers this Christmas

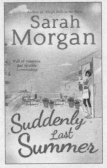

*Fall head-over-heels with*
*24 brand new stories from bestsellers*
*Fiona Harper, Adele Parks, Katie Fforde,*
*Carole Matthews and many more.*

★ *24 New Stories* ★

Truly, Madly,
Deeply

Adele Parks Carole Matthews
Katie Fforde Miranda Dickinson
and more...
Introduced by Jill Mansell

SPECIAL
EBOOK
EDITION
10 extra
stories!

Available now in paperback and eBook at
**www.millsandboon.co.uk**

# *Snow, sleigh bells and a hint of seduction*

## Find your perfect Christmas reads at
## millsandboon.co.uk/Christmas